Kane Unhinged

Wolfwere Series Book 3

Dick Wybrow

Dee Dub Publishing

Copyright © 2023 by Dick Wybrow

All rights reserved.

No portion of this book may be reproduced in any form without written permission from the publisher or author, except as permitted by U.S. copyright law.

Chapter One

Standing at the back of their work van, Consuelo Amaro tapped her foot, her arms crossed. She exhaled, hoping to be rewarded with a plume of mist in the cool night air to give her frustration some physical manifestation, but got nothing.

She repeated the exhalation a bit louder but, apparently, not loudly enough for Edgar to get a clue.

Unless he was just ignoring her. Connie suspected he did that sort of thing.

Tracing her eyes up the dark, five-story office building, she tilted her head back and blew out a longer breath, watching the strands of her long black hair flit and flicker in the moonlight. The sight reminded her of the old car washes, the ones people could drive into, in which the long, mangy dreadlocks of black-mildewed cloth hung down and lazily danced their sorrowful hula, mixing pink froth and grime across the windshield.

Ugh. Even my daydreams are about cleaning. I need to get a life.

There had been a time when she'd wondered if that life might have been with Edgar Duckett.

Well, she *had* a life with him—a business partnership—but that was not what she'd meant when she'd sneaked into her aunt's room and quietly offered a fumbling prayer to a votive candle three years earlier.

After they'd met on the job, at a bigger cleaning outfit, they'd worked closely together for the better part of the week.

She wouldn't have admitted it to Edgar now, but Connie had been a bit smitten.

Anyone who saw them could see it on her face. Anyone but Edgar, of course.

Edgar was a beautiful man with a warm smile and amazing abs. His ebony skin was flawless, and she'd never seen the tight curls on his head out of place. Not once.

This was a man who took care of himself.

This was a man who found joy in life and was quick to laugh.

This was also a man who seemed to have very little interest in her.

Connie had never known Edgar to be with anyone. He'd said he was looking for the perfect girl.

"Perfect?" she'd asked. "How can you tell whether someone you meet will be the perfect girl for you?"

Edgar had flashed his beautiful smile at her. "I'll know her when I see her."

"Har, har."

The pair had quickly become best friends, and after being stiffed one too many times by their former employer, they'd conspired to start their own cleaning business. However, all the big jobs—office buildings, apartment complexes, government annexes—those contracts had been sucked up by the corporate cleaners. The ones with fleets of vans with slick paint jobs and workers loaded down with shiny hi-tech machines that made the staff look like a cross between ghostbusters and South American commandos.

Still, they pursued the dream. At first, they'd picked up single-family homes. But that wasn't going to pay the bills. That wasn't going to even refill the Windex bottles.

Then, they'd stumbled, quite by accident, onto a virtually untapped market: clean-ups at facilities that needed something more than just trash dumping and wipe-downs.

These *required* discretion.

Places that demanded the janitorial crew not just look the other way but forget what they saw in that other direction too.

It had been Edgar, in large part, who'd sold their current client in this regard. The meeting with the bowling ball of a woman with hair like a Troll doll's had lasted no more than ten minutes. Connie had guessed that she was low-tier management if her shoes were anything to go by.

Known to them only as Mrs. Z, the woman with the cheap shoes and cheaper haircut had said she'd never even *heard* of a blind cleaner but admitted that if he could do the job, she found it immensely attractive for her purposes.

To seal the deal, Connie had agreed to hand over every single bit of personal detail to the outfit, which had dangled an *exceedingly* lucrative contract. The private data wasn't just about her but about her family. Brothers, sisters, aunts, uncles, mom, and dad. Everyone.

She'd been told this was merely a very thorough background check.

They'd needed the gig, so despite her reservations about privacy and all that, she handed all of that over eagerly. Only after she'd done that had *all* the terms been explained.

They'd gotten the contract.

But.

But...

If their new employer got any hint that she'd flapped her lips about what she might see inside? Even just casually mentioning to a coffee pal the color of the facility's carpet?

She would die.

However, her family would die first.

All of them.

So she would know that bone-crushing anguish and welcome death when it finally did come.

At that point, it was far too late to back out of the deal. What would they have done if she had? The potential annihilation of her entire family aside, the payout from just this one client was more than they could have hoped to make from ten clients!

And, really, she'd had a lot of Christmases and Thanksgivings with her family over the years. They weren't *all* that great.

Connie chuckled at the thought and offered a small prayer, asking forgiveness. It was fine to joke about those sorts of things, but, no, she loved her family. Even the awful ones.

"What are you laughing about now, Con?" Edgar asked after he'd finally slipped out of the van and begun strapping the back-vac to his shoulders and fastening its fat belt around his waist. "People are gonna think you're crazy, giggling to yourself."

"I only hang out with you, so who cares?"

He spun and faced her, adjusting the straps. "Yeah, and I already know you're crazy."

"I could punch you, and you'd never see it coming, you know."

"Harsh." Edgar laughed with a toothy grin, squinting his gray eyes. "And why would you wanna mess up a face this perfect?" He threw a thumb over his shoulder. "What's the plan, Boss? Do you want to be on top?"

Connie thumped his shoulder, drawing a girlish giggle out of him. She couldn't help but smile.

"You go high, I'll go low."

He nodded as he grabbed his long-handled box with cleaning supplies, rags, an extra telescopic cane in case he lost the one on his belt, and two cans of Diet Coke. Edgar snapped his primary walking stick from his hip and gave it a shake.

As Connie got her gear, she heard the *click!* then *tick-tick-tick* as he walked toward the dark office building. She'd once described the structure to Edgar as a Rubik's Cube the size of a city block but impossible to solve. All sides appeared to be made from segments of black glass.

"Some tech company had owned it," she'd said on their first night. "Now this other group does."

"Right. And what do they do?"

She'd dropped her voice to a whisper. "Let's make that the last time we ever ask the question, yeah?"

"Clean the desks, cash the checks," he said, in a stage whisper matching her tone.

"You got it."

After she'd pressed her ID into the box at the gate and the big bar lifted to let them in, they'd arrived at the back, as they always did. They stepped into a warehouse loading area unlike any warehouse Connie had ever seen—and she'd worked in dozens and dozens of them over the past fifteen years.

Trotting up behind Edgar, she looked over at the loading docks, which had vertical bars that came down *in front of* their big steel doors, not just a roll-away cage to stop people from breaking in. They looked like, well, a cage to stop anyone from breaking out.

"These guys must have a hell of an employee retention problem."

Edgar half turned his head. "What?"

"You're up on six," she said, ignoring the question. "Trash, floor, and glass. I'll start at the bottom and meet you in the middle. Well, probably fifth, because you're slow."

"Whatever, woman," he said as his cane ticked against the double glass entryway. They had keycards and codes to get inside. This would be the first of three doors.

"You starting at the bottom, huh," he said as he listened to the *beep-beep-beep* of his partner typing in their personalized code. "You mean at the *bottom* bottom?"

"No. And don't get started on that again." The door clicked, and she pulled the heavy portal wide.

Edgar gently felt for her shoulder and followed her inside. "Elevator's got a B, doesn't it?"

"No, the 'B' is a one. Some redesign since the last owners, I guess, but I don't know, and I don't wanna know. We start on two and go up," Connie said, approaching the second door. "Two is our bottom."

"Uh huh. Yeah, but aren't you the least bit curious?"

"No," she said, thinking about her family, which tweaked a spot in the middle of her chest. "We're here to do a job and get overpaid, and that's it. No poking around."

They heard the *click-clank* of the door locking behind them and then nothing but their own breaths and shuffling feet. This time of night, aside from a security guard or two, they'd never even seen a single employee. It made the building unnaturally quiet.

That seemed to be a theme.

One evening, when they'd left, both had been stunned to walk into a full-throated thunderstorm. Inside, they'd never heard the torrent of rain or the rumble of thunder once.

At the next set of doors, Connie punched in the second code—different from the first—and as those closed once again, they waited in front of the third. The space between the two entryways wasn't much larger than a walk-in closet and was dark as a grave.

Edgar shook his head slowly. The first week, he'd claimed he'd heard a buzzing while standing here, but Connie had shushed him. This time, he shivered slightly and remained shushed.

A red light glowed just below the ceiling, like the eye of a sleepy demon awakening, and she stared up at the camera. Then she elbowed Edgar, who raised his face, too... in the other direction.

She elbowed his ribs. "Cut it out, freak."

Smiling, he turned his uplifted face to where she'd told him the camera was on their first night.

Sweat had begun to dampen her brow, and she felt a trickle of it skitter down the side of her cheek. Tonight's wait at the camera felt interminably long. She shuffled her feet from side to side, forcing her face upward, which was beginning to strain her neck.

Clank-thunk!

Brilliant light burst from the next room like the headlights of a passing semi that had swerved to run them down. This final door slid open because it didn't have a knob.

Squinting, Connie looped a finger around the strap of Edgar's back-vac and walked them both inside. The door *snicked* back into place the moment they crossed the threshold.

"Breathe, baby girl," he said and put a hand on her arm.

She propped her long box up on a black desk, pulled out a clean rag, and drew it lightly across her face. Already, she could feel dampness beneath the straps of the big vacuum mounted on her back. She needed to get moving, get working, or she'd be drenched before she even started.

Edgar stood at the elevator, humming softly to himself. She smiled at the soothing sound.

Running her keycard over the panel, she punched the button and stood next to him, giving his shoulder a slight bump with her own.

"You want me to do a quick run through six to see if there are any bags on the floor?"

"Nah, nah," he said, smiling. "I know the layout so well, I could draw it for you."

The doors parted, and they both stepped inside. They wouldn't close until she once again passed her card across the interior pad.

Edgar leaned his back-vac against the horizontal metal rail. Connie eyeballed the chips and scratches in the otherwise perfectly polished metal. She knew that behind Edgar, one spot looked bent outward. It must have happened when the building's occupants had moved in the office furniture.

She punched the Six, and then her finger hovered over the Two for just a moment. Thoughts and ideas scattered around her head like coke-head squirrels.

Behind her, Edgar chuckled. Even the blind man could tell what she was thinking. "Do it," he said.

Connie looked at her index finger, just an inch away from the one button. She didn't even know if her pass would take her down to the bottom floor. They'd been instructed from the first day to clean from the second to the sixth. Nothing else. Five floors then get out.

Get paid. Get paid *very* well.

But still...?

Her finger began to slide down the panel, as if compelled by a will of its own. The sound of her own heartbeat began to hammer in her ears.

But then she heard another sound.

And snapped her hand back.

Low, distant, muffled, and... *pleading*?

"Dah fuck?" was all Edgar said. He wasn't smiling anymore.

The door, still open, began to ding like when she stared into the fridge too long, unsure what to take out. Then the chime began to speed up and grow louder.

Connie poked her finger at the numbers in quick succession—Six, Two—then stepped back to the wall next to Edgar. Then she remembered she hadn't run the card over the reader. She leaned forward, extended her arm, and waved it in front of the black box then hugged the wall again.

As the elevator door slowly slid closed, she flicked her eyes up to a camera in the corner of the car. Then she turned, whispering. "What the hell was that?"

His face blank and expressionless, he only shook his head, very slightly, once. More of a twitch than a shake.

"Was that someone..." she said as the door closed and the elevator jostled them, moving upward. "Someone *screaming?*"

"Maybe it's staff movie night," Edgar said with a light tone. His face said otherwise. His next words were barely a whisper. "Sounded far off. Below." He turned to her, his eyes staring at nothing. "Wasn't a scream, though. Maybe... animal experiments or something? Gives me the willies. You're right. Let's stay off one."

The elevator picked up speed, heading toward six first because that was the order in which she'd punched the numbers. She looked at the glowing two and swallowed hard.

Just as the car slowed, she stole another quick glance up at the camera then muttered to herself. "Sounded like a scream."

"Nah," Edgar said, one side of his lips curling upward. "Not a person. Don't worry 'bout it."

"What, then?"

Edgar lifted his silver-and-white cane toward the open elevator doors and tapped both sides. He leaned over to her, kissing the top of her head. Then he started walking forward to start his long night of work.

"Just some animal. That wasn't a scream, baby girl. It'll be some movie or something," he said as he stepped onto the sixth floor. "It sounded like a howl."

Chapter Two

I was having serious second thoughts about being within a thousand miles of Tech Sergeant Gregor.

Hell, by this point, I was having fourth, fifth, and sixth thoughts.

Mostly because he was a horrible human being. Or Enhanced. Whatever.

Sure, this asshole had tried to kill me, but really, the number of people who'd done that in my twenty-five years would be longer than a Grateful Dead set list.

But I could never forgive him for threatening my family. He had invaded the homes of my mom and grandmother by having his people sneak inside and squirrel away cameras in the walls.

After I'd dragged the second dead monster over to him at the smoldering Iowa farmhouse, I'd watched his skin turn from charred to pink. His black-irised and bloodshot eyes—apparently, that latter happens when you're on fire; who knew?—cleared, and his breathing fell back into what I assumed was his normal rhythm.

Before we got on the road to wherever the hell we were going, I'd demanded he'd make a call and get those cameras ripped from my family's homes.

Through still-blackened teeth, he'd laughed.

"You think I can just ring up the Organization and say, 'Hey, take a memo, would you, please?'"

I glared at him, feeling as if my cheeks were growing hotter than his had been. "That's how you probably put them there in the first place!"

"True, true." He nodded, rubbing his face. He watched with detached curiosity as bits of dust and skin drifted into his lap like dirty snowflakes. "But we've just lost the most important asset in this entire operation."

He waved his hand toward the still-burning home, wisps of smoke trailing from his fingertips like an ancient wizard too tired to conjure a proper spell.

"Why we came," I said, barely able to say the words. "Dr. Pental's research is gone."

"Huh?" He scowled at me. "Yes, yes, all that. More than that, Emelda Thorne. So much more!"

I nodded. I knew what he meant. "Kane."

When he looked at me and smiled, I wanted to punch those bloodied teeth in. Had to give him credit. He was no wolf-turned-man, but he'd picked up on my expression and wiped the smirk off his face.

Nearly burning to death probably gives you some perspective.

"Yes, the big guy is like nothing anyone has ever seen. Hell, that—" He flicked his eyes toward me. "Kane is beyond what the program had even hoped to achieve."

"He's not part of your damn program."

"No, yet take a look at him," Gregor said. He cleared his throat and spat out the open window. "And to think I had that and lost it."

"So?"

"By now, the Org will have some idea what's going on. I don't know what Covenant offered Doc Hammer to trade employee name tags, but she grabbed it with both hands and took Kane with her."

"Put your seat belt on." I fired up the Jeep and dropped it into gear. "And tell me where we're going."

"I don't need a seat belt. I am an Enhanc—"

"If you don't put the seat belt on, the damn dashboard dings like a New Yorker waiting at the counter to complain about their dry cleaning."

He glared at me with hooded eyes. "That's oddly specific."

"Which you *haven't* been," I said as he complied, clicking his belt across his waist. Still tender from, you know, being on fire, he winced a bit as he did so.

"The point is that Hammer isn't the first person I've been associated with to double-cross us."

I nodded. "Mon. Monique on your crew."

He snapped his head toward me. "How did you know about that?"

"Me and her had a chat," I said and shrugged. I turned onto the long gravel drive to put the farmhouse in my rearview mirror. In the distance,

I saw a fire truck racing our way. I needed to get the hell off the property before they turned down the street.

"Right, then you killed—no, that was your big friend."

"Of course."

Gregor giggled to himself. I mean *giggled*, for shit's sake! "That... wow, that explains so much. So much!"

"Just can it."

His giggling faded, and he drew in a deep breath. "Mon, then Hammer. And me without any prize to show for it. I know the Org feels it's been generous by supplying me with doses of their serum. That's always been payment on arrears. I had to return Cal Davis or Faria Pental's research. I've got neither."

"And Kane."

He winced again. "Exactly. A goldmine that was snatched out of my fingers." He stared out the window and up at the dark sky. "Two traitors on my team and bupkis to show for it. They'll want me to come in to explain what went wrong, and then they'll incinerate my body."

"Jesus. And you work for those people?"

"Worked," he said. "They'll want their pound of flesh, and the only one left to carve from is me. So no, I can't call up the Org and ask them nicely, pretty please, to pull cameras from suburban tract houses. I've failed them too many times. They'll be searching for me now so they can tie up that loose end."

I growled as we bumped along the gravel road, a bit too fast for my new passenger. He shot his hand out to steady himself.

A few blocks over, I could see two fire trucks, red lights dancing across the low clouds as if we were being invaded by aliens. I pushed the accelerator harder.

Gregor put a foot up to steady himself, leaving sooty shoe prints across the dash. "This isn't a paved road, Emelda Thorne! You're going to kill us both."

"You're Enhanced, yeah? You'll live."

I slowed just slightly when we came up to the main road and heard him take a deep breath then release it. For the hell of it, I jammed in the clutch and revved the engine high. I think a little bit of pee came out of him.

The Jeep bounced as we switched from gravel to the pavement, and I cranked the wheel hard to the right, drifting a little as I did. The double thunk of the asshole's head against the glass filled me with more joy than the laughter of children.

Checking the mirror, I saw the first fire appliance—that's what the fire guys called them—round the corner. We were well ahead of them.

I realized something. "I don't know where the hell we're going."

Gregor sat up straighter in the seat and cleared his throat. "First, I need some vials of my treatment."

I shot a look at him. "Hell no. I'm not going anywhere near the Organization. Not happening."

"I never said that." Gregor rolled something around in his mouth then pulled out a long, blackened tooth. He flicked it out the window, and it disappeared into the dark void. "The Org has warehouses all over the country. Every state."

"They doing Amway sales on the side?"

"Hardly," he said, but then his eyes lost focus. "Huh. Maybe."

"What the hell does that mean?"

Gregor leaned back against the window to look at me. The sight of him propped up like that twisted an icy blade into my stomach. I'd seen Kane do that dozens of times.

Now he was gone.

And I'd let him go. Basically handed him over to Covenant.

"The Org is huge," Gregor said, lifting his palms skyward. "Far beyond your imagination."

"I've got a wild imagination, you prick."

"Clearly. That would explain the purple hair."

I glowered at him. "You think your enhancements can protect you from being pushed out of a moving car?"

He raised his hands in mock surrender, but even when he turned away, I could see his crooked smile.

"This monster hunt Doc Hammer and I were on is just a very, very small part of what the Org does. Covenant too. They are vast, and they are global."

Then I recalled the stupid ditty he'd recited back in the Minnesota bar. "You're an ant rolling a rock over a boot in the back of a closet on a cruise ship on a hurricane sea."

That got a genuine smile of out him. "Yes, good memory. You know, in fact—"

"Please just get to the point."

"Fine," he said and turned to look out the windshield. "Head south. Interstate 380. There's a warehouse space just east of St. Louis. That's where I can get to my emergency stash."

I shook my head. "You think someone wouldn't have found it by now?"

Gregor leaned back into the seat, getting comfortable. For a moment, he fiddled with the belt, then he wiped his hands on his camo pants. Stupid move. The crispy fabric crumbled, its flakes falling onto the upholstery.

At least I hoped it had been from his pants. I didn't need that snake's skin fouling up my floorboards.

"No," he finally answered. "They know all about it. Just.... no one goes there. The stuff will be where it's supposed to be."

I sighed and looked at the gas gauge. I had another two hundred odd miles' worth of fuel before I'd have to stop. Of course, we'd be going through Iowa countryside. Who knew how many truck stops they'd have along the way?

I decided to stop the first chance I got.

"Just to be clear," I said, rolling my shoulders, getting ready for yet another long, long drive, "I'm going to kill you when I get Kane back."

"Maybe I'll kill you first," he said as casually as if he was telling me about his favorite band. Probably a Coldplay guy. "Of course, maybe you won't have to."

"No, that's a promise. I won't change my mind."

"That's not what I meant."

I looked over at Gregor, who'd leaned his head against the window. That pang troubled my belly again, but I ignored it.

"Fine." I groaned. "What do you mean, asshole?"

"What I'm saying is," he said, and sighed, which briefly rolled into a gargle of coughs, "the reason I know the serum is still at the St. Louis facility is because no one goes there." Gregor closed his eyes. "And I didn't actually *leave* it there for me to pick up later."

"What the hell are you talking about, man?"

He looked over at me, and I could see the light reflecting from the whites of his black eyes. "You know about the program, I take it?"

"Cal told us about what happened. They started with twelve, all sorts of Dr. Mengele-level treatments. Only you and Cal made it through. He was far better, of course. Like almost perfect. You were a distant second."

Gregor nodded and leaned back again. "The treatments *evolved* him. Permanently. Not the same for me. If I stop taking the doses, I'll revert. Or die. That's never been clear."

"Can I vote for which one? I'd like to vote. Is there a vote?"

He sighed, his voice weak. "For the group members whose results were suboptimal, those subjects were decommissioned."

"Killed."

"Yes," he said then scrunched his face up. "And, well, no. There was another. Not sure where she came from."

"What?"

"One woman, a Brit or Australian, I don't know. She had a troublesome accent, but that might be because when the virus took hold, she went feral. *Insane*. Not like, 'bitch be crazy,' I mean in-sane. Manic."

"Say 'bitch' in my car again, and I shove a ten-inch steel dart through your eye."

Gregor laughed.

I jammed on the brakes, and we skidded to a halt, my headlights strafing thick tree trunks, and ended up sideways on the road, tire smoke rolling over us like demon breath.

"We clear, you and me?" I stared at him, not blinking.

He licked his cracked lips. "Crystal."

Once I'd cranked the wheel and gotten back onto the right side of the road, we were off again.

Gregor continued. "Her body, her blood, is corrupted. No good use for what the program was trying to achieve."

"Supersoldiers."

"Something like that, yes," he said. "But at least with Martha or Marta, whatever her name is, I suppose, they thought they had *something*. So they put her in some old factory warehouse and shuttered it up."

I saw road signs for I-380, indicating I could take that south. That was where we were headed.

"Martha's blood was a mess, corrupted, but it was all they had." Gregor crossed his arms and let his eyelids fall closed. "They've been keeping her alive until they can work out how to harvest what they need from her. Or find something better. So for the past year, they've been drip-feeding her serum. Comes out of a slot on a timer. Just enough to keep her alive."

My jaw dropped. "*That's* your secret stash? You want to pilfer some doses from this Martha the Monster?"

"If we can," he said, shrugging. "The tricky bit is that the reason they secured the facility is because she broke out of her restraints—*steel* restraints—and killed four armed operators."

"And you want to *go* there?"

"Yes," he said. "And steal the stuff keeping her alive."

Chapter Three

Kane

I do not remember so much weariness in my limbs before.

There is no light until there is.

And when it comes, I do not like it.

Until then, I am immobile. Pinned like a butterfly on a child's corkboard wall. Why would they encourage human children to do these things? Butterflies are very beautiful but do not taste like butter. Not much like fly, either.

However, I would take either right now.

It feels like it has been days since food or water has crossed my lips. Maybe longer. This is impossible to tell. The room I am being held in is endless.

Just a butterfly pinned to a wall.

During the brief, painful flashes of light, I have tried to see the other walls. Left. Right. I cannot tell which way is east or west, and this I find troubling.

When I wait, staring one direction, and the light burns at my eyes, I have tried to squint through that pain and see what is at the far end. Then the other direction. Staring directly ahead, this is impossible, for the light is so very bright, I feel it could blind me.

Is this what they hope to achieve?

What good would a blind wolf be?

For the moment, I wait and listen to my stomach growl. For a time, I also did growl. And yell and howl. But no answer came. The only response was my own voice repeated back to me, weakly. An echo.

I am an echo.

My arms are raised and secured, my legs clamped at the ankles, so that I resemble... What is this pose? Something like one of Mère's old television shows. A man in dark glasses with an impractically long microphone talking to people, street people maybe, who all sit and wait until their name is called.

"*Price Is Right*," I mutter through cracked lips. The words scratch along my dry throat, leaving painful gouges.

The *Price* people, they would hear their name, so excited. Run down dark carpet stairs from the crowd. Even from my seat on the couch next to Mère, I could tell it had been a very long time since that carpet was cleaned.

Then, they would get to a standing desk, the name said moments ago appearing in front of them. And they would jump up and down. Arms in the air. Smiles so impossibly large, Mère tells me her theory.

"I think they spike their Cokes with speed so they're like that."

I ask, "What is speed?"

"Makes you high-energy nuts," she says as we watch the people jumping up and down. They are very excited. "Normal people don't act like that."

I turn to her. "I am not normal people."

"No, baby," she says, squeezing my shoulder in a hand hug. "But you're a good not-normal."

Yet here I am in this very dark, soundless room, and I am like a *Price* people who is suspended in air. Arms up, legs splayed.

However, I have no smiles. No chance to win prizes. Not even the Rice-A-Roni box, which I understand to be a delicacy in the city of San Francisco.

When I hear the thunk, I brace, for I know what is coming. There is but a half second between the thunk and what comes next, and this time, I am determined to stare forward, see beyond.

Then, there is light.

Blinding.

Painful.

I grit my teeth, trying to keep my eyes open.

However, my vision begins to fade even as the light burns into my eyes. Then the thunk, and the light is gone.

I feel drained. Exhausted.

What remains is an odd orange hue this time. The light echo. It is not always thus.

The light from the thunking machine, a massive square of fat bulbs, is too bright to determine a color, but the echo of the light, when the darkness returns, this changes slightly each time.

Next time the light comes, if I have not starved or died of thirst, I hope the echo is purple. I am not sure why, but that color would bring me a small measure of happiness.

Maybe not happiness. Comfort?

Why purple?

My mind swims, and I cannot tell if I am awake or dreaming.

I would like to see purple echo.

Then, I would not feel so alone.

Until then, I will wait.

Chapter Four

Staring into the rearview mirror, I saw that the chick frowning back at me looked haggard. Strung out. And, sure, I know what that looks like.

Not proud of it.

But I was clean and had been for years. I'd done only a brief dance with that devil, thankfully, but I realized I didn't like the music. Or the tempo. Or something. I think I got lost in that analogy.

I was exhausted.

My eyes were bloodshot. The bags under them looked like what the Kardashians might bring for a weekender in Greece.

The purple tint in my dark hair was fading. It had been more than a month since I'd colored it. A bit of joy on the outside that I'd hoped would seep through my skull and stain my brain with happiness.

Still waiting on that. I needed a fresh coat.

Pulling myself from the Jeep, I put a hand out and leaned against the hood. Just needed a few seconds. I stared through the gas station's windows and watched my enemy picking out drinks from a cooler inside.

"If he grabs blue-raspberry Gatorade, I'm leaving him here."

I'll never get used to how you can get *used* to your world being totally turned upside down.

Weeks earlier, I'd just been living in a shit apartment working a shittier job. My shitty ex-boyfriend in prison.

When that had happened, I'd felt a bit lost. Roy had sort of taken me under his wing after I'd left home in a hurry. Of course, that had been a bit of a demon's wing and had started me down a less-than-legal path. But all that criminal stuff had paid the bills.

And, ultimately, it had gotten Roy chucked into a gray-bar hotel.

My accommodations hadn't been much better. I had the basement apartment in North Minneapolis all to myself so that I could suck in car fumes until I died of asphyxiation or cancer.

Then one night, a yippy little dog changed all that. Not just changed but flipped my worldview on its head.

Now I was at a gas station in Nowhere, Missouri, fueling up, with the Organization operative who, just days earlier, had been hunting Cal Davis and gleefully planning my murder.

Well, ex-Organization now. Gregor knew enough about their outfit to know he'd be persona non grata with his bosses. And after the Organization's competition, Covenant, had taken Kane away with *zero goddamn fight* from me, now, I was heading back into that fight to get him back.

Gregor, because he was a psycho, had no interest in helping Kane. He wanted revenge against the woman who'd traded her reserved parking place at the Org's HQ for one at Covenant.

Robotically, I pulled the pump off the pump hangy thingy—Jesus, I needed sleep—popped off the Jeep's gas cap, and pushed the nozzle inside.

Maybe it was because of the lack of sleep, but for the first time ever, I realized that this movie was a bit, um, dirty.

I stared at this mechanical union, a ten-minute stand, as it were, and wondered if the pump man might fall head-over-heels in love with my Jeep. Guys can be like that.

Then Pumpy's texting my Jeep, and she sees the ding, regretting her lapse in judgment after going a bit hard on the Slurpees the night before, embarrassed to tell her friends when they ask who's pinging her.

Damn, I really needed sleep.

As I played pump pimp with the squeeze of my fingers, I stared through the front windows of the service station. Even from here, I could see the woman behind the counter giving Gregor the side-eye.

You could tell there was something off about the guy. And not just that he was cuckoo for Cocoa Puffs, which he certainly was.

With the treatments, Gregor was a big dude. Not as big as Kane but bigger than he should have been for a body like his. Whereas many of the Enhanced monsters I'd seen had been basically bald, Gregor had short-cropped silver hair. I didn't know if it just grew that way because he was Enhanced or if he preferred a style that reflected his former military life. Much like keeping the "tech sergeant" title, which he'd brought up several times on our drive to the middle of Missouri.

When Gregor laughed—at one of his own jokes, I had no doubt—the woman took a half step back. Working third shift, she probably saw all kinds of weird shit. But Gregor's teeth were larger, his jaw distended. And, of course, his eyes had zero color.

Black like his heart.

I raised an eyebrow when I saw him hand over cash—who used cash anymore? He counted out the change in front of her. Whadda douche.

The door chimed as he stepped out, and I leaned between the pumps, getting dizzy on the fumes.

"Ah-ah!" I shouted to him, and he froze in midstep. "What do you think you're doing, man?"

He held up a crinkly bag and a very large bottle of what looked like fizzy water. What an infant.

"I'm not done fueling up." I pointed him back into the service station. "You gotta pay for it."

"I thought you had Kane's bank card."

"I do," I said, watching the digital readout on the pump rocket up like a hundred-yard-relay clock. "But you're paying for the gas. This is on you."

He frowned, started to protest, then buttoned his lip and gave me an exaggerated thumbs-up.

Gregor went back inside, lifting his treats in the air, leaning back as if he was saying, "Women? Amiright?"

What an asshat.

The pump twitched and thunked, finished. I looked down and wondered if it had, in that final moment, whispered, "I love you" as it did.

Poor Pumpy. Another heart ready to be broken.

* * *

The drive from Waterloo, Iowa, to east of St. Louis would take five hours. But I'd already driven five hours to get to Waterloo, had one of the worst nights of my life, and then gotten back on the road.

"I need to sleep," I said to Gregor. He was munching away on Flamin' Hot Cheetos, for god's sake. "We've got about two hours before St. Louis, but if you see a motel or hotel—"

"No, we can't stop!" He turned to me, his large Enhanced mouth chomping on his food. Dude chewed with his mouth open. Another reason to hate him. "We don't have the time."

"I'm tired, shitburger. I'm gonna wreck if I don't get some sleep."

"Fine," he said, taking a swig of his drink, a two-liter of diet tonic water. Who was this guy? Who drank tonic water? "I'll drive."

"No."

"Yes!"

I sighed. "We need to get something straight, you and me. This"—I waved my finger between us—"is not some partnership. Or a negotiation. You would be dead without me."

"True, yes, Emelda. But that doesn't mean you're the boss here. I am—"

"Wrong. I am the boss."

He gritted his teeth and glared at me with those black, hollow eyes. That *would* have been shit-inducing had his mouth not been ringed with Cheeto dust.

"I've risen up the ranks," he said in a queer, childlike voice, "so I don't have to follow orders."

I laughed. "You're not in the military anymore, dude. Or the Organization. You might write 'tech sergeant' inside all your undies, but that's all over. Don't you get that?"

My time with Kane had taught me a bit about reading microexpressions. This, as he'd explained, was how animals communicated. Of course, he'd not said it that way.

"Twitch and flinch. Furrow and frown."

So, yeah, microexpressions.

As Gregor glared at me, I could see the corner of his eye flicker and his mouth slacken ever so slightly. My "you ain't a tech sergeant no more" comment had stung him at his core.

"I don't owe you *anything*, Emelda Thorne," he said, baring those big teeth. "What's to say we pull over so you can take a nappy-poo, and I don't slice your throat as you sleep? Hmm?"

"Because you need me more than I need you, for one. Unless you wanna walk to St. Louis."

He laughed, but there was a tremor in it.

"And I've got an email set to fire off that says where we're going, what we're planning on doing, and where you will be."

That froze him on the spot.

I added, "Each hour, I reset the send time to the next hour. If I don't reset it, the email goes out."

He stared down at the device in my lap. No question he had seen me on it as I drove, a bad habit I'll never shake, and the realization hit him like a slap.

"You don't have a contact at the Organization," he said, pointing a too-long finger at me. "Or Covenant."

"Like Doc Hammer said, I don't *need* to have a specific email address. It's got Kane's name, your name, my name in there." I looked over at him. "You guys have some sort of email net out there, fishing for stuff, right? Sounded like that to me."

Gregor sank back into his seat, all the fight draining from him like a day-old birthday balloon.

"Trawlers. Yes. In nearly every server in every country on the planet. Both sides have them."

"And texts?"

He closed his black eyes, nodding once. "More secure. They've got encryptions, but it's easy enough to get around those."

"Fine. Mine's an email. So if you try to do something asshatty, that email goes out, and your old bosses get to that exit interview they really, *really* want." I put my hand to my mouth in mock concern. "Oh my, I don't think you'd get 'Meets or Exceeds Objectives.' Do you?"

He sighed, blowing bits of orange across the Jeep's dash. "Fine. Before we hit St. Louis, there's a whole strip of places to stay. You can rest up there."

"Good," I said and flicked on the radio to stop my hand from shaking. Fiddling with the dial, I found a classic rock station and gripped the wheel again.

I sighed, dreaming of dreaming. I needed the rest.

And, of course, I probably needed to set up that email I'd threatened him with.

But hell, I really didn't know how to do stuff like that.

Chapter Five

"Two rooms," I said to the insanely old guy behind the motel counter.

He looked up slowly from his solitaire game. Not on the computer; the dude was playing with actual cards. Ancient motel dude looked at me queerly, his lip curving into a hook as he stared.

I'd spent plenty of years on the wrong side of the tracks. Hell, I'd held pool parties over on that side. For the most part, I'd always gotten myself out of jams. I couldn't say the same for everyone I'd been working with, sure, but usually, I came away without any holes in me.

But Gregor's nervousness about us getting found out was rattling my nerves.

A few hours earlier, when we'd made the turn south on the interstate, he'd insisted we ditch our phones. I'd gotten mine from Denny of the farm, good people, so it kind of meant something to me. It didn't have any stickers with tiny flowers or hearts on it or anything, but it was special.

"They'll have picked up your SSID from the phone when they landed the chopper at the farm," he'd said, black eyes extra twitchy. "I mean, who knows what kind of data they picked up."

As we'd walked to the doors leading to check-in, Gregor hadn't once taken his eyes off the sky. Scanning, searching. What had he been looking for? Drones? Planes? Fluffy clouds?

He'd not said a word, but it had made me skittish.

The old guy behind the counter looked at me then at Gregor. He did a double-take on the tech sergeant, and I saw a question form in his mind. It made it all the way down to his Chiclet dentures but couldn't break through.

Instead, he just sighed, writing us off as just some nighttime weirdos.

"Got one suite and..." he said, tapping at his computer. "Well, we've got a romper available. All the other rooms taken. Convention in town. Accountants, so I wouldn't go to the bar next door, young lady."

I laughed. "I gotcha."

Once outside, Gregor headed to his room. I climbed into the Jeep and, for a moment, just stared through the windshield. When the car door *whumped* shut, I got that familiar, cocooning feeling. The safety of my car. My space.

Looking ahead at the dark strip of interstate, as headlights skittered by like lightning bugs, I watched cars pass to wherever they were going.

"I could just leave now," I said. The Jeep muffled my voice, its sound lost in the fabric interior, as if it was conspiring with me.

In my pocket, I had Kane's bank card. Gregor had insisted we pay for the rooms with cash. Maybe they could track my card, maybe they couldn't. But I could get a bunch of cash out, jam it under my seat, and live off that for weeks. Head to the west coast, maybe? Go find Mom.

But my wolf friend would still be trapped. Trapped because it had been my job to protect him from the duplicitous world of humans, and *I had failed*!

Kane had told me wolves don't lie.

Well, humans did, all the time. As easy as breathing or eating Flamin' Hot Cheetos.

I knew that and had been reminded of it every day of my life.

Still, I'd just let him go with Doc Hammer. Had that been just blind optimism? Some false hope that, finally, we had found what we'd been looking for?

Or had some rotten part of me finally bubbled to the surface? Fear? Cowardice? Handing off some burden I could no longer bear?

Didn't matter. I'd fucked up.

Now, I had to unfuck it.

Chapter Six

Kane

Hanging against the cold, dry concrete wall and struggling against the manacles around my wrists and ankles, I try not to pull. If I were to do as such, this can cut the skin. I do not think these people will provide Band-Aids.

Certainly not ones with Hanna-Barbera cartoon characters upon them.

My only company is the intermittent light in the dark. Alas, it is not very good company. The conversation? Not so good.

Thunk-clank!

Again, it speaks only in blinding white. No words. No knock-knock jokes. Or a soft voice telling me not to do dumb things.

However, I do know that I am being observed.

The massive array of lights in front of me makes me temporarily blind. They are so bright! Or it could be that my eyes adjust to the total darkness of this cavernous room when I'm plunged into blackness in between punishing moments of total immersion in what feels like the heart of the sun.

On several occasions, when I heard the tell-tale thunking of the lights, I squeezed my eyes shut. When the *clank* illuminated the room, this made my vision red.

I smile, remembering *mon père* explaining why this is so.

"What color do you see now?"

"*Je vois la coul—*"

"*Non, en anglais,*" he says then laughs with that warm chest sound. "I mean, in English. You must also speak English."

I reposition myself on the flat rock and stretch my short human legs into the tall grass. My eyes still closed, I turn to face my human father. Quietly, he moves around behind me, and I track him. I know he is testing me, and I am eager to impress. He smells of cigarettes, sweat, and aftershave.

He is very easy to track.

Père could run a mile away, and I would still be able to smell him. However, I do not want him to run away.

I open my eyes.

"Closed eyes," he says, pointing at me with his piano smile. This is what I once called it, and I know it pleased him. "What color do you see?"

Once again, I close my eyes and warm my face with the sun. "Je... um... I see the red."

"Just red. No definite article."

"Def—?"

"No 'the,' yes?"

"Yes, no 'the,'" I say, trying to hide a smile. I do a poor job of that and make a note in my brain to practice hiding emotions so they do not give away my intent when I do not wish them to.

I nod once. "When I close my eyes to the sun, I see the color red."

He grunts his approval. "And this is why?"

"Be-because... of that within my eye skin—"

"Lids."

"Yes, within my eyelids, there is tiny tubes..." I scrunch up my face, trying to remember his teachings. "Vessels! And when the sunlight passes through my vessels, it is passing through blood. Which is red."

I snap my eyes open and turn to him, now on my right.

Père purses his lips, trying to pretend he is not proud, but I can tell. Behind that pucker lay the piano smile I like. He asks me, "What does this mean, blood?"

The question catches me off guard. I try to recover, hiding my hesitation by turning on the rock to face him. "It is what keeps us alive, yes?"

"Yes, sure." He shrugs. "But also, what is blood? Metaphor."

I rolled my eyes. "I do not like metaphor. Wolf do not have metaphor and such confusing things."

My father shrugs. "The boy must know these things. The human world will be challenging for you. You must know more but seem less."

"*Pourquoi?*" I say and this gets me a scolding frown. "*Why* must I know more but seem less?"

Père jams his hands into the pockets of his denim overalls and sighs. "Another time. When you are older, I think." He steps closer and drops to a knee so we are face to face. He has a nice face. "This word, blood, is powerful. It may represent passion and vigor. And while, yes, it can mean life, it can also mean taking of that life. Killing."

My chest tightens, and this time, I purse my lips. "This is not so good a word, no?"

"It is a very good word, for it also means something very important." Mon père lays his calloused hand on my small shoulder. "Blood means family."

Know more but seem less.

Can I seem less than a half-naked human hanging from his wrists like wall art? The thought nearly makes me chuckle, but my throat is so dry, I don't dare.

But I do know more.

I am being watched.

Several times, when I closed my eyes against the light, I listened for the secondary *thunk* that would indicate darkness would return. Hearing that, I snapped my eyes open and, for a fleeting moment, saw the circular glimmers around the room. I have counted five.

Camera lenses reflecting light.

They are hidden when the array is blinding me and also when the room is plunged into darkness.

But in this artificial dusk, I have spotted them!

Dusk is a fierce ally of the wolf. The best time to hunt prey.

Doctor Ilsa Hammer is watching. For what, I do not know. But she watches every move through her cameras.

Another thunk, and I brace for another light assault. When it hits me, I am again standing on the surface of a star. White, everything white.

Another clanking sound, but this time, the light does not go off.

The scent of a woman washes over me.

Shampoo and fragrance cover some of this but not all. Neither does the lotion. Other than Emelda, I do not recall meeting a woman who does not use much lotion. Why are they so dry?

If they did not apply lotion daily, would they blow away to dust?

"Hello, Kane," the woman says.

But I cannot see her, not even when I turn toward the voice. I force myself to stare forward, hooding my eyes with my brow to block some of the light.

"Hello, Ilsa."

She clears her throat. "My name is *Doctor Hammer*, Kane."

"But Ilsa is first name, yes? This is the name you tell me when you say 'Come with me in helicopter.' When you say 'I will help. I will cure.'"

Ilsa Hammer chuckles then sucks in breath, sounding very happy with herself.

This I assume, for I cannot see her. If I could see her, I could read the truth words within her expressions. The ones she wishes not to share.

"Please," she says from the darkness behind the light, "we can drop all of that now."

"Dropping sounds good," I say. "I believe I have a cramp in my left arm."

"Noooo." She draws the word out. I hear the *click-click* of a heeled shoe and smell her as she moves closer. "But I will consider... freeing one hand if you give me an answer. And maybe some more clothes than just those hospital pants."

I smile at her and laugh softly, catching sight of the beard on my chin as I do. The dark hair has begun fading to gray. "You taking me to fancy dinner, yes? Why would I need clothes?"

"You must be cold."

"I prefer no clothes."

I hear her take another step forward but not where I can see her. Then her hand passes over the light, just the flicker of shadow. Thin red fingers against white.

I cannot see her face and expressions. This is a disadvantage for wolf. I must rely only on her words. But I now hear a low timbre in her voice. Frustration?

She asks, "Why doesn't the light affect you like it did at Dr. Pental's farm?"

I purse my lips. "And how do you think it affected me?"

"You *changed*, Kane!" Her words come out as if they have scraped flesh from her throat. "You became that... powerful, magnificent beast! How did the light do that?"

Ah. Yes. This explains now why I have been hanging here like a dry, dirty tea towel as light blinds me over and over and over again.

"*Je ne sais pas.*"

"Of course, you must know! That... How do we help that creature come out again? Is that something you can do at will?"

I say nothing.

"No," Hammer says, and I hear a clicking to my left. Moving to get a better look? "No, otherwise you would have done that already. Become the beast and tried to escape."

I lift an eyebrow toward the sound of her voice. "Maybe it is that I am shy."

"You are hanging half naked on the wall in front of me without any problems." She laughs. "I don't think you're shy."

I nod. "This body pleases you, then?"

"Please. Don't flatter yourself." Another laugh, but no joy in this one. "And since you've been here... I mean, not looking so good, Kane."

"You forget, I am more than just a beautiful human man. My sense of smell is far better than yours." To antagonize her, I smile. "But I must decline. For I am betrothed to my wolf wife. And unlike humans, we are loyal. One mate."

"Don't you mock me!"

My eyes are beginning to strain, but this I do not show. The constant, punishing light is beginning to do damage. But I do see a dull flash to my left, from where her voice had come. It flashes again, and I see she is holding a... squished rectangle.

I hear the *thunk*. Good. My eyes can use the rest.

But the light does not go out. Instead, the color, this changes. Still too bright and now more yellow. Then the rectangle shimmers, moving. This is something that Hammer is hold—

Thunk.

New light, feels brighter. More blue?

Closing my eyes, I grin at it. This elicits another low, guttural sound from Doc Hammer.

The clanking of the light speeds up.

Thunk, thunk, thunk, thunk.

Each time, slightly different shade. But then the spot on my vision, a black orb that grows and grows, until I see mostly black.

The light has nearly blinded me. I can only hope this is temporary.

I must squint, but this is not enough. I turn my head slightly, but this does little. The light is so bright! The light is strobing as Hammer cycles through the spectrum.

Thunk-thunk-thunk, thunk, thunk, thunk-thunk.

When I crack an eye open, I can see the squished rectangle shift and shimmy. As the light speeds up, the shift increases, and I can now hear her fingernail hitting glass.

She is holding a computer pad like Dr. Pental had back at her farmhouse. This controls the light.

Oh.

What? It—

The light changes, so fast now, but for just a moment, I felt a stir in my chest and a quickening in my heart. A flickering of amber eyes in my head.

With all my strength, I push that away until the light—*thunk*—changes once again.

Know more but seem less.

Pental did affect me with her large lights. The color, I try to recall, but I only remember what I saw when I slammed my eyes shut against it. Blue. A curious, faint shade of blue. Very faint, but I do recall.

And that light affected me.

However, Ilsa Hammer cannot find same color as Pental had. She somehow knew what color that light...

Ah, yes. Yes.

Moonlight.

This is what she did to me back at her farmhouse. Faria Pental knew to replicate light of moon. However, I did not change to canine, I became the other. The artificial light of the full moon brought forth the part of me Emelda calls the wolfwere.

It is that creature Ilsa Hammer seeks now.

She does not know my origins. However, I am not sure if this would matter. My slipup, speaking of my wolf wife, she ignored as the rambling of a starving man.

Know more but seem less.

I cannot make such a mistake twice.

Perhaps I will not have to. The strobing of the light is confusing my brain. Hurting my thinking.

I can feel consciousness slip away.
Blissfully, my world goes black as a moonless night.

Chapter Seven

Kane

As I awake, I first notice the pain.

It is so terrible, it makes me howl.

But... I do not howl.

Such a strange sound, what comes from me. I do not recognize my own wolf sounds. How queer they are!

To my ears, they sound like human sounds, but this cannot be so. However, I do feel the vibrations through my chest, so yes, they come from me.

And I cannot stop.

The air smells like damp grass, dirt, and *animal*. Horse sweat? Yes, but different scent, like a part of a scent. But, yes, horse. This is a worry. For horse usually means humans.

Lying on my back—such an odd position for wolf—I try to roll to my side, but this is difficult. My movements make crunching sounds, and I feel tiny, poking things in my back.

Ah, this is the rotting-grass smell. Hay.

Why have I lain in hay?

Cannot think straight, my mind a jumble, but I think that is because of the mind-blasting pain in my arms.

I continue to wail, hoping that another within my pack will find me. Help.

But I am in shadow. Have I fallen into a cave?

Staring up, it looks similar to cave rock, but up there, so far away, this looks more like tree. Flat wood like the humans use. Why would—

I cannot think with such pain!

Trembling, I raise my front legs to block the sun, which is peeking through a part of the wood cave at the top.

What is wrong with my forepaws?

Why do my claws look so long and fat and fleshy and useless?

Why am I pink?

Louder, I wail and feel... hesitant. *Not* afraid. Wolf is never afraid. The only fear we know is that which we elicit from our prey.

We are strong. Powerful. Kings and queens of the forest and never—

"*Bonjour, mon ami,*" a strange voice calls out.

Okay, yes, yes, I am afraid.

I have fear.

Fear is me.

This now I have accepted, if only in my head. Now the fear can go, yes. Don't need.

I squeeze my eyes shut because I can smell the human. His long shadow cuts a dark swath across the wood cave. This man smells like sweat and dirt and... car smell. I have sniffed their vehicles before and, yes, he smells like that.

Is he... a car-man? Man who is also car?

"*Doucement, doucement,*" the man says, his voice soft.

I turn to see him holding his large hands back and low. I brace, ready to run, but his expression is... not threatening.

This man's fleshy face is soft. Except for the fur, which is spotted with gray color. It only covers the bottom part of his face.

This I never understood when seeing humans.

How do they remove the fur above their noses? *Why* do they remove it? Such strange creatures, these humans.

With a soft, even tone, he says to me, "*Comment vous sentez-vous?*"

This I know is how humans howl to each other, for I have heard it. When hunters have stomped through the woods in their bright colors and loud, clompy paw coverings. And usually holding onto the sticks that point with noises that can hurt.

However, I do not see one of those in the man's forepaws.

He continues to speak in a flat tone, and his words, oddly, calm me. This I do not understand, for I should run, run! But my...

I howl once again and cannot stop. I look down and squeeze my eyes closed. What is wrong with my body? Why am I bent and twisted and hairless?

Scowling at the man with the half-haired face, I realize my enemy must have pulled all my fur away! Why do such a thing? What fetish is this, fur-taking man?

I do recall an ancestral memory, however. From my before time. My forefathers and foremothers.

They knew of the people who took our fur. Alas, this usually was after wolf had been killed.

I am not that. At least not yet.

Do I look like he does beneath my fur?

That cannot be.

My head snaps toward the man, for I pick up a new scent. This one of flowers and pungent spices and river smells and... so much I cannot identify. But it is a human woman, this I know.

"John, you are scaring the boy," the flower woman says.

But I do not understand these mouth sounds. They jumble my spinning mind, confuse me. But when I think to this time, I can recall those sounds, exactly as they were howled.

John, you are scaring the boy.

What do those mouth sounds mean? And why can I recall them? Before, when hearing humans speak, it was always the same.

"Blah blah blah blah blah blah?"

"Blah blah blah, blah!"

"Blah blah blah."

Just blah noises. Many and only blah noises.

These were the mouth sounds from hunters. Also much burping and farting.

Why can I now hear, discern the sounds, even if I do not understand them?

My mind flips end over end as I wail once again—another wave of pain. I howl from the hurt but also seeking others from my pack.

"You are safe," the flower woman says.

I shift my weight, trying to get in a position to attack or flee. Why is this grass so crunchy and pokey? I let out a low growl but then stop.

Again, this does not sound like my sounds. My warnings to this human woman should incite fear and awe! But they are so feeble.

And she is not scared. In fact, her lips curve warmly.

"You are okay," she says to me, but the mouth sounds mean nothing. "You are safe."

The woman crouches next to me, and I look up at her face. At how she holds her forepaws. The scent coming from her fair skin. I do not detect danger. Something else.

Something kind.

Again, I howl, but it sounds so strange coming from my mouth.

"Owwwww!"

"Yes." The flower woman bobs her head. "It must hurt. May I?"

She extends a hand toward me, but I flinch back. Then, she stops and folds her paws in her lap. She is sitting on the dry, brittle grass, her head slightly lower than mine. Deference. This is what I expect, for I am wolf, and she is... not.

"Do not get so close, Linda," the man says, his words sounding different than hers. Odd and jarring. "*Dangereux.*"

"Hogwash!" the flower woman says, bending her lips upward. It is a pleasing expression. Even on such a furless face. "He's just a boy."

"This is not ... *C'est impossible!*"

Still bending her lips, a comforting expression, the flower woman speaks softly while looking at me. Not hard staring, not challenging. Just observing.

"How can it be impossible, dear, if he's sitting right here?" She reaches out slowly, and I watch. With her claws—no, not claws; they are fleshy, not sharp.

Like I have now! How is this so?

I allow her to touch my forepaw, which is wrapped in material. Like white leaves all stuck together.

"Hurt?"

Growling low, I stare at her pinkish paw hovering above my injury. She does not touch, however.

Retracting her forepaw, she shifts her weight and nearly falls over.

A strange sound bubbles out of my body, unfamiliar.

"Oh, you think that is funny, do you?" she says as if she thinks I can understand.

Alas, I do not.

"Here. Look." On her rear paw, she has a covering. I have seen hunters wear similar coverings to protect their feet. However, just above this, on her leg, I see a shiny strip and some black vines holding it in place.

"Me too, right?" she says, sitting awkwardly, holding up her leg in her hands. "This got me out of the service. I got more busted up than the Ten Commandments." She lowers her leg and points at it then at my bindings. "Mine will never heal. Well, it's done healing, but I'll wear the brace to the grave."

The man growls, "Do not be so morbid."

"Not helping," she calls back to the man then refocuses on the wolf in front of her. If that is what I am anymore. "We are the same, you and me. A couple of wounded animals."

I do not understand her mouth sounds. But her tone is soothing. Comforting. I... *trust* this human woman. But I know I should not.

Slowly, she gets to her feet and stretches out one of her pink paws, dull finger-claws extending. She waggles them at me.

"Come on inside."

"*Ma chère, non—!*"

"Hush, you," she says to the human man. "He's just a boy. And boys don't go living in barns, no matter how they might smell like it from time to time."

I stare at her wiggling pink claws and am surprised when I reach up and place my forepaw on top. Why does mine look like hers?

She then leans forward and gently holds my other front leg, pulling me upward.

For a moment, I wobble back and forth. What is this? How am I upright?

The flower woman laughs softly. "First time standing, love?" She smiles at me. "Don't worry. You get used to it."

I look down and see that I am much longer than I once was. My fur is gone. Only flesh below but uninjured save my two front legs.

"Let's get you some clothes, huh?" she says. She softly guides me from the barn and into the sunlight.

I shuffle my rear paws across the ground. I feel so high up here. Too high.

"Lift your feet, hon, or you're going to tumble on your butt."

She then motions with her legs, exaggerated motions, pulling a paw off the ground, moving it forward, then repeating this with the other. The flower woman is showing me. Teaching me the world ways. The world ways of humans.

What secrets I could learn! And take this learning back to my pack. These would keep us safe. Safe from hunters!

Maybe.

As instructed, I mimic her movements. Lift, push, down. Lift, push forward, down. Ah, yes. I have seen humans walk this way, and it is not unlike how wolf does. However, on hind legs, it feels like you will fall and smash your snout.

I am startled when the sunlight warms my bare body. The warming of the skin calms my shivering and steadies the beating of my heart.

We have moved out of the barn, which is good. Too many odors, so many of which I could not place. Although familiar, they seemed off. I sniff the air and frown. So little scent?

But then I do pick up a scent. One that is familiar. One that is family.

I look to the bushes next to a wood cave in front of us, this one much larger. Such odd colors and shapes, but these I ignore. Staring intently through the gnarled branches and curled leaves, I lean forward and feel myself falling. I pinch my eyes closed, bracing for more pain.

However, I stop in midair.

I can smell human sweat and something sour. Like foul meat.

When I open my eyes, I see a long black strip with a shiny part in the middle reflecting sunlight. Human legs below, but they are a dull shade of blue. This is the man. He must be very cold to have blue legs.

I feel his forepaws beneath my arms, slowly lifting me upright. Of course, I should growl and snarl and warn him back. But his fur—skin—is soft. Not threatening. His eyes regard me, the edges of which are wavy and wrinkled.

Then his lips curl upward. When I shrink back, he seems to remember himself and hide his teeth behind his lips. He nods to the flower woman.

"I think this will take some patience," he says.

I remember the mouth sounds and roll them through my head, but they are meaningless.

Regarding me once more, he blinks, and the corners of his lips lift higher. "On both our parts, eh, *mon ami*?"

Chapter Eight

"Emelda, get up! Get up! Get up!"

I opened my eyes, instantly awake.

"We have to go," Gregor shouted and yanked his stupid face away from mine. "Now, now, now!"

Jumping up, my mind still half in the dream world, I had to put my fingers on the wall of the motel room to not fall over. No good. No wall there, and I tumbled to the floor.

"Dammit!"

"Where the hell did you go?" Gregor peeked over the rumpled bedcovers and loomed over me, his face shadowed by the sun blazing in through the open curtains.

Did I leave those open?

The tech sergeant reached down for me, and I scuttled back. This guy's face was the last one I wanted to see when waking up. My friggin' enemy, reaching for me.

My mind was still foggy. I must have been sleeping hard. I hopped up again and hit the wall with my shoulder.

Gregor stepped forward, lifting my body like a stuffed animal that had fallen off the bed.

Since I was still wobbly, he gripped my arm. The guy had probably been twice my size before being Enhanced by the Organization's program. Now, he could throw me across the room.

He almost did, dragging me to the door.

That was when I noticed glass scattered across the dull-orange carpet like sand sparkling in the sunlight.

The door was wide open.

"Jesus, did you break the window?"

He took a half step outside, then stared up at the sky, his all-black eyes scanning, searching.

"Had to." His voice sounded shrill. Higher than normal. "You wouldn't wake up. We have to get the hell out of here."

I tried to shrug out of his grip, but it was far too tight. Asshole was going to leave a palm-shaped bruise on my arm.

"I gotta grab my stuff—"

But before I could finish my sentence, *he lifted me off the ground* and sprinted for the Jeep, carrying me like a football in the last moments of the state championships with zeros flashing on the clock. With each long stride, I felt my rib cage slam against his hip.

"Let me down, for—"

"No time," he growled at me between breaths. "They're here."

That stopped me. "Who? What?"

He flipped me right side up so I was standing in front of the Jeep's door. I had to throw my hand out and palm the roof so I didn't topple over again. "Who is—?"

Towering over me, he leaned down and growled, "Did your email go out? Did you forget to reset it?"

"W-what? What email?" I blinked. "No. I mean. Yes, I—"

Gregor leaned back, shaking his head. Something flitted across his dark eyes, then he blinked it away.

Then I recalled him checking the sky the night before. I began to tilt my head back, and lightning fast, his massive palm gripped my head.

"Jesus, don't look up!"

I growled at him. "Why not?"

"Not now," he shouted, running around to the passenger side of my vehicle. "Get inside first. I'll tell you, but we've got to split. Right now!"

"I need—" I started to say and saw my keys fly toward me. I snatched them out of the air, more to protect my face than anything else. When I looked down at the keys, I saw a few long, purple-tinted dark strands.

Asshole grabbed me so hard he'd yanked hair out!

I jumped inside and slammed the door behind me.

Gregor was fumbling for the passenger-side shade, finally got it flipped down, then slumped back, breathing heavily. Then, panicked, he burst forward and snapped mine down as well.

"Where am I going?'

"Just drive, Emelda!" he shouted, the pupils of his black eyes pinpricks against a pool of white. "Anywhere."

His fear had finally wormed its way into my brain. My heart was rabbiting as I fired up the Jeep, dropped it into reverse, and punched the gas.

I'd braced myself for it.

He hadn't.

Gregor flew forward and smashed his face into the dash with a satisfying thunk.

Ah, good. Perked me right up. Better than coffee.

I snapped on my seat belt and, before he could do the same, jammed the Jeep into drive and launched toward the motel lot's exit, spitting gravel that pinged off a rusted Buick. Gregor flew back, smacking his head on the headrest. It made a wonderful double clacking sound that warmed my heart's cockles.

Whatever those were, they were warm.

We bounced out of the lot and onto the frontage road. By this time, he'd gotten the message and was holding onto the "oh shit" strap above the window.

"Where am I going?" I shouted at him over the screaming engine. When he didn't answer right away, I saw him looking intently at the red liquid smeared across his fingers. When he'd flown into the dash, he'd bloodied his nose. His breathing hitched as he stared, frozen.

"Hey, man, I need to know—"

Gregor stuffed his fingers into his mouth and moaned.

Shit. Shit, shit, shit.

Maybe I should stop antagonizing him for a little while. Dude seemed, um, hungry. And not for a breakfast burrito.

"Fine," I said, my tone calmer. "Can you at least tell me what the hell is going on?"

That snapped him out of it, and he wiped the saliva from his hand onto his tight green shirt. Yep, Gregor was a tight-T guy.

Is this a surprise? No, it is not a surprise.

Dude dressed like he was still in the military. Green shirt, camo pants with that green-and-yellow pattern. With his black hair so shortly cropped it looked silver—I still didn't understand that, because he couldn't have been more than ten years older than me—he looked like a sci-fi movie extra.

In the credits, he'd be Asshole Military Thug 9 or something.

Thankfully, I'd slept in my clothes, a habit of mine born not from laziness but from the years in which I'd had to race out of wherever I was hiding out the moment my eyes came open.

Well, sure, *some* laziness.

But I was happy to be in a T-shirt and jeans, because I ain't an exhibitionist. No shoes, but I'd always felt better without them anyhow.

Instead of answering my questions, Gregor pressed his face against the window, flattening it, so he could see the sky.

Looking between the road and him slow dancing cheek to cheek with the glass, I let out a sigh of exasperation. "Dude!" I shouted and flicked his ear with the thwack of a finger. "I thought we weren't supposed to look at the scary sky."

Gregor flinched back and hunched low in his seat. Not easy for such a big dude. Not Kane big, of course, but topping six feet. Still, he looked like a kid folded into a car seat. His head was snapping left and right, twitching at every movement. Holy hell, the guy was losing it.

"Right. Too true. Yes." Trying to recover a shred of dignity, he sat straighter. "Head to a town called Rentchler, just east of here."

I reached for my phone, which was usually in the console between the seats, and sighed. "My phone's back in the room."

"So?"

"I don't know how to get to wherever that is! Usually, I just map it and then—"

"No, no!" He said and chuckled, shaking his head slowly. He'd regained his arrogant asshat self in a blink. "Don't use commercial map software, silly girl."

I hooded my eyes. "Call me a silly girl again."

"I was—"

"Do it," I said and punched the accelerator, gripping the wheel so tight my light-brown fingers turned white.

His hand flew back up to the window strap, the other jutting out to the dash, like the dude thought a surf pose would prevent crash injury. "Okay, okay," he said. "I take it back."

I slowed. "Take it back? What? Are you seven years old?"

Gregor raised his hands in surrender and pointed at the entrance ramp. A sign next to it said we were getting onto Highway 15.

"Map applications are a gift to intelligence organizations all around the world. You don't even have to hack into them. You just pay the software company like any other restaurant or gas station or lingerie shop, and they *give* you data. No names, but all you need is a few data points, and you'll get that easy."

"Fine. Whatever."

Sliding into traffic, I slipped between two semi-trucks driving side by side but one lane apart. Running parallel, they looked like they could have been having a shouted conversation through open windows.

Gregor looked between them, his mouth a thin line.

Paranoid as hell, this guy. More little birdlike head twitches. Chewing on his bottom lip. Hands that wandered and didn't know where they wanted to be.

I'd seen stuff like this before. Too much.

Passing the trucks, I draped my fingers over the wheel. "We should get you some gummies or something."

"I don't have a sweet tooth. No."

"Uh-uh," I said. "CBD can help a little with the cravings."

"Cravings?" He scowled at me.

I shrugged. "Yeah. You're jonesing right now, and a bit of CBD can—"

"I... I..." He burst out laughing, bending at the waist, putting a hand to his stomach. "I am not an *addict*, Emelda Thorne."

"Okay. So are we still driving to a hidden warehouse in the middle of Missouri to sneak past some bloodthirsty monster so you can get your stash? Has that changed?"

His laughter died away as his face went slack. But when I looked into his lap, his hand was balled into a fist. Dude was hurting.

"Call it what you like," he said. "We're about twenty-five minutes away. I'll tell you where to turn."

For a while, we drove in silence. I saw him glancing at the radio a few times, at me, then back at the radio. This tickled me a bit. In some small way, I had cowed the guy. An Enhanced human being three times my size.

Good Emelda.

"What happens if you don't, you know, take the stuff?"

My voice startled him a little. Then he blinked those big black eyes at me.

"I've never gone more than a few days," he said, looking at the tiny trees whipping past the window. "I'd gone through the program, months and months of that, but in the end, my body never acclimated fully to the serum. In about seventy hours, my immune system burns it up."

"That didn't happen with Cal Davis?"

He looked like he'd chewed on a dry aspirin. "No. He went through all the same shit I did. The drug manipulation, the stress tests, all of it. When he came out the other side, magic: his body took the virus and its little package of goodies onboard. They became part of him. Hammer posited that his body might have even begun to make little Enhanced blood gremlins of its own."

I grinned. "Not you, though?"

"No, not me," he said, looking down has he finally relaxed his fist, staring at his fingers. "But I am the only other subject who responded favorably to the treatment. I can run faster and for longer than anyone in the world. I'm stronger. Hear better, see better. I am better."

"Yeah, you're neat," I said. "But Bridget Mills and Charlie Boynton—"

"Not the same." He shook his head and let his eyes shut. "Cal had bitten them, so yes, they got the manipulated virus. But they hadn't gone through conditioning. Like it did with that Devil's Dawn moron—"

"Crank?"

"Whatever. For those who aren't properly conditioned, the serum enhances them, but it mangles the body and breaks the mind. *Those* are your monsters, Emelda Thorne."

I nodded, recalling how Bridget had looked. "Mangled" was a good word. And that had been before Doc Hammer had sliced and diced her.

Gregor had physical changes as well, but they were more subtle. Larger hands. Fingers capped with thick, curved nails. Legs and arms unnaturally long. All that could be passed off as just him being a weird dude.

Until he looked at you.

"How well can you see with those crazy eyes?"

He scowled. "They're not crazy. They're *Enhanced*, Emelda Thorne."

"They're like doll eyes. If that doll were Chucky."

"Not true," he said then added softly, "Chucky had blue eyes."

I couldn't help but laugh. "Well, ya got me there!"

He pointed ahead, down the highway about a quarter mile. "Do you see that yellow Honda?"

Squinting, I could see a tiny yellowish blob. From my angle, it looked like a squashed bug on my windshield.

"Yeah. Is that a Honda?"

"It is. A Civic."

"Great, so you can see car makes from—"

"It's license plate reads Y95 4651."

I squinted again. "No way! You can really see *that* far?"

He shrugged. "I can do so many things you cannot, Emelda Thorne. Also, if we do catch up to that car, you should tell them something."

I bobbled my head from side to side. "Okay. What?"

"Their tag expired last month."

Chapter Nine

"Slow down. Somewhere… here," Gregor said, leaning his head over the dash, looking left and right.

He slid one long fingernail across the glass as if he was trying to pick out some discoloration or hidden sign on the side of the road.

The tall grass stood like mottled sentries facing the blacktop, the front line against the encroaching urbanization of humans.

After turning off the main highway, we'd passed through a few long-forgotten neighborhoods. The homes looked as if they'd been rather nice when first built. Small family units, starter houses, all neat and orderly in rows as if some developer years earlier had been a big fan of Monopoly, learned the joy of square units in a line, and replicated that here.

In the decades that followed, the only upgrades offered these structures had been entropy.

Run-down. The paint peeling. Lush front yards had given way to dirt, sand, and rock. Wire fencing surrounded each home, as if the owner had concluded someone must have been stealing the grass in the dead of night and was now trying to prevent anyone else from pilfering what was left.

After a few blocks, the view out my windows changed from homes to an old industrial area. Big warehouses and factories, which stained the air with machine grease and misery.

Most of the parking areas were empty, though. Factories had been shut down.

In one lot, amid all the misaligned wheel stops—some smashed, others swinging around on their rebar—someone had parked a small food truck. Maybe it had been a coffee-and-sandwich stand. Hard to tell, because it had been stripped. Copper and other metals ripped out, sold for pennies a pound. Windows smashed. The vehicle slouched awkwardly, half on the concrete lot and half on dead grass.

All the workers had bailed when the facility had closed down. I kinda felt bad for the food truck. Someone had stolen its wheels, so it couldn't follow. Trapped and alone.

I'd laughed at myself. My heart was breaking, just a little, for a food truck.

When Kane had become a golden retriever, he'd been concerned about a sort of empathy echo it had left behind when he'd become human again. Had I picked up some of that?

No. Maybe I just had a soft spot for things left behind.

"There!" Gregor said, pointing at nothing.

It had taken fifteen minutes of driving around the run-down industrial area before he finally recognized some detail from a previous visit, one he'd been very cagey about. Only when we started running out of structures, where the factories and warehouses abutted a wooded area, did he see it.

"What?" I said, slowing, scanning the side of the road. "I don't see—"

"There's a post. It's rusted, blends in with the dead grass. About fifty feet ahead."

"Post."

"Yes, a post!" he said, eyes blazing at me. Then he blinked, regaining some control.

"Fine, okay. I don't have black-eyed vision like you, so you gotta tell me where to turn."

"At the post, there's a path. Take that," he said, pointing a long finger. "We're only a few minutes away from the facility."

"I don't see anything. Just dead grass." I looked out my window and tapped the glass. "Oh, no. There's a hill. That is also covered in dead grass."

Gregor leaned back in his seat, crossing his arms. "Yes, yes. The hill blocks the view of the factory from the road. But that isn't what I'm worried about."

"Oh?"

He licked his lips. "At the hotel—"

"Motel. Don't try to make it sound fancy."

"—it... Whatever," he said, waving my interruption away. "I heard a buzzing sound."

"We all get to sleep in different ways." I shrugged. "You've got yours, I've got mine."

"I *didn't* sleep well," he said, tugging at his lip, totally missing what I thought was a pretty good joke. Well, pretty average. "But I never do sleep well anymore. Such strange dreams."

"Focus." I snapped my fingers in front of his face. "Weird buzzy sound?"

"Ah, that's the problem. It *wasn't* weird. I knew it," he said, shrinking away from the passenger window slightly. "Hell, I'd used devices like that on countless occasions. Just never been on the receiving end."

"Of…?"

"Drone. Or, likely, drones."

"Wait. You think they're looking for us?"

"Of course they are! We are the loose ends here."

With the help of Gregor's waggling finger, I finally spotted the rusted post nestled in the dead grass. At the top, a bolt. From there, dark chain links dipped then disappeared into a fibrous pool of brown foliage and shadow.

I could just make out the slightest dip where the road had been torn out. Armies of grass, weeds, and thistle had reclaimed the space. A win for nature until the summer sun claimed its own victory.

Crossing my arms, I eyed the tech sergeant. "I didn't hear any drones."

"You didn't hear me knocking on the damn door, Emelda!" Blinking quickly, he stole a peek at the sky then rolled down the window. "I don't… h-hear any now. They are likely doing a grid search, but those things whip along fast. They've got AI scanning the data, but it's far from perfect."

"Who? Who is sending all these drones after us?"

Eyes locked on the sky, he spoke in a hoarse whisper. "Everybody."

"Come on!"

"The Organization wants their pound of flesh from me, and there's a very good chance Doc Hammer fired up Covenant's resources the moment she took your friend. I'd bet she knows I didn't die in the fire."

"How?"

He tapped a long finger at his bottom lip, staring at the dash. "Doesn't matter. We need to get off this road and get your Jeep hidden."

"Won't they check this place?" I pointed in the direction of the hill. "I mean, if they're gunning for us, wouldn't this be one of the first places they'd look?"

Gregor barked out another one of those creepy, schizoid laughs. "No way, no way," he said, smiling to himself as he stared out into the slow, undulating waves of dead and dying grass. "No one would think we'd be crazy enough to get anywhere near Marta."

Chapter Ten

Kane

I am sitting on the chair. No, it is couch, not chair. Chair is the tree thing. Couch is... longer, softer. And humans hide small things down between its soft stones.

Not stones. The flower woman has told me these are cushions.

Cushions, a difficult word to say aloud in English, which I am slowly learning. I prefer the French mouth sounds that the man teaches me.

Not mouth sounds. They are words!

Softly, I say, "*Coussins.*"

Very strange when I say their words. In my head, I get the same image no matter if I use the woman words—English—or the man words. I prefer his words. Far less bouncy.

Sitting *sur les coussins*... Now I am jumbling both human languages, which was the warning that the man gave to the woman. But I can discern. I am pretty sure I can.

I have slept more than two forepaws of nights *dans la maison*. The wood cave, I have learned, is called a house. *Maison*. That one I actually prefer in English because it feels more familiar to wolf. Like calling—

"I don't like it, Linda. I do not like this at all."

They are whispering in the food place. Room. Kitchen. The man makes low barking word sounds. The flower woman's voice is higher but as strong.

I do not think they know I can hear them.

She says to the man, "Well, you can't expect the poor boy to—"

"He is not a boy! This is a wolf who lives in our house, *n'est pas*?"

"No, he is a boy and one day will be a man."

The man laughs. "And you know this how?"

"Because I've had two boys, and that's the generally accepted progression."

"Not always, *chère*," the man said, his voice dropping in volume. Sadness is there. Pain. "It does not always work out so."

They are quiet for a moment. I listen closely, not understanding all of the English words. The man, it was decided, spends more time with me. I think this is because they are afraid of me. And, maybe, they believe the man would endure less harm from a... boy who was wolf.

But I would not hurt either of them. They have been kind.

I turn back to the world box with a show about the French boy who does not like school. He is named Caillou and has a round head. No fur on top, as most humans have. The man often puts me in front of this show to better understand human language.

What I best understand is that French Canadian children are terrible little humans. They do not behave, get into trouble on purpose, and often jump in dirty puddles.

I want to be just like Caillou.

Except he is always very tiny. The man says he is four years old, but after many, many shows, still four years old.

It is not the same with me. I am growing very fast. My first days *dans la*... in the house, I could not reach up to where the woman keeps the glass jar with the tasty, colorful stones. Now larger than before, I can get to these easily when they are distracted.

I believe Caillou would approve.

But it feels like what humans call lying. That is not an animal thing, so I consider telling them what I have done. I fear it may upset.

The whispers have stopped. The man returns from the food room and sits next to me on the couch.

"It seems that you will be with us for some time," he says in his human language. "Do you understand these words I have said?"

"Yes," I say to the man and do the nod thing. Pushing the nose up and down also means yes, but the humans like it, so I do this. "I have learned much from my friend on the world box. He teaches me your words."

"The television?" This gets a chuckle from the man. "From Caillou? I think we may be creating a monster!"

"I am not a monster," I tell him, furrowing my brow. "I am wolf."

"Yes. Yes," he says, rubbing his furry chin. "But for now, you are a human. And my wife believes that we are responsible for you."

My fleshy cheeks warm, but I do not yet understand why. I ask him, "What are the meanings of those words?"

He sighs. "It means that you are here because of our family. Something our son Cal has done to you changed you from wolf to boy. I do not understand any of it, but alas, here you sit."

"I am wolf."

"Yes, but on the outside, you are a teenage boy," he says then scratches at his fur again. "But already growing so fast. My wife believes…"

He stops his mouth sounds. There is a twitch at the side of his mouth, his shoulders slump, and his chest buckles inward.

I extend a… hand to him and place it on his shoulder, as he has done for me. This is to comfort.

"Do you need me to leave? Am I troubling you?"

The man puts a balled hand to his lips and lets out a soft cry. Then he squeezes his eyes together and shakes his head side to side. "No, no. You are a sweet boy," he says and smiles. "Despite what Caillou may have taught you."

"He helped me understand human speaking."

"I hope that is all," the man says, smiling. His eyes sparkle, and I realize there is a dampness there.

I decide not to tell him about the tiny stones I have taken from the clear jar. The darker red-blue ones… purple, I think is the word… those are the best.

But I do not say this.

He continues, "My wife feels it would be best if we gave you a chance in the human world. This means you will have to be, um, real."

"I am real. I am wolf."

"What I am saying is that you will need a name. And documentation."

Shuffling my legs, I wipe my palms across the tops of my jean pants. "I do not know this word."

"It means, well, it means you need what humans call a paper trail," he says then waves his hand in the air to prevent more questions. "Do not worry about what that means. It does not matter."

"Okay. I trust you."

The man draws his hand across his eyes, looks away for a moment, then swallows and nods to himself. This, I have learned, is a human thing. He has made a choice in his head.

"Some years ago, we lost a son. A boy."

"And you want me to help find him. I can—"

"No, no, dear boy." He laughs, but it is watery sounding. He clears his throat and smiles at me without showing his teeth. "He died. As a baby. My wife is a smart woman and knows that if you are to live among the humans one day, you will need an identity."

This is a word they have taught me. "I do have an i-den-tity."

"Yes, yes," he says and rubs his hand over my head.

I laugh when he does.

"You are wolf, this I know. But you must be human. And to do this... you will, at least on paper, be the son we lost."

I frown, chewing my lip. I do not want to disappoint the man. But I am struggling with what he is saying. "I do not understand."

"You will have a birth certificate," he said and again raises his hand in a "don't say anything" motion. "And even shot records. Maybe one day even go to school, but my wife thinks it would be better to maybe learn here."

Nodding, not understanding, I just listen. I know this is difficult for him to say, and I wait with respect.

"The baby died many years ago," he said, his voice quivering, his lips shaking. "We couldn't bear... to speak of it. So the only one who really knows of this is our family doctor. At some point, we will have to visit Dr. Fineman and—" The man belly laughs, and tears sprinkle onto his cheeks. He wipes them away, sniffling. "Will *that* be a conversation!"

I laugh too.

I have no idea what he is talking about.

But I have learned that reflecting the emotions and mannerisms of humans, this comforts them. They drop their guard.

I learned this on my own. Caillou did not tell me of it. Maybe I have left the teachings of Caillou behind.

"Whenever people in town asked of our boy, we did not speak of this. It was too painful, and eventually, they stopped asking," the man continues with soft, gentle words. "So when they see you, they will think you are that boy. If you are to be among the humans, you will have to, well, be among the humans. Learn how they move and speak and act."

I nod. "But you have said to me that I grow very fast. Would your boy have done the same? For your deception relies on this, yes?"

The man claps his hands and holds them to his chest. "You are so clever! Boy, I do not think I will ever get over that," he says, still smiling. "But, yes, this is true. You would be some years older, but human memories are fuzzy. And my wife did not go into town when pregnant because of her bad leg. Carrying that weight was too much."

I point to the television. "This is when she watched her shows. Because she is a TV junkie, yes?"

"Shh, shh, shh," the man says with a half grin. "Let's keep that, um, designation between you and me, okay? Our secret."

"Yes," I say, reflecting his smile. My eyes flick to the doorway, my smile growing, then I look down at my hands. "Okay."

"And since we are conspiring... you will have a name, and it will be the name of our second child. You will answer to that name and repeat it to others as your own."

"And you will have new names for us," the woman says from the doorway, leaning against the frame. When she had approached a minute before, she held a finger to her mouth, so I said nothing.

The man's face reddens, and he spins around to look at her.

"This is not what we agreed upon, chère. We said we would discuss it—"

"No, *you* said we would discuss it, and we did," she says. She is speaking too quickly in English, so I do not understand all of her words. I believe this is why she made her mouth sounds happen in this manner.

The woman limps around the furniture of the living room, sitting opposite the man. She takes my hand in hers, a big smile on her face that fills my chest. I very much like her warm smiles. In French, she says, "You can't keep calling us man and woman, right?"

"Okay," I say, looking to the man. His mouth is a straight line, flickering at its corners. To her, I say again, "Okay."

Beaming, she begins in English, "I will be—"

"*En français*," the man interrupts. "He does not fully understand your language because it is painful to the ears."

"No, it's because you wouldn't let me go near the boy for a week," she says, her French halting and staggering. This is also painful to the ears, but I do not say such. "He is sweet and harmless."

"I do not believe I am either of those things. I am wolf."

"And I will be *mum*," she says in English. She chuckles, eliciting a grunt from behind me. She rolls her eyes at the man and reverts to French once again. "You will call me *Mère*. This lump of smelly man then will be *Père*."

I know these words from Caillou. Mother. Father.

The man I am to call *Père* sighs. "I do not think—"

"No, the problem is you think too much, John!" the woman I am to call Mère says. She softens as she speaks to me, her smile returning. "And from now on, for your own safety, you will be our boy."

Nodding, I point to the man. "Père." I point to the woman. "Mère." Jutting a thumb at my chest, I say, "Our Boy."

The woman laughs musically, and this makes me smile.

"No, dear, dear boy," she says and takes my fleshy cheeks in her hands. "You are Kane. Your name is Kane."

Chapter Eleven

The Jeep had spun a bit as we climbed the rise, kicking out dirt and rock and grass, and I'd eased off the accelerator—not stopping, or I'd never get going again. That was what growing up driving through Minnesota winters taught me.

Keep moving.

Finally, we crested the hill and saw something that looked as if it had come out of the *Walking Dead* deleted-scenes reel.

Enclosing an area about the size of a high school football field, the concrete walls looked as though they'd risen out of the dying earth with thoughts of one day becoming a high-rise. Then, maybe, like the foliage surrounding the structure, they had become starved of either nutrients or the will to live.

The path my vehicle jostled along led to an L-shaped parking lot. The asphalt, split and weathered, bore the scars of neglect. Through the cracks, roots snaked out like skeletal fingers, reaching out from the ground as if trying to drag their prey below.

Faded graffiti tattooed a few of the walls, but I'd seen a shit-ton of the stuff in my day, and this stuff looked off. Wrong. A few half-hearted attempts with overlapping clusters of misshapen letters that seemed to suggest some gang had marked the area as its territory.

Bulbous letter *A*s, swooping *L*s, that sort of thing, haloed by rippling ribbons of color. But the markings were too evenly dispersed. No manic corner bursts here and there.

What tickled my brain was that there had been *zero* artistry to it. No flourish. If there had been a paint-by-number stencil for "graffiti," it would have vomited out this horrific shit.

This had been designed to *look* like graffiti conveying one message: Go away.

Gregor leaned forward, almost birdlike, which was odd for a guy so damn meaty, hands hanging down like those of a little kid looking over a low fence. He pointed to the left.

"Over on that side is a loading area we used last year."

"Last *year*," I said, edging the wheel in the direction he'd indicated. I'd lost any semblance of a path within fifty feet of heading into the grass. Me, I'm a literal trailblazer. "It looks like this place hasn't been used in a decade."

He sighed. "That is the *point*, obviously."

A minute later, I traded dead grass for dirty concrete, pulling into the lot. The building looked much bigger closer up.

Three rows of dark windows stared down at me like hollow eyes, some of their frames hanging slightly askew. None of the glass had been broken, which, come on, was impossible. Hell, I wanted to break a few of the windows.

I wove around the debris scattered across the parking lot. Dead branches and bushes. Busted bits of wood. Rusted barrels tipped on their sides, squished at their openings, so it felt like I was driving through a field of toothless mouths.

And I felt like I had eyes all over me.

"Aren't there cameras out here, watching out for people trying to mess with this place?"

"There were, but a big storm wiped out most of them in the spring. The Organization didn't bother replacing them because they don't have any plans for this place. Basically just storage." Craning his neck to stare up at the building, he added, "Of a sort."

"But, I mean, surely someone would try and bash out a window and get in to see if there's anything worth taking."

He waved ahead again, moving his long fingers in a sweeping motion. "Keep moving. Need to get this thing under cover."

I laughed. "So you don't think the tire tracks gouged through the grass from the main road to here will give us away? From above, that's like two arrows pointing 'They went thataway.'"

Gregor snapped back as if he'd heard a gunshot. Gripping the back of his seat, he stared for a moment out the rear window of the vehicle then twisted back and slumped into his seat again.

"Can't be helped. Just means we've got to move quicker."

When we came around the side, the building blocked out the early-morning sun, and the temperature dropped fifteen degrees. Didn't explain why my hands were damp on the wheel, mind you.

I had to wind around some old wooden crates that had been busted and now lay rotting from the endless cycle of rain and punishing heat. Metal straps that used to hold the containers together had split away, leaving them lying open like broken and rusting rib cages.

At the far end, a carport ran perpendicular to the dead factory. The roof of it drooped at a slant.

Bending around another pile of what looked like mechanical cat vomit, I eased up then slowed to a stop in front of it. Gregor was fogging up his window, scanning up and down the building. His hands splayed on the glass like some kid frustrated by how slow their parents were pulling into the Disneyland parking lot.

"That doesn't seem too sturdy. The roof's uneven," I said, eying the carport. When I didn't get a response, I smacked Gregor's shoulder with the back of my hand.

He spun toward me, teeth bared, and it took everything in me not to flinch. I wasn't going to give him that. Then he blinked the expression away and peered out the windshield.

"It's fine." He straightened his shoulders and lifted his chin, his hands now in his lap. The palm prints on the window evaporated as if left there by a ghost. "Those columns are reinforced. They were installed at that angle."

"Right," I said, easing the Jeep forward and under the awning. "Hard to get good help these days."

Once we were tucked under the overhang, I dropped the vehicle into park and killed the engine.

When I went to grab my phone from the cupholder, my fingers just dangled in that empty space. Felt unnatural. You go through routine moves, and when they're interrupted, it tilts your world a bit. Flick off the ignition, grab phone with one hand, thumb seat belt button with the other, pull handle on door, give it a knee to open, then step out.

Before I could grab the keys, Gregor beat me to it. He held them up and jangled them in front of my face. "Don't need you running off."

"Whatever."

I got out and slammed the door. When Gregor exited, his face was all business. His black eyes stared at the muted blue sky above.

"You hear anything?" I asked him.

"I hear everything."

"What about any buzzy bee sounds that might be a fleet of killer drones?"

He tilted his head then shook it once.

"It's not just drones, mind you," he said as he began walking toward the building, using the carport as cover. "There are eight thousand satellites buzzing around the planet. You'd think all that high tech would be more secure than Department of Defense servers." He looked back over his shoulder. "Easy hack. Actually, come to think of it, so are the DoD servers."

Heading toward a set of stairs, he stepped over an overturned barrel. I didn't have abnormally long legs and had to walk around it. Two burned-out cars blocked the path ahead, so he had to step out from under the cover of the carport, and he picked up the pace. I had to nearly jog to keep up.

At the top of the steps, he stopped at the large steel door and searched all around its edges.

Looking up then back at him, I asked, "You gonna go inside?"

"It's locked, of course."

I pointed toward the handle. "It's got a keypad," I said. "Do you know the code?"

He started reaching into his pocket but then stopped. Then he crouched, staring at the handle.

"I used to have a rotating authenticator."

"Right," I said, sighing. "Probably not enough bran."

Without even seeing his face, I knew he'd rolled his eyes. "An app on our devices that would change up the code every thirty seconds or so. High-end stuff."

"Right. I got the same thing for my Facebook login. Two-factor authentication."

"Ha, no. It's far more complex than that."

I shifted my weight from foot to foot. "Fine. Pull up your thingybob and type in the code."

He stood from his crouch, towering over me, and stared down his nose. "I got rid of that phone back at the truck stop. But even if I hadn't..." He turned his head toward the door. "Punching the code in would trigger the camera."

"What cam—" I said and saw him point.

About three stories up, I saw an odd blister just below one of the windows, a hump that bowed out from the structure. With all the weather damage, it looked like it could have been the bottom pane simply warping. Except for the glint of a glass lens tucked inside.

"You said the cams got knocked out."

"Just around the property. High winds and a power surge that fried their little antennas. That one up there is hard-wired in, and it's a problem." He scratched the back of his short silver hair. Then, he turned to me with the biggest smile I'd seen him wear all day. With those big honking teeth, the look actually made me shiver.

I said, "What?"

"How do you feel about heights?"

Chapter Twelve

Normally, I don't mind heights. And I'd done plenty of less-than-legal things like climbing into windows and scurrying up a drainpipe or two.

This?

I minded this.

"Jesus, what the hell am I supposed to hold onto?" I grunted, digging my toes into his shoulder as he held me steady.

Despite his assurances that the weather-beaten awning of the carport had only been made to look rickety, it was giving me zero confidence it would hold my weight.

"If you fall," he said, pushing the bottom of my foot with his palm, "I'll catch you."

"What if I tumble over the other side?"

I felt his weight shift below me. "Yeah, don't do that."

"Helpful."

When I finally did pull myself up onto the slanted roof, I crouched low. I twisted my head back, and my mouth went dry as I stared the length of the carport. It consisted of a twenty-foot slant that flattened into what looked like a long, dirty banquet table.

Drawing in a deep breath, I started up to the second floor on my hands and knees.

It hadn't rained in weeks, and all the grit and sand and dead leaves made it feel like I was trying to scale a giant air hockey table propped up at an angle. Each time I moved a knee, the metal beneath me complained.

"Lay your palms flat," Gregor said from below.

When I looked down to scowl at him, I noticed he hadn't stepped out to watch. Dude really was paranoid about eyes in the sky.

"Pull yourself along."

"Shut it."

"I'm only—"

"You are *only* shutting it!" I shouted and slid back half a foot. "Dammit."

Slowly, inch by inch, I finally made it to the crest that had been bolted to the outside wall.

The windows were recessed within concrete. On top of that was a layer of metal, plaster, and plastic guards. Most importantly, the closest window was about three feet away from the edge of the awning. I'd have to climb along that thin ledge to get access.

Carefully, I lifted my leg, bracing with the other as I dug my nails into the gap between the overhang and the wall. It felt like a deadly game of Twister.

Right foot to concrete rectangle.

That thought was starting to produce a giggle in me—this was so dumb!—but when my toes slipped, that bit of giddiness evaporated.

Gregor called from below, "You nearly there?"

I didn't bother answering.

When my ex, Roy, and I had done a bit of "finders keepers," as he'd called it, it had always been at night, under the cover of darkness. Sure, we'd scoped the place out in the days before, even taking photographs we could refer to, which felt very James Bond or something.

Those were often pricey houses. So if one of us did fall—and I never did—at least there was fluffy grass or soft flower beds or cheery garden gnomes below to catch you.

I looked down.

My head swam, and I closed my eyes. If I landed down there, it was all busted concrete and rusted rebar.

I sighed, opened my eyes again, and slowly pulled myself onto the ledge. It was about as wide as my foot. Or as big as the center line on a road, and hell, I could walk that simply enough even when kinda drunk.

That theory had been tested. More than once.

But ten feet up, the ledge felt as wide as a nail file. Way, way too skinny.

"What the hell am I supposed to do if I can even get inside?"

I saw Gregor's foot slide into view. Just the shiny black boot and nothing else. He was being more cautious than I was, and I was hanging off the side of a building!

"There's a stairwell on this side of the factory. Just head down, open the door, and we'll go from there."

Of course, in his summation, he'd neglected to mention *she* was inside. An Enhanced woman he'd called Marta was lurking somewhere in there. I didn't take any comfort from his assurances that she had been trapped on the other side of the building.

Standing slowly to my full height, I scuttled along, my cheek pressed to the wall. I felt the porous stone grind against my face and didn't care. Hell, if it took my skin down to the bone, all good with me. Just as long as I didn't take a tumble.

By the time the tips of my fingers reached the window, I could feel pinpricks of sweat bursting from my scalp. Below me, I heard the shuffle of feet. Gregor was watching closely but, thankfully, not asking anymore inane questions.

Pulling myself along, I put one foot on the sill, bent a knee, and moved forward. From here, if I could get the damn window open, I could just swing around and get inside.

Naturally, there were no handholds on the outside.

Very inconsiderate.

But a metal strap of the window's frame had bent and twisted from years of shitty weather. Making sure that I didn't slice my hand open, I tried to pull it up with my right hand. Nada.

I pulled harder, gritting my teeth, and nearly fell back when I peeled the metal strip farther from the pane. My legs were already aching, and I braced myself, my left arm gripping the back of my ankle.

"Pull it again," Gregor called up.

"I almost fell, asshat!" I growled at him. "It's not opening."

"What? No, you did. It's open a crack."

Ah, right. I hadn't seen that.

Maybe that was because I'd jammed my eyes closed, which was always the best plan when seeing what was happening could actually prevent me from dying. But the brain does what the brain wants.

And we'd never really been on good terms.

"There's a gap now," Gregor shouted. "Wasn't there before. You might be able to get a digit or two in there."

I crouched lower as I held onto the strip to get a better look. Sure enough, there was a gap about the width of a finger.

How the hell did he see...?

Right. Those big black eyes.

"Fine," I said and slid my back foot forward, my chin resting on my other knee. Then I scooted my butt along until I was facing the window, staring at the tiny black line at the bottom all the while.

Up on the balls of my bare feet, I wiggled my fingertips into the gap. Then I sighed and looked inside, ready to lift.

Staring back at me was a pair of eyes.

I screamed.

Then I fell.

Chapter Thirteen

My stomach punched my throat as losing all connection to the Earth filled me with electric-white panic.

I felt the snip of the concrete ledge as my feet slid off and then nothing. Such a queer feeling, floating and falling, arms flailing out. My world dropped into slo-mo.

I didn't know if that was some lizard-brain response, stretching out time so I could work something out, or the meted-out sentence from some higher power.

Here, this is where you die, so we're gonna slow the tape so you can see where you royally screwed up.

The only things moving quickly were the lightning strikes of fear lashing my nerve endings, making my body spasm and twist.

The falling sensation turned almost pleasant, like a dopamine hit or some kind of drug squeezed into my veins because I knew what would happen at the end of this.

It was gonna hurt.

This kind of dying would hurt all over.

I felt the impact wrap around my hips and then across my shoulders.

That... didn't make sense.

My neck snapped back, but then I felt something grab it and hold it steady. My hips ached.

Eyes open this time, I stared up at a pale sun and a blue sky that looked like it had been splattered onto a page by a lazy kid with cheap, watered-down paint.

So strange. My legs were dangling in the air. Then I realized, so were my arms.

My world tilted, and the sun got knocked out of my field of vision by a parking lot as I felt two hands set me on my feet once again.

"You almost got it," Gregor said as he strode back under the shade of the carport. Then he spun around, sank to a knee, held his hands in front of him, and intertwined his fingers. "Try again."

He'd caught me.

I had fallen from the second story, and he'd leaped over and snatched me from the air like I'd been an old sweatshirt that had drifted off a clothesline.

Now he was waiting to boost me up once again.

I pointed upward. "I almost died!"

Gregor huffed. "We're always almost dying. Every minute of the day. You didn't, so..." He popped his elbows up and down, lifting his cupped hands. It looked comical, like he was doing a crouched hoedown or something.

I looked at the window where I'd been scared to death—almost literally—by two brown eyes. Not black. Brown.

My own eyes reflected in the glass.

From where I stood, it looked like a mile up. Glancing back at Gregor with his happy hands, I sighed.

Here to there.

* * *

When I finally got the window slid open, it jammed on its runners halfway up. That was no problem. I'd sneaked into spaces much smaller than that. Poking my head in, I stared into a disaster.

I had no idea if this had once been a sales area or where widget orders were taken in and distributed, but it looked like, at one point, it had been a shared office.

It still *looked* like an office, but one in which all the windows had been left open during a hurricane.

A desk was broken into four pieces, smashed, its legs up in the air, bent and reaching, like the carcass of a dead bug.

Oh, and there were actual bugs crawling everywhere. Roaches and beetles scurrying around on the floor.

"Lovely," I said and put my hands out. And, bugs be damned, I rolled inside. I felt the crunch of a couple of ex-roaches on my back.

I scanned my surroundings.

The busted-up frame of the desk was to my left, but its drawers were on the far-right side of the room, their contents strewn everywhere. Food wrappers and copier paper held in stacks by black mold.

I kicked at a perfectly neat ream of paper, and something fat and gray scuttled out.

"Horsefeathers!" I shouted and jumped back.

The mouse raced across the room, over stacks of garbage and shredded paper, running right at the wall, slipped through a crack and disappeared.

"*Horsefeathers?*" I said again, smiling this time. A favorite curse of my grandmother. I reached into my shirt and felt for the locket she'd given me—still there. I rubbed my thumb over it.

I saw an office chair, but it looked as if the leather had been chewed away, leaving only stuffing behind. A few feet away, two old-school wooden chairs, busted up.

Gregor had said that when the Organization had taken over the old factory building, they'd made it look more broken down. Weathered. Of course, I didn't know how much of the damage had been what they'd walked into and how much they'd bash-bedazzled later on.

Whoever had done it could work for a film production company. Or a service that goes in and wrecks your ex's place while they're at work.

Equally respectable vocations, in my mind.

From deep in the factory, a low growl rumbled toward me, making the hairs on my arms stand up. It sounded far off. Thunder maybe? I looked at the cloudless blue sky filling the window.

"Yeah," I said. "Let's go with thunder."

The only seemingly unruined thing in the office was a whiteboard. The markers, of course, were long gone. One of the Org's bust-up guys had probably taken them home to his kids.

The white surface had been smeared to a dull gray, as if a former office worker had haphazardly real-world deleted whatever shipping charts had once been there.

However, in the middle of the swirls and streaks, one area had been wiped clean. In the middle of that, someone had written four words.

I read them aloud. "Here there be monsters."

I guess they thought that was funny.

Another growl.

Marta.

The vocalization was distant, from the other side of the giant building. I looked at the whiteboard again.

Here there be monsters.

"Right," I said to myself. "Then I don't wanna hang around here."

To the left of those ominous words lay an open door. The door itself had been ripped from its hinges.

I peeked out into the hall. Three more offices to my right and, across from me, the wide-open expanse of the entire factory floor.

The place was enormous. I was a terrible judge of distance, but the place looked at least six football fields long and almost as wide.

Stepping out of the room, I put my hand on the rusted rail of the catwalk that led to the offices. To my left, a set of stairs. I leaned forward, carefully, and saw that they did a switchback once and led to the factory floor.

Below me were busted machines of every size, stained with oil, grime, and rust. Larger ones squatted on the left in a grouping of three and then another four. As I swept my eyes to the right, the machines got smaller and, it seemed, more complicated. Then, on the far-right wall, larger once again.

The entire floor was bisected by a brick wall that rose at least twenty feet in the air, as if these were two different factories butted up to one another. In the middle of that wall was a massive cylinder.

From this angle, the big metal cylinder with the walls extending on either side looked like a propeller, as if an impossibly large jumbo jet had crashed and they'd built two sides of the factory around it.

No more sight-seeing. I let go of the rail and stared down at my bare toes.

When Gregor had yanked me from the motel room, I hadn't had time to get shoes on.

I'd spent many summers on my uncle's farm running around barefooted and had long ago built up a good callous. Aside from one pesky nail, there'd been no issues. But all these years later, I could still feel that spike breach my skin. So as I moved down the metal stairs, I kept a watch out for anything that might go pokey-pokey into my foot. Not doing that again.

Halfway down, I turned and peeked around the corner. Just more dead factory. When I stepped forward, the lower flight of steps shifted, and I nearly, um, shifted my pants when it did.

I listened to see if I'd piqued the interest of, say, a bloodthirsty Marta monster. No growls. No shuffling of feet or gnashing of teeth.

At the bottom of the steps, I hooked around what was left of a wall, its concrete busted away at the top like a cracked dragon's tooth. The dim light from the exterior door showed the silhouette of a man, his head twitching left and right.

The window had a reinforced crisscross mesh over it. The glass itself was thick and smoky so no one outside could look in.

I placed my slippery palm on the handle to turn it, but it barely budged. The shadow on the other side of the door flinched and took a step back, head still twitching like a sparrow looking for a worm.

Scanning the handle, I found a thick iron bar that held it in place by piercing the pivot arm. I ran my finger across it and pulled open a cover. Thankfully, it wasn't electronic. I pulled the top of the L-shaped bar down, and it moved freely.

I grabbed the bottom of the L and slid it out, making a dry, scraping sound as it freed itself from the handle.

Then, I pulled. Nope.

I sighed and flipped open another metal casing, exposing three deadbolts inside. Three.

Thumbing those open, I tried the latch again.

Gregor nearly jumped out of his skin when I pushed the door open wide. I waved him inside. "C'mon. I don't wanna hang out in here. This place is creep—"

He pushed me back quickly and stood on the threshold, his body split between shadow and light as he once again scanned the sky. That crazed look had returned. His mouth hung open, exposing his bottom row of teeth, all jagged and unnaturally long. His black eyes didn't blink.

"I can hear one of them," he whispered, eyes flicking left to right from the cover of the doorway.

"Them?"

He groaned but not at me. Like an odd animal whimper. "Drones. Not close yet but not far."

"Fine, then, get inside!"

"Shh!" He spun toward me and put a long finger to my lips, its thick nail dancing between my eyes. It wasn't quite a nail and not exactly a claw, but it was wholly inhuman. Except for *one* thing.

"Dude," I said, frowning at it. "You got your monster nails *manicured*?"

He shot a look at me, snapping his hand back.

His face went flaccid, and he stared down his nose at me. "I take care of myself. No crime in that."

"Fine, fine. Don't care, come on—"

"Aren't you listening to me? If they're doing some high-altitude grid search, they'll be over this area in the next few minutes."

"Yeah," I said, tugging on his elbow. "Get out of the line of sight, then."

Gregor took a reverse step and leaned back, head bobbing left and right. "The Jeep," he said, his voice hoarse. "They'll see the Jeep, Emelda Thorne!"

I pointed at my vehicle hidden under the carport, but before I could say a word, he shook his head like a dog with a dead bird in its mouth.

"No, no, no!" he said then folded his arms. "The heat signature from the engine. If those are the Organization's drones, they'll know what's inside this building, and they've got infrared, and they'll—"

"*Now* you mention this?" I said and started to step forward.

He threw his arm out, stopping me. "I'll take care of it. I saw some old tarps buried in trash when we drove in. I'll drag those over and lay them across the hood."

Happy to leave the creepy factory, I said, "I'll help."

Again, he shook his head so hard I wouldn't have been surprised if one of those black eyes popped out and bounced across the parking lot like a marble. "No, I'll have to take care of this."

"And I hafta pee, goddammit!" I threw an arm up, exasperated. "We both got things."

He ignored me. "You get the serum."

"Me?"

"Yes!" he said and pulled his hand from my shoulder. "I'll cover the car, you go get—"

"I don't even know where the stuff is, man!"

He pointed behind me. "Did you see a massive vat? Right in the middle of the factory."

I sighed, adding a groan at the end. "Yes, saw that."

"At the bottom, there's a red housing the size of a .50-caliber ammo box."

"Like I know what that is."

He started to speak then tilted his head as if he had no other size references on file in his brain. Then he held his hands out shoulder width apart and lifted his eyebrows. "Inside, you'll see three dials. First, turn the left clockwise all the way."

Sighing, I said, "Why don't you just come—?"

He spun around and stomped down the concrete steps, shouting instructions as he ran. "On the far wall, there should be some shelves with metal bottles. Like, uh..." he said, stumbling over a rusted wheel. "Like sports bottles but fatter."

"Man..."

"Put one of those into the glass case," he said, chucking away some boards and revealing a mildewed tarp. "Turn the latch on the case, and it will seal shut. Turn the far-right dial in the red box counterclockwise. That will fill the bottle. Cap it and..." He grunted as he pulled the tarp free.

The moment he did, two huge black birds flew out, and he yelped. Actually yelped. "*Baahh!*"

I couldn't help but laugh. A supersoldier with abilities far beyond those of a human, and he sounded like a soccer mom who'd just seen her kid get an elbow to the face.

"Got it, fine. Put cap on bottle," I said, not bothering to yell back. Dude had super hearing, after all.

"Get *three* of them," he shouted as he dug the tarp out. "Each should last me about a month."

Grumbling, I turned away but then called over, "Wait. The Organization put a serum that can turn people into Enhanced supersoldiers in suburban St. Louis and didn't think that'd be a problem?"

Dragging the tarp over his shoulder, he looked up toward me, frowning. "You can't just drink it like Ovaltine and get"—he motioned down his body—"this. I had to endure conditioning for months. Every damn day. Pain and torture and injections of the virus. The serum only triggers the viral load." He stopped, cocked his head to listen for a moment, then started pulling the tarp again. "If some kid did happen to break in and did happen to work out how to get the stuff out, he'd have a stomachache for a week, and that's it."

I stepped back inside, letting go of the door. "Great. Fine."

"Or die," Gregor said nonchalantly as the door slammed closed behind me. "One of the two. Whatever."

Chapter Fourteen

Kane

C ould my arms be getting longer, hanging here all this time?

Time.

There are no windows, so I cannot tell day from night. The fragrances of earth and wet stone, even though I haven't seen water for what must be days now, tell me I am beneath. Underground.

Yet inside.

Strange.

The blinding light is more infrequent now. Or maybe time is stretching for me. So strange. I now crave the light because in this place, it is my only companion. Alas, not a very good one.

When the light comes, I turn from it and can feel the skin at my neck stretching and chafing. I stare up at my hand, for I do wonder why the pain has shifted closer toward my fingers.

That is another companion. Pain.

One that I welcome in a small way, because it provides its own interaction. Its particular type of conversation. Wolves are social creatures and seek the protection, companionship, and comfort of others.

Pain does not grant me any of those things. Only interaction.

In the harsh light, this shade looks a little bit pink. I can see that the manacle around my right wrist has slipped up to the bottom of my thumb slightly. Before, it was tight around my wrist. Now, it is higher.

I can see the discoloration of the skin, red, raw, and angry, as it scrapes its way toward my fingers.

The cuff is far too small for my hand to slip out of. The first day—or days?—I pulled at it, trying to break free. That is when pain introduced itself and has sat up above me like a gargoyle staring down. Wondering when I might break.

Ah.

My hand has less... stuff within. I do not know the term. It is more bony than before, the skin rippled and wrinkled.

Like when Mère would put me in the tub. So peaceful as I lay there, I would fall asleep floating, only to be awakened by her laughter.

"I've never known a person who could fall asleep floating," she would say.

Blinking awake, I would float and say, "Because I am wolf?"

"Yes, you are," she would say. "And never forget that, Kane. Never ever, ever."

Staring at my hand, it looks now as it did then when I would step from the tub, wrapped in the too-large towel with flower pictures that she would bring me. Always warm. She would make sure it was warm.

I do not understand why my hand would look like it had been in water. I have not seen water for such a long time that when I swallow, I cannot do so fully. My tongue is dry and sticks to the roof of my mouth.

Clank!

The light leaves me cold, and I can feel the buzz in my head. Is this sleep again? Weak now, all I do is sleep.

"You should go to bed," Père says, and my eyes pop open. "You are falling asleep."

I am a boy once again, sitting on the living room couch. I didn't even realize that Mère had gotten up to leave during the show. This is our routine each night. She finds a few shows to watch, and we sit together.

This is my favorite time of day, but I would never say this to Père. He is a hard man, but I think saying this would crack his heart.

No. Break. Break his heart.

"No, *ma père*," I say to him, grinning. "I was only resting my eyes."

"Ha! You are learning," he says and crosses his arms over his barrel chest. "But maybe not the good parts of humans, no?"

"Just a few more minutes, please?" I point to the screen. "The two boys are being chased by the sheriff with the dog. But he will not catch them, for they drive a very fast car."

"*Oui,* yes. The General Lee is very fast. Why are you watching these old shows? Don't we get the new ones?" He laughs again.

I shrug. "They are ones that Mère likes. So I like them too."

He nods and looks down, blinks slowly, then appears as if he's about to say something. Instead, he goes into the kitchen.

On the screen, the farm boys are evading the stupid sheriff, but they do not know that the bridge they are driving toward is out. I now understand why this place they are living is called Hazzard County. Always, the bridges are out.

Something catches my attention. A feeling of—

"It is not healthy, I do not think," Père says, attempting to whisper. But he is angry, and his angry whispers are very loud. Still, I know my hearing is far better than theirs.

"He is just a boy, John."

"No, not just a boy. Unlike other boys, yes?"

I hear Mère soften her voice and can envision her reaching for him. "Which is why he needs to learn. Learn how to be with people. With humans."

"This is fantasy," he says, his voice shaky. "This is your fantasy, I think. I am worried for you!"

She makes the shush sound. "Not so loud. If we don't…"

They continue to speak—argue, it seems—but something else has grabbed my attention. Not from the television because it has gone to commercial break just as the orange car was leaping through the air.

What is that?

A sound?

No. A scent. It is familiar, and I—

"That boy is *not* our Kane," Père nearly shouts. "Our boy is dead. He has been dead many years now, and this now, all of this, just dredges that pain up."

Again, she tells him to be quiet. Softly, she says, "You don't think I know that?"

"Non. No, I do not. I think… In your heart, yes? I think you have replaced my dead son with that boy out there. It is not so." She begins to speak, and he interrupts her. "Ah-ah-hah, non! This will only break your heart, chère. You were in a black place for years after Kane died."

"And you were too."

"Yes, yes, this is what I am talking about," Père says, his voice warbling and watery sounding. "We made it through that darkness. What happens when this boy leaves this place? The darkness, that is what happens. All over again! That pain, all over again. *Mon cœur*, my heart, this it cannot take again."

Mère tries to soothe him, but I do not listen to the words.

I stand from the couch, quietly, so as not to alert my human parents. For a moment, I snap my head back at the thought.

Human parents?

I have never considered this. Is that what they are to me now?

The thought brings a warmth in my chest, so conflicting. One that makes me want to weep and yet also burst with laughter.

Again, the scent steals my attention. Something outside.

I look to the windows and reach for the curtain. Then hesitate.

Père has rules in the house. One of those is the curtains always remain closed. In the weeks that I have been with them, they have had three visitors. One neighbor and two men. Both men were dressed all in brown with brown caps and gave Mère gifts.

They are nice men. The gifts make her happy.

She must have been famous at some point, because both of them asked for autographs. I know a famous person!

The window.

No. Père's rule is never open curtains. He worries that someone may see me, and they are not yet ready to explain my presence. The pull-down blinds, he has pinned to the window sills, but he did not need to. They are rules set down by one of my alphas, and I will obey.

Since entering their home, I have been out a few times, usually so he can show me about cars. Or planting of flowers. Or helping put a shed together.

On *that* occasion, shed building with Père, I learned many new words—both French and English—which he has since forbade me to repeat. He made me promise to not repeat. Not ever.

So I do not.

His other rule is I cannot open the door without permission. This is for the same reason as the curtains. They worry the world is not yet ready for a boy such as me.

Will it ever be?

Something beyond these walls draws me. Outside. It calls to me!

However, my alpha, my human parent, has made a rule I cannot break.
You must not go outside without permission!
Hmm. I must think.
What would Caillou do?

Chapter Fifteen

Just past all the dead, hulking machines, the brick barrier that held the Enhanced Marta on the other side looked like it could hold back a river. From above, I'd thought it might be twenty feet high. Now, it looked twice that.

"They really don't want her to get out, yeah?" I said. Talking to myself was one way I tried to calm my nerves. It never worked, but who knew? One day, it might.

Using the silver vat in the middle of the factory floor as a guide, I wound through the labyrinth of busted and dusty machines and bits of broken wood, strips of leather, and twisted bands of metal. To keep my mind busy—and not think about the monster on the other side of that big wall—I tried to work out what the hell they used to make in a place like this.

Leather? Metal?

I decided it had to have been a gag-ball factory. Sure, not a great chance of that, but they gotta make that stuff somewhere, right? As I crept through the place, stepping over factory detritus, I glanced over at what looked like a conveyor and press machine. Its long belt had been eaten away by mice or rats, the remaining tatters lovingly draped over the rollers in a forever caress.

Winding around a three-door locker that had collapsed onto its side and now rested against a busted-up desk, I saw a machine that looked a little like the industrial dishwasher I'd used at the bars I'd worked at over the years.

"Well, we want our gag balls to be pristine when the customer gets them. Nobody wants a dirty gag ball," I told myself. "Actually, that's probably not true of all gag-ball aficionados."

I was saying "gag ball" far too much.

And just thought the word again right there.

Of course, this was to distract that part of my mind that was waving its arms like a red inflatable stick dude in front of a car dealership going, *"Monster behind the wall! Monster!"*

But hell, I'd been *with* a monster for the past few weeks. No, Kane wasn't a monster; far from it. Still, the dude was next-level dangerous, and we'd gotten along pretty damn great.

Not sure what that said about me.

I recalled those last moments on Dr. Pental's farm. We'd both had so much hope. But sadness too. That may have been the only time we'd ever embraced.

Kane didn't seem like a hugger, really. But like any dude, he could be taught. Just needed the right woman to teach him proper hugs. Or, hell, improper hugs if it ever came to that.

Focus!

After I made my way around a next-level-complicated machine with pulleys and belts and electric motors and buttons of various sizes, I stared up at the giant cylinder in the middle of the factory floor.

"Hello, vat," I whispered.

It looked bananas. Like it had once been a suburban water tower but the legs had given out and it had collapsed to the floor.

This, obviously, had been installed after the Organization had taken over the old building. The vat was shiny, pristine, incongruous with the rest of the surrounding machines that had lost their battle with changing market forces and entropy.

The massive wall came up both sides of it, secured with metal straps as wide as my body. Thankfully, there wasn't any gap for hungry, chompy-chompy monsters to sneak through.

For the first time, I noticed a fat rubber tube snaking from the top of it up to the ceiling. At first, I couldn't work out what the hell that was for until I realized that this was likely how they filled the thing without going inside.

Maybe the crew who came and dropped off more monster juice landed on the roof. Still had to come inside to retrieve the stuff. Seemed like a poorly thought-out system.

Enough stalling.

Spotting the red box Gregor had mentioned, I slid up and kneeled in front of it. It took a moment to work out how to crack it open. Lever on the side. These guys were into levers. Pulled it down, and that disengaged the lock.

Three dials, just like he'd said.

Above that, a readout: 13,741.0. What was that? Gallons? Liters? Number of workplace accidents since 2002?

Didn't matter.

I twisted the far-left dial all the way to the left and the right one...

Shit.

Shit, shit.

"Did he say left one, um...?"

Dammit. I'd been too peeved at him to wholly pay attention. What would be the worst that could happen if I got it wrong?

Not surprisingly, the panicky flailing inflatable red dude in my brain had a lot of answers for that, none of them good, more than half of them deadly.

Twisting the dials inward seemed right. For some reason, when he'd said it, my mind had seen me turning them inward.

I grabbed the left one and cranked it right all the way then did the opposite with the other.

"Bottles," I said and stood up.

Behind me, there was a skittering noise like bits of sand dancing across paper. The hairs went prickly on the back of my neck, and my breath knotted up in my throat like it didn't want to come out. Too dangerous out there.

Slowly, I turned.

Nothing.

I would have said it was probably just my jangling nerves, but that was the sort of thing they said in horror movies, and then *rahr-rahr-chomp*! Nope.

"It's a monster looking to eat me, no question," I said, hoping to spin horror-movie karma back in my direction. You say one way and then the opposite comes true, right?

My logic, admittedly, wasn't based in logic.

I hustled over to a tall shelf unit that was split vertically into three compartments. I gripped one of the handles to open the mesh metal door.

Behind it were five rows of squat silver bottles. Each had a small LCD readout on the bottom reading 0.0.

When I pulled the door open, I heard it rattle. Did it need oil? That would have made it the only item in the entire warehouse that did. *Everything* reeked of grease. Oil stained every machine and had left a film on every surface. I'd been in there just five minutes, and I could feel it seeping into my pores.

No.

The rattling had been me. My hand had twitched as I'd gripped the handle on the skinny mesh door.

Dammit. I had to calm down.

I reached inside and tucked three bottles under my arm. I went to close the door, but screw it, why bother? The quality assurance lady wasn't coming by anytime soon.

Back in front of the vat, I traced a rubber conduit snaking from its base to a glass box. It looked like a tiny version of the public phone booths I'd seen on old TV shows and movies. I pushed the fat little container inside and closed its tiny door.

Another skitter of tiny rocks behind me.

I wanted to shrug it off and laugh away my nerves, but I couldn't laugh. My mouth had gone so dry I couldn't even swallow.

As I tried to calm my mind, another thought snaked its way inside uninvited.

It was the queerest thing.

Something about Gregor's manner. The way he looked, the way he spoke.

"Why is this in my brain right now?" I said, staring in what I thought was the direction of the rustling of tiny stones or sand, waiting for another skitter-skitter sound.

My mind kept rolling back to when I'd been speaking with the tech sergeant. Something about his mannerisms. He was freaked out for sure.

"No. No," I mumbled to myself, frozen as I hunched over.

Of all things, Kane's voice echoed in my ears.

"We do not rely on word sounds," he'd told me. *"Animals express intent with furrow and frown, twitch and tremble."*

Something about Gregor had been off. That is, more off than usual. I'd hung around the ex-wolf for weeks and had begun to feel that I could read *him* a little.

Had I transferred some of that to my subconscious when dealing with others? Had something in my brain seen some *other* intent on the tech sergeant? A twitch or tremble?

Some deception?

In my mind, all I saw was the red inflatable guy waving panicked arms around, banging his forehead onto his chest. No help from that dude.

We were here to get Gregor's go-juice. And the moment he had that, why would he need me? We still had to find where Kane was being held. And I knew without question that Gregor wanted to take down Doc Hammer.

Of that, I had no doubt.

Did he need me to do that?

Maybe.

Maybe.

Slowly, I bent to a knee once again and reached for the right dial. This one, I was supposed to turn counterclockwise to fill…

The red numbers looked different.

I read them aloud, trying to jog my memory. "13,740.7."

That didn't look right. I couldn't remember the number previously, but it had been a *whole* number. In fact, I hadn't even realized it had a spot after the decimal. I was sure of that.

Glancing up at the little glass box holding the bottle, it now looked less like a tiny phone booth and more like packaging for a doll. At the bottom of Monster Juice Barbie, the readout still said 0.0.

"Yeah, because I haven't turned the…" My voice trailed off. Was there a leak in the vat?

No time for that. I'd already spent far too long mucking around with all this.

My hand hovered over the dial. Left. Inward. I was sure of that.

"Mostly sure," I said.

Then the red dude in my head, arms going wild, wasn't so sure. He was all "Danger, danger, danger!" and maybe "Get a Chevy with zero down!"

Something in my mind was sending me warning signs. Big ones.

And not about the dial.

Chapter Sixteen

When I got to the factory door, once again, I could see Gregor in silhouette through the smoky glass. I saw his shadowy head flicker as I came up, obviously hearing my footsteps through the thick metal door.

I grabbed the handle and opened it.

Stepping forward, the tech sergeant filled the entire doorframe as his twitching black eyes stared down at my hands. His lips pulled back, showing teeth.

"One?" He looked over my head, deeper into the facility. "I said three."

I held the bottle up by my shoulder, not ready to hand it over yet.

"Something's not right in there. One for now," I said. "You'll get the other two when we find out where they're holding Kane."

His body tensed, rigid, and he snatched the bottle from my hands so fast I didn't even see him move.

"Yow, man." I pulled my hand back and put it under my arm. He shook the bottle, its contents sloshing inside.

Gregor tilted the fat silver container so he could see the numbers at the bottom.

"0.93," he said and shrugged. "You didn't fill it, but that will do me for weeks. Thank you, Emelda Thorne."

"Great," I said. "Let's go. We'll come back later when—"

But when I turned to head outside, he didn't move back. I pressed on his chest, but he was as immobile as the massive brick wall inside.

The tech sergeant took a step forward as if he was just strolling in the park, looking at the pretty birds and blooming flowers. Twisting his too-tight T-shirt in my fists, I growled at him.

"Back off, asshole," I said, grunting as I put a shoulder into his rock-solid chest. "Lemme out of here!"

I felt him reach down and put a hand on my shoulder. He pushed, and I was launched back into the dead factory. I flew through the air and landed hard on my tailbone, which sent a sharp bolt of pain rippling up my spine and into my skull.

I didn't need super hearing to catch the sound of his chuckling as he slid the door closed. Shadow Gregor bent down and grabbed something from the ground, grinding its metal tip against the concrete.

When he lifted it to the fogged glass, I knew what it was. He jammed the rebar into the door handle on his side then bent it.

"Gregor! You asshole!" I shouted.

The shadow turned away and was gone.

I jumped to my feet, red with rage, sprinted ahead, and banged on the thick door with my fists.

"Get your ass—"

When I heard the growl behind me, I shut the hell up.

I spun around, took two steps inside, glanced to my right, and saw the metal stairs. Without even having to make a conscious decision to run, I was moving. Up the first part of the stairs, I pushed off from the wall and ran up the next, my steps *bang-bang-banging* as I went.

Swallowing hard, I turned back.

No one chasing me.

I had a way out: back into the office and through the second-story window.

Before slipping inside, I looked again to see if anything with teeth and claws had been alerted by the metal slaps of my feet. I'd rung a literal dinner bell.

But I saw nothing.

No Enhanced creature weaving around through the factory detritus. Below me, nothing moved. All was as still as it had been the day the place was shut down.

I looked toward the wall, that massive brick wall. Nothing, not even some supermonster, could jump over that.

Then I saw an odd shadow only about fifty feet from where I'd been at the vat—some discoloration at the bottom of the barrier. My stomach reached up and gripped my lungs, squeezing the breath out of me.

That was where I'd heard the odd skittering sound.

Right there.

No one could get *over* the wall, sure. But someone, some*thing*, had tunneled through the bottom of it. I stared at what was, no question, a hole just big enough to allow something to wriggle under the wall.

"Screw this," I said and spun, taking one quick glance down the stairs.

All clear.

My eyes locked onto the bright light, the warm sunshine beaming in through the office window. I turned to go inside but stopped.

It was closed.

Had I closed it?

A rumbling to my left. No, not rumbling. More guttural and rolling.

Next to the whiteboard, next to those four words in black felt pen, stood the Enhanced monster called Marta.

Like Bridget had been, she was naked from head to toe. Where the other woman had been nearly bald, her hair hung down in strips like greasy vines. Parts of her scalp were showing, red and angry, as if she'd pulled out her own hair.

Her limbs were unnaturally long. Her left leg bent forward like a spider's, while the right pivoted, giving her balance. Her arms were thick and dirty, brown and black substances smearing her skin.

The head was grossly misshapen.

The protruding jaw held teeth too big for her mouth.

Like Cal Davis and Gregor, she was Enhanced. Unlike them, Marta was a distorted version of a human being.

Like Bridget. Like Bridget's secret beau, Charlie Boynton.

Either something had gone wrong with the process or transference, or they had just angered God more than the original "chosen ones," and He'd meted out His displeasure in divine retribution.

No. Not God. The other one, who was, right now, looking up from Hell and laughing.

The monster locked onto me with those eyes, dark, oily circles in pools of white. The woman once known as Marta grinned impossibly wide.

Then, she attacked.

Chapter Seventeen

My body folded into a crouch so fast I smacked my ass on the heels of my bare feet.

The moment those two parts of my body connected, I felt a breath of wind flutter my hair. Marta the monster had been aiming for my chest. I'd ducked low enough that she'd flown over my head.

I knew how fast these things could move. Chaotic and distorted as they were, once they got their blood up, they were after someone else's.

I didn't even turn toward the crash behind me. In my mind's eye, I could see that she'd landed on the bits of busted-up office desk I'd seen earlier, making them even busted uppier.

No time to look.

Arms pumping, I hoofed it out the office door and hooked left so tightly I bopped my head on the frame. I just kept running, running faster. I'd had enough bangs to the head in my life; what was one more?

I tried to listen for the rattling of the creature stumbling back to its feet but heard only the high-hat *bang-bang-bang* of my own feet slapping against the metal stairs as I bolted toward the factory floor. At the switchback, I bounced off the wall with one hand and kept running.

My head, apparently more freaked out than my feet, was moving too fast for my body, and I began to tip forward. The moment I thought I'd crash in a heap, my heels hit the ground floor.

Boom.

Having leaped from the catwalk, Marta landed just to my right. She tumbled to the ground, arms outstretched and flailing, and rolled and rolled until she smashed against something beneath a large metal table loaded down with machine parts.

She wasn't moving.

Then she was.

Her head snapped in my direction, black eyes furious, glaring at me with all the hate in the world.

What the hell did I do?

I bolted between machines covered in greasy dust and filth, unsure where the hell I was going except *away* from the creature that wanted to suck my insides out. Trying to bring up a mental map of what I'd seen from above, I had no idea how the hell I could get out.

And in my panic, my "mental map" was beyond jumbled, like some drawing a kid hopped up on Sugar Smacks might make with all of their markers bunched together in a fist, arm making big swooping motions as their tongue poked out between their lips.

A roar split the air—part human, part animal—and that mental map image went totally blank. The kid in my head with all the markers had apparently shat himself.

Still, I didn't need any sort of map. I knew there was nowhere I could run.

Could I just keep running and running, hoping to find a way out?

Not likely.

According to Gregor—who I was definitely going to kill, no question—Marta the monster had been trapped in the old factory since the year before. In all that time, with all her inhuman strength, *she* had never found a way out.

How was that possible?

The window had been tough to open but not impossible. Had her mind been so far gone that she'd never even tried to work one of them?

No. She'd been the one who'd closed the office window, cutting off my escape, no question. So why—?

It didn't matter.

I had to get back upstairs and get the window open again. It was my only way out.

If I could loop around—

Snarrrnnt!

The large clawed hand swiped from above, and I sidestepped, my heart pouring on the gas as I ran around her grasp like a panicked letter *C*. Again, she'd anticipated connecting and had put all her weight behind the blow.

When her long, clawed fingers sliced through the air, she spun around and fell, knocking over metal crates as she did.

My only weapon, my slingdart, was back at the motel.

Everything of mine was back at the motel! I'd let Gregor drag me out of there, and he'd used my fear of getting caught to… just go with whatever he was saying.

Stupid.

So stupid!

If nothing else, I had to get out of there, to live, just so I could kill him.

By nature, I was not a murderous person. But yeah, I was killing that dude.

More clattering arose behind me as objects big and small smashed to the dirty concrete floor. I heard the unmistakable sound of a collection of hollow rods going *bung, bung, bung-bung-bunging* as they rained down.

Marta's roar split in two, half pain and half frustration.

Her cry echoed around the cavernous factory, bouncing off walls, making it feel as if she was coming at me from all directions and that no matter how hard I ran, I could never escape.

The stairs.

I had to get back up the stairs and to the window.

Gregor had jammed the factory door shut with rebar. Probably did that Superman move from all those old TV shows where superstrong characters bent the metal, face all squishy, and viewers at home shouted, 'That's totally rubber. Fake!'"

This wasn't, of course. I'd never get out that way.

Bending and dodging, hitting dead ends and spinning back, I saw Marta's long arms swinging through the air as she jumped from machine to machine. My only salvation was that every third landing or so, something would give under her weight, and she'd tumble to the floor.

Rounding a corner, I skidded to a stop, finding another cluster of machines and some lockers and another dead end!

Table.

I saw a metal table and a beam of sunlight on the floor. I crouched and crawled beneath it.

Ahead of me, my path was clear.

The stairs were right there!

I listened just for a fraction of a second. Then I leaped forward.

Before I could take my second step, still bent, legs pulling me forward, I felt her before I heard her. Marta's large palm gripped my side, taking me down as she hit the floor. My world kaleidescoped—dark-light-dark-light—until I landed on my back and, once again, banged my head.

No time.

I threw my arms down to push myself up, and, as if descending from the heavens, the large naked woman, covered in dirt and muck and angry red skin, landed on my chest. Her hooked toenails dug into my skin. She arched forward, driving me back.

My shoulders screamed in pain, and I knew that she'd gripped me there too.

I looked up into the empty black eyes surrounded by a sea of white. Spittle dripped from her curved teeth. Her ragged breath washed over my face as she *huff-huff-huffed* from either the exhausting chase or the excitement that she'd finally caught her prey.

With my shoulders pinned, I couldn't move. When I shifted my legs to try and roll her off me, she clenched her toes. I cried out in agony, and she arched forward, baring crooked fangs that were so large, several had split the gum line. Where one of her front teeth had been, there was just a dark hole.

"Listen," I pleaded, "I'm not—"

Like a slap, she pulled her hand from my shoulder and grabbed the side of my head, sending stars into my brain.

As my vision tunneled black, the last thing I saw was her widening her jaw, leaning down. My eyes locked onto the tiny black gap in her teeth as it went for the flesh of my exposed neck.

Chapter Eighteen

Kane

I stand near the door, conflicted.

Mon père has rules that I am supposed to follow. Everything within me demands I do. However, that is the wolf speaking. Now, I am part human, yes?

And outside calls to me! Something familiar, from my previous life. I know I must find out what that scent is.

I catch sight of myself in the mirror, and it startles me for a moment.

Taller than when I first looked into it, much taller. My hair longer and, on my face, I am beginning to get fur like Père, but where his has gray, mine is deep black.

I look away because it is still difficult to... think about how this is how I am. My furless body looks silly. Then, I return my gaze to the mirror.

You must not go outside without permission!

This thought is in my head when I get an idea. I smile at the boy in the mirror and tell him: "You have my permission to go outside."

The boy smiles, and I put my finger to my lips. He does the same.

"But do so quietly and quickly."

From the kitchen, I hear sounds of sobbing, which is distressing. I cannot tell who this comes from. Voices low and comforting.

I must be quick.

Flicking the latch on the door, I pull it open slowly. There is a slight creak, and I freeze then look over my shoulder.

They are speaking once again, in quick tones, sharp words. It is always amazing how fast humans go from emotion to emotion, hopping like insects on the water.

No matter.

Slowly, I ease the door open and push my head through the gap. I blink, trying to adjust my eyes, for it has been so long since I have seen such darkness. Stepping through the gap, I put a foot outside, quietly, quietly, and listen for...

The bushes shake, leaves tremble.

Once again, I freeze, and as I do, the scent wafts toward me. Familiar. Wonderful.

Family.

As my eyes adjust to the night, I see the gray flicker of a tail. When it disappears, I step forward, leaving the door ajar. On the stoop, I search the darkness.

A face peers out from behind the shrub.

Beautiful and perfect. Soft yellow eyes that I know so very well. They are the eyes I wish to stare into after I awake and before I fall asleep.

She steps forward just slightly, regarding me, sniffing the air.

Her head cocks to the side, and I hear her *yip-yip-yip*. This is how we call to each other. I do not look like I did, but she knows my scent.

Of course. My wolf wife will always know my scent. And I know hers. This is what rattled my brain when I sat upon the couch in the human house.

Slowly, she takes a step forward to see me, but I am in the darkness of the porch. I move just slightly forward. When she sees me, she hops back. She turns, shifts her weight to run, then spins back, legs bent low. Her eyes regard me for the briefest moment.

Then she bolts.

"Wait," I whisper. I run down the steps toward her but can only see her tail flicker against the tops of the bushes. She is racing back to our pack!

As I run, I reach for her, but my hand looks so strange in the light. It twists and bends and crumples.

Mon Dieu! Que se passe-t-il?

What is happening to m—

My chest burns, and my brain boils in my skull. I try to cry out, but no sound escapes my lips. It feels like something has snapped my body in half, and I bend sideways, too far over, and tumble to the cold ground. My limbs, they are on fire, burning, burning, twisting, and I can feel my bones bend, bend, bend.

My vision blackens, a void, and I see two fierce amber eyes staring at me. I reach up to swipe at them, punch them away, but my hand is no longer a hand.

It... I have fur again?

My teeth punch through my gums, splitting the hard skin. My lips peel back as if I was about to scream and smile at the same time.

I blink through tears and look at my hand in the light. Dark claws extend and pierce the fur, cutting through that flesh and hair, the pain excruciating.

Then I look past my hand to the light. The moon hangs above me in a mocking smile. Warbling in the sky, it laughs at me, side to side.

Wracked with pain, I scream out, but it is not a scream.

It is a howl.

But... not a wolf howl.

It is less. Feeble.

Embarrassing.

"Kane!" A voice comes from the door, and I turn to see Mère, who is standing on the porch in a panic. Her eyes jet left and right, her arms out as if she might be able to snatch me back from the air. "Kane! Kane, where are—"

"I am here, Mère," I say, getting to my feet, stepping out of my bed clothes, which fall away and pool around me on the ground. "I am here. I am okay..."

Am I standing?

No. I cannot be.

Here, I am barely off the ground, yet all four legs are extended. And—

I am on four legs. Not two.

What is this?

I should be upright, but when I try to walk, I only fall back on my tail.

I have a tail.

Once again, I have a tail. When I turn to look at it, my stomach turns. I will be sick.

My tail is *wagging*.

Swish, swish, swishy, swish.

The tail is not a wolf tail. It is puny and pointy and has fawn and white fur and has a jaunty curve to it! *What is this fresh hell?*

Atop my head, I feel a soothing touch. My heart slows. I gaze up and see Mère looking down at me.

"Kane?" She says, her eyes as big as the wheels on the General Lee car on the TV. "Kane... is that you?"

I nod and begin to whimper—what? No whimpering! Stop this—I cough to cover my indiscretion and say, "Yes, Mère, it is me. What has happened?"

Père appears at the doorway in silhouette, and he has something long in his hands. Not a weapon, I know this. He forbids guns in the house.

Mère grabs my body and pushes me left and right then lifts me off the ground. How powerful she is to be able to lift me. She is so wonderful! Protects me and feeds me.

I want to tell her how happy she makes me feel.

I want to jump and jump and jump and spin in circles and—

No! No spinning!

Not in circles or squares or parallelograms.

"Oh my lord," she says and kisses the fur atop my head. "Look at you, Kane! You are full of surprises, yes you are."

From the door, Père calls out as he brandishes his broom, "What is going on? What is that?"

"It's Kane, dear." Mère laughs and holds me to her chest. "And I think he's a King Cav."

"*Qu'est-ce que c'est?*"

"He's a dog," she says, gripping me tight enough to squeeze the breath from my tiny body. "A beautiful, beautiful dog!"

Chapter Nineteen

Tech Sergeant Gregor slowly sauntered down the dusty concrete stairs, toeing bits of debris left and right in a little dance as he spun the fat silver bottle in his hand.

Behind him, it was like a song. The crashing, the growling and snarling, the occasional yelp or scream from the little girl he'd locked inside.

He hadn't felt this good in days.

Sure, his mind and body were screaming, but now, he had what he needed. *All* he needed. A quick trip to a CVS for a couple of needles, and he was good to go.

He even looked forward to that conversation.

"Oh, I'm a diabetic, and golly, darn it!" he would say, putting on a mask of embarrassment. "I had one of my syringes, but it slipped down between the car seat and the console."

The person behind the counter would gasp. "You poor thing. That's no good!"

"No. I bet I've got coins and keys and the secret to happiness under my seat by now," the tech sergeant would say, smiling with his lips. No need to show teeth. Best not to show his teeth.

Then he would don a sincere, worried face. "Can you help me out?"

And, of course, they would.

Maybe it wouldn't require all the song and dance. Maybe diabetics—which he wasn't because he was the perfect human specimen—could just go in and say, "I need needles," and they'd throw some at them. Maybe anyone could.

But Gregor did love the theater of the idea. The deception.

He was *so good at it*!

All that panicky shit he'd done with the little girl? "They're up there, everywhere! Eyes are upon us, Emelda Thorne! Eyes!"

Spinning his prize in his hand as he hopped from the stairs to the pockmarked pavement, he walked to the Jeep, chuckling to himself.

Yes, sure, there were eyes up there. And he had heard them, or at least thought he had, but they must have been miles and miles away. Up high. If the Organization was looking for him—and it was—it would have a fleet of drones scouring the area.

But he'd used his fear as a weapon. Against Emelda Thorne.

That was what warriors did! Used everything. Even their weaknesses.

Not that he had many of those.

"I should have been an actor," Gregor mumbled to himself as he heard a big crash and a scream from the girl. Probably the last one. Ah well, fun while it lasted.

His smile grew bigger as he dug into his pockets for the car keys.

Still laughing, he switched the tiny bottle to his other hand to check another pocket, although he'd been fairly sure he'd dropped them into the left.

Not in the right, either.

He put the bottle on the Jeep's hood and checked his camo pants pockets again. Patting all four, front and back.

"Where in the...?"

Maybe when he'd been dragging the tarp? He looked over at where he'd tossed it away once the girl had gone inside after she bought his Oscar-worthy acting job. The smile came back with that memory, but it was not as large as before.

Scanning the lot, he searched for the keys.

Not there.

He looked inside the vehicle. Not hanging off the ignition, no. In fact, he'd snatched them before Emelda could. All part of the plan.

Standing upright again, he stared out at the undulating sea of brown reeds swaying in the breeze, just beyond the lot. A grin hooked his lip as he thought this must have been what it looked like to an actor on stage, all those people staring up, adoring him.

Then.

Then he looked to the factory. At where he'd been standing just minutes earlier. There had been a moment when they'd struggled at the door. Did he recall a tugging at his pocket when she'd been trying to push him back?

Maybe.

Maybe.

When he looked back to the dead grass in the neighboring field, it had gone still.

"Goddamn woman..." he muttered. Emelda had snatched the Jeep's keys when he'd been focused on shoving her back inside! "Sneaky little..."

The levity that had buoyed him down the steps and nearly floated him to the Jeep drained out like a birthday balloon left in a hot car.

Gregor licked his lips and could hear the two dry surfaces grind across each other. Snatching the silver bottle off the Jeep's hood, he reached for the door again. Then he closed his eyes and shook his head.

He spun and looked back to the two tire gouges that trailed up the grassy hill toward the factory's lot. How far away might a pharmacy be? They'd driven for at least ten or fifteen minutes through winding streets to get here.

Of course, he could run faster than most, if not all, people.

But already, his pulse was quickening. Swallowing felt like trying to ingest sand.

Could he *drink* the serum?

He nodded to himself. Yes. Yes, that would have to do. Of course, the body would need more of it, surely, than when injecting it into the bloodstream. Ten cc in a syringe, how much then to...

Didn't matter.

He'd take small mouthfuls until he felt right again. Right as rain.

Gregor spun the cap off the bottle, and it skittered to the ground. *Leave it. Doesn't matter.*

His heart sang as he looked inside. This was what his body, his mind needed! That milky elixir that would shift the world, his world, back onto its axis.

Licking his lips, which he regretted because his tongue momentarily stuck there, he swirled the bottle around.

The liquid inside looked *dark*. Or just not the creamy white he'd remembered.

Odd.

Gregor put the silver bottle up to his nose and sniffed.
And nearly threw up all down his too-tight green T-shirt.

Chapter Twenty

I'd always known I was going to die young.

And over the past several years, I'd escaped death countless times doing dumb shit, trying to scrape together cash to just get by.

Of course, I had thought I'd left that life behind after Roy went to prison. I had nearly gone back to his bosses a few times, though, when things got really lean working at the bar. But I never had.

Then, Kane had come along, and my life had changed again.

Definitely got weirder.

After a few days, that old life felt like a story told to me about some other person. Sure, cruising around with a part-time wolfwere hunting monsters was always going to be dangerous. But I'd had a monster on my side.

Still, that feeling that my time on this earth would be short had never really left me.

What was that old saying? Live fast, die young, and leave a good-looking corpse.

That had felt like my path.

Except now, lying on the cold floor of a forgotten factory, I had a distorted Enhanced human crushing my chest with its body weight, claws raking against my skull and teeth bared for my exposed neck.

Live fast.

Die young.

The good-looking corpse thing? Totally out the window. I wondered if I would even have a face left.

Then, I wondered... how did I even have the *time* to wonder?

Why wasn't I dead yet?

Marta the monster's snarling rang in my left ear. I kept my eyes squeezed shut. Something damp drew a line across my neck toward the shoulder. Her nose? Her tongue?

Blech.

But she hadn't chewed into me yet. Hadn't taken my blood as her prize. Was that because she'd been sated by her daily ration of serum from her side of the factory?

The odd damp thing at my neck retracted, and I heard her inhale sharply through her nose.

She repeated the sniff, more deeply this time.

Then more softly.

After that, the sniffing started coming in rat-tat-tat bursts, like a dog that thought someone had hidden a Milk-Bone in a blanket. Searching.

"Ow!" I cried out as she leaned up, pushing my head down so she could get at more of my neck. Marta then put both hands on my head, gripping my hair, holding me in place.

My right hand free, I swung it toward her—why not?—and clocked her in the side of the head.

"Owww!" I shouted because my hand hurt like a mother. Girl had a rock-solid head!

But I could breathe again.

Marta had rolled off me, and I braced, waiting for another leaping attack. When it didn't come, I looked back and saw the Enhanced woman sitting with her arms wrapped around her knees. She was dirty, with bits of hair bursting around her body.

She was a few shades darker than I was, and it was hard to make out all the bruises and scrapes, but they were there, a terrible story written across her skin.

Unlike the other Enhanced I'd seen, her hair was long. Or rather, longer than the others. There were patches of it missing, but for the most part, it was all there.

As she rocked back and forth, her jet-black eyes staring at me wildly, I forced myself to lock onto her face. Ol' girl was nude as the day she was born. And her hands were tugging her thighs open, just slightly, as she rocked forward and back on her muscular butt.

My grandmother's voice wiggled into mind from when I was little. *"Emelda! Close your legs—yer takin' my picture!"*

Enough about that.

I kept my eyes on Marta's.

Rising from the floor, the feral woman twitched a few times as if she was about to leap and hold me down again.

In that moment, I recalled how Kane had approached the moose in the British Columbian forest. Slowly. Calmly. Every motion meaning something. Intent spelled out in finger twitches, leg motions, how the head tilted to the side.

Calmly, slowly, I rose, lowering my chin slightly, never breaking eye contact. I watched Marta for her reactions and tried to complement them. When her head would snick to the left, I fluidly moved mine to the right.

Not thinking. Just reacting. Portraying calm. Not going anywhere.

I tried to force a thought into my mind: *I don't want to go. I want to stay. With you. Here.*

Then I was up, mirroring her pose. Not rocking, just sitting with my hands on my knees.

I waited for her to react.

You're in control, I thought.

Marta took a deep breath and let it out, eyes never blinking. Not once. Then, slowly, she raised one of her powerful arms, which was far too long for a human, and pointed her finger at me. I stared at the mangled nail there, where dried blood congealed into a blob.

She spoke, her voice raspy: "You are we?"

How the hell do I respond to that?

The woman shook her elbow, the blob of busted nail-and-blood dancing like an electrified dot in front of my eyes.

"You are we?" she repeated.

"I am—" I started, hoping my brain would fill in the blank. When it didn't, I improvised. "I am not here to hurt you."

Marta crinkled her forehead, her eyebrows knitting together. Then she rolled back slightly, her hands shifting from her knees to shins, laughing and laughing.

And, yep, all the while—*snap, snap, snap*—like she was paparazzi. Just out of my field of vision. *Eyes up, eyes up.*

"You? You?" she said, howling with laughter. Then she rolled forward again and, thankfully, sat cross-legged. "Could *no* hurt, Marata."

"No!' I said, shaking my head and gulping a breath. "I have no interest in hurting you, Marta."

She stopped rocking and frowned, making a face like I'd just lobbed a cat turd into her mouth.

"No Marta. Marata. Mah-rah-tah!"

I lifted my hands in a surrender pose, which got an eyebrow raise out of her. Slowly, I lowered them again.

"Marata, sorry. Gregor said your name—"

That had been a mistake.

The monster woman named Mah-rah-tah hopped up to the balls of her feet, her arms raised like she was a bird of prey ready to take flight. She growled, teeth bared.

"You and Greg-gor? *Greg-gor!*"

Making myself small, wrapping my arms around my legs, dropping my chin to my knees, I slammed my eyes shut and shook my head. "No! No, no! He trapped me in here!"

For a half minute, I just waited. I could feel a river of sweat trickling down my back.

When I opened my eyes, Marata was still there. Sitting casually, leaning back with her arms propping her up. Waiting for me. I could see the hint, just a hint, of a very tiny smile.

"No Greg-gor, good." She nodded once then turned away like she was bored.

"Yes," I said. "I mean no, right? No way. Yes to that, um, of the answer being no. *Emphatically* no, yes."

Jesus, what was I saying?

Cocking her head, she flicked those black eyes at me and repeated her first question. "You are we?"

"I don't... Marata, I don't understand."

Like she'd been spring-loaded, she leaped at me. I stilled, willing iron rods into my limbs so that I didn't move. Frozen. Calm. Frozen.

Marata bent down and, once again, sniffed at my neck. Two more inhales then a sigh. Kneeling next to me, she tapped my head with the pad of her finger. "You are we, yes?"

You are...

Then it came to me.

I understood. Just part of it, sure, but I understood why she'd been sniffing me.

The night before, that terrible night when I'd let Kane be taken away by Doc Hammer and her new buds in Covenant.

In those last moments, Kane and I had embraced.

It had been tender and comforting. Clearly, this was a man—or a wolf-turned-man—who had been hugged. It was such a warm embrace, like he'd done it a million times before.

And when he'd leaned back, his eyes had been damp. He'd wept. Kane had wept at the thought of leaving his friend behind.

Gingerly, I touched my neck.

That's what Marata had been sniffing. She'd smelled Kane on me.

Minutes earlier, Marata had been ready to split my throat open and drink from my body until there was nothing left.

But she hadn't. I had been saved by the tears of a werewolf. Or wolfwere.

"Whatever," I said, drawing in a quick breath and laughing as my vision blurred through tears of my own.

Chapter Twenty-One

Kane

I stare down at a broken world.

This fragmented realm eludes meaning. A jumble of chaos.
A reality splintered, shattered into a million pieces.
No, wait.
Peeking at the side of the box, I adjust my figure.
A reality, splintered, shattered into five hundred and four pieces. Such a troublesome number. Alas, I *can* at least read numbers. Human written-word sounds are still confusing to me.

Mère chuckles, sipping tea from the couch behind me. "Don't think too long about the one piece. Look at it as a whole, then, you know, slot the bits in where you see fit."

"It is... puzzling," I say.

"Kane, it *is* a puzzle. So if it's puzzling to you, son, that only means we got our money's worth."

I glance up at the television, which is where we spend our nights. Mère had come to join me in here, and I know why. She knows I am still disturbed by becoming that *thing* two weeks before.

And when I close my eyes, I can still see it staring back at me.

Or maybe they are the eyes of another? These that haunt my dreams are fierce and powerful. The floppy-eared creature I became out on the front lawn? It was neither of those things.

These developments trouble me so.

I hear the clink of her teacup upon its saucer and know, for an instant, she has turned away to place the cup on the end table. This is my chance. I reach out for the box top. If I could just get the quickest—

"No peeking, Kane," she says, making a *tsk-tsk-tsk* sound.

I growl weakly and lower my head. A pleading voice captures my attention, and I snap my eyes up.

The beach man is running toward the surf, his long hair flapping in the wind. Under his arm, he holds what looks like an orange football. A very bouncy blond woman runs up alongside him—she caught up to him very fast—and speaks in a breathy voice.

In the water, the dark-blue ocean, a curly-haired woman is bobbing up and down, waving her arms, dipping beneath the surface and then back up again. The screen switches back to the two running people, who are making a plan. My mind, though, is focused on the safety of the woman.

If she continues to run like that, as bouncy as she is, I expect there will be bruising.

"That puzzle will not complete itself, Kane," Mère chides me.

"How am I supposed to make the picture on the box if I do not know what the picture is?" I say, pointing at the overturned box top within my reach. "Before, you let me—"

"Before, dear boy, you'd take one look at the picture and finish the puzzle in less than a minute. Those puzzles are five bucks each."

I wrinkle my nose at her, which earns me a warm smile. "Is that a lot?"

"More than you've got," she says and laughs. Mère leans forward and puts a hand on my shoulder. With her other hand, she gently turns my head toward the broken world on the coffee table. "Sometimes, you will be faced with challenges where you do not know the answer. *Most* times. The world will only give you pieces. Maybe not all of them."

"How are you supposed to finish picture puzzle without all pieces?"

"That's the fun part." She bobs her eyebrows up and down. "When you don't know exactly what the finished puzzle looks like, you look around at what you have. Gather the pieces you need to puzzle out the answer. Your answer."

My shoulders round, and I complain to her, "This picture is missing pieces."

"What?" When I turn to her, she cocks her head to the side. "What do you mean?"

"This puzzle picture is supposed to have five hundred and four pieces," I say, shrugging. "But before me, I only have four hundred ninety-eight."

Mère folds one of her legs beneath her, pulling her knee closer to her chest.

"How... Did you count them, Kane?"

"No," I say, looking at the busted-up, jumbled-up world once again. I wave my hand over it. "Side of box says five hundred and four, but there are—"

When I look back, Mère is holding her hand out, arm bent at the elbow. In her palm, she reveals six pieces.

She asks me, "How did you know?"

I point at her hand, ignoring the question. "Why do you hide pieces? Is difficult much already, *ma mère*!"

She laughs and hands the six bits of jigsaw cardboard to me.

"You are so clever. Clever, clever," she says, her smile beaming at me. "But are you clever enough to finish a puzzle without seeing all the pieces?"

The sound of someone clearing their throat catches our attention. We both turn toward the door to see Père, silhouetted against the sun.

"Can't you just let the boy enjoy the puzzle?"

"He is enjoying it, dear," Mère says, her voice both warm and hard at the same time. She is an impressive woman. Skilled.

Père rubs his half-fur face. "Not everything needs to be a lesson, *non*?"

"But everything can be, *non*?" she says, lowering her voice to sound like he does.

This gets a chuckle out of him.

"Speaking of this..." he says, looks outside, begins to speak, then stops. On his face, I can read hesitation. And something else. Fear? "The boy has been cooped up inside enough now. Is this okay that he goes outside, do you think?"

I spin around and half get to my feet, rocking on my knees toward her. "I would like to go outside. I miss the woods."

"You can't go running off in the woods, Kane."

Shaking my head, I say, "No, no. I will not."

"Do you think it was the woods that did..." Père says, stepping into the room farther. "That made *that* happen to the boy?"

Mère nods slowly, and her gaze wanders the room. I notice the slightest hesitation, the change of heartbeat in her neck vein, as her eyes land on the bookshelf. She then continues sweeping the room, as if she were just casually looking around, considering this.

Hmm.

"No. Not the woods," she says, nodding slowly. Then she looks across the room, her eyes flitting toward the ceiling. "An hour. No more."

"Okay," Père says. "Come, boy."

"John, just one hour, yes?"

I had already leaped to my feet. When I turn, I see she is staring at him, her face stern. "Back before five fifteen p.m. No later. Promise me."

Père looks at me and shrugs then grins. "*Oui, bien—*"

"I mean it."

He nods, all the playfulness gone. Then his face bends in a smile, which is genuine, and on his face, I can read the love he has for his wife.

"It will be done," he says, bending at the waist and tapping his heart. To me, he says, "*Monte dans la voiture, mon ami.*"

Behind me, Mère calls out, "You're pulling the car out? Where are you taking him?"

As I follow him outside and down the steps, he lifts his face to the sun and says, "I am not taking. He is doing the taking."

His strides are longer than mine, so I chase after the man, my heart racing.

"Is this... You will let me drive again?" I say, trying not to sound too eager. "Is okay?"

Père lifts the keys into the air. "If you dent another fender, you will fix it."

"I will!" Then I say louder. "I mean, I will not, eh, dent fender."

"Or bumper."

"*Oui*—yes—or the bumper!"

He stops and looks to the tree on the far side of the property with what looks like a big bite taken out of it. "Both bumpers, which I still cannot understand how you do this."

"No denting."

"You say these words each time, but each time, there is denting. Thankfully, the old girl is made from steel," he says, shaking his head. "But soon, she will need paint with all your bumper-car-style driving, boy."

I stop in my tracks, my heart feeling like it sinks into my shoes.

"I am not 'boy,'" I say and cannot stop wringing my hands together. Why are they damp? It must be the warm sun.

Without turning, he sighs again. "I know. *Oui, bien sûr*, you are wolf. Yes, this I—"

"I am Kane."

His pace slows, but he still does not look at me.

"You never say my name, only 'boy.' *Mon père*, I am Kane. Why will you not call me Kane?"

When he finally turns to me, his eyes are fiery and red. His face appears to be a mask of rage, but I can see more. The shiver of hairs above his ear. When he swallows, how it does not go down easily. Père licks his lips as he tries to speak, and I can see his eyes begin to water.

"No. No," I say, and lower my head. Closing my eyes, I drop to one knee and place both hands atop my heart. "I have no right to say this thing. I have hurt you. This of all things..." I try to speak, but the breaths in my chest come deep and slow, and there is not enough air, and my head is spinning, so much spinning. My eyes water, and my chest aches—

I feel his hand on my shoulder. Rough fingers squeeze me softly, but I don't dare look up. I do not want him to see me as weak. I am not a blubbery boy. I am—

"This... for me," he says, his voice sounding like he is speaking through bubbles. "*Ta mère*, she, I think has a bigger heart than me, *non*? With... with him, when we lose him, so much—"

"It is okay, *mon père*," I say then look up to meet his eyes. "Is this okay for me to still call you Père?"

He begins to speak, but the bubbles in his throat make it difficult for him. He swallows them down, but the voice struggles to come out. Instead, he nods and then nods again.

"*Oui*," he finally says, his voice squeaking as it escapes on the back of a breath. "Yes."

It is hard for me to read his face because my vision is blurred and making rainbows. For now, *mon père* is a puzzle I do not have a picture for. I will wait for him to give me the pieces.

If they do not come, I already have more than I deserve. This I know.

These kind people. Such kind people.

They have goodness and strength, love and fierceness. They both would have made very good wolves.

Père looks back to the long, sleek car and jingles the keys above his head.

"Let us give this another go, yes?" He laughs, getting his voice back. "Luckily, you know where all the obstacles are. For you have hit every single one on the property. And even found a few I did not even know we had!"

My inky sorrow drains from me, replaced by joy. And some trepidation as I stare at the vehicle.

Père opens the driver's-side door and waves me inside.

For as much as he tries to hide it, he is a compassionate man. When I sit down in the vehicle and adjust the seat, he rounds the car and gets into the passenger side and buckles up the lap belt. He yanks it hard, twice, and looks at me.

On his face, a measure of fear. And compassion too. It is there for me.

Firing up the vehicle, its throaty growl filling the car, I fear I am about to test the limits of that compassion.

As my shaky hand floats above the shifter, Père's earthy, assured voice fills my head. A voice that sounds like it comes from all around me.

"Look. Observe," he says. "See everything. *Tout la monde.* Use your eyes."

Pressing my lips together, I nod slowly. Then I remember.

"I should check the mirrors."

He chuckles. "Yes."

I reach up and twist the rearview, the world within flipping oddly, until it fills with a sunburst that hurts my eyes and stings my brain.

"You're not dead yet?" a new voice says. Female.

My body feels heavier than it did seconds ago. Sore. My skin both tight and loose at the same time. The aching at my wrists from where I hang on the concrete wall has returned.

Awake once more, I squint against the punishing light array.

"Just taking an afternoon nap," I say, and my voice comes out haggard.

Doc Hammer is hidden behind the light, but I can hear the *click-click-click* of her walking. Back and forth. Pacing?

"Look. Observe."

She has become frustrated.

"The boys upstairs are taking bets," Hammer says, her voice bending and wavering. "One says twelve hours, another eighteen. I think they give you too much credit."

An old man's voice echoes in my head: *"See everything. See everyone."*

But I cannot see with the light, mon père. It is too bright!

"We do not need eyes to see."

Ilsa Hammer is trying to make her mouth sounds confident, in control. But her anger stains the spoken words. Anger is a powerful weapon.

Especially when you can elicit it in your foe. Many bad choices are born from anger.

"Okay," I say and feel a sting at my lip where it has cracked. "Okay."

The clicking stops. She waits, and I let her wait.

Finally, she says, "Okay? What does that mean, Kane? Are you ready to die?"

I chuckle then cough from the effort. Part of this is theater, sure. But I am also weak and getting weaker. With my hands and feet bound to the wall, I cannot strike. In the brilliant light, I cannot see.

But I can still speak.

I can anger.

"Okay," I say, lifting my head and looking to where I believe she stands. "I will tell you my story. Of how I came to be the man before you now."

Click-click.

"Good. Good," she says. "Who knows? Maybe you won't die after all."

Chapter Twenty-Two

"Gregor!" I shouted from the third-story window.

The former tech sergeant spun in a jerky circle, his arms jutting out as if he were ready to fight off threats from all directions. Like an idiot, he just kept looking left and right. Behind him, out into the distance ahead.

"Up here, asshat!"

"Emelda!" he said, lips peeling back to show teeth. He stumbled forward, his legs wobbly. "I'm so glad you—"

I cut him off. Didn't want to hear his bullshit. "We gotta talk."

"Of course!" he said, beaming a smile up at me, blinking against the midday sun. "I was just—"

"Can it. Open the door down there," I said. "I'm coming out."

When I turned around, I nearly bumped into Marata, who, like a cat, skittered back then raised her arms and extended her legs.

"Don't stand so close, man," I said as I shifted to go around her.

She frowned, looking down at me, blocking my path.

Marata was bigger than me by far. Taller, too, but not NBA basketballer tall like Bridget Mills and Charlie Boynton had been. Sure, she could still comfortably use me as an armrest. But if she were to walk into a Walmart, it was not like every head would turn and gawk.

Well, except for the naked part.

But then again. Walmart? If she had strolled into one of their superstores bare-ass nekkid, my guess was that she wouldn't have been the first that day.

As if she could read my thoughts, Marata crossed her arms over her breasts and looked down her crooked nose. "Why you talk Greg-gor?"

"I need him to do something for me," I said and tried to go around her again. She palmed my head, yep, just like a baller, and pulled me back in front of her.

Arms crossed again, she said, "I need something, too, Greg-gor. Need him to die."

"Get in line," I said and ducked under her elbow, pushing past.

My fear of the monster that was Marata had been put up on a shelf somewhere in my brain. I couldn't forget she was an Enhanced. Not from Dr. Faria Pental's program like Gregor or Cal Davis but a second generation. One that had not gone through the Organization's program.

A body unprepared for the virus that would barrel through it, smashing things as it went.

Marata was a jumble. A doll pulled apart and jammed back together all wrong with muscley He-Man parts that didn't quite fit.

She trailed me down the metal stairs, her clomping steps much louder than mine. I didn't know if that was because she was twice my size or just angry.

I had to watch for that angry part. Marata's mind was like a burlap sack of pissed-off cats with just an old twist-tie keeping them inside. Anger could push her over the edge.

Anger could lead to bad choices, unintended consequences, and terrible mistakes.

And the mistake I worried about most involved her grabbing my head to see if she could chuck it over the brick wall in the middle of the old factory.

Behind me, she talked, alternating between low words and loud bursts. Some of it, I understood. The rest sounded like some foreign language.

Didn't matter.

As much as it pissed me off, I needed Gregor's help. This time, though, I'd be calling the shots.

I trusted him less now than before, and I had barely trusted him then. My mood lightened when I imagined his face when he'd opened that little silver bottle.

Maybe that delicious moment had been caught on camera. I would have loved to see that.

My smile drifted away. There were cameras outside, of course. Had all the noise alerted the Organization that something was happening at the factory?

We had to get off the property.

A few feet away from the door, I felt a clawed hand envelop my entire shoulder. She didn't dig in, but Marata was letting me know she was less than pleased.

"Why Gregor talk?"

"Let me handle this," I said then sighed. Marata needed some kind of explanation. "I lost a friend of mine. No, not lost. I handed my friend to our enemy."

Marata winced, her head snapping back as she glared at me. "Me and you? No friends, 'kay?"

"No! I mean... I didn't *know* they were the enemy."

Behind me, I could hear scraping and the groaning of twisting metal. Gregor was pulling the rebar from the door.

"That scent you smelled on me? That's Kane. He's my friend."

"Know scent. But..."

"It *is* something familiar, right?" I nodded then tried to parrot her own words back to her. "He is we. Yeah?"

Marata cocked an eyebrow at me, one corner of her mouth hooking into a smile. "*He* is we? Kane person we. No you, then?"

"Uh, no-*wah!*" I said, turning toward the door to hide my widening eyes. *Whoops*. "I'm totally 'we,' yeah? I'm *so* we. Like O.G. we, absolutely, for sure."

I needed to stop talking.

Again, I saw Gregor's silhouette through the smoked glass, his head bobbing around like a baby bird or a velociraptor from the *Jurassic Park* movies.

"Back away from the door!"

"It's open, Emelda Thorne," he said, his voice shaky. "I opened it for you!"

I bashed my fist into the metal frame, and he flinched.

"Down the steps, asshat," I shouted. "I'm not coming out until you're down in the parking lot."

Marata snickered behind me, clapping her big hands together once.

When the shadow had cleared out of my view, I cracked open the door. Then I turned back.

"Marata," I whispered, staring into those black eyes. I swallowed. "Do you trust me?"

"No."

"What? I'm... I need you to trust me."

"No." She shook her head. "Friend killer, you. No trust."

I was regretting I'd made the confession. But I thought I'd done that more for my benefit than hers. To remind me what was at stake.

"Wait here," I said.

Her face darkened. "You to lock Marata in. Yes?"

"No, no," I said, putting one foot outside. "I'll leave it open a crack. But stay here."

Without another word, I stepped outside and, as promised, pushed the door almost closed, leaving a gap.

At the bottom of the steps, Gregor had his arms wide, welcoming. Like I was getting off a plane, walking down the ramp. My old friend.

"You asshole," I said, standing at the top of the steps, looking down at him. Jesus, even six steps up, the guy was so big, I felt like I was nearly eye level with him. "We had a deal."

"Still do, still do," he said in that singsong voice. "I think it's a matter of trust. You and me have to work on trust."

"Yeah? It would help if you didn't try to lock me away with a monster."

He shrugged and pointed to the overturned silver bottle in the parking lot, a dark circle forming where its contents had spilled onto the concrete.

"You didn't deliver on your promise, either, Emelda Thorne," he said, clearing his throat. His chin twitched to the left slightly, and his eyelids fluttered. Dude was hurting. "That was not the serum I needed. A nasty surprise. Nasty."

This time, I shrugged. "Told you I had to pee."

"Truce, then." He held up both of his big hands and put his foot on the step. "You get what I need. Then we head to..." Gregor grinned. "There is a hidden installation. Eight-hour drive south. There, I can access the data that will tell us where Kane is likely being held."

"Likely?"

"It's your best shot, Emelda." He advanced up a step, lowering his hands. His face twisted into deep lines. The pupils of his black eyes grew large. "Now, go get me that serum properly this time. If you don't, there are other ways for me to survive. One way or another, you are going to help me."

I dragged in a big breath and sighed, trying to look bored as my heart banged against my ribs hard enough to flutter my shirt.

"Where is this facility?"

"After."

"No," I said, shaking my head. "Give me something here. Where is it?"

Gregor's face lifted, the eyes still burrowing into me, his smile exposing hooked teeth. "Fine. I can always get your help the more violent way. Would you prefer that?"

I'd anticipated he might try something because I didn't have much leverage. Or at least, he didn't think I did.

When he took another step forward, I was already moving, spinning to my left. I landed a few feet down, thumped hard on the concrete, lost my footing, and fell back onto my ass.

From the top step, he stood over me, glaring and breathing heavily. Literal blood lust. If I hadn't peed in the silver bottle, I would have emptied my bladder right there.

"Bad move on your part," he said and bent his knees, extended his hands—

And got yanked back by his short silver hair, head snapping like a crash-test dummy in a rear-ender. He then got tossed forward, flying right over the six steps, and landed hard on the concrete. He yelped then wheezed, unable to draw another breath.

Standing, I dusted myself off and smiled at Marata.

"Nice," I said. "Damn, you're fast."

The feral woman leaped into the air and landed on Gregor's chest. Sure, he was Enhanced like she was, but in a weakened state. Marata could tear him limb from limb and strip off the meat like she was eating chicken wings at TGI Fridays.

"Remember Marata?" she said, pushing her face closer to his as he gulped for air that wouldn't come. Despite her long limbs, she could fold them so completely that her face came close enough that she could chew on her toenails. She looked toward me. "Kill now?"

"No. No kill now," I said, dusting off my shorts. "Maybe later."

"How about," Gregor squeaked, "never."

Chapter Twenty-Three

Twenty minutes later, we were back at the motel.

I rinsed off my dirty feet, dried them, and strapped on my shoes. Outside, the horn on my Jeep blared.

"Hold your horses," I shouted as I grabbed my stuff and chucked it all into my backpack. Standing at the open door, I glanced around the room to see if I'd left anything.

"Ah, shit," I said and stepped back in to grab my slingdart off the TV. Not that I'd gotten any better with the weapon with no time to practice. But it had gotten me out of a jam or two.

As we rolled down the highway, Gregor kept quiet nearly the entire time. If I were kind, I'd say he was brooding. But to him? I was not kind. Dude was *sulking*.

From Interstate 64, we'd take 57 south then 24, which turns into 75 around Chattanooga. From there, straight into Atlanta.

I'd asked him for more details, but he'd only kept up his sulky-kid routine. "Let's just get on the interstate."

He'd calmed down some since he'd gotten his happy sauce from the factory. And, as promised, I'd brought out three silver bottles of the stuff. Enough to keep a junkie happy for, by his estimation, about six weeks.

After he'd spent about ten minutes inside a pharmacy, he'd come out with a black zipped bag. It looked like something my mom used to hold her car CD collection in. Inside the case were three needles secured with tiny straps. I'd had to look away when he'd injected the precious serum.

Marata, for her part, was fascinated by it, staring at the procedure from between the seats, wide-eyed.

When he'd finished, I fired up the Jeep again. "You all good?" I asked. "Got your go-juice and a happy boy now?"

Gregor said nothing. Marata laughed and laughed, falling back into her seat and rolling. "Go-juice! Go-juice!"

I watched her laughter die down, her smile still big as she stared out the window. She took a drag from her sports bottle, then her eyes met mine in the mirror. Despite her imprisonment, she'd been reluctant to leave the factory. Only when I'd explained and re-explained that we could take the elixir with us had she relented.

"Everybody happy?" I asked her but didn't get a response.

We could have taken more of the go-juice, but apparently, when the levels got down below a certain marker, a crew came out for a top-up. Rather, a crew drove nearby and flew a drone up to the roof to do that.

Gregor had plans to return and get a bigger haul before that happened.

I kept my bag open next to my knee, my slingdart within reach. It made me feel more secure. But now that he'd "normalized," he was his same calm, assholey self.

Sure, if he tried anything, I'd never get the slingshot dart out in time. And I still kind of sucked with it, but I felt, sitting a foot away, I could get a steel arrow into his belly if I needed to.

Thankfully, I wouldn't need to.

"Car trip," Marata said from the back seat. "How far?"

I looked over at Gregor, who leaned against the window, eyes half closed. He was trying to look casual, but I couldn't help but notice that he'd dropped the visor, staring at the passenger behind him.

Grabbing the wrapper off the protein bar I'd picked up at the motel vending machine, I wadded it up and bounced it off his head.

That got a husky giggle from the feral woman behind me. "Do again!"

"No. Do not do again," Gregor said, sitting up and touching his hair as he stared in the vanity mirror. Then he flipped the visor back up. "Eight or nine hours until we get to Atlanta."

I shrugged, trying to loosen my shoulders. This entire adventure had started so I could drive for a dude who turned into dogs of various sizes. I felt as if my hands were going to be at ten and two for the rest of my life.

"Stop kicking my seat, woman!"

Gregor glared back, and Marata threw a plastic bottle top she must have found in the back seat. Although she aimed for his head, it hit the windshield instead. Missed entirely.

Still, she let out a throaty giggle, and I heard her take a drag from her sports bottle.

While Gregor had his three pristine silver bottles that he could use intravenously, Marata had never been given needles.

For obvious reasons.

Instead, she drank the Organization's super-secret, billion-dollar serum like it was Yoo-hoo. I'd found an old gas can, dry as a bone, and filled it up from the vat for her before we'd left. When we'd pulled into a station to fill up, I had gotten her a big pink sports bottle from the truck stop.

"Okay, let's come up with a plan here," I said, getting comfortable in my seat as we took the ramp to the interstate. A long, long drive lay ahead. Again. "What is this place we're going to?"

"We have—" he said then cleared his throat and started again. "The Organization has hidden facilities all around the US. Around the world. Most have nothing to do with the Enhanced program."

"Then what?"

He shrugged. "I have no idea. None of my business," he said.

I thought about his vocation. A soldier. I guessed, and it was only a guess, that most were instructed not to ask too many questions.

"Some sites get backgrounded. Still viable but used for a particular purpose, and once that ends, they're secured in case they're needed in the future."

"That's where we're going? One of these 'backgrounded' sites?"

Gregor nodded. "Despite being decommissioned, a great deal of time, money, and effort goes into securing the sites. So even if they are shuttered, they're still connected to the network. In case things go haywire."

"Like what?"

"I have no idea," he repeated. "None of my business."

I sighed, thinking about nine hours in the car with this guy. It was going to be a long, long drive.

Closing his eyes, he eased the seat back, but it abruptly stopped, and I heard it *clack-clack-clack* as he jerked, staccato, forward again.

"All right already!" he growled. "I'll leave it."

Marata grunted and pulled her foot off the back of his seat, dragging her toe claws down the side to make her point.

Maybe bringing her had been a bad idea.

"Hey," I said to the tech sergeant. "You can't sleep because you said we can't use the map software, so…"

"I'm not going to sleep. Don't really need to anymore. Not when you're like I am."

"Really?" When he didn't answer, I got us back to the topic at hand. "So what exactly is this place?"

"It's an old attraction south of Atlanta. Been out of use for decades," he said, eyes still closed. "The Org bought it and all the surrounding land. From what I know of it, no one goes there except a maintenance worker to keep the place tidy."

"Why?"

"Requirement of the city when the property was purchased. They might want to buy the place back, or maybe for insurance." Gregor sighed. "But who really goes to zoos anymore, right?"

"A *zoo*?" I said, almost swerving into the next lane. "You're taking us to a zoo."

Marata made happy growling sounds, rising in tone. "Zoo good! Marata like very much, zoo!"

"You would fit right in," Gregor said, and, yep, got a foot to the face for that. He'd had it coming.

"Will you guys behave?" I said, pointing at each of them in turn. Then I looked back to the road. For the first time, I knew what my uncle had felt like while hauling me and the cousins around the Minnesota backwoods.

No wonder he'd been an alcoholic.

"The zoo has long since been decommissioned," Gregor said. "Up top, it's just empty cages rusting away and crumbling to dust. Deserted for all intents and purposes. But there's a whole underground facility below."

"You mean like tunnels?"

"I suppose. Originally, the zoo people had a few offices there and did some veterinary work when caged residents got sick. Transferred animals in and out." He half nodded. "My bosses probably used the place as a secure conference room or something. But there'll still be power down there. And, more importantly, access to the Org's network."

"Huh," I said, my eyelids already getting heavy. I'd forgotten to get my own version of vat go-juice before we left St. Louis. I'd need to stop for caffeine. A lot of it. "But why'd they go with a zoo?"

"I have no idea," Gregor said.

"None of your business, right?" I finished for him.

A husky peal of laughter rumbled from the back seat. "Stupid people. Zoo for animals."

"Really?" Gregor cracked an eye open at me. "We gotta listen to this for the next nine hours?"

"Yes, Marata," I said, smiling in the mirror. "For animals."

She beamed at me, taking a small sip from her bottle. Then her face went flaccid as she stared out the window, the afternoon sun beginning to lose its will to live.

"Miss them," she mumbled to herself.

Marata disappeared from view, toed the electric window, and propped her heels up on the doorframe.

"Nice animals," she said, her voice heavy with sleep. "Miss them."

Chapter Twenty-Four

"People came all the way out here to visit a zoo?"

When the illuminated signs had said Atlanta was only a half hour away, I'd kicked Gregor awake. So much for not needing any sleep. He'd lifted his big head, dragging his body up with it. Without looking down, he let his fingers dance across the three silver bottles, found them, and sat back again.

Maybe it wasn't fair to call him an addict, no more than a diabetic might be with insulin, but ol' boy had cravings. A hunger for it.

I knew what that was like. Horrifying. I'd felt like my skin was crawling with ants and rats were chewing at my brain. Couldn't really fault him, but it was Gregor, so I did anyhow.

Getting into Atlanta sometime after midnight, I squeezed my shoulder blades together. My body was ready to get the hell out of the car. We'd made just the one pit stop for gas and some caffeine. Gregor had grudgingly whipped out his own cash and paid for everything.

It had taken another two hours to get south of the city, where the old zoo had been located. The tech sergeant had grabbed a map at a visitors' center after we'd stopped so Marata could pee. Gregor had insisted she put on clothes, but she wasn't having it.

He'd said, "What will people think if a woman who looks like her is just strolling past the brochures for the Coke Museum?"

Marata had solved that problem. She had no interest in using the official facilities. Once I'd parked, far from a handful of other cars, she'd made a beeline for the dog park, bare moon flashing in the moonlight, disappearing into the trees. Less than a minute later, she'd come back.

Map out on his lap, Gregor had been navigator, and we drove like some bizarre family on an even more bizarre vacation.

There'd been very little signage for the zoo, which made sense. You didn't want tourists showing up to poke around and just find locked gates and empty cages.

Only when we'd gotten closer could I even tell it once had been a zoo.

Gregor tapped on the dash with a long nail to draw my attention from the tall fence choked with vines, brush, and leaves.

"Down here about a half mile," he said. "I think there's a recess where they used to make deliveries."

I nodded. "You got a key?"

"Hardly."

I pulled the Jeep into the small half circle capped by a gate with a thick rusting chain looping through the vertical bars. They'd overdone it, wrapping the massive chain around and through and back again like a kid tying a double knot in their sneakers' laces.

Standing in front of it, I shot a look at Gregor. "Is that to keep people out," I asked, my voice low as I dramatically raised my eyebrows, "or to keep something in?"

He rolled his black eyes at me and took a step back. I wondered if he was thinking about jumping the damn thing. It had to be twelve feet high.

Could he?

Gregor sighed. "We could ram it."

"What? With the Jeep against Fort Knox here?" I laughed. "It would crush it into a pancake. No, we're not smashing my car."

He stepped forward and leaned in to peek inside, casually putting a hand on the bars. That had been a mistake.

"*D-d-dun-dun-dun,*" he warbled then snapped his hand away. "Jesus!"

I laughed. Couldn't help it. I just liked it when the world hurt him.

Shaking the hand he'd grabbed the fence with, he pointed with the other. "Current going through that."

"I gathered," I said, still smiling, and pointed at the sign farther down the fence that read "Electrified fence."

"Good way to keep the locals out."

"Or," I said as I slung my head low and looked at him sideways, "to keep *something* in."

Gregor bared his teeth at me. "Will you cut that out?"

I shrugged, unable to get the smile off my face, and stepped forward to peek between the bars. There was light above us and none in the park, so it was hard to pull shapes out of the black. Other than crickets, the place was dead.

"Wait," I said, spinning back. "Where's Marata?"

He groaned. "Probably taking a dump. Or eating a squirrel."

Shuffling forward, I peeked into the back seat of the Jeep. Nope, not there. I walked and stood in the road, spinning in a three-sixty. Had I lost a monster?

Jesus.

"We can't... I mean, we gotta get her back."

"Good riddance, I say." Gregor stepped back and sat on the hood of the Jeep, arms crossed, staring at the impassable gate.

"No one asked you," I said, trotting back up next to him. "Not good. Not good at all. If she, you know, chomped anyone? I ain't going through that again."

He shrugged, still examining the gate.

I called out once then again louder. I felt my tongue thicken and my pulse amp up. Now I knew what it felt like when a mother loses her child in a mall. Except this child could start a monster pandemic.

I saw movement in the bushes next to the fence. A moment later, Marata came out, naked and swaying. She had a bounce in her step.

Made sense. The woman—or whatever she was now—had been locked up in a dusty, nasty factory for ages. Just feeling the grass between her toes would be a joy. And girl had some long toes, so much joy to be had, I was thinkin'.

"Marata," I said, unable to keep a scolding tone from my voice. "Don't run off! We gotta stick together."

She pointed at the gate. "No there. Locked and buzz."

Gregor flexed his fingers. "Coulda mentioned the buzz thing before, don't you think? I believe I fried the hair off my hand."

Her arm snapped out, and a small rock bounced off the side of Gregor's face. He grabbed his head with both hands, bending forward.

"Son of a..."

"Marata, let's not antagonize the man," I said and, without him looking, gave her a wide smile and a thumbs-up. She returned the gesture. I pointed at the car. "You wanna chill in the back until—"

"No." She shook her head, the reflection of the moonlight twinkling off her dark eyes. "Go in? You go in?"

"Trying. We'll work it out."

Turning away, she flashed me dirty rumpus again, waving her long arm forward. "This way," Marata said. "In here."

"I don't wanna..."

As she stepped deeper into the bush, she called back, "Small door. Small lock. Smashed with rock." She poked her head through the foliage and grinned her broken smile. "Door open now."

* * *

Pushing through the bushes, I felt each and every branch scrape and scratch at my bare arms. That thought slowed me a bit. My compatriots were both blood-hungry monsters. I didn't need to be slathering on sauce.

"Here door," Marata's voice came as I approached. With the lenses on her eyes wide open, I guessed she could see me coming.

Or hear Gregor complaining.

"Son of a..."

Walking ahead of him, I pushed another branch out, stepped around it, then let go. *Smack!*

"Cut that out!"

For a big, scary dude, Gregor was a bit of a puss. I liked antagonizing him.

Finally, I stepped out into a clearing the size of a walk-in closet. Marata was crouched on the ground, her hands on her knees as she slowly rocked back and forth.

Click, snap.

Blech.

Brushing the leaves and burrowing bugs from my arms, I looked toward the road, just on the opposite side of the line of bushes. From where I stood, the woods had knit shut, but if I looked, I could see a path to the other side about twenty feet away.

I pointed at it. "Why didn't you just say there was a path?"

"Path." She nodded toward Gregor as he came stumbling up behind me. "Path there."

It was impossible to tell how much the treatment or virus or whatever had chewed away at her brain. I was sure she hadn't spoken in broken sentences prior to her, um, change. But—and this had crossed my mind a few times since I'd met her—she did not speak in the hesitating speech other second-gen Enhanced had.

Or rather, the distorted Enhanced. Maybe Enhanced 2.0 was better?

No, because it didn't seem as if those who'd been infected by Cal Davis were any sort of improvement like that kind of numerical system might suggest. They were like bad copies, warped by broken lines of code and artifacts.

When Bridget Mills had spoken, it had been in a staccato manner. Same thing with the Devil's Dawn leader, Crank, when he'd been changed. I remembered hearing him over the camera feed at Dr. Pental's farmhouse, threatening Kane.

Not Marata.

She'd lost some verbal communication, sure, but what she had was confident. No stuttering or hesitations. Somehow, she was different.

"Nice find, Marata!" I said to the crouching woman.

She turned her head to hide a grin. A shy monster?

I'd seen Gregor get all googly-eyed from grabbing the fence and hesitated. Crouching, I saw where, indeed, the fat lock had been smashed away.

I looked around for the rock and didn't see it. When I spotted the look on the crouching woman's face, I caught her crooked grin.

She knew what I was thinking. *Where's the rock?*

The toes of her right foot wiggled ever so slightly. Yep. Beneath her heel, hidden mostly by her large foot and smashed-down grass, was a stone the size of a softball. She'd shown me and not Gregor.

More and more, I liked this woman. Or monster.

Behind me, the tech sergeant was grumbling to himself as he pulled bits of twigs and leaves from his camo pants and T-shirt.

Stepping up to the door, I scanned around. Marata cleared her throat as I did. Got it.

Reaching forward, my back to Gregor, I held my hand there. "Hmm. Wonder why this part of the gate isn't electrified?"

At that, Gregor pushed around me. "Make way. Let's get this over wii-i-i-i-i-i-i—"

After two full seconds of trembling and shaking, his oversized teeth chattering in his oversized head, he let go of the wrought iron door and tucked his hand under his armpit.

Marata rolled to her left, sprawling on her side, laughing. She sucked in big gulps of air, busting a gut with joy.

From the dirt and grass, she pointed at Gregor. "Do again!"

I could feel his breath making the hairs on the back of my head flicker as he leaned in. Without turning around, I said, "Back off, big guy."

Another burst of raucous laughter from Marata.

Once again, I stepped forward and held a hand out to the woman, whose peals of laughter had slowed but gone up in register, almost in song.

"Rock," I said.

She gripped the rock with her toes and flicked it toward me. I caught it.

Using the rock to push the gate open, I leaned into it. I struggled, since grass had grown up wildly at the base. I felt the heat of Gregor's body as he leaned forward, putting his hand over mine, swallowing my fingers entirely.

But there was no threat. He was merely pushing. I felt a pressure on my palm, but I guessed that he was happy to have the rock and my digits between the hurt-owie fence.

After a few seconds of us both pushing and grunting, we had the gate wide enough that we could slip through. Behind me, I felt Gregor inch forward. I pointed at Marata.

"You found the door, my lady," I said. "You get the honors."

She looked up at me, blinking. Marata then pursed her lips and grunted her approval, slipping through the gate like she'd done it a hundred times before.

Watching her step deeper into the run-down zoo across a craggy path, I drew in a deep breath and exhaled.

"There ain't no tigers and bears or anything inside, is there?"

Gregor stepped around me, pushed his face to the vertical bars, and gazed back and forth.

"There's nothing in here. It's a dark site," he said. "That's not to say there aren't alarms or cameras around, though, so let's get in and out quickly."

"Once we've found where they're holding Kane," I said. "You really think we'll get that here?"

Gregor eased through the gap between the gate and fence more cautiously than Marata had, avoiding the metal sides as if he was playing the world's largest game of Operation.

He looked back at me with a frown. Even with that expression, his teeth showed just a little.

"From what I know of it," he said, his voice low, "this place hasn't been used in more than a year. Who knows what secrets it holds?"

Chapter Twenty-Five

Dr. Ilsa Hammer smiled as she looked back at the man hanging off the wall behind her.

When he'd first been latched to the wall, days ago now, the guy had been an Adonis. Like something out of an eighties action flick. All toned muscles and power.

But that was not what she'd wanted to see.

She wanted that beast!

That beautiful, powerful creature she'd seen take out at least four of the Enhanced back at Pental's farm. Sure, Gregor's wannabe gang-bangers hadn't been properly conditioned before the virus had slammed their circulatory systems. They hadn't gone through the Organization's program with its litany of powerful injections. The endless therapies, physical and mental, that she and Faria had perfected after years and years of testing.

Even so, those lesser Enhanced could have taken on *ten* humans without a problem.

But Kane's beast had dispatched all of them like they were scrawny ten-year-olds.

Now?

Opposite where he hung from his bonds, she placed her palm on the black glass wall and was rewarded with the satisfying soft click of the door opening. Stepping through the gap, she stopped at the second step so she could turn and see just over the light array as it continued to cycle through the variations of light.

She had been so sure one of those frequencies had triggered the beast! Increasingly, doubt began to worm its way into her mind.

The man hanging on the concrete wall had once been perfect. Powerful. Even beautiful.

Ilsa Hammer muttered, "What a difference a few days makes."

Now, she didn't even recognize him. She doubted that stupid little girl, Emelda, would have.

Walking up the stairs to the second floor, Ilsa sighed.

It didn't matter.

The compounds in Kane's blood were already working on the subjects she'd brought from the training facility. Not just working, they were thriving! A half dozen Enhanced, better than she'd ever seen before!

But she *wanted* the beast.

Kane would last, maybe, another day without water or food. If she didn't get that beautiful creature, well, she had more than she could have hoped for.

And now, she had had an idea about *how* he'd become that creature. Her plan had worked, and he had finally told her his story.

As fantastic as it sounded.

"Doc Hammer?" the young tech said, straitening up at his station.

She looked around the room to see all three of them. Brothers, triplets, she'd been told. Dirty-blond hair, watery blue eyes, and big, stupid moon faces.

But all brilliant, loyal, and, most importantly, borderline sociopaths.

Not killers, it seemed. They just didn't care.

Perfect for what she needed.

Triplets, she mused to herself. *More like twins and a runt.*

The one at the closest workstation, Paul, was the boldest of the brothers yet somehow shorter than the other two almost by half. He removed his AR goggles and spun his chair toward her.

"You look pleased, ma'am," he said, nodding toward the black glass.

From up on their perch, they could see Kane against the wall below, bathed in unnatural light.

He looked like he'd called out in anguish. But from here, they could not hear him. Ilsa Hammer always wanted to keep her conversations with the man private. There would be recordings only she could access, or grant access to, however.

So the trips, as everyone called them, waited to hear the news that had brought a smile to her face.

Hammer sat on the edge of an empty desk and crossed her arms.

"He told me."

"Told you?" another of the young men said. She looked at his desk and saw the nameplate that read Peter. "He told you how he turns into the beast you saw?"

"No, not how," she said, her voice lower. A quick glance at the man below. He was bare chested, with only thin hospital-style pants covering the bottom half of his body.

She returned her gaze to the trips. "But he told me how he was... imbued with such power. It's a fantastic story, and if we could replicate..."

"Wait," Paul said, always the mouthy one of the brothers. Probably trying to make up for being the runt of the litter. "He told you? Why now?"

She laughed. "Because he'll be dead within a day. I don't know, maybe he thinks I'll give him a glass of water."

"What did he tell you?" the other brother asked. She couldn't recall his name, and his desk was so cluttered if there had been a nameplate, it was buried deep. Or dissolved.

Ilsa Hammer smiled and slowly told them what Kane had revealed. How he'd become the magnificent creature that could turn into that wonderful, wonderful beast!

At first, they were wide-eyed. Staring. Mouths hanging open.

However, as she continued to tell the tale, they began to shift uncomfortably. Shooting glances at one another. Whereas at first, she enjoyed telling the fantastical tale, their fidgeting began to disquiet her.

When she wrapped up, they all stared.

Finally, she broke the silence. "Can we replicate that process?"

All the brothers looked to each other, as if the freaks could somehow communicate with their minds. Brother thing or trips thing, she didn't care.

"Well?" she said more loudly, glaring at Paul the runt.

He cleared his throat and rubbed his mouth. When he went to look at one of his brothers, she leaned forward, gripped his stupid, weak chin, and pulled his attention back.

"So you *can't* replicate what happened to Kane? Why did I even—?"

"No, no, ma'am," Paul said, clearing his throat again. "It's... I just want to understand the process."

Ilsa huffed, rolling her eyes. "Fine."

"You said his—" He looked around then continued. "His wife got into a car accident. Trapped beneath the vehicle, and when he couldn't lift it from her, she died."

"Correct."

"Uh, but he'd heard of many people, in moments of stress, being able to lift cars. Mothers saving babies. Stuff like that?"

"Yes, yes!" she said, rolling her hand.

"So he... went to his lab and bombarded himself with, um, gamma radiation," Paul said, his tongue tripping over his words, "hoping to replicate, uh, that strength. But it all went wrong. He got overdosed.... And that's how he became the... beast?"

"Yes! He refuses to tell me what triggers it. But I saw him change with light—"

"Are you *sure*," the moron called Peter interjected, "it's not, uh, triggered when he's, maybe, angry?"

The third brother, the no-name one added, "You wouldn't like him when he's angry."

The three of them laughed. Laughed at her.

She reached into the desk drawer and pulled out a handgun. She shot No-Name, and he slumped to the floor. The other two stopped laughing.

Pointing the pistol at Paul, the mouthy one, she asked, "What's so fucking funny?"

Chapter Twenty-Six

A gloom pressed down onto the entire complex, making it tough to pull in a full breath.

Or maybe that was just my nerves.

Once inside the zoo, we crept along a black tar path that bisected the damp grass. It had grayed after the months of punishing rain. Mud and silt from flooding had dragged its way down the surface, giving what had once likely been a pristine walking path a mottled sheen.

Every dozen feet or so, there were short poles on either side, capped with misshapen baskets. At one point, those had had little trash cans within so zoo visitors didn't drop their garbage all over the place.

Those cans were long gone, and now, the wooden baskets were falling apart, filled with dead and rotting leaves from the previous fall.

I scanned left and right then ahead, trying to discern what might lie at the end of the snaking path.

"This must lead from one exhibit to another," I guessed.

"Probably," Gregor said, walking past me. "No time to dillydally."

"Do you know where you're going?"

He stopped and put his hands on his hips, looked back to where we'd broken in, then ahead again. He pointed a little to the left. There, I only saw darkness.

"From the busted sign by the gate, it looks like the admin buildings are in that direction."

"Right," I said, wandering up to him. "But you said we're looking for the underground part. Is that where access would be?"

Gregor frowned down at me. "Of course."

But when his eyes cut to the left, the opposite direction, I realized he wasn't so sure.

Marata, thankfully, hadn't bolted off once again. Instead, she'd run ahead and found an old wooden bench to sit on. When I looked at the back of her head, I could see her taking it in, enjoying the newfound freedom.

Leaving the path, I had to step over a mound of earth that ran in a long line, parallel to the strip of black tar.

I'd seen similar crests zigzagging across the dirt and grass all through the complex. My sleep-deprived brain imagined them to be long, winding banquet tables for fancy squirrels.

More likely, some crew had been preparing to install a sprinkler system before the whole place got shut down.

A project never finished. I'd had plenty of those.

I walked up behind Marata and put my hand on the back of the bench. It was slick with dew, and when I pulled my fingers away, they were peppered with flecks of dark-green paint.

I wiped my palm on my jeans and, with a smile in my voice, asked her, "You wanna go see the monkeys?"

Her chin lifted toward me, and she raised an eyebrow. She slowly blinked, calmer than I'd ever seen her.

"No monkeys. All gone."

"It was kind of a joke," I said and rounded the bench to sit next to her. Then I thought about the muck on my hand. I stood in front of her.

"You, um, you can... smell better now, right?" I said, trying to find the right words. "I mean your sense of smell is sharper?"

"Yes. Smell you."

"Ha, right." I chuckled. Of course, I hadn't forgotten that my body odor bouquet—or rather, Kane's—had saved me from becoming her snack earlier that day. "Anything else?"

"You no shower." She grinned at me, poking the tip of her tongue through a gap where the front tooth had been. "Ripe."

"Me?" I said to the woman covered in dirt, grease, and various stains I tried *not* to identify. I kept those thoughts to myself. "You're right. Jeez, it's been a few days. I gotta be rank."

She nodded and shrugged casually, as if she was just hanging out in the park, watching her kids play.

I realized I knew nothing, nothing at all, about Marata. Did she even have kids?

"There are cages or enclosures all around here," I said, waving an arm around. "You smell any, you know, tigers or anything?"

Marata drew in a deep breath through her nose, exhaling with a tiny smile. "Dead things. Rotting things."

"Great! Great." I nodded, letting out a breath I didn't realize I'd been holding. "Just to be clear—no living animals we have to worry about?"

Marata looked at her long, dirty hands and sighed.

I crouched in front of her. "You like animals, huh?"

"Yes." That got a small smile out of her. "Animals first."

Smiling back, I said, "Have to agree with you. My best friend is a wolf."

She popped her bushy black eyebrows and smiled more widely.

"That's Kane. He's a human now, a big human, actually," I said. "But we're trying to find him because some pretty shitty people have him locked up. But at one time, he was a wolf. I'm hoping to help him find a way back to that."

"Good."

I stood up and extended a hand to Marata. She looked at it but didn't take me up on the offer. We weren't there yet.

We started walking again, and I thought about her reaction to what I'd just said. "Did you understand what I said to you? A wolf who became a human?"

"I understand what you say."

Nodding, I stepped over the thick root of a tree. "And that made, um, sense?"

"Make sense," she said, walking next to me, kicking away leaves as she did. "You *haurangi*."

"Hau-what?"

With a big smile and sad eyes, she said, "You a crazy person."

* * *

When we'd arrived at where the admin building was supposed to be, we only found the decaying latticework of a wooden fence.

Butted up against that was a concession booth. The punishing elements had warped its awning, which gave it the look of having furrowed its brow, confused at why no customers came to visit anymore.

Around it, a massive stone bib was pinned on each of its four corners by picnic tables, as if their weight was all that held it down. The center of that concrete slab had buckled and cracked where the roots of nearby trees were trying to reclaim the earth.

The tables themselves were a wreck, busted up with pieces hanging from their metal frames. It looked like this area hadn't been used in a very long time.

"How old is this place?" I asked Gregor, who was poking around at the fence line. He'd been so engrossed in his search that it had been the second time I'd posed the question.

"What? The sign said 1985, I think. Old."

"No, I mean," I said, staring up at a faded sign with a cartoon depiction of a happy ice cream cone. Big gap-toothed smile as it handed one of its tiny children to an eager cartoon kid. "How long has it been closed down?"

He sighed, slumping his shoulders. "I don't know. A decade maybe."

It looked like it.

At one time, the zoo had been teeming with excited families and squeals of laughter as they went from one collection of fantastic creatures to the next. Now, not even their echoes remained.

We'd passed a few animal enclosures during our ten-minute trek across the zoo. No cages, but I'd spotted several sunken areas with waist-high fences. I'd looked over one of those, staring down, and saw the incongruous blue concrete that, I assumed, had once held a pool of water. Now that it was paint-chipped and covered in mildew and leaves, I couldn't even imagine what animals had once made this their home.

Atop a short concrete pole, the rectangular info display was basically a blank picture frame. Years of wind and flying debris had smashed away the window that was once there. A single rusted staple remained, holding just a scrap of curled paper.

The only words left that I could read, in Comic Sans font, were *"their natural habitat!"*

Nearby, poles that had once held posters were dotted with nails, ringed by darkened bits of material that hadn't yet fallen away.

A small booth on the side, now listing closer to the enclosure after time and weather had beaten it down, looked like a place where you could maybe buy food for the animals.

Did they let you feed the animals?

Peering in farther, I could see vertical lines on the concrete walls where the thick paint had been stripped away. The exposed concrete here didn't look as mildewed as below.

As I stared longer, they looked less like strips and more like scratches. Claw marks.

I decided I'd done enough exploring.

"Here!" Gregor called out, and I turned toward him.

He stood at the lattice of wood, yanking away as if he were trying to pull it down. But at the top, I could see a slight indentation. As he struggled with it, inching it out, a black crease formed as the hidden door slowly came open.

Marata leaped down from a low branch in a nearby tree, locked her clawed fingers into the crisscross of wood, and pulled with him.

A moment later, they had it open.

"I *already* had it," Gregor said, scowling at her.

She chucked a handful of damp leaves at his head as he slipped inside. Marata followed.

I trotted up, having zero interest in being left in the spooky zoo alone, and as I stepped through the gap, I looked back, wondering.

What sort of creature might have left scratches in concrete?

The space between the false fence and the real one was about the size of a hotel hallway. I could see Gregor keeping his distance from the electrified bars, which made my heart sing just a little.

At the far end, sticking out of the ground like a squared-off thumb, was a big metal door.

The tech sergeant bent before it, brushing away cobwebs and leaves.

"Damn, I was worried that might be the case," he said as he punched at the tiny silver buttons.

The entire zoo had been dead, no lights or electricity. Except for the exterior fence, of course.

During the long drive over, he'd warned me getting below could be a problem. If the underground bunker were secured by an electric lock, it would be impossible. But he didn't think that'd be the case.

The zoo had become some emergency bolt-hole of the Organization. If shit really hit the fan and they ended up there, left to the mercy of an electric lock without the benefit of electricity, they'd have been sunk.

So instead, just below the doorknob was an old-school punch lock, a brushed-metal keypad with twelve raised dots. Four high, three across. The numbers had long since faded away, but it was obvious that the top three rows represented digits one through nine. Zero would be in the middle of the bottom row.

I'd used a pad like this hundreds of times at the various bars I'd worked at.

Type in your code and push the bottom-right button. Or left. Didn't matter. We could try both.

Of course, you did *need* a code to punch in first.

Dropping to a knee, I looked around his shoulder. "Lemme guess. You don't know the code?"

Gregor rubbed his chin.

Then he punched in six digits and pressed the one on the bottom right. When he tried to twist the knob, it moved about a quarter inch then seized up.

I asked him, "What did you type in?"

"It..." He shook his head. "I tried my birthday."

"What? Why would it be your birthday?"

"I don't know!" He glared at me. "Any bright ideas?"

I stood and went around the door. From the side, its shell covering dug into the earth. The back of it was thick curved metal, like a capital letter D that had been cut horizontally across the middle.

Clearly, the door opened to a ladder or stairs that descended at a steep angle.

When I kicked at its side, it didn't even ring out. It was like knocking against concrete; the metal was crazy thick. Sure, we could look around for an axe or hammer, but we'd never tear through it.

But it had to be bolted to something, right? And with all the rain and constant damp...

Bending down, I brushed away leaves from its base with my hand, snapping it back when I felt a weird silky tingle brush across the tops of my fingers.

"*Holy mother of shitburgers!*"

A second later, a very pissed-off spider, half the size of my palm, burst out of the debris and, thankfully, skittered to my right, slipping beneath some pile of rotting leaves there.

Gregor peeked around the side of the protruding doorframe. "What?"

"It... Down there, might be a seam or something."

Yeah, no way I was telling him spiders freaked me out. Your friends think stuff like that is funny. It's not. Never is. What would an enemy do with intel like that?

Okay, that was sounding paranoid even to me.

But, I mean... spiders, right?

Fuck them. They all must die.

Standing again, I brushed my boot up against the side, stripping away the leaves, which got damper and darker the deeper I dug. At the bottom, sure enough, there was a metal seam bolted to the concrete base. Gregor came over as I cleared the detritus away.

He pulled out his phone and flicked on the light, scanning it up and down.

"Looks pretty secure," he said then stopped at the far end. "That bolt, though. Looks rusted away."

"It was probably one of the last covered. Exposed to the air."

Gregor moved some more leaves away, and we saw two more bolts next to it, also stained with rust. They didn't look loose, but maybe they might be brittle.

He turned and gave it a horse kick and, impressively, this time, it did clang. He repeated the move in the same spot.

When he spun back, he shined the light at the spot he'd kicked. No dent. Nothing.

"Look," I said, bending down and pointing. Next to the rust bolts was the hint of a darkened line parallel to the metal lip. "Did you shift it?"

"Hmm."

He glanced toward Marata, who was just standing at the door, arms crossed as she watched us. I could see his internal struggle. Even as a distorted version of the Enhanced, the woman was nearly as strong as he was. But his ego was even stronger. No way he'd ask for her help.

I'd picked all of that up from just a quick look at his face. Twitch, furrow, and frown.

Throwing a thumb over his shoulder, he said to me, "Push or kick or whatever. Let's see if we can move it."

Pushing it would do jack, I knew that, so I lined up next to him, and we both started bashing the metal cover as hard as we could. I felt stupid.

When Gregor would hit it, the thing would rattle and shake. When I'd hit it, the only thing rattling was my shin, all the way up my thigh to my neck.

For a half minute, we bashed and bashed and bashed away at it. Both heaving huge breaths, we turned, and he pointed the light again.

"Nothing," I said. "I don't think—"

"Door open."

We turned toward Marata, who was already going through, disappearing below. The huge metal door was heavy and closing fast.

Gregor leaped forward with a hand out before I could even come up with the idea of grabbing it. Jesus, with reflexes like that, he could take over the world.

Which, I suppose, was the idea.

I came around behind him as he pulled the door. Below us, a mouth yawned, promising total darkness below. We could hear Marata's bare feet slapping against metal stairs.

He stared down at the handle then back at the void ahead. "How did we...?"

"Dunno," I said and brushed passed him. "You heard the lady: door open."

Chapter Twenty-Seven

I put my hand out to the rail angling down with the steps because they were brutally steep.

The moment the door above me clanged shut, we were blanketed in darkness. I slowed my pace, fumbling for the phone in my pocket. Before I could pull it out, a harsh white light burst from behind me.

"Thank you," I mumbled, my voice echoing off the walls.

"What? I didn't do that for *you*. I can't see!"

I turned and looked up at him. Well, looked in his general direction, but all I saw was a tunnel with a brilliant light at the end of it.

I was not a fan of that imagery because it kind of felt like a death experience. I especially didn't like it because this tunnel angled sharply downward. If one day I were faced with that particular afterlife trope, how shit would *that* be?

Decades of slogging through life and finally, you get your eternal rest, but to get there, you've got to take the stairs?

"You know," I said, shading my eyes from the glow of his phone. "You could have said nothing, right? That way, I get the false impression that you've actually done something kind and you can see so you don't fall to your death. Win-win."

The light bounced as he started to descend once again.

"Don't want you thinking I'm handing out favors left and right," he groused. That was not a word I'd normally think to use, but no question, that had been grousey.

"Don't worry, asshat. You will never be accused of that."

As I closed in on the bottom, my shadow grew longer and longer, cast down upon the metal steps. That was good because at the bottom, there was a quick turn to the left. I'd let my shadow make sure everything was just fine down there first.

With each step down, it felt as if the temperature dropped another five degrees. The underground facility couldn't have been more than twenty feet below the surface, but it felt like we were walking into the bowels of the earth.

Smelled like it too.

The walls were slick with mildew and green grime.

I trailed my fingertips across the top of the handrail, but I wasn't touching the wall without a syringe full of antibiotics.

"Marata," I called out. "Don't go too far, 'kay?"

At the bottom, I hooked left and once again was plunged into darkness. Now I did pull my phone out, swiped into my flashlight app, and clicked it on. Not surprisingly, I didn't have any bars down here. However, my Wi-Fi indicator told me that there were connections available.

I thought of pinging one—did the super-secret spooky evil spy group the Organization have a "GUEST" account?

Then, it occurred to me that my phone was likely pinging that local Wi-Fi for info, and I quickly tapped that connection off. If my phone was knocking on its virtual door, I didn't want anyone inside—virtual or real—to hear that.

We found another door at the bottom, this one wide open. How far had Marata gone ahead?

She, of course, didn't have a phone because she, of course, didn't have pockets. Or any clothes in which one might have pockets. But with those all-pupil eyes, she might have no problem seeing in the dark.

Crossing through the opening into the adjoining hall, I realized this wasn't your run-of-the-mill office door. Strong, thick steel, and I had to step over a lip. The door's opening didn't go all the way to the floor.

It was more akin to what I imagined submarine doors looked like. Or, at least, the ones I'd seen in movies. And I'd seen *Aquaman* a dozen times.

Still don't know what the hell the movie was about. I'm not any sort of comic book nut.

I am, however, a Jason Momoa nut.

That really needed no explanation.

Anyway, oval door and lip thing. I rapped my knuckles on it.

"The door is *open*, Emelda Thorne. What the hell are you knock—?"

"Shut it," I said, splaying a hand at him so he didn't try to shove past me. "This is as thick as a regular door, but it's solid steel. Seems a bit overboard, don't you think?"

He twisted his light to the door then back at my face. Gregor said, "It's a clandestine organization that manipulates half the governments on the planet and is experimenting with a way to create superhumans in a lab." The light danced for a moment, his impatience growing. "That door probably isn't thick enough."

Despite me straddling the frame, he pushed past me, pressing my body against the open door. I elbowed him as he slipped through but only ended up hurting my arm a little.

What a dick.

I turned to follow him then had a sudden thought.

I stepped back outside and looked at the front of the door. Like up top, this had a handle with a keypad. Had it already been propped open? Or had the last person out forgotten to reengage the lock?

"Pull the door closed behind you," Gregor said, his rectangle of light advancing down the hall ahead. "If we alert anyone to us being here, I don't want to literally leave the door open for them."

I stuck my tongue out at him.

His voice echoed back to me. "I heard that."

"Can you hear this?" I shouted, extending a middle finger.

He didn't bother answering. I took that as a yes.

As I shut the door, I heard the handle set back into its lock cup and then, a moment later, a *thunk-thunk*.

Shining my light up then down, I saw that two steel clamps had gripped the door like the latches of a Tupperware lid.

Three locks on the door?

Didn't matter.

We had to get in and out as quickly as we could once Gregor discovered where Kane was being held. *If* he could find that out.

I held my phone in front of me as I walked, scanning the walls. These were mostly pristine and not damp and mildewy like the ones on the other side.

Ahead, I saw Gregor round the corner to the right, which would put us beneath the main part of the park. I flashed my light up ahead and, yep, another L-junction.

However, when I cast the beam down, illuminating the walls, I saw groupings of thin gouges on the gray concrete. They varied in depth and consisted of virtually horizontal lines in short strikes.

Not many, maybe a half dozen groupings. Keeping up my pace, I regarded them as I walked.

Some had three lines, a few four. One of them five? Or two sets of three overlapping. It was impossible to tell.

"More scratches," I mumbled to myself.

Of course, this had been the zoo's underground system before the Organization purchased it through some shell company—which probably belonged to another shell company—and then took it over. The scratches would be from when they'd transported animals, big cats maybe, from below to topside.

Through the door?

Me, I'm not a zookeeper. Maybe they do just walk the animals up the stairs. *Come on, penguin, hop to it!* Or the service elevator might have been out at some point. If they had a service elevator.

There had to be more than one way out of this underground, um, lair. Yeah, sure. An evil organization owned it, so I thought that ticked all the boxes for "lair."

I picked up the pace, and a few feet from the juncture, I saw the next hallway light up.

When I rounded the corner, there was a short pass-through then a large room like a common area. Gregor was leaning against a wall, phone still in hand, arms crossed over his green T-shirt, taking in the room.

I guess I didn't really know what I might find when we got to the hub of the underground lair.

Maybe a dark room with navy-blue walls, neon tubes of light around the edges. Giant video screens showing maps of the Earth with video feeds displaying ongoing operations for their campaign of global takeover.

It looked like the home office of a corporate accounting firm.

That would, *technically*, also qualify it as a lair, mind you. Sure, that might have shown a bit of anti-accountant bias on my part, but those guys did voodoo. Didn't trust them. Not one bit.

It was basically a rectangular room, split down the middle.

On the far half, there were two long tables with workstations all along them, four on the closest side, five on the other. Like many of these sorts of setups, the delineations between workspaces were thigh-high three-drawer shelves.

Equidistant between the metal drawers were computers, each with dual monitors. The one on the far end had a long vertical monitor, which had probably designated a supervisor at some point. Bigger monitor, bigger paycheck, right?

I could only guess. I'd never worked in an office, so all my knowledge came from bad TV shows set in offices.

Shoved against one wall was another workstation about a quarter the size of the main one. With four computers there, it would be significantly more cramped.

Interns. Had to be, right?

Staring down at the interns from the concrete wall were two big boards. One was a whiteboard with smears and erasures all over the place. A chipped cup on the far right held markers, which I could only assume had long since dried to dust.

Not that decades would be needed to have done that. I'd had some experience with whiteboard markers as a bartender and waitstaff. Most whiteboard markers would dry out within six hours of popping their caps. I was pretty sure the manufacturers made them that way.

To the left of the white surface was a corkboard, just as large, holding enough paper to qualify as a fire hazard. Multicolored pushpins held their captive papers in place. I wondered if each color designated the importance of a task.

On the half of the space closer to where I was standing was a raised table with a black stone top. Three gooseneck spigots peered down into their silver basins. Between the basins were coffee cups and tumblers.

I stepped into the room. Gregor didn't even look at me. He just stared into the middle distance, frowning.

When I rounded the long table, I could see where the pipes of the basins had been hidden by white plastic boxes that fed from the top to the floor with gaps between them. One had a fridge.

When I popped the fridge open, I regretted the decision.

No one had used the tiny fridge for a long, long time. And no one had cleared it out when whoever had worked in the space had left. Two tiny bottles of milk sat in the door. At least, they'd been milk at one time. Now, they were just green goo.

The same delightful color decorated a plastic-wrapped sandwich on the middle shelf. Its owner had written their name in marker across the top. It was unreadable since the dark green below made the letters impossible to make out.

A few cans of Diet Coke. Those never expire, right?

I grabbed one, and it was cold to the touch. I closed the fridge, popped the can open, and took a sniff.

Gregor flicked his eyes at me, his mouth hanging open. He scowled, tongue tip braced against his bottom teeth.

First, I took a tentative sip, then I slugged a big gulp.

Still good.

Another big swig, and I balled a fist, thumped my chest a few times, and belched.

The tech sergeant made a hitched gagging motion then turned away.

It's the little things.

Can in hand, I pointed at him. "You want one? There might be a Fanta in here. You look like a Fanta Orange guy."

He shrugged. "What's wrong with Fanta?"

Huh. I shrugged. "What are you doing, man? Let's get to this," I said, nodding to the computer station. The screens were dark, but a shake of the mouse might bring them to life again.

"I was worried," he said and showed me his teeth, "that portions of the floor might have been electrified. The Org is big into throwing 220 volts into floor seams in case of intruders."

Stepping back, I heard the heel of my shoot click against, yep, a long metal strap in the floor. I hadn't even seen it before. I pulled my foot away.

"You didn't think to tell me?"

He shrugged. "Doesn't matter. Either those are from the previous owners, or whatever might have been plugged into them doesn't work. Or was turned off."

Gregor had his elbows up on a black shelf that ran the length of the far wall. Behind him were three framed photos. One, black and white, featured an old dude. Next to that was another old dude with similar features, this one in color. The final one looked like it was a woman with dark hair, cropped short. The top of her head was wrinkled slightly, indicating she was grinning like a maniac. The background portrayed a leafy scene, probably taken up top in the zoo somewhere.

I couldn't see her face because another piece of paper, slightly yellowed and curled inward, hung in front of it. Above that picture were the words "Employee of the Month."

The spots above the two other pictures had rectangular discolorations. Probably "Founder" and—what? "Manager"? "Head Lion Tamer"? Either those plaques had fallen off or someone had ripped them down years ago.

To Gregor's right were two glass-walled offices with similar setups as the long table but for sole occupants. They looked identical: wastepaper baskets, comfy chairs, desktop phones that would never ring again.

The one difference between the two offices was the naked feral woman in the closest office, slowly spinning on the aforementioned comfy chair. Round and round and round, arms in the air.

I watched her for a few rotations, which made me dizzy, and just when she was slowing to a stop, she put the pad of her dirty foot on the glass and spun herself again.

When I turned to Gregor, I saw he was watching Marata too.

"Well," I said, "the chairs aren't electrified either."

He shot me a grin that didn't reach his eyes. He thumbed a button on the side of his phone and pocketed the device.

"Turn your phone off," he said, nodding toward my hand. "Don't need it pinging anything down here."

"Probably too late."

"Turn it off anyhow, Emelda Thorne," he said, his voice dropping into that singsong tone he loved to use. I knew this to be his "I know more than you" tone.

Whatever. I thumbed mine off and stuffed it into my back pocket.

Casting an arm toward the rows of desks, I said, "Computers, so many to choose from. Get those fingers clacking away and find out what we need to find out, man."

He sighed. "They're dead."

"The computers? Give the mouse a shake."

Gregor, arms still crossed, nodded forward. I huffed and walked over but couldn't find a mouse. Or keyboard. I opened one of the drawers and found some old coffee cups, stained and smelly. In the top drawer was a keyboard, which I pulled out and put on the desk in front of one set of monitors.

Between them was a very small HP computer, about as big as a hardcover book.

Then I noticed something. I glanced back at Marata, still spinning, then frowned at Gregor.

I stepped back, regarding the space in front of the line of computers.

"No chairs."

He grinned at me, a real one this time, and tapped his forehead with a long, pointy finger.

Great. I'd worked it out. What I'd worked out, I had no idea. But the no-chair thing, that was a thing, right?

"So...?"

"So," Gregor said, bumping himself off the wall to step forward. As he did, the paper in front of Employee of the Month fluttered slightly. "So it means we've got to find the real office. This is just... I mean, it's supposed to look like an abandoned office."

"It *is* an abandoned office, ass-kettle."

He turned to me, blinking those black eyes just once. "The beating heart of truth is buried deep within a grave of lies. Everyone knows that, Emelda Thorne."

"Right. I'm not a fan of everyone. Actually, I don't like people very much at all."

From her glass enclosure, Marata growled. "Animals first."

I pointed at her, my eyes not leaving the tech sergeant. "She's feeling me."

He chuckled. "I doubt she even remembers how we got here."

"Fine, whatever," I said. "So what now? Where is the other office?"

Gregor shrugged. "We'll have to look around," he said, nodding to another door. "Might be down that hall there. But it won't be—"

"Second office?" Marata said, now standing not ten feet from us.

I jumped back. I hadn't even heard her come up! The look on Gregor's face told me he hadn't noticed, either.

"Yes, Marata," I said calmly. "We're looking for Kane, remember?"

She waved a hand, nodding. "Remember, yes."

"Well, the information we need to find our friend—he is we, right?—is on some database in that office."

"Second office," she repeated.

"Right. Something like that."

The Enhanced woman got a big grin on her face, and she nodded slowly. Her eyes twinkled slightly, and she blinked quickly to clear them. "Yes." She nodded to herself. "Second office."

I gave her a thumbs-up and looked to Gregor. "So where do we—?"

He held a hand up and snapped his head to his right, his eyes trailing after Marata. On the far wall, next to the glass-walled offices, was a massive wooden bookcase holding what looked like technical manuals. She grabbed one side of it.

"Marata! Don't shove things around," I said, trying not to shout. "We don't know if they're monitoring or…"

My voice trailed off.

The feral woman pushed and shoved on it, grunting as she did.

I stepped forward. I could see she was getting agitated. "Marata, it won't be underneath anything like that."

She ignored me, pushing harder. Leaning, she dug the claws of her feet into the floor, leaving gouges in the concrete.

I stared, transfixed, because they kind of looked like the ones in the adjacent hallway.

Then, the bookshelf shuddered.

I shouted, jumping back. "Oh shit, it's gonna—"

A crazy loud scraping *screech* filled the room. Then the giant floor-to-ceiling bookcase moved more freely. Evenly. As Marata pushed, I saw metal grooves in the floor.

Tracks.

She shoved it to the end, and it stopped.

Then she stood in front of a windowless door.

"Holy shit," I whispered.

Had she smelled something beyond the door? Heard, I dunno, the whirring of computer fans?

No.

I expected her to turn around like a little kid happy with herself. Instead, she reached for the door handle, twisted it once, then thumbed the keypad. Five digits, then tried again.

The door opened, and Marata disappeared inside.

Chapter Twenty-Eight

Marata had walked through the hidden door behind the shelving unit into total darkness. It looked like she'd stepped right into some giant's open mouth to willingly let herself be swallowed. No hesitation. No break in stride.

Just waltzed right in.

I began to further suspect those black eyes that she and Gregor had picked up from the Org's program gave them some sort of night vision. Would that work in a room devoid of all light?

A moment later, fluorescents began to flicker in the room, a harsh wash of unnatural white light.

One look at Gregor, and I knew that he was working hard to keep his face neutral. I hadn't known the guy long—and had zero interest in knowing him a second more—but I could already pick out some of his tics.

He was easy enough to read. He'd clench his jaw when he was trying to come off as impassive. The result was that his lips pursed a little, and the cords in his neck bulged like ropes.

And dude was pursing and bulging big time.

Marata hooked out of sight to revealing a long white counter loaded down with complicated devices. Above that were what looked like shiny black cupboards with button-shaped keyholes above each handle.

I stated the obvious. "She's been here before," I said, my voice just above a whisper.

"What difference does it make?" He sneered, but his eyes never wavered from the open door. I could tell his mind was racing as well.

"I like to know who the hell I'm traveling across the country with!" I said, throwing a hand toward the open door. Yeah, we still hadn't gone through. "It's kind of a rule I got."

Finally, he looked at me, a self-satisfied sneer on his face. "Is it, now?"

What a dick.

But he was right. I knew nothing about Gregor. Hell, I didn't even know his first name, but it wasn't like I wanted to be book club buddies or anything.

"Come on," he said, stepping forward before I could will my own feet to move. "The data I'm looking for will be in there."

I watched him go through the door, look left and right, then go in the opposite direction Marata had.

Yep.

And there I stood. By myself. It felt odd. Like going forward would be stepping into another universe. In a way, it was.

Once inside, I'd be in a world that belonged to the Organization. Their turf. Even if they weren't around anymore.

Weird. I'd never felt territorial like that. I suppose that came from hanging out with a wolf-dude for the better part of a month.

"Get a grip," I mumbled to myself. I took two or three steps, finally crossing the threshold into the hidden room. As I stood there, taking it all in, the panicky part of my brain, the red car-sale guy flapping in the wind, warned me that any moment, the door was going to thunk closed behind me, and I'd be trapped in here forever.

It did not thunk closed.

Whereas the room I'd just left looked like an accounting wing of some law office or shipping firm, this was otherworldly.

For one thing, it was massive.

Three times the size of the other room, this was a space where a dozen people could work all day without ever bumping into each other. You'd have to raise your voice to get someone's attention across the room.

I could see four long tables, a bit like the ones outside the door, but these were thick and white, with massive sinks at either end. They had odd sloping basins, not the square bowl shapes you'd find in a restaurant kitchen.

On the side next to the table's edge, that part was vertical and deep. From there, the basin sloped up to the white tabletop.

On the two tables on the left, I could see instruments. Not flutes and trombones, mind you; knives, clamps, massive tweezers as long as my forearm. Tubes and masks. And each of those tables had a recessed metal bed in the middle, which fed down to the sinks at the end.

Instead of being neat and orderly like the fake office space, here, all the stuff was scattered. A lot of it was broken.

The far right two tables had similar sinks but were loaded down with devices I couldn't make heads or tails of. I'd seen similar stuff in news stories about medical treatments, though.

Devices to examine blood or tissue samples. Old-school microscopes with next-gen updates. A large tablet secured to the side of another machine with more dials and readouts than a cockpit.

That had been smashed, its glass face spiderwebbed with cracks.

Along the far wall, Gregor had pulled up a rolling chair. He grabbed an overturned wireless keyboard off the floor, wiped it with his shirt, and got to work. His back to me, he was hunched down and pecking away. The vision was very incongruous with the impression I had of the guy. It was as if some mafia hit man had lost his gig to downsizing or AI and had to slum it and take up a data-entry job. Even with his back to me, his long arms bent sharply at the elbows, I could tell that dude was typing with two fingers.

"Can't get access to many of these documents, dammit," he said, chewing his words. "I've found a folder with what looks like video clips. Not much else."

"Keep looking," I said. "Our answers are there or nowhere."

I waited for a full minute, staring at the back of his head. I shifted my weight from foot to foot. Looked down at the floor and saw a dark smear. I looked away.

I'd been avoiding looking at the opposite wall, and I knew it.

Finally, I swung my head in that direction, and the red guy in my brain rattled his big inflatable arms in the air and covered his eyes.

Wuss.

But I empathized. The giant rectangular box was... confronting. Huge. It looked like half the size of a railroad container. It had a thick metal frame. One half of the front was clear like glass. The other consisted of thick vertical slats as wide as my forearm.

In the harsh florescent light, I could make out warbling striations in the thick glass.

That was when I picked up the hint of a smell. Not quite rot or stench. More like sweat. Or some kind of body odor.

Marata was standing in the corner, her back to the wall, next to the giant box. She slowly turned toward me, a queer, far-off expression on her face. She looked lost, as if she was trying to remember the name of a song that was quietly playing on an overhead speaker.

Her head snapped up toward something in the opposite corner of the room. As she crossed in front of the giant box, I finally realized the striations I'd seen in the glass weren't any kind of discoloration.

Scratches. They were thick scratches.

It wasn't a box. This was a cage.

"What kind of animal was that...?" I said then turned to see Marata slipping her arms through a coat of some kind. Next to her, a rack on the wall held three others like the one she was putting on.

Why was she putting on clothes now?

Marata walked forward, hunching as she did, her long limbs pulling her across the floor. She jammed her hands into the pockets, eyes out of focus.

This was something familiar to her. She just couldn't reconcile it in her feral brain.

When we'd popped open the door up top, it hadn't been our doing. Marata had known the code. And she had obviously known the one for the second door in the tunnel. She'd also known about the hidden door behind the shelf.

She hadn't picked up the scent of anything. She'd known it was there because she'd been here before. Not just been here.

As she stood awkwardly in front of the cage, sniffing as she hitched her head left and right, I realized she'd put on a lab coat.

Her lab coat.

Marata had worked in this lab.

Then it all came flooding into my brain. This was how she became an Enhanced. One of the program candidates had been—what? Held in the cage and gone nuts and bitten her? Or they'd been tied down on one of the lab tables...

No.

The participants of the Org's program had been at another facility. That was where Cal and Gregor had been. This was another.

An earlier program.

And, of course, this had been a zoo, which came with all the necessary infrastructure needed to house animals.

In the early stages of the program, they would have tested out a battery of treatments and therapies and serums. This was where they'd done that. This had been the final step before human subjects were put through that hell.

When I looked up, I saw Marata had turned to me, that faraway expression filling her eyes. But a hint of something else. Something familiar.

She had been here, in this lab, in those early days. The first stages of the Enhanced program.

Nodding, as if she could read my thoughts, she said, "Animals first."

Chapter Twenty-Nine

Kane

I hear the *thunk-clank*, and the light blasts me once again. There is a low noise, a rumble of something.

Then, I realize it is me.

A breath? A moan?

Am I losing control of myself?

Another banging sound, but this time, it is not from the light array. I hear the clicking and clacking of hard plastic smacking against the cold concrete.

"You think you're funny?"

Ah, yes.

I knew this would be coming. For the first time in as long as I can remember, my face stings. It is a mild pain I welcome because it has been too long since I have smiled.

Ilsa Hammer is striding toward me, her heels punishing the floor beneath her, one of her arms looking unnaturally long in silhouette.

"My lackies tell me your story, the story you claim is yours, is from the plot of a television show!" she says as she speeds up.

I cannot see her face, which is in shadow. But I do not need that to know she is very angry.

When I try to speak, I only get out a croak. My throat feels seized. I have not had water in days.

"*The Incredible Hulk*?" she screams at me. Actually screaming, her voice ringing in my ears. "You think that's *fucking funny*?"

I can now see her eyes, for she is close. Behind them, I can see—

Zzznnnttt!

My entire body explodes in pain, my muscles tense, and my spine feels like it has burst into flames and is now trying to burst from my chest.

The pain stops briefly, and I slump back to the wall, my breath lost. I feel dizzy. I try to pull in air, but it will not come. As my head lolls forward, I see a long metal pole in her hand.

Yes. Yes, I remember this. Gregor had used it on me back at the Minnesota mall. Pain stick. Electricity from twin barbs.

"I will not be made a fool of! Not by you, old man! Not by anyone!"

Too weak to even lift my head, I shift my arms. She is close. So close. If I could just—

My eyes widen as I see her stab the teeth of the pain stick into my wrinkled stomach. She leans in, tearing some skin. Then she hits the button on the shaft, and light explodes into my brain. I squeeze my eyes against it, but instead of darkness, I see only starlight.

My head swims, swims, swims, and I am floating. The pain subsides.

When I open my eyes, I see stars.

Not like in the cartoons that I much enjoy watching with Mère, however. For such a kind woman, those tend to be surprisingly violent. And those stars often come from an often unprovoked, quick-fire attack that the prey did not see coming.

Me, I have never seen stars when enduring a skull smash.

Nor have I seen tiny tweeting birds encircling my head. I believe I would prefer the birds.

The stars I see above now carpet the sky. Various sizes and shapes and luminosity. These are not the same light-dot patterns I recall from my nights in the forest. The quiet evenings with my pack. With my wolf wife.

Of course, those memories are a jumble. As if old thoughts are an entirely different language, like the troublesome English, and when I try to recall them and translate to my now-mind, the memories of the past are cryptic and unreadable.

But I do remember the comfort the stars granted me. Yes, I can recall the feelings of the past, if not always the circumstances or environs.

The stars made me feel... peaceful?

Yes, I think so.

I believe this is why Mère has placed these different stars upon the ceiling of my den.

Room. Humans have rooms, not dens.

Last week, when I changed into... that puny animal, I was distraught. Frustrated. Angry.

"I think you look very handsome," Mère had said when we'd returned to our home. I'd been unable to move, for I was so shocked, and she had carried me to the couch and sat beside me. At first, when she began to stroke the fur of my head, I balked.

But then I relented. Her comforting touch almost made me forget that I had become such a lowly creature.

"*Regardez-moi, Mère!*" I had said, squeezing my eyes closed, trying to make it not real. "*Je suis un chien!*"

Mère chuckled and scratched my ear. Involuntarily, my tongue lolled out. Betrayed me!

"English, Kane. You must practice English," he said. "And yes, you are a dog. So what? They are beautiful, majestic creatures."

"I know of dogs. They are the lesser of we. Their hunting instincts stripped away, which they have happily traded away for gelatinous food that comes in cans," I said, growing angry. "What sort of vile creatures can be so happy to eat meat tubes?"

"*Clame-toi!*" Père said, swirling the amber liquid in his thick glass. His third that particular night, so as he moved the glass, a slosh of liquid lapped out. Even several meters away, I could smell its acidic aroma. Funny, I had never smelled this when a human boy.

Mère shot him a look. "Nobody ever calmed down from someone shouting 'calm down,' John. The boy's upset."

"He is not a boy. No longer a boy, he is..."

I looked at Père and nodded. "Yes. I am dog. Eater of tube meat. For now, my life is sucking on tube meat!"

"Uh, maybe," Père said, clearing his throat, "you don't say that anymore."

"*C'est vrai!* This is true!" I said, snapping away from Mère's caress. "Television has taught me I am good for eating from pink bowls, chasing cars, licking my privates, and getting help for little boys who fall in wells!"

"No, dear, sweet Kane," Mère said softly.

"Why would such animals pick companions who fall into *clearly* marked holes in the ground?" I said, lowering my head and covering it with my soft, fluffy paws. "Caring for someone so clueless, this sounds like endless heartbreak. I do not want to be this... *thing*."

I felt the soft touch of Mère's hands on either side of my furry jowl as she lifted my face. Reluctantly, I opened my eyes and met her gaze. She had bent down, putting her nose to mine.

"You will never be a *thing*, my beautiful boy."

"But Mère," I said, my voice shaking. My vision getting blurry. "I don't want to be—"

"You will always be you. On the inside."

I sniffed. "On the outside, I am soft fur and floppy ears! Is beautiful, yes, but... but... I am a dog, *ma mère*. A dog!"

"You are not."

"*Oui!* Look at me—"

Mère smiled at me, rubbing my nose with hers. I felt a flood of warmth, my heart singing. She spoke softly to me then, words I will always remember.

"You are wolf," she said. "You will always be wolf. It doesn't matter what skin you have or clothes you wear."

"I do not like clothes."

"Yes, yes," she said, clearing her throat. "You do need to get over that. When you do meet others, they prefer you to be wearing clothes." She then got a twinkle in her eyes. "Most of the time."

"Mère, please!" Père said, taking another very large swig from his glass. "Is this not already strange enough?"

She stroked my head to get my attention, and my eyes returned to hers. Her warm, enveloping gaze.

"Say it."

"*Quoi?*"

Mère took a deep breath and steeled me with a look. Her eyebrows pressed down as she gripped my paws with hers, feeding her determination into me. And, yes, I felt it. Felt that flow through me.

Is this the power of mothers?

To feed the younger their strength? To give power?

She said, "You. Are. Wolf."

I nodded, and when I tried to look away, she placed her fingers on the side of my snout and pulled me back to her gaze.

"Say this to me."

Grumbling, I told her, "I am wolf."

"Again."

Louder, I said, "I am wolf."

"Who is Kane?"

"Kane," I said, then blinked, my vision blurring with prisms of light, "is wolf."

Mère grinned, tilted her head to the sky, and shouted so loud it hurt my floppy ears, "I am wolf!

As she fed me her strength, I felt it flow through me, and I matched her volume.

"I am wolf!"

My smile falls when something in my brain wrestles me from the memory. I am no longer a dog, grateful for having returned to the form of a human boy. Alas, still not a wolf but—

A sound. A clatter.

Waking from sleep, I push the foggy memories of my dog days behind me and focus. My instincts are what I must focus on now. I must pay attention to my surroundings. Not only in this room, this bedroom they have gifted me, but extend my senses out through their home.

My home.

I flinch at the sound of breaking glass and leap from the bed. I glance toward the window, cocking my head to listen. No. No, the crash did not come from outside.

Downstairs.

Something is wrong.

I lift my face and sniff the air. Upon it, I can smell the comforting odors of my human parents. The roast Père cooked the night before. The smell of flowers outside drifting in.

And other scents I do not recognize.

Strangers are in the house.

Chapter Thirty

I stared at the monitor, my mind reeling.

Wobbly, I almost put a hand on Gregor's shoulder as he sat in front of the computer to just steady myself. Instead, I drew in a deep breath, trying to process what I'd just seen.

The only files Gregor could access on the hidden lab's computer were some video clips on the computer's desktop. His best guess was that this had been some security-feed backup that had dumped them on the drive if things went wrong.

And they had.

Holy hell, had things gone wrong.

The static image on the screen, the last moments of some nameless lab worker, was a distorted mask of fear and resignation frozen in time.

I jumped back, startled, when that horrified face blinked away. A message popped up in its place, white letters on a black background:

END OF FILE.

Dropping onto a stool next to one of the disheveled lab tables, I stared at those three words, both willing them to tell me more and wanting to hear none of it.

Gregor spun in his roll-away chair to scoot up to me, kicking his feet out like a kid pulling himself along after his snow sled had gotten to the bottom of a hill and he didn't want the ride to end.

"There are other video files in the folder," he said as his black eyes danced in his skull. "Dozens of them."

When he started to scoot back, I stuck a foot out and hooked his chair with my heel.

"You want to see *more* of that?" I swallowed and rubbed the back of my hand across my eyes. "I've... I've never seen so much blood."

The tech sergeant shrugged and muttered, "I have. Years of that."

"Whatever. No one wants to hear any stories about your Cub Scout summers," I said, putting the other foot up next to the first. "We're here to find the Covenant facility. Do you think you can find that, or is this some stall of yours?"

He swiveled his head down to look at my feet gripping his chair. I dropped them away. He spun and slid in front of the keyboard once again. For a moment, he just stared at the open folder.

"That vid is date stamped as the last in the collection," he said, tapping away with two fingers. "Seems like all the good bits might be in the one we watched anyhow."

Good bits?

The guy was a monster even without the physical distortions, sounding like he'd been disappointed he'd seen the one good episode of some shitty Netflix series.

As he poked at the keyboard, I stood and approached Marata. She'd been mostly silent the entire time the video carnage had played out. At least twice, I heard a low moaning. I thought it might have come from her, but with all the screaming, snarling, and dying on the video, it had been impossible to tell.

The feral woman stood there, stooped slightly forward, as if she still wasn't used to the longer limbs that had sprung from her shoulder and hip sockets. Her arms hung forward, and her head hung slightly down like it was too heavy for her neck.

Her black eyes were off in another world.

After seeing her animated for the past twenty-four hours, borderline jumping off walls, it was eerie to see her in this fugue state.

I wondered if the lab coat she'd slipped into had once been hers, when she'd worked in this facility. Before the chaos.

The once-pristine white coat had grayed. There were a few dark streaks across the sleeves and breast of it. After seeing the video, I knew what they were.

Her arms poked out of the sleeves to the forearm. The bottom hem, which normally would drop to the knee—at least from what I'd seen in *ER* reruns, it would—instead hit her just above mid-thigh. It hung open.

I wondered if she found some comfort in wearing the old uniform. Something familiar.

When I looked up from her coat, she was staring at me with those dark eyes. I smiled at her, trying to assure the woman that I was a friend. She just nodded and raised her long arms, trying to shift the sleeves pinching her skin. As tight as it was, the garment had to be a bit uncomfortable.

As she shifted around, she seemed to finally notice she was exposed, and at that moment, that appeared to bother her. She tried to pull the garment closed.

Watching her twist the buttons between her long, ungainly fingers, I stood. Marata tried pushing one button at the flap on the other side. Then she repeated the motion.

I realized she wasn't necessarily trying to button it up. She'd been staring at me as she'd done this.

"Yeah, Marata, sure," I said and lifted my hands toward her, paused, and got a slight nod, then secured a lower button. She was too big for the outfit, really. On a woman as unnaturally large as she was, it looked less like a lab coat and more like a kid's karate outfit without a belt.

As I latched a second button, I spoke softly to her. "You worked here. I saw you on the tape."

"No see," she said, taking a half step back.

I raised my hands. "No. No, we won't play it again. Just... we had to know, okay?"

"O-kay."

"I'm sorry about your friends," I said, knowing that staying on this particular memory was not a great idea. Still, I felt she needed comforting. "That must have been hard."

Marata grunted and turned to the wall opposite where Gregor was typing.

He grunted and smacked the keyboard with his palm. I ignored him.

Then, I realized something about the moment back at the old factory that had likely saved my life.

"I thought you'd picked up Kane's scent and recognized Cal within it," I said, standing and regarding her. "You look great. Very professional."

That got a smile out of her, which I kind of regretted. A lot of teeth. Except for the gap.

"You were, um, bitten by one of the animals here?"

Another grunt, but this time, a hitch of her head.

"I think that's why you recognized the scent," I said, staring at the empty cage. "Kane is a wolf. A man for now, but a wolf. Your, um, *glow up*... that had come from an animal. So I guess you recognized that smell on me. He is we, yeah?"

The dark-stained coat arms slid against her body as she shrugged. "You are we?"

"Right. Right." I nodded. No need to contradict her and, I mean, that would be rude of me, right? Still, I had a question that hadn't been answered by the tape. "What... I'm sorry, I know this is hard... What kind of animal bit you?"

Marata winced, then her face softened. She smiled sadly. "Mindy. Mindy bit."

"Mindy?"

She nodded. "Mindy... meer... meer-kat."

Despite how awful it must have been, I had to suppress a laugh. "Okay. You got bit by an Enhanced meerkat? Named Mindy?"

"Mindy friend."

"But your friend bit you, yes?"

Marata waved her hand in front of her face. "Mindy not self. Go-juice made crazy. Angry. When..." Her eyes flickered to the monitor where the tape had played out. "When trouble happen. More crazy. Mindy bite."

"I'm sorry, Marata."

"Not Mindy fault. Go-juice make crazy."

I didn't bring up that she'd been swigging that same go-juice for months. I wondered if she'd made that connection.

Of course, I wanted to know where Mindy the meercat had gone. The cage was empty. Two more smaller cages lay on the floor in the corner. Those had been more traditional, all metal. Now they lay with their wires bent and jagged. Doors swung open at odd angles.

Before I could ask her, Gregor growled loudly.

"This is useless," he said, smacking the keyboard with his fist. "The video files, I can get to. *Some* of the lab tech notes. But that's everything in this folder."

Walking up to stand next to him, I stared at the screen. "Try another folder."

"I did that, Emelda Thorne," he said, hissing his words. He drilled me with those black eyes, the skin between his eyebrows like a tiny fist waving at me. "They're all locked. You need a passcode to access them."

"Marata," I said, turning, "do you remember the code for this computer?"

"Pu-ter?"

"Right. There are folders we need to get into to find Kane. But they have a passcode. Or a password," I said, smiling warmly at her and pointing at the monitor. "Do you know what that is?"

She pointed. "It pu-ter. You say that." Marata shook her head and chuckled. The expression on her face looked like she might go, *"Sheesh. Get a load of this lady, amiright?"*

I tried again. "Yes, but do you remember the passcode? For the folders?"

"Fold-ders," she said as if toying with how the word felt in her mouth. "Fooold-ders." She smiled.

"Well, that was informative," Gregor said.

I shot out a backhand that thunked his head, one that I knew he could have blocked but didn't. Odd.

"Don't do that. And this is a waste of time."

"No!" I said and put my hands on his shoulders to stop him from getting out of the chair. This time, more gently. Less smacky. "No, please. It has to be here, right? Or we go to another location and see if what we need is there."

He sighed and shrugged. "Even if we found another location with access, we'd run into the same problem. It's useless, Emelda Thorne. Dead end."

I refused to accept that.

At that moment, Kane was being held captive. Treated like an animal, just like the ones we saw on the...

"Hold on," I said to Gregor. "Pull that video up again." To Marata, I said, "Are there bottles of water or something for us to drink? Do you know?"

She grinned at me, nodding. "Yes. Know. I get, yes?"

"Yes, please. Thank you, Marata."

She went to the door next to the cage, opened it with a flourish, and disappeared down the hall, the dirty hem of her lab coat flapping behind her.

I told Gregor to replay the tape.

"Listen, I agree, it's a hoot to watch," he said, poking at the keyboard. "Love to download it somehow and put it up on the big screen. But if the Org is paying any attention to activity on this computer, we're on a countdown clock."

I barely listened to the last part of what he'd said. *A hoot to watch?*

"You got issues, man," I said then hooked a thumb in front of the screen, jerking it left. "No, back, back. Before the attack."

"But *that's* the good part."

"M'kay. Go to about a minute in," I said, swallowing back the bile that had risen in my throat. Being this close to the guy, leaning in, was turning my stomach. When he'd reached the right point, I tapped the screen. "Stop there."

He hit the space bar.

On the screen, lab assistants were milling around, working as a group but clearly each in their own world. Maybe each approaching the problem, whatever it had been at that moment in time, from their particular training aspect.

On the left, two people in pristine white coats were muttering while taking turns staring through a bad-ass microscope. The thing looked powerful enough to see an electron give you the finger.

A woman with flowing dark hair was bent close to the barred half of the cage, her face crazy close to the animal inside.

It was Marata. Before she'd become a monster.

The meerkat had been swinging around, grabbing ropes above then landing as if ready to attack.

I'd always thought the animals looked cute. Hell, in photos, they always appeared to be smiling. The way their heads would bop up and peer around, as if they were searching for a good time.

Mindy the meerkat was not one of those.

Not anymore.

In this early stage of the program, she had been altered. The long, lean body was now bulkier. Claws at her hands and feet, long and thick. She stalked toward Marata, who was leaning in toward the cage, with its massive head down, shoulders raised.

As Mindy moved forward, it looked less like walking and more like she was clawing the ground and pulling the helpless world toward her. As her black eyes settled on Marata, her head shifted. Even in the small image, we could see spots where electrodes could be attached to the skull.

Two short metal poles stuck out on either side of her brow.

Cal Davis had said they'd used light therapy in his treatment. Torture, really. It had been designed to trigger some rewiring of the brain. Obviously, that process had been developed from these experiments. Conditioning to soften the mind, make it more pliable, so the serum could do what it did.

The tabs on either side of Mindy's head could have been where they might have clamped down tiny goggles she wouldn't have been able to pull off.

When the Enhanced meerkat got within a foot of Marata, her demeanor changed. She blinked her black eyes, and her tense shoulder muscles slackened. She licked her lips, tiny black tongue tracing in a circle, and then went back up on her haunches, sitting upright.

Despite her grotesque changes, she looked, for the first time, like an actual meerkat.

My attention was drawn to the far side of the screen, just barely out of frame, where another lab worker was writing something on a clipboard.

Recalling what I'd seen the time before, I tapped on the screen. "I think I know who that is."

Gregor just grunted, arms crossed. This was the boring bit for him. He wanted to go back to the carnage.

On the far left of the screen, Marata and the meerkat stared at one another, like some silent armistice. On the right, the woman in the lab coat scribbled away on a chart.

No. Not scribbling.

"She's not writing anything," I said slowly as I squinted at the image. Then, I saw it. "Holy shit."

Gregor leaned forward, the chair complaining under his bulk.

On the screen, the woman with the lab coat reached under the clipboard and extended her arm enough that the light pink of her undershirt stuck out.

Then she slowly pulled at a metal bar and dropped her hand.

I took a step back. "She opened the cage."

"Maybe she's putting in food or..." Gregor's voice trailed off as we watched the woman hang the clipboard on a hook next to the glass portion of the cage.

We watched as she then stepped over to the computer, the same one we were on now.

Her head was down, so all we could see was her raven-black hair twisted up into a ponytail that would have made my eyes water. I hadn't worn a ponytail since I was eleven. But my mother, tired of my wild hair, had bound my locks like that.

The more I'd squirmed, the more tightly my hair was squeezed into the tiny noose. I learned not to squirm, lest I get rivulets of blood in my mascara.

"Damn." Gregor tapped the screen with his long fingernail. "That's Doc Hammer."

"Yep. I *thought* I saw her earlier," I said, pushing my nose closer to the video. "What is she doing?"

"Can't see from this angle."

On the screen, we saw Doc Hammer stand up, wipe her hands down her lab coat, and then jam them into her pockets. We both jumped as her voice burst from the tiny computer speaker: *"Anyone want a coffee?"*

The only person who'd even acknowledged her had been Marata, who languidly waved a hand in her direction, indicating she didn't.

All the others in the room just went about their business, engrossed in their work.

Hammer looked around, shrugged, and wiped her mouth, then jammed her hand back into a pocket.

"I'm going to get one, then."

She spun away from the computer and strode to the adjacent door, the very one I'd sent Marata through for water minutes earlier. Yanking on the handle, Hammer pulled it open. As she exited, her hand flung out and nabbed something hanging on the wall.

"Did she take her bag? To get a coffee?" I said.

Gregor leaned into the chair and threw his head back. "Jesus." He started laughing. Like gut-bust laughing, pointing at the screen. "That crazy... woman. She's leaving."

I put my hand to my mouth.

"She did it." I looked toward where Marata was leaning toward the cage. Mindy the meerkat dropped from two legs to four once again.

"Mindy. Over here, love," she cooed, and for the first time, I detected an accent. Like British but twangier. Australian? *"No, don't muck about with—"*

My hand flew out, and I punched the space bar. The screen in front of us froze.

"Why'd you do that?" Gregor sat up, wiping his eyes. "This is where it all goes to hell."

I elbowed him out of the way and bent over at the computer and nabbed the mouse.

"We've seen it," I said and shuttled the video back to where Hammer had been on the computer. Just before she stood up to leave. Pressing the space bar again, I searched the screen.

"There. Timecode says it's August 13 at 21:42:56." I frowned. "Which is..."

"A few seconds before 9:43 p.m." Gregor shrugged, leaning over my shoulder.

"Oh, good." I shuffled my feet in the chair, pushing him back. "All those years of military training paid off."

I could feel him seething behind me. "Oh, I learned far more than just how to read a clock, Emelda Thorne. Far more."

"Right," I said, clicking away on the keyboard. "Is it supposed to be scarier if you say it twice?"

He grunted.

I pulled up the web browser and searched through its history. Scanning down, I came to the same date and time that Hammer had been on the computer. That wasn't hard. It was the last entry in the browser's history.

I tapped the screen, thumping the entry with the pad of my finger.

"Google maps. She was planning her escape route." I shook my head as I clicked a few more times, bringing up the page she'd looked at. "Damn. Ol' girl left it late."

Behind me, Gregor snickered. "What's that supposed to mean?"

"She *opened* the cage, shitburger," I said. "Hammer knew she'd only have a few seconds, maybe a minute. If she'd been ramping up to that moment, surely, she'd have planned better."

The tech sergeant shuffled a little closer. "How could you know that?"

I shot a look at him. "I don't! I'm guessing here, man. But if she was planning on causing that kind of chaos, she'd have her escape all laid out. This looks, I don't know, last minute."

"Maybe she saw an opportunity and just took it? That is kind of her way."

When the map page opened, right in the center, a giant red pin poked into the digital earth below. Instead of identifying the name of the structure, it showed coordinates.

Gregor leaned in. "Southwest Atlanta. Near here but out a ways."

"It won't let me get to street view. Look."

I grabbed the little yellow dude on the map, and it showed green lines up and down the roads everywhere on the screen. But in the two blocks surrounding the map pin, the streets were red. I held the little yellow dude at the tip of my mouse pointer, and he hung there, dangling above the red line.

But when I went to drop him, yellow dude flew back to his home at the bottom right of the screen.

"It's probably private property," Gregor said with a sniff.

"For two city blocks?" Then I had a thought and turned to him. "Does the Organization have any influence to get info like that pulled?"

He laughed. "Are you joking? Of course. I don't think you realize just how pervasive the Org and Covenant are, Emelda Thorne," he said, steepling his long, gnarled fingers. "They own us. Every bit."

"Right. Well, there are ways around that."

Opening a new tab, I typed away, my fingers flying across the keyboard. Finding the sites I needed, I went through a few mirror backups until I got to where some lovely nerds had backed up map data from around the world.

I double-clicked on the images I needed.

Gregor leaned back. "What the hell is that?"

"Well, in a former life," I said, clicking and dragging, "my old boyfriend, Roy, and I used to like exploring sites that people didn't want us to visit. And the best places had some big money, so they could petition map sites to take their stuff down."

"You mean estates," he said in a tone I didn't care for. "You were looking for layouts of people's high-dollar properties."

"Sure. Not all of us are born with a silver dick in our mouths, Gregor."

I saw him tense, rolling his hands into fists. Had to force myself not to laugh.

"You can't go into million-dollar homes without good intel. Well, unless you don't care about getting out again." I copied and pasted the coordinates from the first tab into the nerd-data page and hit Enter. The pin dropped once again.

"Come on, yellow man. Let's take a look."

This time, when I dropped the little hangy guy, he landed on his feet, and the screen flipped and spun. It resolved into a street scene. A few drags of the mouse, and we were staring at the image of what looked like a five-story office complex.

At the front was an electronic gate but no guard. I hit the arrow on the screen to get into the lot, but it was private property. The little Google Volkswagen Bug with its big eyeball camera had not been allowed to slip inside.

"The sign," Gregor said. "Go back to the sign."

Zooming out slightly, I cursored over to a long white sign, nestled into the long Georgia grass. Gregor read it aloud.

"Deimos Industries." He sighed. "Okay, yeah. That's them. That's Covenant."

"How could you know that?"

"They love their lesser Greek gods. Never understood it," he said and kicked the stool I'd been sitting on earlier, sending it crashing across the room. "That bitch. When was this again?"

"About a year ago."

I turned toward Gregor, and he had his hands up on his head, gripping his short silver hair.

"A year ago?" His eyes were wide, the pupils shrinking to pinpricks. "*A year!*"

I'd spent too many years with dudes who lost their shit. I knew better than to say the worst two words in the world to guys in that sort of state. I temporarily deleted both "calm" and "down" from my vocabulary.

And I'd learned that to get a dude off his rage train, you ask them to tell you something they know and you don't.

"That's the nearest Covenant site, then?"

He blinked and dropped his hands. "Yes. It would have to be." He looked around the lab space. "She basically lit the match and bolted to her new bosses."

"Do you think that's where Kane is being held?" I asked.

But instead of answering, he leaned against the lab table and slumped to the floor, burying his face in his hands. Through his fingers, he mumbled, "She'd been working with them for *a year*?"

"Gregor... um... I don't even know your first name. I can't keep calling you Gregor. We ain't on a soccer team together." I laughed.

He let his hands fall. "Anton," he muttered softly. "Named after my grandfather."

"Okay, Anton," I said. Yeah, no way I was calling him that. But for now, I needed him calm. I pointed at the screen. "Do you think Kane is there?"

He sighed and leaned forward, regarding the screen. Slowly, he nodded. "There'll likely be a subbasement in a place like that. If that's where Hammer ran to last year—*last year!* And I took orders from her the whole—"

"Focus, man."

"Right," he said and nodded, getting his mojo back. "If that's where she bolted to from here, that's probably where she'd been assigned. The Org and Covenant liked compartmentalizing. Millions of moving parts. If she went there last year, then that's her patch."

I jumped up. We knew where Kane was!

Touching the screen with my fingertips, I whispered, "Hold on. We're coming for you."

That was when I realized something and scanned the room.

"Where did Marata go?"

Chapter Thirty-One

Kane

As I stand, the thought takes over my brain. Enrages me.

Strangers are in the house.

The human part of me insists I run for the door, but I am more than human.

"I am wolf."

And I use my wolf sense, dulled as a young man but still there.

Sniffing the air, I can detect... wood smoke? No, not from wood. Another kind of smoke smell. Acrid and unpleasant.

There are low grumbling sounds, word sounds, then a crack.

No more time to evaluate. I have learned all I can, so I pad to the door and slowly open it. It is dark in the hallway. The room across from mine is open, and from here, I can see the bed of my human parents.

It is empty.

Have they gone downstairs to argue? I fear that my presence here does create discord in this home. I have heard the whispers from Père, admonishments. He is kind to me but wary. Not of me, I do not think, but of how Mère cares for me so.

I pick up those new scents once more.

Body sweat but not of Mère or Père.

People who do not belong in our home in the middle of the night.

With a glance to my right, I can see light spilling across the bottom of the stairs, a burnt-amber glow. Shadows flicker and dance. A voice.

A man is speaking, but I cannot pick out the words.

Slowly, I creep forward, trying to listen. Trying to hear.

The voices are louder, and resting my hand on the wood banister, I close my eyes to draw them in. One man speaking. Another with him. But closer now, I can detect the sweat smells of three. There are three.

And they are with my human parents.

Friends?

I have never known them to have friends. Or at least none that come to the house. Only Dr. Fineman, but we have only visited him at his clinic in town.

Another small step forward, and I let out a small cry. My foot has dragged against the jagged metal lip of the carpet runner at the top of the stairs. There's a shuffling below, and a man leaps around the corner. He punches at the wall, and the light bursts above me.

"Who the fuck is this?" he says, a long black pipe cradled under his arm. I know what this is. I have seen it in the *Dukes* TV show. Shotgun. Dangerous and deadly.

From the living room, I hear Père call out, "He is no one of your concern. A boy staying with us. Leave him—"

I hear another crack and Père cry out.

My head swims with a haze. I can feel my hands ache, my arms throb, as my blood pumps harder. My ears fill with the *thud-thud-thud* of my quickening heartbeat.

"Come down here, boy!" the man with the shotgun says. He waves the weapon toward the living room, and I see a tiny sparkle in his ear.

I hear Mère struggle then say, "Let go of me!" and she appears in the doorway to the living room. "It's all right, Kane. Just come on down. They won't hurt you."

A voice from behind ma mère says, "I'll be the judge of that. Get him down here, Van!"

"You heard him," the nasty human named Van says, pressing the stock of the weapon to his shoulder. I put my hand on the rail and slowly descend. My bare feet are sweating, my palms tingling. A queer feeling takes over my brain.

I want to rip this man's throat out. *Need* to.

As I pass the family photographs lining the staircase, an object on the wall catches my attention. When I see Van turn to another intruder, the two planning and scheming, I reach up, grab it, and hide it in my cupped palm.

When my arm retracts, Van snaps his attention toward me, scowling. He senses something is up, but I can smell the alcohol on his breath. Stupid human has dulled his senses and only waves the weapon.

"Get moving."

Stepping past him, I transfer the object to my other hand, holding its length against my wrist.

Something occurs to me.

Something forest animal.

I know I cannot appear as a threat, or I will be treated as such. Instead, I must show weakness I do not feel. This will lower their defenses when regarding me.

Wrapping my arms around my chest, I hold this feint. And also, it helps me hide the object in my hand.

Before me, Mère and Père stand in the middle of the room. Van the alcohol drinker is behind me, shoving me forward. Another of the long-haired men is nearby, pointing his shotgun at the ribs of Père.

Mère's face is a vision of fear.

Fear for me.

I know this.

"You didn't say we had company," a bald man on the couch says with more swagger than a tiny man like that should have. He grabs one of Mère's couch armrest coverings, slips off his spectacles, and wipes them. This gets a grumble from ma mère, but she says no more. "I asked nicely if anyone else was at home, and you both said no."

Père shakes his head. "He is only here few days. Passing through. It slipped out of my mind."

"Ha, no. No, I don't believe that," the bald man says. "I get you want to protect the boy, sure. But I value honesty above all else. In fact, I see it as a virtue. Even from those I'm robbing."

Mère reaches for me, and I go to her. She wraps an arm around my shoulder, putting her body between me and the man next to Père.

The spectacled man on the couch leans back and puts his dirty boot on the coffee table, earning a groan from Mère. He smiles, enjoying this. "Anyone else in the house you're not telling me about?"

"Non," says Père.

"You sure? Nobody? No little girls hiding anywhere too?"

The man named Van chuckles. "I do like little girls."

"No," Père says, his voice a growl. "No one else is in this house."

"Right," the bald man says. "Just the boy."

"I am not a boy," I say, frowning. "I am wolf."

The men all look at each other then burst out laughing. The man on the couch stands, steps on the coffee table so he is looming over us, then drops to the floor right next to me, loudly, hoping to frighten me.

Wait. How is it that I know this? His intent. Confusing.

"Great. A crazy kid," Bald Man says. "Keep an eye on him."

"Just take whatever you want and leave us to our home," Père says.

The short man with the loud stomping boots reaches out and puts a hand on my human father's shoulder, giving it a squeeze. When Père does not react, he squeezes harder.

Still, there is no response.

The man in the glasses tries to hide his scowl with a smile, but it is forced. The edge of his lip is twitching, and his eyes have narrowed. A tiny crease folds in the middle of his brow. I see his elbow twitch.

He is going to—

The bald intruder pulls his hand from Père's shoulder and grips the older man's neck. Père's eyes widen slightly, but his face is stone. He is afraid. But not... not for himself.

He is fearful of what these men might to do Mère. To me.

How is it I know this?

"We see this here as transactional, my friend," the bald man says. "All we want is what you've got."

This gets a laugh from the two other men, the barrels of their shotguns lowering slightly. I feel the cold iron pressing against my wrist, waiting for my moment.

"You see," the leader of the bad men says, releasing Père's neck. He wraps an arm around my human father's shoulder and faces the other two. "These fine gentlemen, Van in particular, couldn't help but notice that vintage automobile you've got. Crazy-lookin' thing, that is."

"Zephyr," Van pipes up, grinning from ear to ear. "A 1939 Lincoln Zephyr."

Père growls. "1940. Bigger engine."

Van takes a step closer, nodding quickly at his boss. "Even better. The '39 I looked up priced at a quarter-mil."

"Takes a fair bit of money to fix an old jalopy like that up," the bald man says, squeezing Père in close like they are best friends. They are not. "So here's what you're going to do. My associates here will take the keys to that fine automobile and anything else of value around the house. If you don't give them any problems, you'll wake up tomorrow cozy comfy in your beds."

"How are we supposed to believe criminals?" Mère says, getting a look from Père, who shakes his head. "People that take never stop taking."

Bald Man thumps Père's shoulder and nods to the man's wife. "You gotta learn to curb your bitch, sir. Otherwise, she'll get you into all sorts of trouble."

This elicits another garble of laughter from the two shotgun men.

Turning from my human parents, the leader faces the others. "Get what you can, and I'll meet you back at home, boys," he said, looking between the two of them. My eyes move to a patch of skin on the side of his head that puckers. The tongue flicks his teeth; his jaw drops and shifts. *After, you have my grace to kill these people. Quickly.*"

Wait.

Wait.

"If they cooperate," the bald man's voice splits through the haze in my mind, "just leave these fine folks in peace. Capeesh?"

My head swims, and I blink quickly to clear my eyes and get control of my brain, which is a jumble of confusing thoughts and emotions.

The man has said... two things? At the same time?

This cannot be so.

Why do I hear both things so differently?

Anger boiling through my veins, I arch my arm around, the metal object in my hand clasped firm, my eyes focused on a spot on his neck, where I can see the artery pumping and throbbing. I will strike this man down!

Inches before the metal tip hits his skin, I feel a strong hand lock onto my arm.

How has this man stopped me? Turned away, he cannot—

"Non," mon père says to me in a low voice. "Non."

The bald man shrinks away, ducking from the metal cross clenched in my fingers and hanging midair. My arm is suspended by the grip of my human father.

"What the hell is that?" Bald Man says, and the other two lift their weapons high. "Van, didn't you check him for weapons?"

"He's a kid!" Van shouts back, his trembling hands making the shotgun barrel shake.

Père looks at me with soft eyes, slowly shaking his head. "Once you go down that path," he says softly to me, "you do not return."

The three intruders watch as Père holds his hand out. In his palm, I place the cross made of horseshoe nails, a trinket Mère once told me she purchased at a fair from a local blacksmith. My heart sinks, as I am now without a weapon.

"Listen to the old man," their leader says, laughing. But his face is red, and he is sweating. He looks to me, and I hear him speak, but his mouth does not move. "*I fear you, boy, but will not tell you such a thing.*"

I squeeze my eyes closed, confused by such strange things.

What is happening to my mind?

The man named Van steps forward and grabs the cross from my hand, smashing it across my brow, which sends me sprawling to the floor. When Père leans forward, the shotgun butt lifts and comes down on his shoulder.

He cries out, grabbing his arm.

"Leave them alone!" Mère shouts, the cords in her neck straining.

Van spins the gun around and aims it at Père, pushing it closer and closer to the man's forehead. Père does not move. Does not shrink back. Only stares at the man, meeting his eyes.

Face down, I hear Bald Man clap loudly and laugh. "Spirit! Yes, such spirit in this house. So nice to meet the family."

Turning my face, I see his boots pass me, then his voice trickles down from above.

"They'll have accounts. Oldies like this always do," he whispers. "Get that and finish up here."

"You got it, Crank," the other says.

I watch the boots as they clomp toward the front door. When I lift my head to look at the bald man in spectacles, I see him glance at me. A strange expression passes over his face, then he leaves, closing the door behind him.

A moment later, I hear the sound of a motorcycle firing up.

Inside the home, everyone is silent as we listen to the motor putter away until it's gone.

Mère speaks first. "Can I please look and see if my husband—"?

"You can look after him once we're gone," the second man says.

When I start to rise, I feel the boot of the other press into my back.

"You stay down, junior," Van says. "You've been enough trouble."

The other addresses my human mother. "Where are the keys to the old car?"

"You won't get anything from me, you jerk!"

Père lets out a breath. "They are hanging on a hook in the coat room. Take those and go."

"That, sir, is just the appetizer," Van says, laughing. "You got some bank records around here, right? Old people love their records. I just want a peek at those."

"If you promise to leave," Père says.

Before the other can answer, I say, "They do not promise these things. I heard the bald man say they will kill us."

"What?" The voice from above is strained, high in the register. The boot comes down to the middle of my back, heel first. "You keep your trap shut or I'll shoot you right now, boy!"

"I am not a b—" I begin to say and get another sharp smack from the boot.

Behind me, I hear a growl that rolls into a roar. Then a scream.

"You leave Kane alone!"

Mère.

Mère is screaming at the men, charging at them. I can hear her uneven gait—the clank of the metal brace on her leg banging against the floor.

"Non, Mère!" Père shouts, and I hear a strike.

When I turn my head, I see this lovely flower woman tumble over the end table and land on the couch, smashing her face into a cushion.

She is not moving.

Chapter Thirty-Two

I looked around the chaos of the lab and stepped up to the cage.

On the video, the premonster Marata had stood right here, watching Mindy the Enhanced meerkat, before things went to hell. The scratches made more sense now. Inside the cage, the floor was covered in wood shavings.

Some of them were darkly stained. I could guess what that might have been but decided to take all those thoughts and put them in a cupboard way up high in my brain. I could think about it later.

On my phone, I had a picture of the screen showing the coordinates. For now, that felt safer than plugging anything into my device's map software.

We had to find Marata before we left. I'd asked her to grab some water so she didn't have to see the video playback again. But it wouldn't have taken this long, so where had she run off to?

Turning back to one of the long white tables, I peeked underneath. All I saw was busted lab shit everywhere. More dark stains the same color I'd seen in the cage.

And, I was pretty sure, a part of a finger.

"Let's get out of here," I said, standing and fixing my shirt so it met my jeans again. When I turned, I saw Gregor back at the computer screen, his limp arms hanging by his sides.

Time to go.

I walked to the door Marata had gone through earlier and stood there. The tech sergeant didn't move. His big black eyes had creases around their edges. He looked like his mind had taken a trip to another planet. Or another time.

"Gregor," I said. Then, louder, "*Anton*, let's go, man."

"How could I have been so foolish?"

"Too late to do anything about that now, man."

He swiveled his head toward me. "I never saw it. Hammer had worked under Dr. Pental. And when Faria split, Ilsa took over the project like it was her own. And all that time, she was working with Covenant."

As I yanked open the door, I thought my shoulder might pop out of joint. It was hard to pull, like when I closed the fridge, remembered I forgot something, and tried to reopen it right away.

It even made a faint sucking-slurping kinda sound.

"Who knows?" I stared down the short hall. *Where the hell is she?* "Maybe they had some recruitment drive or something. Gave her more money and a parking space."

Gregor twisted his chair toward me, thumbing his chin. His eyes cleared a little as he nodded.

"You know the odd thing about stealing someone else's research? You don't know what it took to get there. Along the way, you discover"—he waved a hand around the room—"where the pitfalls are. The no-go places."

"Yeah, sure," I said, pulling the door wider. "Can we just—?"

Gregor stood and did his double hand wipe down the camo pants. I wondered if it was some sort of tic of his.

"I think she will push your friend harder than the Org might have." He walked up to me, staring down. Reaching over my head to push the door wider, he stepped through the gap. "Push him all the way, I reckon."

"You trying to make me feel *more* like shit for letting him go?"

Hitching his shoulder, he said, "It passes the time."

The door closed behind us with a slurping thump, and I heard the *clack* of the lock reengaging. Didn't matter. I was happy to leave that hell hole behind.

The hallway was maybe fifty feet long.

The only break in the wall on the left side was a door with faint light emanating from a long vertical window. Gregor bent down to peer in, and I elbowed him out of the way to look.

I said, "Nice. The creepy scientists had a break room."

"Vending machine and fridge," Gregor said, gazing inside over the top of my head. "Coffee maker. Microwave. All so normal."

"But no Marata." I sighed. "I would have thought she'd have gone in here to grab the water."

"Fine by me," he said, striding down the hall to the bend. "We don't need her."

I need her because she'll keep you in line, I didn't say.

Around the corner was another hall about twice the length of the first. A few of the overhead lights had been busted out, their entrails littering the floor below. At the far end, another set of stairs led up and, I assumed, to the surface.

On the right, I saw a gap where a door used to be.

The edges of the metal frame were ragged and torn. When I looked closer, I saw deep, parallel gouges in groups of three or four. Claw marks. Mindy the Enhanced meerkat must have come down this way and just started tearing the place to pieces.

I looked back, wondering how she'd gotten out of the lab.

Just inside the door on my right, I got my answer.

It looked as if this area—back when it had been just a zoo and not an evil lair for the Organization's scientists—had been a type of animal hospital. When residents got sick, they got taken down here so they could be attended to.

The Org had used it to house *their* experiments, of course.

Animals first, as Marata had said. I needed to pay closer attention to what she was muttering about, but listening to her was like plugging into an audiobook of someone reading a Jackson Pollock painting.

Two cages on the far wall, all metal and no glass, had been bent and smashed. One had been up on a black stone pedestal of some kind. Claw marks ran all down the front of it, and its cage lay on the floor.

The other pen was huge, probably for two animals. It looked nearly big enough to drive my Jeep into it without scraping the paint.

One end of that had been crushed.

Mindy the meerkat had been powerful and pissed off. Once freed, she took her revenge, which had included the two people on the floor. Or, at least, what I could tell from what was left of them.

Their lab coats were stained with long-dried blood. The hands and wrists sticking out of their sleeves had been chewed down to the bone. By this time, it had been maybe a year since the attack, so it wasn't clear to me if that had been all Mindy or if a parade of bugs had come in for a picnic.

I had to fight the bile rising in my throat.

"That's how she got out," I said, staring down at the remains of the lab techs. "These two ran out, she chased them down, and…"

"And lunch," Gregor said, walking into the room.

Unable to look at the bodies, I lifted my head to the ceiling and noticed something in the top corner. Up there, something gnarled and dark purple, dried and withered, was stuck. I thought it might have been an ear.

"Oh god," I said, putting a fist to my mouth. "Let's get the hell out of here."

Gregor swept his long arm through the air like he was in a showroom of new appliances. "No smell."

"Does it really need that?" I said, pressing my back against the wall, willing my stomach to stop dancing around. "I've never seen anything like it."

"You normally would have a lingering stench," he said, dragging in an exaggerated breath through his nose. "Must have a duct system pulling the bad air away. Interesting."

"Is it really?" I asked. I spun off the wall and staggered toward the stairs. "Let's go."

Gregor called out from the room behind me. "Hold on. There's a sliding door here," he said then grunted. I heard the scraping of metal against concrete. "No, it's a service elevator. Huge."

I looked up the long flight of stairs—no extra door here—and turned back. Such a long way up.

"Looks like the rest of the crew hid in here." He grunted. "More flesh on these. Ah, there's the smell."

Despite how sickened I was, the image in my mind hurt my heart. They'd spent their last moments seeking refuge in the big metal box. But if it were a service elevator, why didn't they just ride it safely up top?

Gregor answered that for me. "Buttons don't work. I'll bet Hammer shut them down when she left." He chuckled, his voice bouncing off the cold concrete walls and making my gut twist tighter. "Three or four of them. Hard to tell. Looks like the basement of a mannequin store."

I'd heard enough.

My hand up on the wall, I climbed the steps, being sure I lifted my feet high enough. There wasn't any handrail, and I had no interest in tumbling to the bottom. The coolness of the concrete under my fingertips felt good.

Above us were only a few dim lights covered in wire mesh. I had to pray there weren't any, um, bits of people splattered on the walls. I'd been barely holding my insides in.

At the top, I stared down and had to shoot my hand out to steady myself.

"Whoa, easy, easy," I muttered to myself. Looking down was giving me vertigo. I shouted, "Let's get the hell out of here, man."

Concentrating on not yakking everywhere, I'd briefly forgotten all about the missing Marata.

I pulled down on the handle and shouldered the door open. It didn't move easily. As it slowly swung aside, I heard the crunch and scrape of grass, rock, and bramble against the bottom of the door. When it was finally open, I stepped out and drew in a deep breath of the cool Georgia air.

As before, it was dark as death outside.

The only light from above came from a million miles away.

"You know, this is all your fault," I said to the moon, which just grinned its Cheshire Cat smile down upon me with not a care in the world.

With a quick survey of my surroundings, I saw that we'd crossed to the far end of the fence. I saw more of the wood lattice but a gap on the side. Not a natural break—years of rain and rot had eaten it away, as if Mother Nature was slowly devouring it, savoring it, and taking her time.

Just above the fence line, I could see the silhouette of the tip of the ice cream cutout at the top of the food stand.

Stepping forward, I whispered, "Marata? Hey, where you at?"

Silence.

Could she have taken off? The woman—former woman?—had been trapped in the warehouse for months. Likely the better part of a year. Now finally free and out in the open? Hell, I probably would have run too.

"Dammit."

I looked back when I heard the *chut-chut-chut* of feet brushing against dry concrete. Gregor was finally coming up.

That should have been comforting. I was not alone in the spooky zoo by myself. But it was Gregor, so... not so much.

I took a few strides, stepped through the hole in the fence, and once again saw the massive expanse all around me. The grounds undulated, split here and there by walking paths and the raised mounds I'd seen earlier.

Four cement blocks just ahead of me looked like they had once been for a food cart. I supposed they opened it up when the place got busy on the weekends. Once the zoo closed down, it likely got rewheeled and dragged away.

I scanned left to right and was about to call out again when I saw Marata.

From behind, seeing her hair wild and her body draped in an ill-fitting lab coat, I recalled how confident and easy-going she'd looked on the video. Now, her body was large and awkward, bulging unnaturally with muscle and too-long arms and legs.

As always, she hunched as if waiting to attack whatever might try to attack her.

Maybe that was how she saw the world now. An alien landscape of threats and dangers.

Instead of calling out, I slowly walked up to her. Her fingers twitched, and I saw her head tick in my direction ever so slightly.

Good. She knew I was there.

Hell, I hadn't showered in a few days. She could probably smell me.

"You were supposed to get the water," I said, pressing a smile into my voice. "And here you are taking in the sights."

She flicked her hand into her lab coat pocket, not even looking, and I felt the cool plastic bump up against my hand. I grabbed the bottle, spun the cap, and took a big swig. I held it out to her.

"You want any?"

Marata didn't respond. She just stared out across the zoo.

I realized then she didn't have the "go-juice" with her. I had no idea how long she could go without it, but at that moment, she seemed calm. Serene.

In fact, it was the quietest, most still I had seen her since we'd met.

Gregor appeared from behind the wooden fence, stepping through the rotted-out gap, and headed our way.

"You okay?" I said quietly before he got too near. I knew she'd wind up a bit the moment he sidled up next to us.

The woman just stared, her black eyes distant, her face flaccid.

"Hey, Marata," I said. "We know where Kane is being held. We can get out of here." I looked in the direction she was staring, but it was all a dark void in that direction, deeper into the run-down zoo.

Finally, she grinned slightly and grunted. "You friend? Good." She nodded once. "More we."

"Right. Right, exactly."

Somehow, Marata saw Kane as similar to her. She'd been infected by an animal, and Kane, well, he had *been* an animal. I supposed in some way, that made them like kin.

"Can we get out of here now?" Gregor stomped passed us. "This place smells like animal shit."

I said, "It's. A. Zoo."

He threw a hand in the air and kept on walking.

I considered putting a hand on Marata's shoulder to shake her out of her reverie. I decided against it because I liked having all ten fingers. It was then that I realized what might have been on her mind.

"What, um, ever happened to Mindy?" I asked. She'd obviously been close to the animal, given the way she'd cooed at the creature on the video. Even when the meerkat had become an Enhanced minimonster, Marata had still been sweet to her.

The feral woman lifted an arm, pointing to some Dumpsters about fifty feet down the fence line. That was where she'd been staring.

What an unjust way to end the tortured creature's life. Chucked in the garbage.

"I'm so sorry, Marata." I began to step forward. "But we've got to—"

Marata's other arm shot out, and she laid her clawed hand across my belly. I flinched, my heart in my mouth. If she squeezed...

But she didn't just hold me.

She held me *back*.

I looked at her. She shook her head and said, "More we."

Oh shit.

Oh shit oh shit oh shit.

"Where?" I asked, crouching low. "Where? Here? In the zoo?"

Again, she pointed toward the massive steel trash bins. Lower to the ground, I could see movement, skittering and shifting.

Then, two sets of long, sharp claws lifted out of the opening and wrapped around the rusted metal, damp and glistening in the moonlight.

I shifted my weight back and forth. Where to run?

But I couldn't take my eyes off the claws as they spread apart, leaving scratches as they dragged across the side of the Dumpster. I didn't want to look, but I was frozen in place.

The top of a head appeared first, the fur mottled and split in a patchwork of hair and discolored skin. Following that came a snarling face with a thick black tongue lolling out of a mouth full of piranha-like teeth. Above them gleamed two sets of piercing black eyes.

Staring at me.

"Is that..." I said. "Is that Mindy?"

All I got was a humming grunt from the woman off my shoulder.

"Marata," I said, my voice shaking. "Will she attack?"

"Yuss."

"Jesus," I said and spun around to look at the gap in the rotting fence. If I could just—

"More we," Marata said, and I slowly turned back. She took in a deep breath, holding her arms out, her smiling face turned up to the black sky above.

"*More?*" I dropped into a crouch. This wasn't happening! "How many more?"

She just stared upward, a beatific expression on her face lit by the half moon in the sky.

"Marata, how many more of... *we*?"

The feral woman said nothing, just drawing in deep breaths through her nose then exhaling like she was doing monster yoga, for chrissakes.

She struggled, trying to say the word. "It—t-t-gnn..."

I bounced on my heels, staring at the meerkat who was, so far, just peeking out of the giant trash container. Observing. But as I stood, the creature pulled itself up and forward, leaning into the light.

I'd seen meerkats in late-night nature documentaries on TV when I was too buzzed to sleep. Sweet-looking fuzzy creatures. Tall and skinny.

Mindy was not that.

Oh, tall. Hell yes, tall. Twice the size I would have expected. But she was meaty, arms and legs and body bulging with muscle like a bear cub.

One hand still on the Dumpster, Mindy stepped up to its lip, her toe claws digging into the metal. Half my size, she still looked like she could tear my arms off my body.

As she had done to the people down below.

Down below!

I had to get back to the safety of the lab. I had no idea what to do then, but at least I'd have a moment to think of a way out.

Marata had stopped trying to speak and instead extended three long fingers in front of my face. I stared at them and swallowed.

"Th-three? Three of we?" I said. "Three of them?"

Marata looked at me and smiled. "Th-three. Th-three." She nodded, happy with herself.

Gregor was off to our right, almost parallel with Mindy.

Dammit! He *had* smelled the animals in the park earlier, but I'd played that off as, well, zoo. Now, he was merrily trotting along, heading toward the gate we'd come in.

Mindy looked from me to Gregor.

"Oh, shit." I sucked in a deep breath. "Gregor! Mindy is still in here!"

With impressive speed, he spun toward me, arms raised and fists curled. "What? Where?"

The Enhanced animal answered for me. She leaped from the Dumpster and flew through the air, claws extended. She hit the ground running and burst toward him.

"Back to the lab," I said and pulled at Marata's coat sleeve.

She raised an arm, pulling the fabric from my grip. With her sorrowful black eyes, she said: *Run*.

I didn't need to be told twice.

Sprinting toward the wooden fence at the back, I started to see pinpricks of light at the edges of my vision. I sucked in air, forcing myself to breathe. My footfalls rang out so loudly in the dead leaves and branches that I felt like I was ringing a goddamn dinner bell.

But I couldn't look back.

I heard a grunt echo around the park.

Gregor.

Some part of me felt bad she'd gone for him but, in truth, not a very big part. I knew where Kane was being held now, and if Gregor provided a distraction…

I got to the rotted-away hole in the fence and stared into the safety of the darkness beyond.

Three. Three of we.

Didn't matter. If something was waiting for me back there, hell, I would deal with it. Or get chomped. But I knew a very real threat was behind me. Hopefully, it was chewing happily on Anton Gregor.

Holding my breath, I stepped through and chanced a look back.

Gregor had gone down to a knee, bracing for Mindy the beast-meercat's charging attack. As she leaped forward, the tech sergeant braced and spun, kicking the massive creature in midair. It shot off at a right angle, landing and tumbling, but was back up on its feet in seconds.

Mindy turned back and charged again. The creature's roar rolled across the waves of dirt and grass and made my ears ring.

"Yeah, screw this," I said and bolted toward the rear entrance of the underground facility. I gripped the door, yanked it hard, and… nothing.

Locked.

I looked down at the handle and saw the same keypad as before. This one, though, in this damper area of the park, had corroded and rusted. Even if I'd known the code, the buttons had long since flaked away to dust.

The other door!

It was down the fence line on the far side, but I couldn't see it from where I stood. It looked like there might be another fence, perpendicular to the one on my left, that cleaved the rear space in two.

Or there may have been bushes or old, busted-up equipment stacked in the middle. I squinted and saw something sparkle in the moonlight. Metal? Glass?

Then the shiny bits moved. Something growled.

"Yeah, fuck this."

Spinning around, I bolted in the other direction, back where I'd come. Behind me, I heard odd thumping then a single clang and another thump like someone was banging a bag of rotting potatoes against wood and metal.

I dove through the gap, catching part of the wood fence with my shoulder, and stumbled but didn't fall.

As I ran full steam away from the threat, I heard another growl behind me.

Marata was right where she'd been before, now crouched, hands across her knees, just watching the Gregor and Mindy Show.

The tech sergeant had the meerkat by its hind legs and was spinning in a circle as the furious creature clawed and swiped at him. Each time it bent at the waist, trying to reach his fingers, he spun faster. Even from here, I could see she'd already slashed him, splitting open the skin on the backs of his hands.

That was when I noticed something around Mindy's neck—a thick ring that gleamed like black glass. I'd only seen it because it had pressed up against her chin. She'd inadvertently hooked her claws under it several times while trying to get at Gregor.

The snarling behind me rose and was now coming from higher up. That didn't make sense.

"Marata," I shouted, huffing with each stride. "Marata, run!"

She casually looked back toward me, and then, as if bored with the old show, she tuned into this new one.

Watching.

In the trees above me, I heard something racing across the branches, leaping, and then grabbing another. Its breath sounded ragged and throaty. Christ, I could hear the air scraping across its sharp teeth, whatever it was!

I burst past Marata then realized I was running right toward the spinning Mindy, her claws slicing through the air.

"No good!" I shouted to myself, trying to get my stomach to stop punching me.

When I hooked hard to the left, I felt the whoosh of something fly past my neck. Then came the *rumpa-thump-thump* of a meaty body tumbling across the grass.

I had turned a fraction of a second before the whatever-it-was would have landed on my head.

Pumping my legs, I got to the fence line, sucking in heaving breaths, and realized...

I did not have a plan.

The gate we'd come through was on the *other* side. And the fence was electrified, so even if I could scurry up the bars, I'd get fried with megavolts that would make the little purple tint I had left in my hair turn black.

Another quick hook this time to the right and, as if on cue, I heard a smash-rattle behind me then the scream of the animal as the electrified fence punished it for its mistake.

I glanced at Marata. She was rolling back and forth, banging her oversized hands together.

Yeah. She was *clapping*. One big show.

With nowhere else to go, I bolted for the Dumpster, put a foot on the metal support bar midway up its side, and leaped over the edge.

I landed in damp, gooey leaves and rolled to my back. Putrid slime covered half of my face. I wiped it away, gagging, and slung it against the Dumpster's interior.

Smell and gunk be damned, I wanted to burrow under the leaves and hide like some gopher. No good. I had to get out.

I reached up for the rear wall, lost my grip, then slid back down, my shoe piercing the top layer of leaves. My foot slid into cold, damp sludge.

Years of rotting garbage, leaves, and branches seeped down my shoe and into my sock and gummed up my leg. Bracing my left foot on a metal lip, I tried to drag my right leg out. As I lifted, the thick layers of filth felt like a cold, wet mouth had wrapped its tongue around my shoe and swallowed it whole.

But my leg came free.

A smash against the side of the Dumpster rattled my teeth, and I fell forward into the sludge. My predator had shaken off its electrocution and was back in the game.

Looking up, I saw two thick hands. Ropey, muscular fingers twisted down into fat, dark nails.

Unlike Mindy's, these claws were short. Hooked.

The creature pulled itself up quickly, braying at me, its wide mouth showing off two sets of piano-key teeth, each coming to a point. When it closed its mouth, I saw the distorted face of a primate.

A goddamn chimp.

Its head was thick and lumpy, unevenly bulging, as if it had taken knocks from a baseball bat. Red-rimmed black eyes stared at me, and saliva flowed from its blackened bottom lip and drizzled onto its chin.

Lifting itself higher, it exposed the top half of its body. The thing looked like a mini gorilla, but one that had been tossed into a nuclear waste dump. One arm was longer than the other. Its left hand was a fawny orange, its right jet-black.

No question, it could crush my skull with those.

Lifting itself up, it could see I was trapped, and its breath quickened. It was excited for the meal covered in rotting gravy.

I arched back up and reached for the metal lip, but stuck in the muck, I couldn't get to it.

The monkey-beast screeched at me, and I slapped my hands to my ears. Then I could only watch as it bounced up and back, up and back, swinging on the lip. I knew what was coming.

All I could do was hope a punch in the face might stun it. I cocked my fist back and glared at it, baring my own teeth.

"Come on, fucker!" I screamed at it, my arm wrapped around a gap in the metal, my other hand trembling as I readied to give it everything I had in one punch.

It screeched its battle cry then arched all the way back, raising its powerful, misshapen arms above the head. It crouched and leaned forward to exact its primal violence—

Like a balloon stuck with a pin, it curled into a tight ball, arms and legs snapping inward as if on springs. I could see blue electric light dance across those sharp piano-key teeth. Its black eyes fluttered, and it slumped, half in the Dumpster, half out.

As its head fell forward, I saw a black collar like the one on Mindy thunk against the base of its skull.

The creature hung there, motionless.

Whatever. I wasn't waiting around.

Outside, Gregor was screaming. And then silence.

I dug my hand deep into the muck where my leg had been and reached for my shoe. It came out with a slurpy *thwop*. Sure, I had a killing machine taking a quick siesta just three feet from my head, but that shoe had cost a hundred bucks!

Well, it would have cost a hundred bucks if I'd paid for it. But hell, I looked damn good in those shoes! I wasn't leaving one behind.

Footwear in hand, I climbed out and, of course, landed hard on my ass. Getting to my feet, I slipped the shoe back on in time to see Gregor wobbling to his feet. On the ground next to him, Mindy looked dead.

I glanced over at Marata. She lifted her arms in the air, swinging them as if I'd just scored a goal for my intramural soccer team.

I'd have to reevaluate this idea of Marata having my back.

"What the hell happened?" I shouted to Gregor, lumbering over to him.

Unsteady on his feet, he was gripping his head and staggering around. "Some—wow—some sort of ch-charge," he said, moving one hand to his jaw as if to reset it.

I came up next to him. "*What?* These monsters can shoot lightning or something?"

"No. Why would they stun themselves?"

I threw my hands up. "I don't know. This is my first animal attack. All new! Every bit."

"That collar," Gregor said, rubbing the back of his neck. "I felt the electricity through her body. She got the lion's share of it."

I shot a quick glance over my shoulder to the Dumpster then down at the animal on the ground.

"Are they dead?"

"I don't think—"

"No, the animals are not dead." The voice had come from some hidden loudspeaker, booming through the park. "Guests of the park, please go to the visitors' booth one hundred meters to your west."

Gregor and I exchanged a look.

"You will see signs for the visitors' booth to your left. Follow those to me here," the voice boomed in accented English.

"Should we trust the guy?" I whispered.

Again, the voice rattled the fried-out speakers. "The animals will revive within sixty seconds, if history is any guide."

We both looked around for the source of the voice. I muttered, "I feel like Dorothy looking for the Great Oz."

"That makes me the Tin Man." Gregor grinned. "I'll take it."

"No, you're more like Toto, because—"

"Also if history is any guide," the voice, sounding exasperated, cut in again, "they will awake and be quite angry. I suggest you hurry."

I glanced at Marata, who was staring up, likely wondering what the over-modulated Sky God wanted from her. She would be fine. The animals seemed to have no interest in her. Me and Gregor were a different story.

We ran for the visitors' booth as fast as we could.

Chapter Thirty-Three

Kane

As I lie on the floor, my cheek pressed to the slick wood, anger rises within me. A howling rolls through my mind, calling me to the hunt.

My heart sings when I see Mère slowly begin to move, settling herself onto the couch. No groans or complaints. She will not give these men such treasures.

"Everyone needs to calm the fuck down," Van shouts. He pumps his shotgun and fires into the ceiling. Bits of plaster rain down into my hair and fall to the floor. "Especially you, lady!"

But Mère is not paying attention.

She is looking up at her curtains, which were disturbed as she fell. The kind woman runs her fingers over the soft, sheer fabric lovingly, caressing, as if she were trying to comfort the material. Smoothing her hands over the pleats, she mutters softly to herself.

"Old bat's lost it," the other man says and points at Père. "Go find those bank records, or the kid—"

"He," *ma mère* says, twisting her neck and scowling at the thug, "is *not* a kid."

The two men trade looks, unsure, then they laugh.

I can feel a growl build in my chest.

Mère stretches up, hooking her leg brace under the sofa's arm, reaching up as high as she can. She grips the hanging fabric with both hands and, with a grunt, yanks her precious curtains down from the wall.

"What in the hell!" the second man says, stepping back as the woman tumbles end over end, wrapped in the curtains, rolling to the floor. "Jesus! Lady's lost it!"

I look at Mère, wanting to call out and comfort her.

But something is happening. My mind is swirling. My blood is on fire. I turn from *ma mère* on the floor, wrapped in her beautiful curtains, and look back to the window.

Outside, the peaceful night.

Stars in the sky.

And the light of the moon.

Around me. Time slows. My vision turns red. I can feel my arms and legs throb painfully, twisting muscles beneath my skin. When I try to call out, my voice hitches and freezes in my throat.

The dented white eye in the dark sky locks me with its gaze. My vision rolls, and for a split second, I am plunged into darkness and see another set of eyes, menacing and angry, staring back at me.

Then they are gone.

My limbs twist and bend, and I feel myself lift from the floor. I hear a low growl. Then a snarl.

A predator!

I must protect—

No.

No.

Those sounds are coming from me.

"Jesus, wha... what the hell is that?" Van says.

I lift my head toward him. No longer lying on the floor, I am standing on four legs. I look down at my feet and see brown-black fur covering my paws, which are capped with thick, curved claws.

"Shoot the damn thing!" the other shouts, struggling with his own weapon. "Whatever it is."

I growl at both of these intruders. These weak men.

I say, "I am wolf."

When I leap toward the first man, he is struggling with his weapon but gets a shot off, which blasts over my shoulder, singeing some of the hairs, but I do not feel pain. I place a front paw on his forehead and another on his chest as I land, and he tumbles back and takes a lamp down as he falls.

On top of him, I breathe heavily, saliva dripping from my open mouth onto his face.

His fear turns to rage, and he lifts his shotgun.

"Move out of the way, man," the other man, Van, shouts.

I can *feel* his heartbeat. I can hear the sounds of his slick fingers against the trigger, searching for a shot.

"Slide out."

I spin around and growl at this other.

He lifts the shotgun to his shoulder, moving slowly.

No, not slowly. The wolf within has taken over, and I have slowed the world around me. Sniffing the air, I can smell the fear on him. The panic.

A rivulet of sweat wriggles down the side of his face.

My ears prick, picking up the sound of his damp finger pad sliding across metal, and hear his muscle flex. In that split second, I leap to the side, away from—

Boom!

Several pellets impact my hindquarters, but I roll away and leap quickly to my feet.

Van stares, his mouth hanging open, eyes wide and unblinking. The air smells like warm copper, an odor that thrills me, feeds something deep within. At the same time, it births a hunger, a deep need, that intoxicates me.

"Oh my God," Van says, his lower jaw grinding side to side. "B-Blaine?"

Snarling, I turn to look at the man on the floor and see him spitting up blood. Not spitting; it is bubbling from his chest and neck. The lower half of his mouth is missing.

No, not missing. I see it there. Stuck to the wall.

Mère will not like that.

Van wakes from his trance and points the weapon at me, his hands trembling. He racks the shotgun and fires, missing me.

I leap to the window sill—not the couch because my paws are slick with blood and I do not want to stain Mère's upholstery.

Facing away from him, I can hear the twang and thrum of his finger muscles.

Père calls to me, "Kane, watch out!"

Heeding his warning, I jump to the side and land, the claws of my feet skittering across the floor. Behind me, the window shatters, and Van screams as he racks the weapon again.

I cannot give him another chance to fire.

I launch myself at his body, and my paws land hard on his chest.

The weapon explodes, hitting my shoulder. I wince. This is painful, but I must protect my human family. Predators will seek the weakest of the pack, and if I do not dispatch this man, he will target them next.

The soft flesh in my mouth begins to split, and I feel the stubble of his chin rub against the side of my muzzle. I growl as I tear and tear and tear.

We are falling together, intertwined.

Snapping my head back, I feel the skin and bone and cartilage between my teeth and a lovely, intoxicating warmth across my tongue. Something in my brain fires off sparks, urging me to swallow.

I hear Mère nearby, and she is whimpering.

When I look to her, she has a hand on her mouth, eyes watching me. Not in fear of me. I can see in her eyes. There is fear but not of me.

For me.

The man beneath me struggles to breathe, tries to lift his weapon with a weak hand.

Crawling up his body, I place both of my heavy paws on his shoulders and roar into his face. A moment later, his eyes flutter, and the life behind them flickers out.

For the next minute, I stand on the chest of the man, which has gone still.

Père regards me as Mère speaks soothing words, helping him up into his chair. She limps to the kitchen and returns with a damp towel and a glass of water.

The water is for her husband.

Then she turns to me and kneels, rubbing the damp towel down my bloodied shoulder. It should hurt, I know this, but it no longer does. Is this the power of a mother's touch?

"I am sorry you had to do that, Kane," she said, stroking my head as she cleans off the blood. "You know as well as I do that they had no intention of letting us live."

"Yes," I say, nodding my head, which feels heavy. Large. "The man said as much without... without his word sounds. Other words."

Père sits forward in his chair, puts his head in his hands for a moment, then looks at me.

"You do never cease to surprise, my boy," he says, the hint of a smile on his face. He looks at the dead man, sniffs once, and looks back at me. "How is this? How can this be?"

I shrink back, ashamed. "I do not know."

"Kane is a special boy," Mère says. She folds the damp towel in her hand, rubbing at my neck as if she were merely wiping away dirt. "And more than that."

"I am wolf," I say, nodding to her, repeating the words she has taught me.

Père points at me. "But this is not wolf. This is... I do not know what this is!"

Mère stands slowly, favoring her leg. I try to stifle a whimper. "Are you hurt?"

She waves the question away. "No more than before these men came into our home." Reaching into her bookshelf, she pulls out a large volume. A large, laminated book.

On the front, there are nine pictures of various animals. No, not animals. They are dogs.

She holds it up to me and asks me to read the words on the cover. Turning away, I shake my head.

"I cannot. You have tried, but written words make little sense to me," I say, my head down. "Please read to me."

Pointing out the individual words, she says, *"Big Book of Dogs."*

"Mère, is this the time?" Père says, motioning to the men on the floor without looking at them. *"Maintenant?"*

"Now is as good a time as any," she says, paging through the book. "We must always make time for learning when the opportunity arises."

As she flips through the book, Père points to my shoulder. "I thought he hit you, *non*?"

"*Oui*, I believe..." I say and lick at the wound. But where there should be an injury, there is nothing.

"I cleaned away the muck," Mère says, licking her thumb to turn another page. "There was a tear and some redness, but it stitched itself up. You're just fine, dear."

"This is"—Père waves a hand around the room and takes a big gulp of water from the glass in his other—"less than fine."

Ignoring him, Mère spins the book around, holding it up. "This is you right now."

I look at the animal on the page then down at myself. Same creature, it seems, my fur lighter than what's in the picture.

"What... what is that?"

"At the moment, you are..." She pauses to spin the book around and read the caption then spins it back. "A Tibetan mastiff."

"Is a dog?" I say, shuffling my feet. "Again?"

"Different dog entirely. Very clever of you," she says and folds the book up, returning it to the shelf. "And very beautiful."

"And why is this?" Père says, looking at his wife. Or avoiding looking at me. "How is this? Wolf who becomes boy becomes dogs?"

Mère laughs, full of joy. "Because Kane is a wonder, dear. A beautiful wonder and a gift from God. Tonight, he saved us."

I look down at the body below me. "I killed two men."

"Hmm, technically, only one," Mère says casually, pointing at the man across the room. "This one shot that one." She holds up a single frail finger. "So, just the one."

Père leans back in his chair and sighs. Weakly, he points at the window. "You knew. You knew the sky would change him."

"Not the sky, John," Mère says, wagging the finger. "The moon. Old legend. But there is always some truth to the legends, yes?"

Shaking his head, Père says, "But how could you know this?"

Mère approaches me, kneels, and puts her hands on either side of my head, stroking my thick fur. "A mother always knows."

Slowly, Père gets to his feet. He looks out the window for a moment and then down at the two men on the floor. "Okay, does a mother know how we handle this now? They will return once they know these men have not!"

Mère kisses the top of my head, steadying my heartbeat. She stands and sighs. "We have to leave," she says, shrugging. "We've done it before. We take Kane and—"

"No," I say. "You cannot leave your home."

"Our home, Kane," Mère corrects me. "But there is no—"

"Yes, always a way," I say and leap off the man to look at the other. "Why have these men come?"

Père walks up next to me. "Thieves. Gang members. Devil somethings, I can't recall. But I've heard people in town talking of them."

"Thieves," I say, nodding. "I know of this from the surfing-beach show Mère likes. With the good-looking man who takes his shirt off much."

Frowning, Père turns to her. "David Hasselhoff?"

She waves his question way in the air as if it's a flying insect. "Yes. Same as that."

"Bad people. Untrustworthy, yes?"

Nodding, crossing her arms, Mère walks closer. "Yes. Yes, they are."

Bending down, I sniff the man's body. There is alcohol and other smells, strange and chemical. Those same scents in his sweat. "*Comment*... how do thieves, together, trust one another?"

"Ha. I think they are only bound by the promise of shared loot," Père says. When I look at him, he clarifies. "Treasure. Money. Things."

I nod my head. "So... to understand... It could be that these two got treasure but did not want to share."

Mère smiles at me and clasps her hands together, nodding. "And? Go on!"

"The other man, the bald man, thinks they will return," I say. "But what if he thinks they have taken the treasure, your treasure, and they have left with it? They would have no reason to return."

Père laughs. "That... is actually clever."

"Of course it is," Mère says, digging into the jacket of the other man and coming out with his phone. "Our boy is very clever."

She taps on the screen for a moment then sighs. Flicking the man's cap off, she exposes his face and holds the phone to it. With a grin, she stands.

"I can see texts here from his boss," she says, typing into the phone. "I'll just reply to him... that he and his friend have what they need and want to start a life. Together. Away from here. Finally, they can live as they always wished. Happy, in love, and unable to be found."

Père shakes his head, frowning, "Mère, this is—"

"The only way," she says, nodding. "I agree." Her hand hovers over the phone for a moment, then she nods to the two bodies. "But before I send this, you need to do something with our uninvited guests."

"Me?"

"Yes," she says. "I have to clean up this mess. And iron my curtains. I worked very hard to get those pleats just right, and I want this place to look just as it did."

Père sighs, shrugs, and laughs. "I know of a place. But I will need your help, boy."

"Kane needs his rest," Mère says. "And he is not a boy." She smiles at me, holding her hands to her chest. "He is wolf."

"And sometimes dog," I say, my tongue lolling out.

"Well, dog can help me, yes?"

"No opposable thumb." I hold up a paw. "This would be very hard."

"You are both conspiring against me," he says, looking between the two of us. Then he turns serious and sighs. He looks at me. "This cannot happen again, Kane. Must not. If I am to go along with you and your... your mother, you must make me a promise."

Standing, I nod vigorously. "Anything, *mon père*. What is it you would have me do?"

He reaches out, and for the first time, he strokes my head. Tentatively at first, then long, tender caresses.

"You will remain in this home until, one day, you must leave. As all young men do," he says. "But until that time, you must stay out of the moonlight. This is a promise I need from you."

My eyes watering, my heart singing at his touch, I nod. "Yes. For you, *mon père*, I will do this."

Chapter Thirty-Four

Of course, Gregor had flown past me looking like he'd barely worked up a sweat. And he'd veered right in front of me, so I started spitting out bits of dirt and leaf fragments in between heaving breaths.

The one advantage I had he didn't?

I was *panicking*. Big time. The human flight-or-fight response had made its choice, and all systems were go. I was pumping my arms so fast that my tiny fists felt like they might explode. My legs ached like a mother.

At some point, if this was going to be my life for the foreseeable future, I'd have to get on a cardio program.

Or not.

Routinely running for your life with some form of monster chasing after you is, in fact, a form of cardio. Maybe I could write a fitness book one day and make a mint.

Focus!

I ran with the disgusting shoe tucked under my arm. My hair was already damp with sweat, and the parts that weren't glued to my head tapped out a rhythm on the back of my neck that felt like John Bonham on a three-day coke binge.

And each *thwop* of my own damp hair felt like the bloodied fingers of some creature reaching for me from behind.

The good news? This only made me run faster.

Ahead of us, I saw the white steepled shack with a Visitors' Center sign on top. Closer to the drooping trees, the sign had black sludge oozing down from top to bottom covering half the words, but I could see enough letters to identify it.

It also had a large italicized letter *i*, lowercase, in a green circle. Designating this as "information," I supposed.

Gregor slowed his pace, but he was still much faster than me, so I had to peer around him as I ran up.

It looked like a house built for one. It was an A-frame style with a tiny fake chimney, which that lowercase letter *i* had been plastered to.

Instead of windows like on a house, the top half of the door was open. The bottom part formed a long counter so hapless animal lovers could lean on their elbows and ask where the lions were.

Oh shit. Lions. Don't think about lions.

A late addition to the welcoming Visitors' Center was a very unwelcoming thick steel mesh that covered the entire opening. It now looked like a cage for humans.

Iron bars on either side had been bolted to the structure and, it seemed, drilled deep into the ground. More metal piping ran across the top and bottom. In the middle of the unbreakable rectangle was the cross-stitched mesh.

Within, I could see a faint blue glow.

Gregor made it to the front of it and hit the brakes, banging his hand on the mesh, which rang out way too loudly for my already-jangled nerves.

He looked left and right then spun back to look at me.

No. Not at me. Past me.

And the look on his face? Not great. Edvard Munch could have made a *mint* off that expression.

I didn't look back. What, I was going to run faster? My legs were screaming, and I had hit max velocity fifty feet earlier.

A silver door popped open on the side of the tiny white house.

Gregor continued to stare over my shoulder, black eyes going wider and wider, as he stepped back and pressed against the steel mesh.

I pointed toward the door as I ran.

"On the side. Someone's opened a door," I tried to say. Instead, because I was breathing heavily and so wrung out with exhaustion my tongue was sweating, it came out a bit like: "Sidethn. Mnnf, doorp."

He got the message and spun around the side, disappearing inside.

Behind me, I could hear a *thuda-dump, thuda-dump, thuda-dump* of something closing in. Evil meerkat or killer chimp? Didn't matter.

When I got to the side of the white shack, I leaped through the door and was swallowed by the darkness. A figure behind the door slammed it shut then shut a second door in front of that.

Then the entire structure shook. Something had smashed itself against the outer door.

I lay on my side, sucking in breaths, but couldn't get enough air. My vision was beginning to sparkle. I felt Gregor's tender hand on my shoulder.

No. Not Gregor.

He didn't have tender hands—dude basically had claws—and he'd never gently put a hand of comfort on anyone. Unless it was ironic.

"You need to slow your breathing, miss." The man's silky voice filled my ears. "You are hyperventilating."

I shrugged the stranger off and blurted, "Monsters, okay?"

He chuckled, and I should have been a bit pissed, but it had sounded kind. I heard him rise, his knees cracking with the effort.

"Take a moment. You are safe for the next few minutes, but you cannot stay here."

In an electronic blue haze, I could just see the side of the man's face as he spoke. And his voice was a bit strained or shredded. It sounded like he'd been shouting all day at his kids' soccer game, like he needed to clear his throat.

"There is a chair just behind you."

I heard Gregor shuffle his feet. "Thank you."

"I did not offer the chair to you, sir," the stranger said. "And I am surprised you would take it before a lady. That is not proper."

"Ha, lady?" Gregor actually *chortled*. "Let me tell you—"

"Sir, I would suggest you consider your next words carefully," the man said, and I saw his hand in the air, pointing. "That door is an exit as well as an entrance. And I hold the key."

I rolled onto my side and sat on my butt, leaning against the wall. "Thanks, Sir Lancelot, but I don't need defending."

As my eyes adjusted to the darkness, I caught the man's wide smile. In the blue electronic glow, the only light inside the one-room Visitors' Center, his skin gleamed like brushed ebony.

Finally catching my breath, I asked his name.

He nodded once and said, "I am Ganiyu."

"Is that a first or last name?" Gregor asked. A minute earlier, the dude had looked like he was about to piss his pants, and already, he had his razor-sharp sneer back.

Ganiyu glanced at him and didn't bother answering. Instead, he crouched and reached under a table. Just above his head, I saw what had been emitting the blue electric light. Six screens, one stacked upon the other, rested on a table.

The monitors weren't fancy. Long, with louvers on the side, they looked like they'd been built in the last century. I could hear tiny fans whirring inside them.

Ganiyu shuffled over and handed something cold and damp to me. I thanked him for the water, twisted off the top, and guzzled half of it down.

Wiping my mouth, I said, "You run this place?"

"Ha, no. I do not." He leaned against a table leg and ran a hand over his bald head. "I maintain the park."

"What does that mean?" Gregor asked, arms crossed, still eyeballing the chair.

"When something needs repair, I fix it." Ganiyu sighed. "And most importantly, I make sure the fence is in proper working order. And deter anyone who might come to look."

I laughed. "How do you go about doing that? I mean, this place is miles away from anywhere, but you've got to have the occasional teenager showing up to do, you know, teenage shit."

The man shrugged. "If people come—and yes, rarely, they do—I do what anyone else does."

"You shoot 'em," Gregor said, nodding.

The zoo's maintenance worker twisted his head toward him. "Do you work at being unlikeable? Or is this a natural trait?"

"Ha, well, he's one of the Enhanced. He was probably unlikeable before, and now he's *super* unlikeable," I said. "So, yeah, mission accomplished."

"Why are you with this man? Are you from the Organization?" Ganiyu looked at me. "You broke in, so you could not be Covenant."

I ignored his question. "You're with Covenant, obviously," I said, looking around the small room. "So we can expect a bunch of those assholes any second, I bet."

Ganiyu grinned at me. "No. I do work for them, but I'm not a part of them."

"How do you figure that?" I asked him.

He sighed and lifted his shoulders, then a frown pulled at his face. "I have family back home. They needed someone with animal experience and, most importantly, someone who would stay quiet."

I took a slug of my water and waited for him to continue. After a moment, he did.

"I do what I am instructed. If I wavered, I would be punished. And also my family back in Nigeria."

"They can go and find your family there?" My pulse quickened again, remembering how the Org had put cameras in the homes of my mother and grandmother. It seemed Covenant used all the same tactics.

The man tilted his head to the side, regarding me. "Miss, they are *already* there."

"I've tried to explain that," Gregor said with an exasperated sigh.

"Where I am from," the man explained, "they are known as Masu Kula. And they are everywhere."

"Which one is that? The Org or Covenant?"

Ganiyu stretched with a groan. "Does it matter? One English equivalent would be 'the Guardians,' and I believe the moniker is used for both groups. Impossible to tell one from the other."

I watched as he pulled a stool from under the table and sat before the monitors.

"The Guardians? As in protectors?"

"No," he said, his weak smile lit in blue. "Propaganda. But I think they don't realize it means something else. More appropriate." He turned to me, his smile gone. "Masu Kula also means 'the Controllers.'"

We stared at each other for a moment until Gregor finally broke the silence.

"Great, fine, *so interesting*, yes," he said and leaned over Ganiyu. "How do we get the hell out of here?"

Before the man could answer, another metallic thud rang through the shack, knocking my head against the wall.

"Ow, shit," I said, rubbing my scalp. I rolled to my knees and stood. Then I picked up the half-drunk bottle and poured some of the water over my shoe. A bit of the stanky muck came off, but it would need a serious scrubbing. Good enough for now, so I slipped my foot in.

Ick. Some Dumpster juice slid between my toes. Now I would need a serious scrubbing.

"There was a third with you," Ganiyu said. He typed on the keyboard, changing the camera views on screen. "I fear she might have been taken by the animals."

"No, she's got sharp-tooth immunity," I said, getting a queer look from the seated man. I waved a hand in the air. "Far as I can tell, she went beast mode after getting bit by Mindy sometime last year."

"Interesting."

"And it seems they can sense the animal strains of the whatever. Virus. Evil. I dunno." I nodded to the screen, grimacing a little. The squishy stuff between my toes was so gross.

"Well done you for working that out," Ganiyu said. "That had me curious. They never attack one another. All of them act as if the others are barely there. Just another animal. But on occasion, a squirrel or rat makes it through the gate. A small flock of ducks one time."

"What happened?"

He clicked his mouse, dragging the cursor, which turned one of the cameras left then right.

"I only saw the aftermath. Twelve-hour shifts, you see," he said. "When I watched the tapes, well... a lot of feathers. Not much else."

"Blech," I said.

"The animals don't require any health checkups, thankfully. Just feeding." He pointed to a metal sign nailed above the monitors. About the shape of a license plate, it had the words Happy Coat with a smiling cartoon dog.

"You feed them dog food?"

"Ha, no. That is a Covenant operation," he said, squinting at an image. On the screen, Marata was on a swing set, kicking her feet to move back and forth. "But, of course, you would never see their name on the manifest. But shipments of animal parts are delivered, and a few dozen cans go out to make it look legitimate. The rest keeps the animals here fed."

"The bloodier the better?" I said, looking at the innocent sign.

"Of course, yes."

Gregor slammed his open palms on the table. I jumped. The man at the computer didn't.

"Leaving? Go time, yes? How do we do that?"

Ganiyu sighed. "The meerkat and spider monkey—"

"Spider monkey? Really?" I said, shivering. "Can we just say 'monkey' or 'primate'? Really, we don't need to make it *more* horrifying."

He smiled, looking at his hands as he typed. On the upper-left monitor were the images of a meerkat and a primate. Monkey. I wasn't even thinking the other word.

Next to each was a bar like a status meter. At full, it was a four. Halfway, two. Both, at the moment, were at a one.

"Mindy and Sammy have one jolt left in their collars," he said, sighing. "You have about six hundred meters to cross in sixty seconds."

Gregor chuffed. "Easy."

"Except for all that landscaping from the sprinkler work," I said, rubbing my chin. I stared out the wire mesh and saw two red-rimmed black eyes staring back. I turned away. "It's like running over moguls on a ski field."

Ganiyu raised a hand, snapping his fingers above his head. "Ah, I can drop a load of food! They know the sound and will likely be attracted to it. It is at the far end of the park. That will buy you some time. But the moment they smell you—and the wind does not favor you tonight, so they will—I expect they will leave the dead stuff for the living, breathing stuff."

"Hamburger versus fillet mignon."

The Nigerian man nodded, cracking a grin. "Extra rare, yes."

Crossing the short room, Gregor reached for the door then hesitated. "We'll have to time this, Emelda Thorne. Maybe we run for the fence line and dart down the side. Less landscaping leftovers there."

I was ready to get out of there, so I walked over and stood behind Gregor.

"Can we do this now, Ganiyu?" I said. "You're a lovely man, but we would like to leave."

"Yes. I'll need a moment."

Gregor stepped forward, his demeanor turning dark. "How do we know you won't just let us get ravaged out there?"

"Why would I let you in, risking my own life, only to lead you to your death?" Ganiyu shook his head. "You used to be in Covenant, then?"

"The Organization," Gregor said, sneering. "Not anymore. I'm out."

"That would explain the paranoia. Probably why you are still alive." The man at the keyboard nodded. "I have no part in this. You leaving this park is good for the animals, and my job is to make sure they are content."

"So... you aren't planning on telling your bosses?" I asked as nicely as I could.

"If you leave and the animals are no worse off, there is no reason to tell Masu Kula about your presence here." He turned to me, nodding once. "I have no loyalty to them. Only to my family. But this does not endanger them. As long as you leave quickly."

"That's the plan, man!" Gregor threw his hands up.

It took a few minutes for him to type away at the keyboard until he was ready. Then he pointed at the door, telling us to hold.

"Dropping the food now."

Over the tinny speakers, we could hear the *clank-chunk-clank* of some metallic system dropping animal parts and blood into—what? Giant bowls with *Mindy* and *Sammy* on them?

"I will wait until they are eating," he said. "Then you go. Once they start chasing, I can monitor here and can hit their collars. That will immobilize them for about a minute. But with the prospect of live dinner, I wouldn't trust that time frame. Maybe thirty to forty-five seconds."

"Right," I said and punched Gregor on the arm. "Let's run down the path. I don't want to trip over the jacked-up landscaping."

He shook his head, showing me teeth. "Winds around too much. I can leap over those tiny hills easily, and I'm twice as fast. I'm going straight for the fence and rocket to the gate."

I muttered, "Asshole."

"The fence may be better anyhow, miss," he said, and I realized he'd never asked my name. Fine by me. He was Covenant, even in a small way. "That landscaping, as you keep calling it... that is not so."

"Oh?"

"No. That is the other animal in the park," he said and slowly shook his head. "One that does not have an electronic collar because its skin is far too thick. It can tunnel underground."

"What?" Gregor's voice shot up two octaves. "You're only telling us this now?"

The man shrugged. "How would it have made any difference?"

"What else is out there, Ganiyu?" I said. "Some sort of Enhanced gopher?"

The zoo's maintenance man held up a finger, watching the monitors. We couldn't see the images but heard the snarling and slurping.

"Are you ready?"

"Yes, ready," I said, holding out my hands in a stopping motion. "Wait! You didn't—"

"No time!" Ganiyu shouted and slammed a button next to his keyboard. A red light appeared above the door, and we heard the latches disengage.

Gregor yanked open the first door then the second and bolted out, moving faster than any human ever could.

Ganiyu pointed wildly at the door. "Go!"

I shook my head, defiant. "First, tell me! What made those tunnels, Ganiyu?"

"Hugo," he said, closing his eyes and opening them slowly. "Hugo made those tunnels."

Then, I ran.

Chapter Thirty-Five

Kane

When I awaken, my body is no longer covered in fur. The fond memories of my past have slipped away. The familiar scent of my human parents lingers for just a moment then is gone.

I feel a shiver ripple up my legs and torso. The pain in my hands has returned. I hang, my arms stretched to the point that it feels as if my bones might pop out of their sockets.

The figure comes to me and leans in close. Her features are a wash of black in the starburst of light behind her. Something sparkles at the sides of her throat.

"Ah. So you're not dead," Ilsa Hammer says, her voice cold and dismissive.

My mind searches for a witty rejoinder, something to say that is smart and bold and will cow her and wipe what I know is a smug smile right off her face!

"No," I say.

Hmm. Not my best work.

When Dr. Hammer turns away, the light again assaults my eyes, and I fight not to squeeze the lids shut. I watch as she steps, slowly, feigning confidence. This is the first time I have seen her since being hung upon a wall in this place. Before, I always saw just the light and heard her voice.

I can read hidden things in a voice, but seeing my enemy is far better.

And no question—this is my enemy.

I see the way she steps as short heels scrape across the dry concrete floor. The sway of her hips. The way a stiff hand pulls reading glasses from her face then lets them sway from a chain. The ripple of her jowl.

She is trying to portray confidence, even indifference. The scientist even chuckles to sell this lie.

But she cannot hide her true self.

I see you, Ilsa Hammer.

This is a woman who is anxious. Frustrated. Angry.

Pulling a computer tablet from beneath her arm, she taps away on its screen. Before me, a light array the size of a bed mattress goes dark. Far above, softer lights illuminate my prison.

For the first time, I can see where she has been keeping me chained to this wall.

Blinking the spots away, I look around. We're in a large, empty room wherein one could fit three long-haul buses. Maybe four. The only object is the massive light array that faces me.

In the center of the floor is a drain, but this I knew. Trapped as I was, I had to urinate while hanging from the wall and did hear this drip and drain into pipes below. It has been a long time since I have had to relieve myself.

Alas, without water, there is no need.

Hammer clicks her heels as she walks to the far wall, some fifty feet away from me.

But I see you now, Ilsa Hammer.

Momentarily stepping behind the dark array of lights, she continues her attempts at manipulation.

"We are almost finished with you, Kane," she says, and I watch her feet as they pass under the apparatus. "The blood we extracted from you has been very helpful. And the results are... pleasing."

Her heel touches the floor before the toes do. The ankles are stiff. She is trying to control her emotions, to portray strength when she is weak.

"That bit of magic inside you," she says, and I hear the tapping on the tablet's glass once again, "looks to have come from one of the Organization's prodigies. At one time, Cal Davis's blood might have been the most valuable substance in the world. Of course, he's dead."

She steps around the array so that I can read her body words as she speaks.

"Alas, that strength and power also flow within you but even stronger! Better! Now that I have stolen that power, soon, I will have no use for you."

I smile and feel my lips crack. "This is good. I am looking forward to leaving. I believe I will get a cheeseburger."

Nodding, Ilsa Hammer leans against a wall made entirely of black glass. Very faint light glows behind the top half. Does someone else watch from behind there?

They would not need to, for I have seen cameras all around this large room.

"Where is the mighty warrior you showed me on the property of Dr. Faria?" she asks with words and expression.

After days without water, my eyes have blurred slightly, but I can still pick up some of what is not said.

"Can you no longer do that because...?"

Hammer points to me.

I am unsure of what she is saying. For some time now, it feels like dry cotton has filled my head.

"*Quoi?*" I say, because I don't understand.

She's smiling—this time, I can tell this is a real smile. And one I don't like. She thumps away at the tablet, and I hear a clanking noise and brace for the light. But it does not come.

This time, the light array levers downward, slowly lying flat on the floor. Why has she...?

Yes.

Yes, I see.

The black glass reflects my image, and I see myself for the first time. I struggle not to cry out.

I am so old.

Withered.

My beard, once full and black, is now haggard. Like my long hair, it is more gray than black. My chest is sunken. My arms and legs are shriveled.

Can this really be me?

"I would say," Ilsa says, and I cannot take my eyes off the stranger in the reflection before me, "that you look—what? Maybe sixty? Seventy?"

I can only stare, unable to blink.

"I admit, you were kind of, well, *fit* when you first joined us. But after a few days..." she says, lifting a limp hand toward me.

When I turn to her, the expression is one of distaste, and it is not a feint. I close my eyes against it, but still, she continues.

"We can no longer even get blood out of your veins, probably because of the 'no water' thing, right? But if you just would bring out that beautiful monster…"

"You are the monster here," I croak out, and the words feel like vomiting broken glass.

When I open my eyes, she is slowly walking toward me, tapping on her tablet. Her gait is different now. More confident. Menacing.

"I have a surprise for you," she says, looking at me over the rims of her glasses and holding the tablet between us. "If you don't give me what I want…" She turns the screen toward me. On it, I see a woman running through a place with many machines. What is… Then I realize who that woman is.

I try to speak but then am wracked by a coughing fit. My eyes sting but do not water. Still, I do not break away from the video on the screen. Emelda running. And being pursued by some creature. A monster.

Dr. Ilsa Hammer then pulls the tablet back, holding it to her chest like a nuzzling child. Her face beams with pleasure as my mind screams and screams.

"That fun little film is from yesterday. We've done a flyby at the factory," she says and shrugs. "No body cut to ribbons as far as we can see, but my little birds out there are searching for your friend. We'll find her."

Spinning around, she steps back to the array and presses the side of it, returning it to its place. More light. Alas, I have endured her punishing lamps before, so this is…

But she does not engage the light. Instead, she slips the computer tablet behind the array. When her hand returns, she is holding a metal pole. I have seen this before. She sways it in the air, back and forth. Electric arc light ripples between the twin tines at its end.

"You've felt the bite of this little device of ours a number of times," she says, holding the button down long enough that I can smell the electricity in the air. The ozone. "But all it's gotten me is a limp man and a bit of drool."

I crack a chapped-lipped smile. "I have no interest in your home life."

"It—what?" Her smile flips upside down as if I've thrown a switch. Creeping closer, she thumbs the button again. The arc light flickering in her cold eyes. "What if I jammed this fun stick into the gut of your friend? How long would I have to hold it until that moronic purple hair of hers began to burn?"

I can feel my heart pump blood into my extremities, my hands throbbing. No. No. I must not let her control my emotions. I am in control. Breathing deeply, I close my eyes.

Her heels clack louder, and I can hear her breath quicken.

"How long would it take for her eyes to," she says, stepping closer, and I feel the steel fangs under my chin, "pop out of her head?"

Slowly, I pull in a deep breath, slowly, slowly, and she pushes the tines deeper into my neck.

Snapping my knee upward, I feel the skin on my foot scrape and slice. But, so much thinner now, so frail, I pull until I hear the crack of the bones in my ankle. My foot comes free, and I wrap my leg around her waist.

"Ugggngh!" she cries out, the breath pushed from her lungs as she depresses the button on the shock stick.

I roar in pain, fighting the darkness trying to take me, then drop my head and go for her neck, my teeth bared. She shoves me with one arm, and again, she depresses the button. My body seizes, shaking, convulsing, and she pulls away.

I bite down, but I can no longer hold her, and she tumbles back away from me and falls to the floor.

The electricity stops, and I wearily open my eyes.

Defiant, I crunch at the plastic in my mouth. The sharp edges cut into my gums and inner lips, and I can taste thick blood. I spit out the broken pieces of her glasses, which land on her sheer white top, leaving a bloody stain.

A door flies open behind her, and a small man is standing there with a pistol in his hand. He is pointing it at me.

"No! No, don't shoot him," Ilsa Hammer shouts back to the man, hand held in the air. "I'm not done with him."

The short man lifts his weapon higher, aiming down the sights. I am not afraid of death, for my wolf ancestors await me. In this moment, there is no fear, but I *am* curious.

This is a man I cannot read.

He betrays no thought. No emotion. What a curious creature.

"He's got a foot loose, Doc Hammer," the man says, nodding toward me. "Maybe I just shoot the leg?"

The woman on the floor makes a sound of disgust and pushes the bloody, broken pieces off her once-clean shirt. Getting to her feet, she calls to the man. "Paul, put that down and clean this fucking mess up," she says, flicking off bits of plastic.

The short man holds his stance for another few seconds then pockets the gun. Using his shoe, he pushes the bloody pieces into the mouth of the floor drain.

"Those glasses were two thousand dollars," Ilsa Hammer says, glaring at me. "For that, I will make her suffer. Then, if you're still alive, I will bring that recording here. Her pain will be the last thing you ever hear, Kane."

The short man is already walking to the back wall. "What about him? He's out of one of the bindings."

"Tighten the others ten percent," she says, following him to the wall. Then she turns back to me, and she cannot hide her rage. And fear. There is so much fear there. "Make it fifteen. Let it hurt."

Paul the Short Man presses a spot on the black wall, and a panel lifts, but then he steps in front of it so I cannot see what he is doing. To his left, a portion of the wall rises, and Ilsa Hammer steps through, ascending a set of stairs.

He does not immediately follow. As his hand works within the panel, I feel the three cuffs restraining me tighten. The bones in my right wrist splinter, but I do not cry out.

The pain is making me dizzy, and just as I'm about to pass out, the light array fires up again. Brilliant white light, brighter than I remember. The lights above extinguish, and I am left with the mini sun blasting me.

But I am smiling.

I hope she is watching on the camera, because I am smiling. Blood trickles down my mouth, but I do not part my lips to taste it. The temptation is there, yes, but I resist.

Instead, I focus on the feel of the brass-colored chain, the coolness of it, the salty perspiration of a desperate woman, as it brushes against my teeth and tongue.

Chapter Thirty-Six

Sprinting across the zoo, literally running for my life again, I cursed my stupid brain.

I'd heard an odd little fact about perception once. Probably in one of the moments I'd been a bit too stoned to get off the couch and some nature documentary came on and I couldn't find the remote.

So I'd been sitting there, eyes half crossed, after Netflix decided that me watching *John Wick* on a loop was what an assassin might call "grooming," and suddenly, I've got some show with facts and researchers on the screen.

My first thought: I could kill that science guy with his pen.

But the second thought had been spurred by something the pen-twirling dude had said. Humans are animals, and all animals, when threatened, transition into a state of heightened perception.

Sight, smell, hearing.

Taste, too, I suppose, but I don't have any idea where that might come in handy.

This ain't French vanilla, it's just vanilla!

Deeper in the zoo, I heard a rumble then a throaty shriek, stretched and rising, roll toward me, up and down the curves and contours of the grounds like a runaway bowling ball. It smacked into my chest.

I pushed myself harder, feeling my neck muscles tense as I forced myself to keep running and not look at what might be coming.

This documentary science guy said that the heightened-sense thing was a survival instinct that evolution had cooked up over millions of years. The ones that developed it survived.

And they ate the ones that hadn't.

Coming up a rise in the zoo's near-total darkness, I had to duck whip-crack fast to avoid smacking my head into a sign hanging off a low-slung tree branch.

Gregor, as promised, had run straight to the fence line impossibly fast then cut left. Dude passed right cross my field of vision like he was on roller blades. Motorized roller blades.

"Shit!" I spat out between gasps of air.

Another animal wail, this one closer. The screeching seemed to come from all around me, and I couldn't tell what was actual beast and what was echo.

Didn't matter.

I ran up over another long crest, winding around the deep grooves in the ground where it had collapsed. It did really look like some lawn outfit had come in to dig trenches for a sprinkler system but never gotten around to finishing.

Too much dodging and weaving. I could now hear thudding footfalls coming my way.

And something else. A grumbling, rumbling sensation.

I had the queerest sensation that the Earth's stomach was growling as it eyeballed me for its next meal.

Ah, bringing me back to my senses.

Much better to think about that than about the teeth and claws that would rip me apart at any second.

So now, I was in this heightened state, my senses sharper than at any other point in my life, probably overclocking human capacity to one hundred fifteen percent, and *yet* I wasn't using that super perception to dodge beasts or work out the perfect vector of my escape route or burst wings from my shoulders and fly away.

No.

Tears streaming from my eyes, my breath now audible moans, my muscles shredding from bone, and all I could think about was the letter *H*.

There'd been Mindy the meerkat. Sammy the spider monkey. Got a theme there.

So what the hell was Hugo?

Speaking of Mindy, I'd just seen her off to my left, running on all fours, fat head bobbing, teeth bared with bits of whatever animal parts she'd been eating still tumbling from her open mouth. She didn't care about that stuff; fresh meat was on the menu.

"Jesus," I shouted and dropped to a knee, rolling forward just as she leaped at me, careering through the air over my head. I felt a claw reach out and nick my shirt, then I heard her smash into the ground.

Somewhere in my brain, I put a Post-it note. Without even thinking, I'd ducked at the last minute, rolled, and gotten back to my feet. Not planned. No thought, just reaction.

Where had that come from?

Heightened-senses thing?

No, not likely, because most of my brain processing was running through all the animals that began with the letter *H*.

Hugo the hermit crab? Hugo the hyena?

Mindy flipped over and landed on her feet, crouched and clawing into the ground. She roared at me. The meerkat roared!

Worst. Zoo. Ever.

Racing past her and turning from another trench, I had to switch directions and jump over. Arching my head so I could keep a bead on Mindy, I looked down into the gap and saw grass. On top.

How did Hugo the whatever take scoops out of the Earth and leave the topsoil behind?

Hugo the honey badger?

Hugo the—

Mindy bolted for me, its paws as big as a dock worker's hands, clawing at the earth, but I couldn't run any faster. When she dipped lower, I knew she was going to pounce again. And she wouldn't leap high; she'd have learned.

She'd go straight for my legs.

Ten feet away!

Out of the corner of my eye, I saw her leg muscles pull farther forward, folding her long body in half, preparing to jump, but the moment she began to extend her legs, I heard it.

Znnnnt!

I could smell the burnt fur, hear the crackle of animal sweat frying as the collar lit up, sparkling at the edge of my vision.

"She will be down for less than a minute." Ganiyu's voice came from a tinny speaker inside the open mouth of a massive cartoon duck at the top of a rusted pole. "Apologies that I didn't hit her collar sooner. My water bottle rolled under the table."

I glanced up, cursing and thanking the duck simultaneously.

Then my mind went back to...

Hugo the horse? Did they have horses at the zoo?

Hugo the...

A screeching ripped through the air above me, ahead at my ten o'clock. I cast a quick glance up and saw only the reflection off Sammy's teeth and the whites of its eyes. Just a sliver there, as its black pupils had ballooned in their sockets.

The monkey extended an arm and swung, which made me flinch, but it was using its momentum to not leap at me but instead corkscrew down the tree. It made wider and wider swings, twisting its body back to front to use its other elongated arm, kicking off the branches and trunk, speeding up as it spun around.

Leaning forward, I leaped again, extending my leg forward. And again, I glanced at the trench that wasn't a trench. Somehow, Hugo had made that.

Sammy bared its teeth, eyes totally black now, swinging impossibly fast, round and round and round.

I clenched my hands into fists and screamed at it as loud as I could, the force of the call tearing at my throat. I felt the blood flush my face.

Wood spat from the tree as Sammy leaped, arms up, legs spread, hooked claws cutting through the air. I rolled into one of the trenches and smashed into the grass below.

As Sammy sailed over, I heard the electric collar engage and a staccato howl that ended with a thump on the far side.

"Those are the last charges for both animals," Ganiyu's voice rang out above me. "You must run. There is nothing more that I can do. Run fast. Good luck to you."

I pressed my hands into the grass, and it finally occurred to me. Grass hadn't grown atop the cutout trench because it wasn't a trench at all. A tunnel.

Whatever Hugo was, it burrowed underground! And after it passed, the topsoil collapsed behind it.

Tunneling creatures!

Hugo the hamster?

Hugo the hedgehog?

But the tunnels had been so wide, I couldn't imagine—

"RUN!" the voice from the sky screamed, and I heard the speaker pop and sizzle.

I ran.

Up over the lip, I pushed my muscles harder, but they were already giving out. My feet were landing not exactly where I'd planned. I was tiring.

When I glanced forward, I could see the gate we'd come through. A hundred feet away, maybe?

My heart sank. Closed.

"Fucking Gregor," I muttered, but I was committed. One way or another, I was going to make it to the door. Even if I got torn to shreds by these Enhanced beasts, my goal, right then, was not escaping.

Just the door.

I make it to the door, and I've won.

Here to there.

The earth hit my stomach high as it burst up in front of me, and I tumbled over the top of it. Too distracted! I hadn't seen the hill.

Then I heard the rumble of earth, the crumbles of rock and mud falling to the ground. No, not a hill.

Hugo had tunneled right in front of me, cutting off my path, and knocked me to my feet. My head spinning, I tried to get my eyes to focus.

Leaning forward, I grunted and screamed, willing myself to get up.

On my knees, I flicked my head toward the door.

Closer.

Here to there.

I heard a rumble to my right and snapped my head at the approaching wave of earth. Fear gripped me, and I froze. Not a hamster or hedgehog; this sonofabitch was huge. Massive.

As earth shifted and twisted, it wasn't coming straight for me but bending and curving and doubling back. Toying with its food.

Some creature the size of a sofa was burrowing underground and screwing with me.

I jumped up and turned just as the earth exploded. Soil and rock and twigs and damp leaves rained down on top of me. I halted because I had to look.

The speaker above me, up in a massive oak tree, just bleated out high-register buzzing noises. It seemed that Ganiyu had fried the speakers screaming at me to run, and all that was left was a bleating alarm.

Bzzzt! Bzzzzzzt! Buzzzt-buzzzt!

I forced myself to turn and look at Hugo. I had to see.

Hugo's head was as large as my torso. Its eyes, white around the edges, big black circle in the middle, bulged from its head, the size of softballs. The small ears, I knew, normally poked up on either side, but its transformation had slicked them back to slits. Just two long cuts in its skull, covered by a flap of trembling skin.

I recognized the creature, but somehow, the treatments, the experiments, and that serum had compacted all the power into a creature half its normal size. But it was still one of the largest I'd ever been near.

Its two front legs were up in front of its massive head, and I saw now why it didn't run on land. The feet should have been more pawlike, hairless. Fat arms terminated in fat pads.

From stump to shoulder, Hugo's long limbs looked almost human. Muscles bulged on either side of the elbow joint. Instead of padded feet, Hugo had long, fat, twisting claws extending from bloodied stumps. Running above ground would have been difficult—the spikes at the ends of its claws curved like scythes as long as my shin.

This was what the treatment had done. What had happened after the lab techs with their white coats and clipboards and break rooms full of overpriced snacks were done.

Hugo was a heartbreaking abomination.

Dumbstruck, I was shaken out of my trance when it roared at me, spittle flying, and the jaw hyperextended impossibly wide as two rows of teeth bared, ready to tear at flesh and bone.

Like the mouth of a shark.

On a hippo that could burrow underground.

Chapter Thirty-Seven

For a fraction of a second that stretched into eternity, I stared into the warped creature's bulbous eyes. Instead of being nestled in, they rose higher on its head, white beach balls with a black, swirling center that grew. When it blinked, I could hear the thick flaps of skin slide down, drawing over the half spheres then peeling back with a wet, sickening sound.

"Nope."

I jumped up, pushing off with my right foot, launching myself to the left. I'd half expected it to burst through the ground, its upper jaw extending and chomping down on my leg as if it were an errant white marble.

Yep. My only knowledge of the feeding habits of hippos came from a kids' tabletop game.

I wasn't sure but felt pretty sure that sort of wisdom wouldn't help.

Passing between two trees, I was now running parallel with the fence. Not the direction I wanted to go. The one thing working for me was that with the Enhanced beast's transformations, running over ground looked difficult if not actually painful.

Hugo didn't leap out of the ground, teeth bared, but dove back down into the Georgia soil as if he were swimming out in the sand of the Serengeti.

The ground shook. Just behind me and off to my right, it sounded like a rocket launching. I heard a rolling, almost deep gargling sound as Hugo chewed through the soil. When I glanced over, my heart twitched and tried to hide between my lungs.

The earth was bulging then collapsing in the wake of the creature.

I didn't know if it was merely pushing the dirt aside, compressing it, or, hell, eating it as it went. Like that mattered.

Hugo was coming up beside me, moving as fast as I was, and most importantly, blocking my path to the door.

With a quick glance to my right, I saw the gate we'd come through earlier.

"Gregor!" I shouted between breaths as I ducked under another low branch. "Swing the gate open!"

The bulge in the earth seemed to respond to my voice, hitching right at a sharp angle. For a moment, I thought Hugo might go for the opening door. But, of course, the door didn't open.

I was alone.

Wait. Where the hell was Marata?

I briefly wondered if she'd gotten eaten by a meerkat and a monkey. She'd disappeared.

Pushing my already exhausted limbs, I tried to juke to the right, but Hugo raced forward.

"Goddamn it!"

Veering left, I tried to think if there might be any other—

Bzzzt! Bzzt-Bzzt-Bzzzzzzzz!

Great! Was some prehistoric insect about to swoop down and chomp my head off now? Really? *Really?*

No. Ganiyu was yelling into the mic, but the fried speakers only offered ear-splitting white noise. I didn't need to know what he was saying; the message was clear.

A moment later, I heard them.

Shrieks and wails of anger, rage, and hunger. The other Enhanced beasts had awoken from their electro-shock daze. And they were coming.

My eyes watered. I'd come all this way to just get caught between three impossible animals, split into three like some KFC family pack.

Jamming my heels into the ground, I flexed my arms and screamed, "Noooo!"

I turned to face the soft bulge that was moving in a serpentine pattern, probing and prodding through the earth. Hugo was screwing with me.

If he'd wanted to take a straight path right at me, he'd have been chewing at my pricey running shoes in a matter of seconds.

At that thought, I shivered and had to grab a nearby tree to steady myself. Waiting for him to surface, I stared and cocked my head as I watched.

Why wasn't it just rocketing beneath me then leaping up from the ground to swallow me whole? Then I looked at my palm.

The trees.

Hugo wasn't circling around in that earth like it was water, lining up its strike. The ground wasn't water, of course.

"No," I whispered. "You can't get to me." I looked up at the giant tree beside me, its branches flaring out, arms reaching to the night sky as if in triumph.

I patted the trunk.

"You can't get past the roots."

Just off to my right, I could hear the thudding advance of the other two creatures, and I scanned the area by the fence line. Up ahead, the trees curved around and met the fence. Two park benches faced each other. At one time, it had been a place where families could meet up and eat the lunch they'd hidden in bags and purses.

At least, that was what my family had always done.

Well, the one time we'd gone to the zoo.

I crouched into a runner's starting position with one leg back, one bent forward, and sucked in a big breath.

Once again, I ran.

I sped down the tree line as fast as my weary legs would go. I could see movement up ahead to my left. To my right, Hugo was chewing through the soil beneath me.

As the trees arced, I began to turn with them. Hugo wasn't turning.

Shit, if I'm wrong about this... well, at least I won't have a lot of time to berate myself. Hippo turds don't really have the capacity for self-reflection.

Finally, I was moving toward the fence in a slow arc. I screamed, pushing my fear deep into my empty belly, and blinked away tears and sweat.

Hugo was arcing slightly but not giving up.

Of course. He knew this park, knew the ground. I had to get from this hook of trees to the next, and I'd be home free.

But to get there, I had a ten-foot gap.

Hugo knew about the gap.

And I could see crisscrossing uneven earth there. It was a well-worn path he'd used before.

No choice. The other animals were closing in on my left, coming at me from the other side, maybe a hundred yards away. I could see teeth from here, for god's sake!

The gap was approaching, and I focused on it. I would have to jump high or end up lunch. The huge bulge in the earth twitched to the right a little then jagged and turned, slowing slightly. Why was he slowing?

How did he even know where I was? The crazy abomination didn't have a friggin' periscope to look up and find me.

I looked down at my shoes.

Right. Of course. He could hear my stomping feet. Nothing I could do about that. I took a few deep breaths, readying myself for the gap.

Three seconds away.

I began to growl, the rumble rising up in my chest.

Two.

My body tensed. Me versus a thousand pounds of muscle, claws, and teeth. Hugo made a quick arc and headed straight for the gap, its form almost bouncing in anticipation of my blood and bone in its mouth.

One.

Screaming in pain, I jammed my heels into the ground, leaning back and pinwheeling my arms to keep my balance, stopping just inches from the grassy gap.

In that moment, Hugo burst from the ground, mouth wide, teeth gnashing, roaring as it brought its blade-like arms forward.

I watched as it flew through the air, its thick eyelids peeled back wide as if it had wanted to witness me go down its gullet. The creature's thick and sinewy oil-black flesh passed me just inches away. It crashed back to earth and rolled on its side, end over end.

Stunned that it had come up empty.

"Bye."

I ran across the warped ground because I did not have the strength to jump. In the cover of the trees and branches, I screamed, just twenty feet from the gate.

"Open the gate! Open the gate!"

Behind me, I heard the thudding. I could feel it in my legs. One of the other creatures had gotten ahead of the other, closing in. The ragged, panicked breathing was so loud I could almost feel its hot breath.

I shouted again, dizzy from exhaustion. "Open!" A grunt of exhalation burst behind me, and I shouted again. "Open the—"

But the gate was open.

A figure burst out of the dark gap ahead. As it leaped, I rolled to the ground beneath it until my legs smashed against the door. My eyes rolled back from the electricity that rabbit punched my body.

I'd only touched it for a second, bouncing off the metal, and I felt like every cell in my body had exploded.

Breathing heavily and with my vision blurred, I lifted myself and stared back into the zoo. I'd rolled right through the gap.

I was out.

Through the open gate, I watched a massive creature slam its fist into the meerkat's snarling face, stunning it. Then it kicked the beast in the stomach, bending it in two, getting a slash of claws across its leg.

I blinked. "Gregor?"

The tech sergeant, twice the size of the Enhanced meerkat, grabbed it by its legs as he had before then turned with it but not to put it into a dizzying spin. Crouching, he arched upward with the body of the first creature, slamming it into the second as it leaped through the air to join the fight.

The screeching beast-monkey howled as it flew back and smashed against a tree.

All I could do was stare.

Mindy flipped over and swiped her hind claws, tearing into Gregor's calf. He screamed in pain then kicked the beast, sending it flying too.

He turned toward me, grabbed his side, and started running.

Time to move.

I hopped up and looked at the half-open gate. I grabbed the rock Marata had used earlier and braced it, ready to slam it closed.

Gregor's eyes grew wide as he ran toward me, his mouth opening in an unspoken question.

"Come on!" I shouted.

He leaped through the gap and rolled to the ground. I banged the gate shut. I fumbled around for the busted lock and hammered it through the loop, getting another teeth-rattling electric shock.

I fell back.

On the other side of the fence, we could hear the animals growling, but they knew they'd lost. Going near the fence was pain.

As I heaved for breath, a buzzing sound split the cool night air.

Zttt Zttt.

I have no idea what the zoo's Nigerian maintenance man had said. But in my mind, he'd congratulated us on not dying.

Well done.

I glanced over at Gregor as he sat up, wincing.

"Why'd you do that?" I said, my voice trembling with exhaustion. "Why did you risk yourself for me? I thought you'd run, leave me behind. But you didn't. Why?"

Gregor turned to me, frowning. He shrugged then stared back at the creatures as they slipped back into the darkness of the forgotten zoo.

Running his hands through his short, silver hair, he nodded at me and said, "You've got the keys to the Jeep."

Chapter Thirty-Eight

Kane

I drift in and out of sleep for hours, waiting.

The light does not change. Does not extinguish. She has left me here to die.

"Give it another go."

In the silence, some time ago now, I heard shouting from above. Behind the black glass. Or at least where I thought the black glass was, for I cannot see. I only see white. Spots of red and shadows. Am I going blind?

"You'll never learn sitting and staring at it," Père's voice echoes in my head. "Put your foot on the brake—"

"The only thing I can do is to put my foot on the brake!" I growl at my human father, and it darkens my heart. It is not he who I am angry with. "Too many things to move with the hands and feet."

"And eyes," *mon père* says, putting his strong, calloused hand on my tiny shoulder. "It is not only what you do but the others around you. You have to account for their choices as well."

Blinking, I can see his face as he leans against the car window. One corner of his mouth is raised. Ever the patient man.

"It is too much to know," I say, muttering through chapped lips as the past and present mix as one. "Why cannot I take the bus?"

This gets a laugh out of the man. "One day. For now, just focus on—"

"I try to focus. It is so much!" I bury my face in my hands. Are my hands free now? No, these are young hands, when I was a boy last year. So confusing. "Lever and wheel and feet pedals and... too much."

I feel his soft touch as he strokes my hair. It's grown long now because Mère does not trust her trembling hands with sheers anymore. She says I look like a rock-and-roll singer. Like a beach lifeguard on TV. This she approves of.

"It is like *ta mère* says," my human father says. "Get one puzzle piece in place, and that can lead to the next. But if it doesn't, so what? You got the one piece in! That is more than you started with."

"This is not enough," I mutter into the steering wheel's plastic.

"It can be. Kane, sometimes you just need the one win. Just the one. In life, very many difficult times you will face, as we have. As everyone does. If you get the one win, a small win, the day is a success."

Slowly, I lift my head and look at his face. The kindness of his eyes.

"One win."

"*Oui*," he says and tousles my hair. He points out the driver's-side window. "You hit that stump there. And the rock a few meters away." A finger goes to the windshield. "The flower bed is now three flower beds with tire tracks down the middle." He hooks a thumb over his shoulder. "My tool shed has a dent in the side of it the size of my bumper and my bumper a divot the side of a tool shed."

I put my hands to my face. I feel his fingers lace into them and pull them down again. He holds my hands in his larger ones.

Tilting his head, he motions to the barn where I first awoke months ago with these two beautiful people waiting to care for me. In a human sense, it is the place of my birth.

"You have not yet hit the barn," he says, grinning at me. "Let's give the driving another go. If you do not hit the barn? That is a win. You just need the one."

I nod slowly, my neck hurting. The blinding white of the room returns. So does the pain in my crushed wrist. My leg is buzzing, hanging loosely. It has fallen asleep.

"One win." I croak the phrase out, the tiny reading glasses chain stuffed between my cheek and lower teeth. When I try to swallow, I cannot.

I am dying of thirst.

Then that is the win I seek.

Freeing myself from this place, I cannot do this. But I can get a win. Just the one. If so, I will have bested Doctor Ilsa Hammer.

That will be enough.

It will have to be.

Slowly manipulating the brass chain in my mouth, I dribble the end of it from my lips. Feeling around with my dry tongue, I slowly push out one tip. As I move my jaw and teeth, the end hangs farther and farther out.

It moves slowly, glued inside my sticky mouth.

"One win," I say, or maybe I have only said this in my mind. Fighting exhaustion, I push the chain farther, squinting against the light. More shadows have formed in my vision like a computer screen on which the tiny squares flicker out.

I can feel the end of the chain as it rolls across my tongue, and I push it farther out. The other end rubs down my chapped lower lip, dangling across my beard. Slowly, slowly, I sway my head back and forth to get a feel for how much length is now extending.

I feel the chain clasp graze my chest. Almost enough. If I can get the end to my front teeth...

It slips out. I feel the jagged end nip at my bottom lip as it falls.

I groan, "*Non!*"

But there's no clattering sound. No clinking to the floor. I feel the weight of it on my chin. Holding my head perfectly still, my neck straining with the effort, I rotate my eyeballs down to see the chain has caught on my gray, scraggly beard.

The chain will be my win.

And it's stuck in my beard!

That is not enough win. Water, this is my goal. One gulp of water, and that is my win. But I need to get the chain back into my mouth.

Extending my tongue across sandpaper lips, I lean my head forward, just slightly, trying to reach the dangling—

It drops.

Time slows in my head. Below, I can see the chain growing smaller, sparkling in the light array as it falls, falls, falls from me.

"*Non!*" I shout and will my leg to move. Spreading my toes—no, they are claws, I must think of them as claws!—I place them beneath the sparkling chain as it falls.

It keeps falling, passing my paw, foot, claws, toes, and I strike out, kicking at it with all my strength while clasping with my feeble toes.

The chain stops.

It's hanging between my big toe and the next one.

What is this toe called?

Index toe?

No. I do not know. What I do remember, very young, early days, *ma mère* told me the jobs these toes had. The larger, it did the shopping.

"This little piggy went to market."

The second—

"This little piggy stayed home."

I smile and stare down at the toe that has caught the chain. "Good. You did well, shut-in piggy."

Sucking in a deep breath, I glare back at the light, pressing my will against it.

"My turn," I say, growling at the array.

Ignoring the searing pain, I twist back and forth, swinging my leg, back and forth. I will have one shot.

"One win. Just the one."

My back bangs against the cold concrete behind me, but I bury the pain deep in my mind. I twist my secured ankle, feeling the skin tear, to get the momentum I need.

I count the swings, seeing the chain glitter and sparkle as it crosses in and out of the light's glare.

"Three," I say, extending my leg forward.

My hips bounce hard off the wall, and I push. "Two."

Crunching my stomach muscles, gyrating my hips, I shout as I give it one go, one last go. "One!"

I release the chain with all my remaining strength, watching it tumble and flip end over end. There is a wispy shadow, a thin golden line.

I see the sparks before I hear the crack. Glass shatters, bits of it spraying to the floor.

Two of the large bulbs have burst. In another two, the glass has cracked and fallen away. Tiny bursts of light crackle there.

Good. Good.

Nearly there.

I will my leg to lift and use all the piggies now.

"Come on, shopping piggie, meat piggie, hungry piggie," I say, my mind drifting in and out of madness. With my toes, I grip the hospital pants that cling to my right leg and pull and pull until they tear. Lifting my knee, I yank harder, and there is more tearing.

I only hope it is fabric and not muscle.

Not that this matters any more.

"One win."

Forcing my right hip back, I yank hard with my left foot, screaming in agony until I hear the rip. I grip the shredded pant leg between my toes.

"One win."

This time, I do not have the strength to count. Holding the fabric against my leg, I scrunch as much of it as I can to create a ball. Then the piggies tire and begin to cramp.

It will have to be enough.

I pull back my left foot, my toes clenching the scrunched-up pant leg, and will every last bit of strength into my thigh.

"Aaagrhh!" I scream and hurl the fabric ball at the sparks. It lands, catching on the teeth of broken glass.

Now, I can only watch and hope.

Nothing more for me to do.

There is a spark. Then another. Beneath the white pants with their thin blue lines, I see a darkening. Then a wisp of smoke.

"One!" I shout at it. "One win!"

Then flame!

When the tiny fire hits the spots I have soiled, the flames shrink. Then the equipment begins to smoke. More smoke, billowing up. Another bulb explodes, which ignites another part of the dirty fabric.

Two parts smoking now.

I can smell it, and maybe this is enough. The smoke lifts from the array, disappearing into the darkness above.

Is this enough of a win?

To damage the array?

It might have to be. But I want—

Blan-blan-blan-blan!

Red lights rise from the corners of the room. Next comes a siren so loud it hurts my ears, splitting my head in two.

"Arrrgh!"

The very tiny, upside-down trees begin to erupt. Water cascades down, falling like a spring rain.

Lifting my face to the shower, I let it wash over me. Then I open my mouth for my victory. The water burns at first then cools. It is hard to swallow, but I let it refresh my mouth and tongue. I feel cuts within, but the feeling is glorious.

There's a whirring in my brain, but I ignore it.

The water has soaked the light array. It sparks and snaps, and bulbs explode! With a mouth full of water, I laugh, and half of it gurgles out onto my chest.

I swallow the other half.

The cool wave rolls down my throat. My eyes no longer sting when I blink.

The final bulbs on the light array burst, and it goes dark. The room now glows like a sunset. Emergency lights, I believe they are called.

Sticking my tongue out at it, I gather more rain.

"Two wins," I say to the dead lights. "I have defeated you as well!"

I tilt my head back. I will never leave this place, but this I have done. My father was right. You just need the one win.

I open my mouth to take in another swallow of water, one of my last on earth.

"Hello?"

I ignore the voice in my head. I have no more time for—

"Hello?"

In the dim red light, I twist and turn to peer into the far corner of the room, which is hard to see from my vantage point.

"Hello?" a male voice says. "Where did this car take me?"

The young man steps out of a strange little room with a large pack on his shoulder and a metal stick extending from his hand.

Chapter Thirty-Nine

For a long, long moment, I lie back, just trying to slow my breathing. Staring up through the thick canopy of trees above me, I could see a flicker between the leaves.

"You stay out of this," I grumbled at the moon. "You got me into this mess."

"What?" Gregor said, rolling up to his knees. "You were the one so desperate to find your boyfriend."

Ugh, this guy.

"No, not my boyfriend."

The tech sergeant wobbled forward, putting his hand on a tree to stand. I could see gashes across his arms and chest. What looked like a bite mark gouged his leg, as in a *chunk* missing, blood oozing out.

I tensed at the sound of rustling in the bushes, snapping my head toward it.

A moment later, Marata burst from the foliage, arms in the air.

"Not dead!"

"No," I said, sitting up. "Not yet. No thanks to you."

Marata grinned, poking her tongue through the gap where a tooth used to be, as if she didn't understand a word I'd said. Then her smile dimmed, and she turned toward the fence. When I looked over, I could see a giant bulge in the dirt about ten feet on the other side of the gate.

Sure, Hugo had tried to make me an appetizer. And he'd chased me until I thought my heart might burst out of my chest. But now that same heart ached a bit.

These twisted beasts, driven by bloodlust, had never asked for this. In fact, it had been a crew from the Organization, which Marata had been a part of, that had warped them into this living hell.

Marata seemed oblivious to all of it.

Or, at least, oblivious to the fact that I could have—should have—died. I had to remind myself she wasn't exactly on my side.

Whose side was she on?

I didn't know.

Gregor stomped down the path, cursing the branches biting into his skin as he stalked back toward the Jeep.

Watching Hugo slowly dip low and disappear, I crawled up to the fence and looked at the bottom of the gate.

A very small gap showed me a sliver of the zoo beyond. The gate door was about an inch from a steel plate that seemed to be jammed deep into the ground. That made sense, I supposed. Given that Hugo could dig deep, if they hadn't buried a barrier, he might have slipped right underneath.

Standing again, I pointed at Marata to head back to the Jeep.

She spun around, her too-small lab coat flapping as she did, and disappeared back into the brush.

I cast one final glance into the zoo.

It wasn't right. At some point, I would have to return and see if I could do something about Mindy, Sammy, and Hugo.

What I would do I had no idea.

After fighting with prickly branches and nipping leaves, I finally burst out of the bushes and saw Gregor lifting his shirt. In his hand he held a syringe. He jammed it into his belly, squeezed just a little serum in, and sighed.

As I got closer, I pointed at his face. "You've got a fleck of green in your eyes," I said. "Is that just the light?"

He shrugged and then shivered, closing his eyes.

I watched the skin knit itself back together across his arms. The red welts shrank and disappeared. The chunk out of his leg began to fill in, but it looked like that repair would take longer.

Gregor hitched and twisted like he might vomit. When he finally opened his eyes, he stared at me, defiant. I looked at his pupils and, yep, all black again.

The far-side Jeep door slammed, and Marata put a foot up on the passenger seat, sipping from her sports bottle.

Gregor glanced at her and half gagged. "Vile creature. How does she drink that?"

Pointing at the needle he was slipping back into its case, I said, "You're doing the same thing, just in a different way."

"Hardly," he said and sighed. "Okay. Now for the hard part."

My eyes went wide, and I laughed. And… I caught the tiniest hint of a smile on his face. The guy was impossible to read. Or maybe I was just making it impossible.

"All right, Anton," I said, pointing at the road ahead. "Let's go get us a wolfwere."

Chapter Forty

Tiffany Maitland opened her mailbox with her elbow. Or she tried to. Orlando's afternoon rains had come and gone in an hour that, sometimes, she felt was a collection of angels who'd looked down upon the city and just wept.

Orlando had that effect on most people.

A beautiful landscape, so beautiful someone thought it should have a price tag on it. Now it was riddled with tourist attractions of all flavors, T-shirt shops whose garments didn't last a single ride in the wash, and soulless architecture that looked like someone hadn't quite finished the blueprints but built the places anyway.

She didn't care about any of that.

With the humidity above one hundred, the mailbox was sticking. And she'd just chased Mr. Underfoot down the block because the cat needed to go to the vet and was having none of it.

After trying to get it open the third time, the lip of the mailbox nipping at her skin—while the cat clawed at her shoulder—she finally got it open.

Empty.

Sweat trickled from her armpits and down her ribs. She'd only been outside for five minutes!

Right. She'd also been chasing the cat.

Elbowing the mailbox closed, she spoke softly, cooing to the fuzzy animal, trying to get it to calm.

Then her phone buzzed.

"Owwah-whaa-owww!"

Mr. Underfoot knew a threat when he felt it, and the buzzing prompted him to dig his nails in deep and leap from his owner's arms, taking small bits of flesh with him.

She watched him run the other direction down the street and took in a breath to call out or curse but then just let it roll into a sigh.

"Fine," she said, ambling back to her one-story bungalow with its chipped paint and lopsided shutters. "Can't afford the damn vet anyhow."

When she reached for the door, she realized she'd forgotten about the buzz in her shirt pocket. Must have hung up.

Inside, the cool air blasted her, filling her with temporary bliss. She closed the door, let her eyelids fall, and leaned against it.

Then her phone buzzed again.

When she pulled it out, she saw that it wasn't her mother. Good. She might take this call, then.

In fact, the call had come from the VizionMe app on her phone.

"Oh shit," she said and crossed the room, fumbling for the phone and reaching for the headset on her kitchen counter. Thumbing the accept button, she strapped the headset on and powered it up.

"Hi, this is—dammit!" She dropped the phone, and it bounced once, twice, then landed at an angle on the cat's bowl, spilling kibble all over the phone. "Aw, shit."

Later. She'd deal with it later. Right now, someone needed some help.

Adjusting the headset, she got the speaker over her ear and bent the gooseneck microphone to her lips.

"Hi, hello, yes," she said, speaking as she picked up her phone from the floor. "I'm here. Who is this?"

The voice on the other end was laughing. "Hello. Seems like you and me are having the same sort of day, Ms. Dammit Awshit."

"Ha, it—the cat was, I mean, I was running before," she said, realizing she was still a bit winded. "Then, you know."

"Right, right," the voice said calmly. In the background, she could hear a strange alarm. *Blan-blan-blan.* "My name is Edgar. My visual impairment level is total. If you've got a moment, I could use your eyes."

"Yes, of course. Yes, that's what I'm here for." Tiffany grabbed a tea towel off the counter and wiped her forehead. She remembered then that she'd used it earlier to clean something up, something sticky, then stopped wiping and forced herself not to remember what that had been. "My name is actually Tiffany, not that other thing. I just lost it for the moment. How can I help, Edgar?"

Edgar said, "Well, I have an unusual situation here, Tiffany."

"Great," she said, her breathing finally slowing down. She stared at the screen as the camera icon swirled with the word "connecting." "I've got the usual situation here and can use the break."

"Happy to help. There's supposedly a keypad behind this panel in front of me. And I just—"

"Wait, what is that noise? I can hear it in the background."

"Oh, don't worry about that," Edgar said.

She tried to picture him. She could just ask him to point the camera at his face, but that would be weird.

"It's just a fire alarm."

"Fire alarm? Are you in danger?"

"Too early to tell," he said, chuckling into the phone. "But not from the fire. Fire's out. A bit of smoke, but we are fine."

We?

"Okay, where are you, Edgar?"

Another chuckle. "Well, I don't one hundred percent know that. I'd been on the elevator to the top floor of the building I do some cleaning in. Just before I got to the floor, the fire alarm went off, and the car went into emergency mode and took me down to the first floor."

Tiffany pulled on her lip, waiting for the camera to fire up. Why wouldn't it connect? Must be a bad signal.

"Do you need me to help you find the way out?"

"Ah, no. Not at the moment," Edgar said. Then Tiffany could hear another voice, distant and low. "This place, this building, was once some tech hub or something. They got new owners who changed the place up. I think I'm in what used to be their old subterranean basketball court."

"Subt... the elevator took you to the basement?" Tiffany asked, rounding the couch and sitting with a squeak. She threw the cat toy across the room, and it bounced off the wall with another squeak. "It should have brought you to the first floor. Are you—?"

"Don't worry about all that. My guess is the old tech guys monkeyed around with it. But that's neither here nor there."

"If there's a fire, Edgar, you gotta get out."

"No fire," he said, the smile still in his voice.

She liked his voice.

"Just need help with the panel. I can't get it open."

"It's just that the cam—" she said, and the screen came to life. The entire screen was washed in red light. "I got it. Show me the panel." She stared at the image. The caller moved the camera back and forth, but in the dim light, it was hard to make anything out. "Looks like just a wall. Are you sure—?"

Another voice called out, more distant. Edgar had had her on speaker. "*Yes. Panel in wall,*" the deep, craggy voice said.

"Is someone else there with you, Edgar?"

"Yeah, I'm trying to help him out."

"You're helping him?"

"Well, I think you're helping both of us," he said, the ever-present smile making his words sing. "He says there's a panel on this wall. It's hidden."

"Hidden panels? You live a life of mystery, Edgar," she said and turned up the brightness on her screen. "In front of you is a dark wall with large squares. I can see your hand on the wall, so... they're about two hand-lengths long and wide."

"Great. One of these is supposed to open," he said, pushing on one then another.

"Right, um, if they've got a hinge, it'll be on one side," Tiffany said. "Find an edge and press there. Then run your fingers across and try the other side. If one square doesn't—you got it!"

She saw a thumbs-up on the screen. That was when she noticed Edgar's hand was wet. "Are the sprinklers going off?"

"Yes, but it's all good. Didn't take a shower before I left."

Tiffany pulled her knees up and wrapped one arm around her legs. "Are you sure you're okay? You've got red lights and fire sprinklers going off. That doesn't seem like a good situation."

"I'm better off than the other guy," he said, chuckling, a deep rolling sound. "Can you tell me what's behind the panel?"

Tiffany squinted at the screen. It was dark, and the red lighting wasn't helping. "Can you turn on the flashlight on your phone?"

"Sure," Edgar said and swiped his phone.

Tiffany heard the voice-assist echo off the wall. "*Settings. Display-key-board-input-flashlight.*"

A moment later, the light came on, and she described what she saw.

"Okay. Okay. You've got another panel the size of a dual light switch. There are twelve buttons on it. Four across, three down."

Edgar sighed. "Ah, damn, don't tell me it's a keypad."

"Hmm. Not quite. No numbers. There are symbols on them but like... hieroglyphics or something. I can't tell—"

"Do you see anything that looks like... um... a bracelet? Or a cuff?"

"A what now?"

Edgar's phone shook as he spoke to the unseen person then came back. "Just anything that looks, I dunno, maybe circular?"

Tiffany put her face so close to the phone, her nose nearly shut down the app. She pulled it away slightly, squinting at the image. "There... yes, sort of. The top row, they all look like... um, the letter *C* but the open part is facing downward."

"Right," Edgar said. "You mean like the Greek letter omega?"

She smiled. "Been a long time since I wrote in Greek, but yeah, let's go with that," she said. Then she told him to move the phone down slightly. "Okay, the row under that, they're flipped over."

"Okay. So like the lowercase of the letter upsilon."

"It looks like the regular ol' letter *u*."

"Right. Same thing."

Tiffany frowned. "Then why didn't you just say 'letter *u*'?"

"I'm trying to impress you, I guess."

Before Tiffany could speak, she heard the man's voice in the distance again. "*Please stop flirting with lady phone voice. Manacles, please.*"

Tiffany thought, *Manacles? What the hell is going on?*

"Okay, okay," Edgar said. "So... as you look at those two rows, which do you think might... I mean, if you had, let's say, clamps or something, which ones would open the clamps?"

She put her feet on the floor then pulled them back again. Her heart began to beat a little faster. "Edgar, are you okay? This is just—"

"I promise you, I am fine, Dammit."

Tiffany frowned. "Now, I don't like to be cussed at. If we could—"

"No, that isn't any cuss," he said, the smile back. "Earlier, you said your name was Dammit Awshit. Maybe I was being a bit forward using your first name and all, but—"

"I told you, it's Tiffany. Stop playing, now," she said and stared at the images. "I can't tell which is, well, open and which is closed. Maybe facing down is closed?"

"Okay, let's try that," Edgar said, and a yell that sounded like a howl erupted from behind him. "That ain't it."

"Move your finger down one and try that."

He did.

She heard a raspy cheer go up off screen.

"You are an angel, Dammit," Edgar said.

"Stop calling me that, now," she said but knew the tone of her voice told him otherwise.

She watched his fingers dance over the pad, find the four buttons in the second row, and depress all of them at the same time.

His voice muffled, she heard him yell out, "Did that do it?"

"Yes. I am freed," the other man said.

What the hell was going on in that room?'

"Are you sure you're okay, Edgar?"

"Totally sure. I met a guy who needed a bit of help, and I think we're good."

"You need to get out of that building. Like now."

He turned the phone to his face, and Tiffany smiled. Edgar was a good-looking dude. And he didn't wear sunglasses, which she'd seen several blind people she'd helped over the past year do. His eyes were kind. His smile was beautiful.

"We're good, Tiffany. Just going to help my friend to the elevator, and we'll—"

"No, you can't take the elevator, Edgar," she said, rolling her eyes. "Fire alarms going off. Elevator won't work."

"Aw, shit."

Cocking her head, Tiffany said, "Um, that's Ms. Awshit to you, Edgar."

"Got you." The smile on his face dimmed a few degrees. "So how are we...?"

"Listen, if the elevator took you down to that floor, there'll be a way out," she said.

Edgar called over to the other man, who she hadn't seen yet. He spoke too low for her to hear it. Then he said, "Here?"

The camera dropped as the man ran his hand up and down the black wall, fingers probing and searching.

"Edgar? What are you looking for?"

As his palm swept left and right, he said, "There's a door here too."

"I just see more black squares. Not a—hold up. There's a black ridge about the size of a vape pen."

"Vape pen?"

"Up, up, right," she said, directing him. "There."

Edgar pulled on it, but it didn't open. He pushed on the panel next to it then another. Nothing.

His voice muffled again, he called out, "I think it's locked from the other side." Back to her, he said. "I gotta go, I think. We have to find—"

"I'm not leaving you there, now," she said. "If the lights came on, so will the emergency exit signs."

That got a laugh out of Edgar. "I don't think the folks who took over the building maintained emergency exits."

"Doesn't matter. When the building was constructed, it had to have them," she said. "Ask your friend if he sees the word 'exit' in red anywhere around the room. It'll be lit up."

He did and got back a growling response.

"Hmm. Yeah, he says he doesn't read so good."

"It's four letters!" Tiffany said, throwing her hand in the air. "Fine, fine. Point the camera around the room."

Edgar did as instructed. When she saw what she was looking for, she called out for him to stop. "See? I told you."

"All right!"

Tiffany told him to walk forward then hitch left a little to avoid some big metal apparatus she couldn't quite make out in the dim light. She could hear a shuffling off to his right. The other man.

"You need help?" Edgar asked the unseen man.

"No. I am fine. Ankle broken. Wrist broken."

"That does not sound fine, old man."

"Not old man. I am—"

Tiffany jumped in, "Hold up! You're about three or four feet away. The exit should just be in front of you."

Edgar ran his fingers over the panels, Tiffany directing him. No handle. She told him to push each of the black glass squares, and he did. Nothing.

"Point the camera higher," she said and he did. There was the exit sign, *behind* the black paneled glass. "Um, I think... the new owners put the black glass wall over the emergency exit. That's not—"

She never got to finish her sentence.

A fist came into view, smashing into the wall, which spiderwebbed and split. The hand splayed out, and she saw the other man, at least part of him, for the first time. Old guy with gray hair up and down his arms. His knuckles had split in places with the impact.

Then the hand pulled away and once again struck the wall. It shattered but didn't—

"Get back, Edgar," she shouted into the mouthpiece. "Take two or three steps straight back."

As he did, the wall collapsed, thick glass pieces falling away. She caught a glimpse of the other man, his foot suspended in air, hanging awkwardly. As if the man had sensed she was watching, he hopped back out of frame.

Edgar asked her, "What do you see?"

"Once you get out, I'm going to make some calls," Tiffany said, her free hand balling into a fist. "They can't build stuff in front of emergency exits. That's against—"

Edgar laughed. "Hold off on the call, I'm thinkin'. I'll send a memo or something. What do you see?"

"The glass wall has broken away, and there's a door just behind it. A horizontal bar down the middle, as an emergency exit should be. Give that a push, and it should take you outside."

"Is the, um, glass okay to go through?"

"Yes. Yes, it... Your friend bashed away a lot of it," she said, squinting at the red-tinted screen. "You should duck down a bit, but there's plenty of room. The hole is your basic omega shape."

"Is it now?" Edgar said, chuckling. "Thank you, Tiffany."

"You are welcome, and thank you for using my proper name, Edgar," she said then held her finger over the end call circle. "Hope we get to chat again."

"Yeah, I'd like that. Maybe under different circumstances."

She laughed. "I don't know what kind of circumstances you are in!"

"If I'm being honest," Edgar said, moving forward, "I really don't either."

Chapter Forty-One

Approaching the Covenant building, I found myself creeping along, holding my breath, as if the slightest twitch of a muscle might cause someone inside—if there was anyone inside this time of night—to see me and sound the alarm.

But someone had already sounded an alarm.

There was no sound, but there were spinning red lights at the top corners of the building. I wondered what that was about.

"No, you cannot," Gregor said behind me, making me jump. "Leave it alone!"

Marata growled, and I turned to see her scuffling with him as they walked.

I whispered as loudly as I could, "Would you two cut it out? We're trying to be stealthy here!"

"Go-juice empty," Marata said and pointed at the tech sergeant. "He has more."

Empty? That wasn't good.

"What do you mean empty? You finished all of it?"

The Enhanced woman leaped at Gregor, but he was too quick, stepping back and knocking her to the ground. Instantly, she was back on her feet again. Hands *and* feet, looking like a predatory animal hungry for a meal.

I stepped forward, waving my hands. "Marata, no," I said.

Too late. She leaped at him, legs and hands sprawled. This time, when Gregor swung, she was ready, ducking his blow and bashing him in the chest. Both tumbled to the dusty road, rolling end over end. When they stopped, Marata was sitting on his chest.

"Cut it out, Marata!" I said, trying to keep my voice calm. "No eating people. That's the rule."

She tilted her head at me, eyes searching the sky. "Who rule?"

"Just a basic rule. Really the biggest one there is," I said, trying to sound confident. "Don't eat your friends."

She sniffed a laugh. "Greg-gor not friend!"

The tech sergeant pushed her off as he stood. "That, we can agree on."

Marata flipped backward and landed on her hands and feet again. Why was she favoring all four limbs?

"I don't like being out here, exposed," I said, waving them forward. "Can we go?"

Gregor looked up at the building and, without a word, passed by me, heading toward the lot. Marata watched him go, her black eyes glassy.

"Are you going to be okay without that stuff—"

"Go-juice."

"Yes, yes," I said, motioning her to walk again. "Will you be okay without it for a while?"

She nodded and grunted.

"Good," I said.

"Just need to kill Gregor and drink his blood."

I sighed. "Can you wait until we save Kane, please?"

She shrugged then wobbled her head from side to side.

"Marata?" I said.

She trotted farther ahead. For a moment, I thought she was going to leap on Gregor again, but instead, she brushed past him, giving him a knock with her hip, and kept going until she reached the parking lot of the Covenant building.

When we caught up to her, she was standing upright, arms arched in the air, sniffing.

Standing just outside the lot's pool of light, I stared at the building. It stood at least five stories tall from what I could see. On the left side were some loading docks.

In front was the main entrance facing the parking lot. Opposite that ran a short road with an electronic gate that allowed or denied entry. I'd parked the Jeep a quarter mile away, and we'd hoofed it over.

"Great, now we're here," I said to Gregor, "how the hell do we get in?"

He crouched down, rubbing dirt between his hands. "Not through the front door. That keypad will have a code. Or a passcard. Or both."

I squinted "What keypad?"

"To the left of the door. Right under the 'No Sales. No Entry. No Trespassing' sign," he said, sniffing his fingers. "Through the glass... I can see at least one more entryway. Also with some sort of lock."

Taking a half step forward, I squinted. "How the hell can you see all that?"

"I am Enhanced," he said, but for the first time, that declaration hadn't been dripping with arrogance. When I looked at him, he wore no cocky smile.

"Okay," I said and threw my hand toward the building. "How do we get in?"

Marata took a few staggering steps forward, sniffing the air. I told her to stay back because we didn't want to be spotted. Not even looking, she waved her hand back as if she were shooing away a fluttering moth.

"I don't have any idea," Gregor said, slowly standing and brushing off his hands. "But you're clever, Emelda Thorne. You'll think of something."

I spun around. "What? I don't think you've ever said anything nice to me. Ever."

He grinned, the cocky expression back. "Well, I'm putting this impossible task on you. If we don't get in, it'll be your fault."

"Great. Great," I said, groaning. "It's not like I can just raise my hands and say 'Open sesame' and the place..."

To the left of the building, a red light grew larger and larger.

"Um," I said. "Okay."

We watched as a shadow ambled up a ramp, leading from beneath the building. The man there held something in his hand, waving it back and forth.

* * *

I stood there indecisively for about three seconds.

Then, I realized, hell, life gave me something to work with, and I didn't have anything else, so screw it. I ran for the red glowing chamber to hell.

Gregor called after me, "Where are you blah blah blah?"

He didn't actually say blah blah blah. That was only what I heard, because whatever derision he was hurling my way, I didn't need anything to fan the flames of doubt already raging in my head.

Crossing the parking lot, running full steam, I rounded the building in a wide arc. I didn't know if there might be cameras watching the lot.

"Hey!" I shouted, waving my arms.

But the guy coming up the ramp didn't even look over. His head twitched left and right, but it was as if he was searching for where the shouty girl might be.

Why isn't he looking at me?

When I got about fifty feet away, a woman hopped out of some kind of cleaning crew van, holding a weapon. She pointed it at me.

"Hold on!" she shouted. "Stay back!"

When I slowed but didn't stop, she lifted the strange weapon higher and said, "I mean it. Stop where you are!"

"Connie, you threatening people again?" the man on the ramp asked as he came up over the lip.

When I looked closer, I finally saw what was in his hand. Dude had some type of metal cane he was moving left and right in front of him.

"Hey, man," I said, finally stopping and breathing heavily. "Did you just come from inside?"

"I dunno. I didn't see a thing," he said and flashed me a sparkling grin.

Before I could say another word, the woman called Connie gripped her weapon tighter. "Don't talk to him. Stay where—"

"Is that...?" I said, pointing and staring. I noticed she had the same pack on her back as the guy with the tappy-tap stick. "Are you threatening me with an industrial vacuum cleaner?"

"No!" she said a bit too quickly.

This got the guy laughing, and she turned her attention to him.

"It's clear from where you are to me."

"Thank you kindly," he said and moved toward her voice.

She shot me a hateful glance then looked at her friend. "Why are you wet, Edgar? What happened?"

"I was in the elevator, heading up, when the fire alarm went off," he said, high-stepping toward her across the concrete. "Then the car stopped moving and slowly dropped to the bottom floor. A robot voice came on and said I should push the call button, and I must have hit every button *but* that one." He laughed as he reached his friend.

She put an arm out and embraced him. She was still pointing the tube of her vacuum cleaner at me, by the way.

"Ended up on the bottom floor," Edgar said, leaning against the van. "Some basement."

Connie nodded, keeping one eye on me. "You found a way out, so—"

"Nah, I didn't find a way out. Some old dude was in there. I mean, a dude hanging on a wall. You wouldn't have believ—"

"Wait, wait," I shouted, tears starting to bubble in my eyes. "Did you... I'm looking for my friend. Did you talk with him?"

"Leave us alone," Connie growled at me.

I ignored her. With my hands up—yeah, I knew it was a vacuum tube, but whatever I had to do—I walked closer.

"Those assholes trapped my friend inside. That's why I'm here," I said, and Edgar turned toward me. "Is he okay? Is he hurt?"

"You don't come any clos—" Connie said.

Edgar shushed her. "That dude got me out, so I owe him that much," he said to her. "Or I suppose we both got ourselves out. And I may have even met a girl in the process."

Connie and I both said, "What?"

For the next minute, Edgar explained what had happened. My heart broke and mended a thousand times in that minute.

As he spoke, Gregor slowly came up behind me, listening.

When Connie got a look at him, I saw her eyes widen. I'd forgotten how off the guy looked compared to normal people. She raised her vacuum tube. He gave her a crooked grin and flashed his hands to show he wasn't armed.

By the time Edgar finished, I was standing just a few feet away from him. Connie had finally dropped her "weapon" and attitude when she saw my damp eyes and red, blotchy face.

"Why would he go back inside?" I said, my voice a harsh whisper.

Edgar dabbed his damp face with a towel Connie had pulled from their van. "Dunno. Dude was kind of hard to understand. He sounded French."

"French Canadian," I said, but I have no idea why.

"Yeah, that's what I said." Edgar gave me a wry grin, then it fell away. "He said something about whatever they'd done was his fault. And that he needed to stop them."

"Who?" I stepped closer. "Stop who?"

"With the siren blaring and all the water raining down, I had a hard time making sense of it," Edgar said. "But he said something about blood and creatures or some crazy stuff like that. I have no idea—"

"Monsters," Gregor spoke from over my shoulder, and I jumped. "They've used Kane's blood to make more Enhanced."

I looked to the ramp and the blood-red lights spilling out from within, flashing like a warning. Danger.

"We've got to go get him," I said to Gregor.

The tech sergeant laughed. "Pulling Kane out is one thing. But if Hammer has a bunch of Enhanced in there? No way—"

I stepped forward, jamming a finger at his pointy nose. "I thought you were the best. You said you were one of the very best the program ever put out."

"True. Of course," he said, his eyes slits.

"Time to prove it," I said. "I'm going whether or not you're man enough to go."

"Whatever. Fine."

I looked past Gregor and into the dark lot beyond. "Where the hell did Marata go now?"

"I have no idea." He looked toward the ramp. "And don't really care."

Didn't matter now. It *would* matter later if she had run off into the city. Jesus, I hoped she hadn't. I spun back and asked Edgar if there was anything else he hadn't told me.

"Met a girl on the phone named Tiffany." He smiled wide. Guy had a great smile. "She sounded very cute."

Frowning, Connie punched him on the arm. "What girl?"

"Please!" I said, putting a palm between them. "Did you see which way he went?"

Edgar just stared past me, eyes pointing somewhere over my head, off in the distance.

"Okay. Okay. Poor choice of words," I said. "I'm sorry, I didn't mean—"

"Yeah, yeah," he said, the smile back. "I get what you mean. No offense taken."

"Thank you. Sorry."

"It's fine. Don't worry about it," he said, pointing back toward the ramp. "He's still down there, maybe. But halfway up the ramp, I was pretty sure I heard metal sliding against metal."

I gulped. "What does that mean?"

"I think he got into the elevator that took me to the bottom floor."

Chapter Forty-Two

Kane

Once again, I am trapped.

    A wolf in a box.

No. Not a wolf.

I stare at the strange mirrored wall and see an old man looking back at me. An old human man. Gray hair, dirty gray beard.

Where I once had power, shapely tone, and muscles, adored by all who laid eyes upon me, I am now sunken. Frail. Withered.

I had poured all my remaining strength into merely standing. But once I got imprisoned by my own hand, all that vitality bled out of me. Lying like a meat-sack beanbag chair, smashed into a corner of the very tiny prison, now, I cannot get away from my image.

This is a torture chamber.

Or my mind has finally cracked.

Everywhere I turn, it is the old man looking back.

Hollow eyes. A face that has forgotten how to smile. Even now, as he stares at me, his expression sours into a look of utter disgust.

He is right.

He is right.

I have become something vile. Low. Is it because I look like a bass player from a seventies arena-rock band? My father would have hated seeing me like this. In part because he hated bass players.

Thankfully, the red lights and sirens have stopped punishing me. They, too, felt like judgments, as if I had been on one of Mère's old game shows.

I shout to the indifferent universe, "Big money, big money, no whammies!"

But, alas, it is all whammies. I am swimming in whammies. Half naked, with gray hairs puffing from my chest. One half of my hospital pants torn.

Here I lie in whammie jammies.

But no.

No.

I must fix what I have done. Not by my hand but my blood. My choices. I trusted Ilsa Hammer, and she betrayed me. However, that is on me. My decision.

Within this building, somewhere, are monsters. Monsters that came from me.

"Do good work," *mon père* used to say to me.

With what little strength I have left, what shred of my will remains, I will do good work. Fail I might, but I will try to destroy the abominations created from my body.

As I roll up to my knees, my bones make strange cracking and popping sounds. So odd. How did the little cereal men, those three strange tiny people, get into my bones? What were they called?

It doesn't matter.

I will take them with me. Together we will—

"Arrggh!"

Pain shoots through my brain, turning my vision white. Instinctively, I stuff my hand beneath my armpit, coddling it there. Protecting it. Still, it screams with agony.

When I slowly pull it out, damp from my watered body and sweat, I see that the wrist has turned bright red. The hand itself hangs at an odd angle.

Broken. Crushed.

No matter.

The ankle on my opposite foot, this also is lame. But I will push forward. Fix what I have done. Rolling to the knee on my good leg—the one with the pant fabric—I lean upward. A long rail surrounds this room. What is the purpose of such a piece of metal in a tiny room like this?

I can only imagine that from here, they chain their prisoners. And yet, this is the room I stumbled into?

An open door had been awaiting me. Where the man with the metal stick had come from. He is gone now. Safe.

That is good.

However, the moment I went into the room, I saw no exit. The next moment, the silver doors slammed me within, sealing my fate.

Leaning forward, I paw at the doors, but there is no handle. Nowhere to grab. No way to force them open.

I must stand. That in itself would be a small win. I press my knee into the ugly carpet and thrust forward, too fast, and begin to fall like a building ready to topple.

Throwing my hands out to stop my collapse, I grab the silver wall again and howl in pain.

Behind my eyelids, I see an odd illumination. When I crack my eyes open, I see my finger has hit a circle. And now that circle *glows*?

What strange voodoo is this?

I squint because there is a number here. On a button. Which number is this? I know the difference between numbers and letters but don't know, don't know, don't know!

Calm.

Calm.

Number that looks like snake. What could—?

The room shudders.

I know what has happened. This room of torture was waiting for me to decide my fate. I lean back, arms wide, staring at the ceiling with its tiny recessed bulb, also mirrors up there, and await the snakes my choice has wrought.

They are coming.

I will fight them!

My legs feel heavy, pushing against my body. How is the room moving? Moving upward!

I stumble to my feet.

Wherever I am going in this movable room, I will fight these snakes with one arm if I must.

Chapter Forty-Three

We stood by the ramp, a gaping red mouth in a sea of darkness around us. However, the red flashing lights at the top corners of the building had stopped. Had they been on some sort of timer, or had someone shut them down?

I had no idea.

"Why would this place even have *whatever* this is?" I asked, staring down the ramp but not expecting an answer.

Gregor frowned, the blood-colored wash making the expression look more menacing than it normally was. "How would I know?"

"Zip it," I said. "It was a rhetorical question."

"Why do people even bother asking rhetorical questions?"

I looked over at him, a half second away from responding, then caught it. He saw my hesitation and couldn't stop the tiniest smile from tugging at the corner of his mouth.

"This is why no one likes you," I said and spun around, my arms folded. Where the hell did Marata go? Had I just unleashed yet another monster upon this world?

No time for that.

As I stared off into the dark beyond, Connie seemed to think I'd turned to her, waiting for an answer. Really, I was just stumped about what to do next. She answered my question.

"A few years back, this was some tech bro's place. Got gobbled up by some other big whale tech company or something," she said as she helped Edgar into the van. "I've never been down there, but I bummed a cigarette off a guard who said there used to be a basketball court at the bottom."

"Basketball court?" I asked.

"Yeah. Rich dudes, right?"

I pivoted and looked back into the angry mouth. The sprinklers within seemed like they'd just stopped, but moisture was still belching from below in a hazy steam. It looked like the open mouth of a dragon.

"What's there now?"

Connie slammed the passenger side door and crossed in front of the van. "Who knows?"

"Not a basketball court, that's for sure," Edgar said from the open window, his elbow resting casually on the door.

"Then what?"

He shrugged. "Don't know, but the old dude in there said he was, um, restrained. I found a way to get him free, and he must have found a way out."

"But he didn't come out!" I was exasperated. And obviously delaying going down into the devil's mouth.

"He said he had to fix what he did," Edgar said and tilted his head like this might be explanation enough. "Hard to tell with the accent."

I nodded then smiled at him. "Thank you for helping our friend."

"*De nada*. Be careful in there."

That got my eyebrows up. "Oh?"

Connie rounded the van and opened her door. "We only met one of the administrators, but these guys here are kind of next-level paranoid," she said and put a leg inside. "This was our only gig. They paid us really well, but I guess that's all over."

I shook myself lightly, preparing to go in. "Right. Thank you again. My friend's got a bit of cash, so maybe we could pay you, I dunno, a finder's fee or something. If you want to give me your number—"

Connie laughed. "I am not giving you our number. We don't want any more trouble than we've got."

"I've already got it," Gregor said over his shoulder.

I spun toward him. "You do?"

"What? You think you're psychic or something?" she said with a chuckle that had no humor in it. I'd already seen her looking at the tech sergeant strangely, noting that his arms were too long, his jaw bigger than it should be, and it would be hard to miss those eyes.

Maybe she thought he really had ESP or something.

"No," Gregor said and threw a thumb over his shoulder, not bothering to look. "It's written on the side of your van."

Connie and I tilted our heads and looked. Yep.

"Right," she said. "Please keep us out of whatever this is." She waved a hand in the air, fingers flicking like she was trying to get something nasty off them.

I watched her slam the door, fire up the van, and drive off without another word.

As she bounced through the parking lot, I suddenly wondered why the fire alarms had been going off but I hadn't seen any fire trucks barreling down the road toward us.

Whoever got the alert there was trouble, it seemed, wasn't the fire department.

Then the bleating siren inside stopped. The red light turned to a harsh white. My heart skipped a beat, because I felt like, the next moment, the ramp would close, and our only way in would be gone.

Without another word, I ran toward the opening, dipped my head low, and thumped down the metal ramp into the chamber below.

* * *

Of course, I had no illusions that I'd find Kane waiting there for me, that he would grab up his stuff, give me a big wave, and we could just leave the way we came.

What I saw crushed my heart.

The place was soaked, filled with the smell of damp concrete and oxidized air. I'd had to step over a big pile of thick, busted glass to get inside. Bending down, I could see some blood on a few of the sharp edges.

Gregor stood over me. "If he busted the damn glass wall out, why didn't he just leave?"

"Kane thinks he's got to fix something. Whatever that is."

A shadow passed over me, and I realized he'd stepped over my head to get farther inside. Rude.

Standing at the threshold, I just stared as the tech sergeant walked around, his boots making tiny splashes in the puddles that had formed on the bare floor.

If this had been a basketball court, at some point, the floorboards had been pulled out, exposing the concrete beneath.

On the right side was a wall of black glass. It looked similar to the pile of busted pieces where I crouched. Above us, the emergency lights had switched from red to piercing white. More lights glared from behind the wall.

It was hard to make out what was within, but if the thick glass weren't there, it seemed the upper half might be some sort of viewing area. Likely a hangover from when it had been a basketball court.

A faint column down the middle was a staircase that led from the one-time court to the seats above.

But through the glass, it didn't look like bench seating. More like an office. I could see desks and a fridge in the back. No people, though. That was good.

Why was I so focused on that side of the room?

Because the other side made me sick to my stomach.

On the opposite wall—not smooth glass but bare concrete—hung four metal brackets. Not brackets, of course. They were manacles. I tried swallowing, but my throat had gone dry.

"They hung him up there," I muttered. "Why would they...?"

A tiny popping sound snapped my head to the middle of the room. There, Gregor stood in front of a giant panel of stadium lighting. Just the one unit on a swivel arm in the middle of the floor.

The tech sergeant had pulled one of the massive bulbs out and dropped it on the floor. Bending forward, he prodded at a dark spot.

"What the hell is that?"

More glass tumbled away as he poked at it. He said, "Some of these bulbs were busted. There's a chain in here or something. And some ash and cloth." He stood straight and looked to the corners of the room. "That's probably where the smoke and fire came from."

I blinked away the blur from my eyes and smiled. "Kane started the fire," I said.

Gregor scoffed. "No, something must have..." But he didn't finish his sentence. Instead, he pointed up. "Cameras. I count at least five of them."

"So they were doing something to him here. Monitoring."

"Maybe, whatever," Gregor said. "Point is, we're on TV, Emelda Thorne. We can't stay here."

"Right, yes, totally." My brain back in gear, I crunched over the glass and jogged toward the far wall. I'd spotted the elevator that Edgar had mentioned. When I got there, I went to push the button.

But, of course, there was no button.

I scanned around, searching up and down. I ran my hand along its edges.

"Probably controlled by a remote," Gregor said in my ear, and I nearly peed myself.

I jammed a finger in his face. "Stop sneaking up on me!"

"I'm not sneaking up on you. You don't pay attention to your surroundings, Emelda Thorne," he said and stepped up to the closed elevator doors. "That's going to get you killed one day."

"Whatever," I said, stepping back as he examined the brushed steel. "You see a way to open them?"

"Nope." He turned and crossed his arms.

No joy there, so I ran past the busted stadium lighting to where I'd seen the staircase hidden behind the dark glass. I heard him crunching and splashing behind me.

At the wall, I ran my fingers around and found the edges of what seemed to be the way in. It looked like just another large rectangular panel of smoked glass. But how to get in? There had to be—

"Step back," Gregor said from behind me.

I did.

The tech sergeant looked up then down then left and right. He took a deep breath, stepped forward, and punched the glass wall. It cracked but didn't break. He straightened up, and with a grunt, he struck again.

The panel shattered, its pieces cascading down like rain, revealing a staircase behind it.

When I saw Gregor pulling glass shards out of his hand, I winced.

"Holy shit, man," I said. "That looks like it hurts."

"Not much." He was digging in his pocket with his other hand. Then he reached around and checked his other pocket. "Goddamn it."

"What?"

"Nothing," he said and flicked his fingers, spraying a line of blood across the concrete floor. "I must have left the syringe in the Jeep."

"You know," I said, stepping over the busted glass and starting my climb up the stairs, "that kind of forgetfulness will get you killed one day."

"You're probably right," he said. "As long as it's after I kill Doc Hammer, I'm good with that."

Chapter Forty-Four

I could smell the blood before I even got to the top of the landing. The three-tiered seating area had been converted into a small office space with desks. No tiny figurines or flowers. No pictures of family.

Just as I'd seen from below, there was a fridge in the back. A sink. Coffee pot. In the far corner, what looked like a computer monitor nestled into a long sheet of steel that ran floor to ceiling.

I saw six desks in three rows of two, one of them splattered with congealing blood.

"What the hell happened in here?"

Gregor breezed past me without a word. He'd spotted the door in the upper-left corner and was now a man on a mission. Whatever that was.

Part of me wanted to rummage around to work out what we were getting into. Not the tech sergeant. When he got to the exit, he reached out and hissed when his hand touched the door.

"What?" I said, trying to look around him. "Is it electrified or something?"

"No. It's fine." He levered the door open with his left hand while flexing and unflexing the fingers of his right.

I ran up behind him and saw a short, dark hall with another exit at the end.

Gregor strode through, thrust his shoulder into the door, and shoved it open.

"Jesus, man, slow down," I whispered, trailing after him. "We don't know what we're walking into."

What we'd walked into was impressive. Dark marble floors and massive columns stretched to the ceiling. I looked to my right and saw two steel doors. Somewhere beyond that lay the front entrance.

When we stepped farther into the atrium, our footsteps rang off the stone walls.

A long counter took up half the far wall. Walking closer, I could see the backs of three chairs on the other side. At each station was a large touchscreen showing a rotating image of a landscape.

"Huh," I said, walking up to one. "Even evil lairs use screen savers. Who knew?"

Gregor stood in the middle of the cavernous space, craning his neck back to look up.

Above us, four identical floors opened to the atrium below. Each had long, generic walls dotted with cheap art. At the far corners, hallways led into darkness.

Next to the door we'd come in was a stairwell leading up. Its twin was on the opposite wall.

I thumped one of the screens to life with the pad of my thumb and blinked at the image. Trying to swipe left or right didn't change it.

"What does it say?" Gregor asked, his voice raspy.

Tapping it a few more times, I got no response. Just the five tiny circles. Ah, right.

The top four were in a lopsided arch. Then a bottom circle on the left.

Holding out my hand, I hesitated as my thumb and fingers hovered over each of the five circles. Was this a dumb idea?

Ah hell, what did I have to lose?

The screen throbbed once, twice, three times, like a pulse, then the edges turned red.

ACCESS NOT AUTHORIZED.

"Yeah, no big shock," I said and turned around to look at Gregor.

He stood rigid, one leg back, one forward in a boxer's stance. His hands weren't fisted, but they were raised and ready for a fight.

"What are you doing?"

Gregor blinked. Then he blinked again, staring up at one of the floors. "Something's up there," he said. "I heard…"

I waited for him to finish. He didn't, so I asked, "Heard what?"

"Something. Damn ringing in my ears won't stop. I have no—"

At the sound of an echoing scream, I nearly pissed myself. I ducked then realized I'd recognized that scream. It was mine.

When I spun back to the desk, all three monitors there were showing a movie. No, not a movie.

I walked up to the middle screen, frowning. "Some security feed," I said. "That's from the zoo."

On the screen, I saw the nighttime images of me running full tilt from one camera angle to another and another. The screen froze momentarily, and I saw me and Gregor disappearing inside the Visitors' Center and slamming the door.

A second later, the Enhanced monkey raced in and smashed against it. The creature stalked back and forth for a moment. Then the screen flipped back to the five circles once again.

"I thought for sure that you'd have been chewed to bits by our pets," a voice called down from the second floor. "We made bets here. I lost five bucks."

Ilsa Hammer stepped forward, her hair pulled into that severe ponytail, looking down at us. Despite her attempts at a perfect appearance, even from here, I could see that she had been rousted out of bed when the alarms had gone off.

"Where is he?" I shouted up at her.

"Our zookeeper?" she asked with an expression of mock concern. "Yes, you're right. He should not have helped you. That would normally go on his upcoming performance review: Does not meet expectations. But after we're done here, I'll just have him fired. Or rather, terminated."

"Doc Hammer," Gregor said, his hands now balled into fists. "You look awful."

"You look far worse, Tech Sergeant." She grinned down at him. "Yeah, a bit of trouble at work, you see. I'd only been sleeping for an hour and had to race back in to take care of a minor issue. Which I'll do now."

Hammer grinned as she held out a computer tablet, thumping the screen with big, swooping gestures.

On three sides of the atrium, paneling slid away to reveal steel doors. In the huge cavernous space, I could hear the echoing whir of motors. A moment later, the doors opened.

From the elevators, five Enhanced soldiers stepped out, dressed in military fatigues, their too-large eyes black as death. Their mouths hung open, and spittle drizzled through sharp teeth, dripping onto the stone floor.

They looked more animal than the others I'd seen before. Their faces were narrower and more angular, and their ears sat farther back.

The claws at the ends of their fingers were twice the size of Gregor's. I turned to look at the tech sergeant.

He scowled at the pair closest to him. He'd always seen himself as the alpha Enhanced soldier. Well, maybe the beta after Cal Davis. But now, with Cal gone, he was the apex predator of this world.

Not anymore.

These five were larger, stronger, and more lethal. Like Gregor, they sported short-cropped hair. Several of them had vaguely feminine features.

As the two nearest me advanced, one of them growled. Its teeth were familiar. Nowhere near human. More like—

"I'll give you a chance to live," Hammer said, shrugging nonchalantly. "Join me, and you won't die here."

I shot her the finger and shouted, "No way, you asshole. Why would I—?"

"Ha! Oh god, no." Hammer laughed and winced like she'd just sucked down a mouthful of curdled milk. "Not *you*. Gregor, you've been disowned by the Organization. Rumor has it, they kind of want you dead. But you were always loyal. Come work for me with Covenant."

The tech sergeant took a half step forward, shot me a glance, then looked up again at her without saying a word.

"Of course, you would be required to wear some new jewelry my people have designed. Very effective," she said, nodding to the five snarling creatures in front of us. Just below their jaws, I could see a series of flickering lights.

Collars like the ones that had kept the animals at the zoo in line. Their torturous experiments on those creatures hadn't really ended a year earlier. They'd used them to develop the collars.

Now she'd put those devices on people.

Not people, no.

"I will agree to your terms under one condition," Gregor shouted up to Hammer and turned to me with hooded eyes.

I shot back a look that could have melted granite. "You prick," I whispered, slowly shaking my head.

Above us, Hammer shrugged. "Name it."

"I'll sign on," he said, his signature singsong voice returning, "if I'm permitted to cut off your head, prop it up on a broom handle, and use that fucking ponytail to clean out the cobwebs in my apartment."

I couldn't help it. I busted out laughing, partially out of relief and partially because *that* was a hell of an image!

Hammer just sighed and lifted her tablet. "Fine. Have it your way."

She tapped away at her device, and the creatures in front of us shifted their weight, the collars at their necks dancing with light. I heard a slight buzzing sound as each rattled.

Blam-blam-blam!

I flinched, going down on one knee to prevent myself from falling over entirely. The sound of the handgun left my ears ringing.

Gregor stood there, his pistol trained on the three Enhanced soldiers he hadn't yet shot. They looked toward their comrades, who each had a hole in his or her chest and was howling in pain.

Yeah. *Howling.*

Then, in unison, they stopped their keening, flexed their arms, and roared back at the tech sergeant. The blood flow on their chests stopped. In the one nearest to me, I saw the dark hole in the tissue begin to knit itself back together.

Gregor fired a round into a fourth creature, this time hitting it in the skull. I heard the bullet ping off the far wall. It had ricocheted off the monster's head, leaving only a bloody line across its brow.

Like the other three, tendrils flickered and danced in the air, and the skin began to repair itself. Within a few seconds, it was like she'd never been shot at all.

As she grinned at me with those animal teeth, I saw something just past her shoulder, moving fast. A high-pitched battle cry split the air.

All five turned and looked at Marata as she landed on all fours. She sneered at each of them, the fabric of her dirty lab coat brushing against the stone floor.

"What the fuck, now?" Hammer said, trying to lean over the rail and see what was happening.

That was my chance.

Crouched on the floor, I reached around to the back of my pants with my right arm, and with my left, I dug into my thick sock and gripped one of the three long metal tubes I'd stuffed there.

I brought the slingdart around and slapped an arrow into place. Lifting it at a forty-five-degree angle, I fired.

Hammer, trying to peer into the chaos below, never saw it coming. She wailed as the steel dart pierced her shoulder, which burst red with blood. She lost the grip on the tablet in her hands, and it tumbled, smashing onto the marble below.

The Enhanced soldiers didn't even budge, apparently locked onto the last order they'd been given through the collars. They crouched, ready to pounce on Marata.

She sniffed the air then lifted her head and sniffed again.

Above, Hammer tilted forward, the red oozing from her shoulder and dripping down her arm.

I screamed in my mind, *Just fall! Just fall, you asshole!*

But she didn't.

She let out a low yelp as she fingered the dart in her shoulder and stumbled back. I heard her collapse, her moans echoing through the atrium.

The Enhanced on the far left lifted its face to the air and began sucking in breaths. Then, it broke away from the group and bounded up the stairs, heading toward the woman who was wailing in pain.

Seeing his chance, Gregor chased after it. I knew he wanted to get to her first.

"Dammit, Gregor!" I shouted as I jammed another dart into place.

Fine. I was ready for a fight. But then my heart froze when I caught the look on Marata's face.

"No," I said in a strained, pitiful whisper. "Marata, no."

She sniffed the floor around the remaining creatures then stood, arms hanging at her sides. In turn, they drew in her scent.

All four then turned toward me, snarling.

No. Not four.

Five.

"Marata!" I said, my eyes filling with tears. "You... you can't. Please!"

Frowning at me, she slowly shook her head, looking more animal than before.

"They are we." She pointed at me with a sharp claw. "You are not we."

I swallowed hard and shook my head, slipping a hand down to my ankle. "No, no, no! We're *friends*. I saved you from that awful place! Don't you remember?"

Marata blinked and looked down, and a confused expression passed over her face. One of the Enhanced put a clawed hand on her shoulder. When she looked at him, I knew I had lost her.

Pulling my hand up, I slammed the steel arrow into my slingdart and, in one quick move, pulled the rubber cord back and fired it at the closest monster. It sailed right for the chest, center mass, but then it stopped.

Midair.

The creature turned the arrow in its hand and stared at it. How had he grabbed it so fast? I hadn't even seen it move.

Marata snarled. She then blinked and rubbed her eyes.

Above us on the second floor, I could hear a scream. Not Hammer's this time. It was Gregor.

Marata took a half step back as if searching for the source of the scream. No, she was *sniffing* at the air. It wasn't the sound that had caught her attention.

Then I heard it.

The low grumbling. The deep, rumbling tones. A throaty growl that had come from the darkness above.

One floor up from Hammer, I stared up at a figure. A massive human being I knew to be six-foot seven and French Canadian. But... *but*...

"Oh, Kane," I said, my voice cracking. "What have they done to you?"

Slouched over the edge of the railing, he looked ancient. His once-black beard was now a mottle of white and gray. His skin hung over his arm, loose and wrinkled. When he looked at me, he smiled, his face creased and sunken. But those eyes, those amber eyes, were still Kane.

He looked *ninety*. Barely able to stand, he called out, but the sound of it was hollow and thin, dying in his throat. My friend leaned forward, arms hanging down over the railing. His shoulders hitched.

"Kane, wait, what are you—?"

From the third floor, he lifted himself with a grunt and dropped. All I could do was watch. There was no way he'd survive the fall.

But instead of smashing onto the hard stone floor, he landed on a softer surface. Three of the monsters tumbled to the floor under the impact.

The Enhanced wailed in pain and frustration. Another, still standing, looked at me. She'd seen her meal and was happy for the others to take care of the new guy.

"Marata!" I shouted, standing and shuffling a few steps back. "Marata! Help me."

She couldn't look at me. Her eyes darted around, watery.

"Then help…" I said, my voice watery sounding, "then help Kane!"

"K-Kane?" Marata cocked her head, confused.

The three creatures my friend had knocked down leaped back up and pounced on Kane as he'd stood, leaning heavily on one foot. One caught him in the flank and once again, they tumbled to the floor. I watched as he tried to swing his bony arm, but the Enhanced easily blocked it.

When the other two crept forward, the one pinning Kane growled for them to stay back.

With the monster soldier stalking me, relishing the smell of my fear, I shouted to Marata, "He is we! Kane is we, Marata!"

She looked around and sniffed the air again. Then her jaw dropped, and she jammed her hands into her coat, flapping them excitedly like some strange bird.

Over the shoulder of the approaching monster, I saw Marata jump into the air. She'd pulled a small knife from her pocket and was aiming for the monster pinning Kane.

Then, I realized I was wrong.

"No…" I said as my back hit a thick marble column. There was nowhere left for me to run.

As she landed with her weapon, she didn't attack the Enhanced soldier. She stabbed Kane, who buckled and wailed at the impact. The knife stuck out of his shoulder, and she reached for it to stab him again.

No. She didn't lift it. She *pushed* it.

The handle of the knife moved as if retracting into the blade.

My eyes went wide. It wasn't a knife. It was one of Gregor's syringes.

Marata raised her arms in the air and shouted, "Go-juice!"

Chapter Forty-Five

Kane

My paper-thin skin puckers as I feel what must be a killing blow. The strange knife buries deep into my shoulder and drives broken-glass spikes of pain up my neck. My brain clutches into a fist, and my ears ring. A high-pitched whine that rises and rises and rises until I hear nothing else but the song of my defeat.

In my lesser state, I knew this to be impossible.

So many of them, and I am now a withered old man.

However, my death could give Emelda a chance to escape. Flee this awful place. I know she has come to save me, so brave, but soon our pack of two will be one.

Strangely, the fire in my shoulder grows, burning hotter each second. The whining in my ears is drowned out by a roaring, *roaring*, in my mind.

The flames within explode from my shoulder and surge through my extremities, pulsing and searing across my body. An old man's feeble arms stiffen and throb. Legs flex and grow. My mouth aches as my teeth enlarge, and *I relish the pain of it.*

Eyes clear, and I can see graying skin give way to twisting purple-black flesh. Power flows through me as my muscles bulge and my senses sharpen.

The roaring in my brain now fuels my heart. The beating heart of a warrior once again.

I am wolf.

No. I am the wolfwere.

When I look up, the monster soldier upon me has its teeth bared. I grip the upper and lower jaw, and spread my arms, sending the top half of its skull clattering across the floor. Its blood has splattered across my chest, and the scent of it is intoxicating.

I leap to my feet, ready to challenge the other two Enhanced soldiers. A squeal, just behind me, catches my attention. But I cannot turn from my foes.

"You are we!" The voice cries out, then the slapping of feet. Whoever spoke those words is gone.

The next soldier leaps from its crouch. This is good. Had they attacked as one, this would have been far more difficult. But they are not a pack. They are mindless drones.

But deadly nonetheless.

I twist my body to let it pass, and, towering over the other creature, I thrust my hands forward, anticipating the charge of its brethren. Catching it midair, my claws raise up and pierce its neck. The monster's black eyes go wide and unsure then roll back.

Its lip twitches with a question, never spoken.

A scuttling behind me.

Dropping to a knee, I spin the limp body toward the first attacker, knocking the monster out of the air, and it smashes into the far wall. The creature I'd used as a weapon, dangling from my claws, now feels lighter.

When I look to my hands, dead eyes stare back.

Then I notice its body a few feet away. I chuck the head over my shoulder and run toward the downed attacker, leaping into the air with my fist raised.

Its eyes widen as I come down.

"Knock, knock!"

My fist smashes into the stone floor, but it has gone through the chest of the creature to do so. I pull my hand out and flick the blood and gore away.

"Kane!"

Before Emelda can cry out a second time, I leap again to cross the room and land on the shoulders of the Enhanced woman reaching for her.

"Oooofff!" the soldier cries out but does not fall. She braces against my weight and reaches up to slash me with her claws.

I dig my own in. *The piggies are so powerful now!*

My talons hook into her back and shoulder flesh as she swipes at me, trying to stop the attack. Too late. Gripping tighter, I reach down and grip her jaw, twisting.

Like batteries pulled from a toy, she collapses, and I tumble to the floor. When I spin around, only her dead eyes stare back.

I feel a hand on the fur of my back, but I know this touch. And I have missed it.

Emelda says to me, "Hiya, Kane."

Chapter Forty-Six

Kane put a clawed hand out, indicating I should stay back for the moment.

I did.

"I would prefer you not watch me do this," he said in a voice that wrapped me in an audible bear hug. His massive body hovered over one of the dead monsters sprawled in a heap on the floor. He bent to a knee as if he were about to subjugate himself to some benevolent god, then lowered his mouth to the bloodied corpse.

"Okey dokey," I said, catching the sight of Gregor stumbling down the stairs. When he bumped against the stairwell, I saw what looked like a bag under his arm. Without turning back, I said to my friend, "Hey, Kane?"

He smiled at me, and my heart sang. "Yes, Emelda."

"Good to see ya."

My friend let out a low chuckle and began to drink.

"You asshole," I shouted at Gregor, pointing at him. In my other hand, I gripped my slingdart and considered smashing him over the head with it. "You just left me to—"

He fell the last three steps, his feet buckling beneath him. The bag he'd been holding bounced, once, twice, three times, then rolled across the marble floor.

My stomach twisted. The bag's black eyes stared up at me. Yeah, not a bag.

"You yanked off its head?" I said, grimacing at the face of the Enhanced soldier, its tongue lolling out. I looked across the room where another skull lay on the marble floor. "What's with you two and head pulling? So gross, man!"

Gregor had landed on his back and leaned up against the side of the stairwell. He chuckled.

"Only way... the damn thing would die," he said, his damp breaths coming in heaves.

I nodded, softening my tone. "Doc Hammer?"

He pointed at the head. "That's why I killed him. He got to her first." He laughed, and a fine, red mist hung in the air for a moment then drifted onto his tight T-shirt. "She'll bleed out, so I left her to die."

I gave him a wan smile. "Well, you're showing restraint. Pretty human for a monster."

"No, I wanted her to suffer more."

"Hmm... also kind of human, actually."

He pointed at the head again. "*They* are farthest from that." He winced, holding a dark patch on his side. Blood seeped through his clenched fingers. "They're so strong, so fast. Different somehow. They're—"

"I think they come from Kane," I said. "His blood."

A man's words echoed off the walls. "Better! So much better!"

I turned toward the sound of the strange voice. Kane, blood covering his wolfwere face, looked up, pushing red fingertips to his mouth.

At the long, stone reception counter, I saw a face.

A man, maybe in his midfifties, appeared on all three screens, his head, oddly, just floating in the middle of the space, surrounded by black and shades of red.

"Can they hear me?" The big floating head said, looking somewhere off screen. "I don't think they can hear me. What?"

I stepped forward. "Who the hell are you?"

"Ah, yes," the man said to someone off screen. "The mousy one just spoke. I think you've fixed it."

"Who the hell you calling mousy?"

Gregor cried out in pain, but when I turned, he held up his free hand and just shook his head.

"Okay, listen, I'm very busy. All this business," the man on the screen said, waving his hand. "So much mess and trouble. Needs to end. I have other things to attend to."

"Screw you," I said and punched the middle screen, smashing it.

That really, *really* hurt my hand. Not broken but damn it hurt like a mother!

"It would be better for everyone if all of you just... went away," the head said from the remaining two screens. I was wondering how he was seeing us. Cameras above?

Walking to the left screen, I glared at the guy. As he moved, hints of a suit and tie warbled in and out of sight, like he was using some crappy Zoom green screen. The dude oozed corporate asshole.

"We're looking for something," I said, jamming a finger at the screen. "A way to—"

The head was joined by a floating hand, gold cuff links sparking from some overhead light. He waved away my words, interrupting me. "Yes, yes. To make your friend human again, I know, I know. I saw all that in some memo or something."

Human, no. But I wasn't going to split hairs with the guy. I listened.

"Thanks to your dying compatriot there, we got what we'd been searching for," the man on the screen said, hooking a finger to point behind me. I turned and looked at Gregor, raising my hands as if to say, *What does that mean?* He looked away. The man on the screen continued. "A loyal little soldier, he uploaded the data that had been stored at Dr. Pental's home. Damn near burned to death while doing it. That was a goldmine!"

I took a few steps forward, toward Gregor, my fingernails digging into my palms.

"Wait, you *had* it all this time? You had the cure for—"

Gregor held up his bloodied hand, shaking his head. "No. No. Uploaded it... to the Organization. They have—"

"Ah, no, actually," the head's voice sang out, and I turned back toward the screen. "We had a digital net around that entire farm house. The whole property. When you sent out those valuable details, all that lovely data, we snatched it."

"We want it!" I shouted, spinning back and holding a fist at the left screen. "Give it to us now, or—"

"Fine, yes. You can have it."

I stopped and looked over at Kane, who slurped from a piece of ear. Blech. He looked at the screen then back at me, waving his hands, encouraging me to speak further.

"Okay," I said, leaning down to the screen. "What's the catch?"

"No catch, Emelda," the man said, with a big car salesman's smile. "We just want you to go away. Because of your efforts, we have everything we need! Consider our disagreement with you at an end."

"Screw you!" I shouted and smashed the screen with the handle of my slingdart. It went dark.

The voice from the third screen *tsked* at me. Dude actually went *tsk-tsk-tsk*.

"Without you, I doubt we'd have ever discovered the location of the creator of the program. The people I put onto that task? So disappointing. Heads will roll, I can assure you."

I looked to the floor, and the Enhanced soldier's dead eyes stared up at me.

"Fine, great," I said to the prick on the screen. "So you've got it now, and—"

"Not just that." The face leaned closer to the lens, the eyes growing larger. "So much more. The compounds from your big friend's blood are even better than Dr. Pental created! Next level, as you kids say. His body *made* them better."

The screen flipped to a drone-shot video of three green airplane hangars nestled in the lush foliage of what appeared to be a crater at the top of a mountain. As the camera angle rose, it revealed blue sky and a valley below. Far off in the distance, hazy buildings, one with tall pink spires. In the foreground, tiny people in lab coats shuffled from building to building.

Two of the workers were pushing a gurney. Atop that was a large humanoid creature with an IV drip feeding its arm. The late afternoon light flickered off the restraints around its wrists and ankles.

"You're making more of them," I said through gritted teeth.

"And thanks to your friend's blood, far superior to any cohort before. Nature is an alchemist!" The man on the screen blinked and looked off screen. "Oh, I like the sound of that. Nature is an alchemist. Write that down somewhere so I don't forget it. Hmm, yes."

To my left, I heard Kane groan. When I looked at him, he slowly shook his head.

"Is my fault. Yes?"

"No, Kane," I said then held up a hand to him. I mouthed *Talk later*. "So, where's this cure you're promising?"

"In the next room over from where you're standing. You, um, came through it to get to where you are now," the corporate guy said. He sounded distracted, like he was focusing on some other action item in his agenda. "But, no, it's not a cure. Can't cure a virus, but we can stop... um... technical mumbo jumbo stuff. Whatever, but it will render the virus and its manipulations within dormant. Then the Enhanced become, um, normal. Or whatever."

I looked at Kane then back to the man on the screen. "Bullshit."

"No, no. Not at all," he said and lifted a hand casually. "Go see for yourself. The new compound is secured in a wall safe. Black panel thing."

I'd remembered seeing that in the corner of the room. Not a monitor. Wall safe.

"All you need is Ilsa Hammer's fingerprints, and it will pop right open. There should be two or three doses in there. Give one to your weird-looking friend and the effect, I'm told, is almost immediate."

I blinked and looked up to the second floor where Hammer had been killed. Well, if we just needed the fingers...

"I don't trust you people," I said, frowning at the screen. "Covenant has made promises before and lied."

"Why would I? More than *anything*, I want your friend to use it."

"Why?"

"Because outside of decapitation," the head said, with a frown and an accusing finger that pointed behind me at Gregor, "the next-gen Enhanced are unstoppable! Well, they were until your friend dissected four of them. Once he's gone, they're, um, back to the unstoppable thing. So please, yes, take the compound and go back to the squalid life you lived before."

"How do we know it won't just kill Kane?" I said, frowning at the screen. "I can't take your *word* it'll work. I don't even know who you are!"

The head leaned into the frame. "My name is Steve Janus," he said, raising an eyebrow. "No? Doesn't ring a bell? Well, I was once quite well-known in some retail circles. No matter. What I'm telling you is true. No use in my lying to you."

"I just—"

"Sorry, I've got another appointment," he said, waving a finger in the air in a circle. "No more time to chat. Bye now."

With that, the screen went blank.

Chapter Forty-Seven

"Put... m-me down," Ilsa Hammer said, her eyes blazing at me as her head bounced on Kane's shoulder.

"Gladly," I said and tapped the arm of my very large friend, who dumped her on the floor next to the wall safe. The black hair of Kane's shoulder was slick with her blood. She had slashes across her chest, neck, and face.

Still, that damn ponytail remained perfectly in place. Maybe I'd cut it off and make a keychain.

"Okay, put your hand on the screen," I said.

She spat out blood. "N-no."

"Fine." I turned to Kane. "Rip her hand off so we can put it on the screen."

"*No*, all right," Hammer said. She lifted her hand and stared at her own trembling fingers, as if mesmerized by them. Like they were somehow alien.

I grabbed her elbow and pressed her palm to the glass. I had to push her fingers into the five circles.

The first attempt got me a red screen and a buzzer.

"Dammit, hold on," I said and rubbed her fingertips across her hair to get the blood off. I placed them back upon the circles.

Buzzt.

"H-h-ha," she said, red-streaked drool dribbling down to her chin. "J-J-Janus... locked y-you... oww-t."

"No," Kane said in a voice that sounded like it had come from the bottom of a dry pit. I turned to him. As the wolfwere, he was taller than the room and had to bend forward just to stand upright. His neck had to be as thick as my thigh. Atop that, a muzzle of teeth framed by purple lips that would have sent any sane person running.

But, as always, his amber eyes told a different story. Kind and warm. And, at that moment, sad.

"She is changing," he continued. "The virus has taken hold."

Of course, he was right. Doc Hammer's jaw was beginning to spread. Her fingernails were growing thicker as they transitioned into yellowed claws.

I sighed. "The screen doesn't recognize your fingerprints. They don't match anymore."

She shook her head, her grin fading. "N-n-no. Janus, h-he cha-changed... it."

I bent down and looked into her near-black eyes. "No, you are becoming a monster."

Hammer tried to laugh, but it came out weird. Distorted. When her gaze shifted away from mine, I realized she'd already known. "Then, y-y-y-you will not get inside. Safe is imp-imp-imp...'"

I didn't even flinch when the massive black paw swung over my head and smashed the screen. The glass shattered. The safe wall behind it bent inward like a metal flower growing in the darkness.

Kane reached in, pulled out a black case the size of a hardcover book, and handed it to me. Just as Steve Janus had said, there were syringes inside. I held one up to the light and stared at the dark yellow liquid within.

Searching for this magic elixir, we'd traveled thousands of miles. Been shot at, nearly burnt to death, and electrocuted. I'd been hunted by monsters and clandestine paramilitary outfits and nearly been eaten by a hippo that could burrow underground.

I looked up to my friend, then down the stairs that cut between the office desks. Through the jagged hole that Gregor had smashed in the dark glass, I saw a black stain about the size of a six-foot-seven man, framed by four open manacles. Kane hadn't yet told me what he'd endured when held captive. There would be time for that later.

"I'm worried it's a trick," I said, staring into the yellow serum. I twisted my head up to see Kane's face. "I mean, it could be poison."

Hammer waved her long fingers in front of my face to get my attention. When I stared at them, she snapped her hand back.

"Y-you to test," she said, struggling to get her tongue to behave. "Test it out on me. Y—yes."

"That's an idea," I said, and her face lit up. I looked at Kane. "But not on her."

Chapter Forty-Eight

"You got what you wanted, Gregor," I said, leaning over the dying Enhanced soldier. I had one hand up on the stairwell wall to balance. In the other, I held the syringe. "I helped get you here, so can you at least do this one thing?"

"I did *not* get what I wanted, Emelda Thorne," he said, his voice sounding like two steel wool pads being rubbed together. Where his fingers holding his side hadn't been stained red, the flesh had turned pale. The once gushing wound had turned to a trickle. "I heard her complaining as your boy stepped over me to carry her from the upper floor. Doc Hammer needs to be dead."

"I've got a better plan for her. I promise."

The tech sergeant stared at the needle in my hand, his face bent in a frown.

"You're out of your go-juice," I said with a crooked smile. "And I'm not dragging dead bodies to you again. Once was enough."

His black eyes stared at the yellow liquid in the tube, and he let out a long, damp breath. "I don't want that anyhow. I'm tired. I'm done." He raised an eyebrow, his decision made. "I can face death and go out like a man."

I laughed. "You'll go out as an asshole," I said. "But, yeah, a human one. *If* this works."

"That's your sales pitch?" He chuckled and coughed out red mist. "It needs work."

Spinning the needle around, I held the thin metal fang above his arm. When I looked at him, he gave me the slightest nod. As I stared into those oil-black eyes, a question in the back of my mind made its way to the front.

"When we were going down the dark steps into the underground bunker at the zoo, you didn't need the light did you? You turned that on so I didn't trip. Why?"

He tried to shrug but only managed a slight twitch of his shoulder. "Needed you ahead of me. If Marata got hungry, you'd be first on the menu."

"Uh-huh, right. You know, if you and I had met in the street without all this stuff going on," I said, nodded, and pressed the needle tip to his skin, "I'd probably have run you down with my car and backed over your corpse."

The tech sergeant gave me a blood-soaked smile. "Good. You're finally getting the hang of this world."

I laughed and jabbed him with the needle, depressing the plunger.

Gregor buckled and coughed. As his eyes slammed closed, his mouth sprung open in a silent scream. His entire body began to shake so violently I had to step away, pressing myself against the opposite stairwell wall.

I watched as he seized and shook and flopped around. Then, like a switch had been thrown, it all stopped.

For the first time, he looked like a young man. A man who'd made so many wrong choices he'd been so sure were right. That very notion had led to the death of countless nations since the dawn of civilization.

I supposed the world had gotten lucky. His bad decisions had only ended himself.

Gregor exhaled his last breath and, as he died, stared up at me with emerald-green eyes.

Chapter Forty-Nine

When I got back to Kane, he was staring down at Hammer, large hairy arms crossed over his barrel chest, as she lay slumped against the wall. Despite all she had done to him, whatever that was, he looked concerned.

Sure, she didn't look so hot. Her breathing had changed to panting. Her face was flushed and damp with sweat. The woman's legs poked out from under her gray skirt, twitching and flexing, as if she were trying to run in place.

I could see striations in the skin on her thighs as her limbs began elongating. She was becoming one of the beasts she had created.

"It worked," I said, smiling at my friend. I strode over to the nearby desk where I'd left the black case. I pulled out a full syringe. "You ready for this?"

"Tech Sergeant Gregor is now cured?" Kane asked, his pupils shrinking to pinpricks. "He is human once again?"

I smiled. "Happened right before my eyes," I said. My grinned dimmed slightly. "Uh, right before he died."

My wolfwere friend laughed, baring his teeth. "A strange cure, then."

"He died from his *injuries*, Kane." I put a gentle hand on his muscular arm, and the purple-black skin rippling at my touch. "After he'd become human again."

"Wait," he said. "Will this make me human or wolf?"

"W-w-what?" Hammer said, her darkening eyes bouncing between the two of us as she struggled to control her body.

"I don't know," I said, shrugging. "But that Janus dude said it would return you to what you were before, right?"

When I leaned forward, holding the needle above his arm, Kane shook his head.

"No. No. I cannot."

"Kane, we've come all this way. This is what you wanted!"

"Yes, but I cannot. Those creatures in that video, they are from my blood. I am responsible. As the floating head said, I am their only threat. I must destroy them first." He put his hand on mine and gently pushed the syringe away. "Then we can do this. End this."

I sighed, took a few steps back, and sat on the edge of the desk. I rolled my eyes.

"How did I know you were going to say something stupid like that?" I muttered, took a deep breath, and blew it out slowly. "Well, you can't go all that way on your own. You couldn't even drive across the parking lot without crashing!"

He smiled at me. Sure, he had twice the teeth I did, but in its own way, it was beautiful. Terrifying, but beautiful.

"Fine. Okay," I said. "We'll do it together."

"Of course. We are a pack of two."

Spinning around, I put the syringe back into its black case and closed the lid.

"Y-you d-d-don't need both," Doc Hammer said, her voice coming in grunts. "Give me the other, and I promise you—"

"No," I said.

She glared at me with eyes that looked all pupil. I smiled when I noticed a tiny strand of hair had wriggled out of her perfect ponytail and clung to her damp face.

With the case under my arm, I said to Kane, "You ready for another long-ass drive?"

"I do not think," he said, looking down at his body, "I will fit in your puny Jeep."

"We'll work it out. Maybe I'll tie you to the roof?" I said, stepping closer to him. "I'm gonna need a passport, but I know a guy who knows a guy back in Minneapolis. I'll need one before we head across the border."

Kane raised his thick, furry brow. "We return to my homeland, yes? Back to Canada. This is good. You have yet to try poutine."

"Another time," I said and grabbed my slingdart from where I'd left it on the counter. "In that video Janus showed us, I recognized a building off in the distance. It's a big pink cathedral in San Miguel. I'd seen it in old photos my grandfather would pull out when he got loaded."

"Where is this?"

"Mexico," I said, the word tickling something in my chest.

When my friend stepped forward, three large tiles shifted above his head and nearly fell from their brackets. He crouched lower, so he didn't drag the entire ceiling down with his big wolfwere melon. He pointed at the panting woman at his feet.

"What of her?"

"Oh yeah." I crouched low to meet her at eye level. With a smile growing on my face, I said, "I have a fun idea."

Chapter Fifty

Standing outside my Minneapolis apartment, I dug my fingers into the soil beneath one of the many dead plants outside my door. Then I uprooted another. The key was hidden somewhere in the dirt, but it had been buried so long ago, I'd forgotten where.

I kept searching, desperate to get inside so I could crawl into bed and sleep. I told Kane to wait in the car because if I couldn't find it, we'd have to find a hotel for the night.

When we'd left the Covenant building two days earlier, we'd looked for Marata, but she'd hightailed it away. I knew that was going to literally bite me on the ass one day.

Maybe.

As for Dr. Ilsa Hammer, her team had devised some restraints specially designed for the Enhanced. It had been some of those which held my friend chained to a wall for days. We'd used those to bind Hammer, then Kane threw her into the back of my Jeep.

I'd opened both back seat windows and Kane had lain down, feet sticking out one, head out the other. We could have waited the two hours for sunrise, but I didn't trust this Steve Janus person.

When he'd blinked off the screen, he'd seemed to be attending to other matters on his to-do list. If he checked the live camera feed, I wanted to be gone so he'd think we were out of the picture. Of course, if he had one of his underlings check the tapes, they'd know we were coming.

Yeah, that was a realization I wish I'd had before talking about plans to head south of the border.

Under the cover of darkness, we drove about a half hour west and got a few looks from locals, but this was Atlanta. A guy apparently dressed as a werewolf chilling out in the back seat of a Jeep probably wasn't the weirdest thing they'd seen that week.

I'd headed to an old construction site I knew rather well from my previous less-than-legal lifestyle. A good hiding place. We spent the two hours waiting for the sun to come up trading stories about what we'd each been through the past few days.

Kane, the big softy, had wanted to go *help* the Enhanced animals at the zoo.

"They tried to eat me!" I'd said.

"This is not a fault of theirs," he'd replied. "This is their nature because of what was done to them."

"Kane, they wanted to strip my bones like it was Buffalo Wings Wednesday at Applebee's!"

"Hmm," he said and flashed his grandma-eatin' teeth at me. "Isn't today Wednesday?"

When the sun came up, I grabbed some clothes I had for him in the Jeep and let him get changed. I didn't need a naked French Canadian in my passenger seat, no matter how many people would have been just fine with that.

I'd worried he might transform into geriatric, shuffleboard-playing Kane, but thankfully, he was back to his prime physical shape.

Hammer had fallen unconscious a few minutes after we'd left the Covenant parking lot. The virus coursing through her body put her in a fever coma for about eight hours.

However, she'd struggled and fought when Kane lifted her out of my vehicle and chucked her into a faraway factory in southeast St. Louis. Inside, I'd crawled through the hole in the massive wall that bisected the facility and found the tether that had once held Marata in place.

Kane had pushed Hammer through the gap and then climbed over the wall before she could get to her feet. We secured her metal bracelets to the tether.

It seemed she was *not* happy. Her virus-born vocabulary consisted of growls, grunts, and howls, so she couldn't elaborate on her displeasure over the new accommodations.

However, I did point out the buffet, which consisted of a metal spigot covered in dried crud and mold. A twist of the tap and she would have all the go-juice a growing Enhanced monster needed.

I smiled at the memory as I looked at my Jeep idling on the Minneapolis side street behind my apartment. Kane was fiddling with the radio, and that made me smile wider. The radio was the only thing he could work in the car that didn't end up crashing it.

Turning back, I was just about to dig under another dead plant when a light flicked on inside my home. Through the dirty curtains, I saw a man coming out of my bedroom with a sheet wrapped around his waist.

Well shit.

He got to the door, peeked out through the curtain, and grinned. I frowned back, and he opened the door.

"Hello, stranger," he said.

"Hello, Roy," I said. "When did you get out?"

###

Acknowledgements

My everlasting, heartfelt thanks to my Beta readers: Claire Armstrong-Brealey, Ron Daniel. Bill Thompson, Megan Rang, Mark Bunbury, Michael Pelto, Joe McCormick, Donna Cronin, Steve Lewis, and Peter McCloud. You make the book better and not just in the places where I've royally screwed up. Thank you, thank you, thank you.

Thanks also to the kind folks at Red Adept for helping make my words more prettier and sense making.

And much love to the newest members of Kane's wolf pack, my friends at Podium Audio. Thank you Annie Stone, Alicia Aldridge, Taylor Bryon and everyone else. Dear reader, if you haven't checked out the *brilliance* of what Maria McCann (Emelda) and Tim Campbell (Kane) have brought to the story, you are missing out! Go grab it on Audible!

Finally, to my lovely wife, Tiffany.

We are forever a "pack of two."

Pre-order *Kane Unchained* on Amazon.

Coming early 2024!

Also by Dick Wybrow

THE HELL INC SERIES

Hell inc
Hell to Pay
Hell Raisers
The InBetween
The Night Vanishing
Past Life
Ride the Light
The Hangman
Hell's End (coming 2024!)

MELODY SUNDAY SERIES

Live Shot

Printed in Great Britain
by Amazon